SHADOWS FROM THE FIRE

Also by Mary Ryan

Into the West
Whispers in the Wind
Glenallen
Mask of the Night

SHADOWS
FROM THE FIRE

Mary Ryan

St. Martin's Press
New York

Library of Congress Cataloging-in-Publication Data

Ryan, Mary.
Shadows from the fire / Mary Ryan.
p.   cm.
"A Thomas Dunne Book."
ISBN 0-312-13168-2
I. Title.
PR6068.Y33S48   1995
823'.914—dc20   95-2827   CIP

First published in Great Britain by Headline

First U.S. Edition: August 1995
10 9 8 7 6 5 4 3 2 1

To my dear 'Plato'
with love

ACKNOWLEDGEMENTS

My grateful thanks to the following whose inspiration and help contributed so much to the writing of this book.

Paulyn Marrinan Quinn for an inspiration central to the whole story, Bernadette Moran for confirmation on radio-therapy treatment, Clodagh Corcoran whose pamphlet *Pornography the New Terrorism* was the basis of my information on 'video nasties', my family and sisters who listened patiently, my former editor Caroline Oakley for her commentary and my new editor Cate Paterson for her enthusiasm and encouragement.

For in and out, above, about, below,
'Tis nothing but a Magic Shadow-show,
Play'd in a Box whose Candle is the Sun,
Round which we Phantom Figures come and go.

from *The Rubaiyat of Omar Khayyam*
Edward Fitzgerald

Prologue

May 1969

The young hikers stopped on the hill. An otter which had been following them along the ditch disappeared furtively into the hedgerow. Patricia saw the slinking tail, laughed and turned to Paddy. 'We've lost Mister Curiosity!'

He put both arms around her and she leant her weight against him, aware in an excited and nervous way of the prospect of their being alone together all evening, all night. They did not openly advert to it, behaving like two people who were merely out for the day. But in her stomach Pat had the floating, free-falling sensation of someone who has driven too quickly over a hump on the road.

It was a fine summer evening. Behind them the warm tarmacadam stretched beyond Laragh towards Annamoe, Roundwood and Dublin. To the right was the road up to the Wicklow Gap. Before them was Glendalough. It was here, in this sheltered valley of two lakes among the mountains, that the monks of a thousand years before had built their chapels and monastic cells. It was here, overlooking the monastic ruins, that Patricia and Paddy were going to camp.

The bus had brought them as far as Laragh, and from there it was only a matter of walking the remaining mile or so to the valley of the lakes.

They had been to Glendalough often as children, with their families; parents and grandparents, summer Sunday outings with tea and scones and sibling fights and car sickness on the homeward journey over the twisting Military Road back to Rathfarnham. But now they had freedom. They had jeans and back-packs containing sleeping bags, tent and food.

From where they were standing they saw the valley below them

1

and behind it the sheer escarpment of the mountain.

'Isn't it beautiful?' Paddy said, gesticulating. 'It's no wonder they call Wicklow the garden of Ireland.'

'When I was a child,' Patricia said, 'I never noticed. But now it takes my breath away.'

They reached the Royal Hotel, turned the corner and then trudged up the steps to the monastic graveyard. In the graveyard they looked at the eleventh-century round tower, used by the monks to escape marauders, at the ruins of early churches and the ancient Celtic cross. Paddy tried to embrace it, threw his arms around the carved limestone upright.

'If you can put your hands around it so that your fingers touch you will have a happy marriage! That's the legend.' She tried it too, laughing, and also failed. 'You'd need arms like a Neanderthal ape!'

They picked their way among the gravestones and then crossed the bridge to the woodland path beyond. The path followed the edge of the lower lake, through woods, of oak, birch, hazel and sally. It was six o'clock in the evening; there was hardly anyone else about. Patricia had told her mother she was going camping with her friend Bernadette.

'I'll be back tomorrow.'

'Where are you going?'

'Glendalough.'

'Is it safe?'

'Of course it's safe . . .'

'I don't like you camping. What if you meet unsavoury types? I remember in England, during the war . . .'

Her mother was English and had vivid memories. Pat had sighed out loud. 'Oh, Mum, the war is over . . . This is Ireland: May 1969.'

Her mother hesitated, unwilling to risk confrontation. Patricia knew that she regarded her as headstrong, had often heard her complaining to her father, 'That girl is so headstrong! You can't tell her anything!' But this time her mother made no further demur. 'Wrap up well. It can be very cold at night,' was all she said.

'Don't worry. The forecast is good.' Pat glanced at her mother there in the kitchen, a swift, sidelong glance. There was a mirror near the door, which had once graced the inside of a pub, an old mirror with PADDY written across it. PADDY, according to her father, who liked Jameson Twelve and obscure Scotch whiskies, was made of razor-blades, but he was referring to the whisky, not the young man who came to take his daughter out. Since her relationship with Paddy had started, the mirror amused her, seemed absolutely apt, and she enjoyed the sight of her face staring back at her through the letters of his name. She caught a glimpse of herself now as she turned to assess her mother's reaction, saw a girl with thick, curly, auburn hair and blue eyes, her face animated, her eyes bright. I look beautiful, she thought with surprise. Well, beautiful if it weren't for the filthy freckles! Normally, when she caught herself unawares in the mirror, she liked to linger for a moment in sly self-appreciation, but right now she wanted to be sure her mother suspected nothing. So she studied her parent covertly and was satisfied. She knew from the way her mother held her head that she was preoccupied with the white sauce and that she did not entertain the least suspicion that her daughter was going camping alone with a young man. Tendrils of grey hair had worked their way loose from the 'french roll' at the back of her head. The set of her profile, the way her head was bent over the saucepan seemed to Patricia suddenly to be innocent and trusting. Recently Pat had begun to feel very worldly wise; she had begun to suspect that parents knew very little. Suspecting this she wanted to kiss her mother in a sudden rush of love. Instead she set the table, listened to the news and kept her ears open for the weather forecast.

The weather was balmy, as predicted, a summer evening with pink streaks across the sky. A tall youth was fly-fishing by the shore and cast his line up and out into the water with a crake of his reel, swish of the line, and the circling ripples where the fly landed, one of a million ripples because the Mayfly were up. Midges congregated in small dancing fogs over the edge of the lake. Further out there were reeds, bulrushes, a few shy water-hens. There was the sharp chuckle of the coots, the cawing of the rooks. All around them the birds were singing the evening chorus, half demented with joy. Paddy held her hand.

'We'll hear the sound of the water all night,' he said. His hand squeezed hers. It had a warm, firm clasp she loved.

'Where are we going to camp?'

'In the woods near the upper lake. I was there once before.'

'On your own?'

He looked at her, smiled, lowered his head. 'Are you jealous? No . . . With Tom Curran.'

She knew Tom, who was a friend from his year in college.

'Did you enjoy it?'

'Yes. It was great. We camped in a clearing in the hazel woods. We could see the stars.'

The path was stony, winding up and down the inclines and arriving eventually at a deserted grassy sward with a ruined chapel where a few sheep were grazing. Beyond this was the upper lake, a dark blue mere with a sandy shore, merging back to the shadows of the mountain. The waterfall was frothing in the distance as it decanted itself down the cliff in a long white torrent.

They stood on the shore, threw pebbles, watched the ripples; circles starting, widening, dying.

'Just like life,' Paddy said.

'You mean the ripples?'

'Of course; a small stone hits the water and eventually sets up eddies in the lake. Same as life! We're the small stones!'

'Is that supposed to be profound?'

He laughed, turned to look down on her. 'Of course it's profound!'

On one side the cliff rose, a tree-clad precipice rising steeply from the water. Paddy raised his hand and pointed. 'That's Kevin's Bed.'

She looked up, trying to find it, the cell of St Kevin, the hermit who had retreated here to fast and pray and who had been followed by the woman who loved him. But he had been a holy man and had thrown her down into the lake, to her death.

'What was the name of the woman?' asked Patricia. 'The one he drowned?'

Paddy shrugged, waved his arms to drive away the midges. 'Let's get out of here before we're eaten alive!'

As they walked, Patricia glanced at him, watching his face, his deep-set eyes, his assured way of moving. He put an arm around her shoulder, stopped suddenly in mid-stride so that he almost unbalanced her, and kissed her on the mouth. Pat felt the surge of electricity all the way to her toes. His lips were warm; there was the faintest hint of stubble on his chin. He smelt of life and certainty. He smelt of the future, of love, of excitement, of hope.

'You make me dizzy,' he whispered after a moment. 'You are one beautiful bird and I am going to sleep with you tonight.'

4

Patricia tensed at the flippancy.

'I'm not a bird.'

He looked at her quizzically. 'What's wrong with being a bird?'

'Nothing,' she said crossly, 'so long as you've feathers!'

He laughed. 'I'm teasing you, idiot. I can always get a rise out of you.'

They climbed the slope into the woods. He walked in front and she watched the way he moved, his maleness, his certainty, the glamour which invested all his movements, like an invisible cloth of gold.

'I think this will do for our resting place!' he said, indicating a dry open space among the trees. He took off his rucksack, sat on some gnarled roots, began to untie the tent.

Patricia stood staring at him, suddenly feeling intensely shy. 'Our resting place!' A knot gathered in her stomach; the voices of all her mentors, all the warnings about sex, about mortal sin, clamoured in her brain.

The night was purple. She had never seen a violet sky, but there it was above her head, studded with stars. From below them they could hear the unending song of the mountain torrent. The two lakes lay like sheets silvered by the moon. Woodcock whirred close by in the darkness. They had pitched the tent, and sat beside the Primus stove heating their supper: Heinz baked beans and frankfurters and tea and bread. From the woods around them came the sounds of life: little rustlings; wild, startled, rust-red retinas suddenly in the light, then gone. They had a storm lantern and the white moths clustered about it, winging around and around it, with small flashes of fire as they were caught in the thermal and incinerated. Beyond the circle of lamplight were the waiting shadows. They listened for a while to the rushing water.

'It's all music, isn't it?' Patricia said, her voice low. Her head was cradled against his shoulder, her curly hair full of little bits of sticks from the snogging session before supper. 'Like in *Song of the Lotos-Eaters*,' she added, reciting in a whisper,

'There is sweet music here that softer falls,
Than petals from blown roses on the grass . . .'

She bent her head forward to drink some beer out of his bottle, and when she had finished he put the bottle down, turned towards her, reached under her jumper for the fastening of her bra, pulled up her jumper until her pale breasts were exposed, touching them with wonder, kissing them, suckling them.

'Beautiful, beautiful,' he groaned after a moment. 'Christ, Pat, I want to make love to you so badly that I think I'll die. Let me make love to you . . .' He began to pull at her jeans, opening the zip.

Patricia found the drift of her consciousness into some alternative reality abruptly arrested. She moved awkwardly to cover her breasts, to put down a hand to stop him.

'Not now!'

He lay back, sighing. She had a mental picture of herself as a prude, or a tease. It was just that she desperately wanted it to be right, and for him to know what it really meant. Maybe she shouldn't have come. It had been like this too the day in Dollymount when she had torn away from him and run down the beach.

I wish I wasn't so afraid, she thought. I wish I wasn't so afraid. I wish he wouldn't ask. I wish he'd kiss me until I melted into the earth, kiss me everywhere, kiss me very gently and so slowly that I would not have to try to keep up with him. If he kissed me like that how could I resist?

'It's all right,' he whispered eventually, his normally pragmatic voice very gentle, his arm cradling her tenderly. 'We'll wait. We have a lifetime.' He took out what she thought was a cigarette and realised as he lit it that it was a joint. He took a few drags and offered it to her. She took it gingerly; it was uncharacteristic of Paddy to need any kind of crutch.

'I didn't know you smoked this stuff.'

'I don't. I've only tried it once before. It stops you being horny! And I am very very horny!' He sighed. 'Tom gave it to me and I thought I'd bring it to keep me quiet. It makes all your troubles go away!'

After a while he said: 'Say it again, the *Song of the Lotos-Eaters*.'

Patricia obliged, reciting the first verse slowly. When she stopped they were both very still.

They passed the joint between them in silence. After a while came the peace, the sense of belonging to the night and the singing water and the gentle rustling sounds around them and to each other. Patricia felt as though she had soared up into the violet space above her, into the whispering night. She heard his words of love: 'I love you, Patricia, I love you and I love your name and I love the patrician in you and I love the queer little thumping of your heart'; heard her reply, 'I love you Paddy Johnson.'

After a moment he added in a low, teasing voice which struggled with suppressed laughter: 'I think the two of us are hewn from the same bit of old bog oak!'

Pat laughed into the darkness. 'Speak for yourself!'

Later they got into their sleeping bags and slept side by side, holding hands, kissing blindly in the morning.

In Dublin on that May night in 1969 a girl named Sarah dreamed of school. In the dream, Sister Martha was scolding her. She had narrow, witchlike eyes like the queen in Snow White, and long curved nails. 'You've no future, Sarah Dempsey,' she was saying. 'No future in this school or anywhere else . . .'

'I'm sorry, Sister. I didn't mean to forget the homework again . . .'

Sarah woke with a start, her heart pounding, and then she remembered that she had done all her homework for tomorrow and that Sister Martha was not a witch, or at least not a witch like the absurd queen. She was a right old bag in many ways, but there wasn't enough evil in her to make her that interesting. But all the same she felt sick with horror, horror disproportionate to the dream, horror pressing down on her. There was an apple tree outside her window and the leaves brushed the pane with a small scratching sound. There were shadows cast by the tree on the curtains and they moved suddenly in the night breeze.

I'm fourteen, too old for this. She thought of her parents in the next room and of the days when she would flee to them – 'I had a scary dream' – and her mother would sigh and move over for her and she would listen for a while to the comforting sounds of her parents' breathing, her father's intermittent snoring, until sleep reclaimed her. Why do I have to grow up and leave everything safe behind me, came the half-formed thought, and then she remembered that she did want to grow up because then she would be free.

Not far away in another Dublin suburb that Friday night a young woman called Joan was studying late. She worked best at night, when there was total silence, except for the neighbour's dog which she longed to strangle, as it howled and whined and groaned.

Her Leaving Certificate was only a couple of weeks away. She had her future mapped out for her. She wanted to be a lawyer; she wanted to understand how everything worked; she wanted to ensure that she would never feel the powerlessness of childhood again. Soon she would be in college; she would be free then to see David as well, the art student she'd met in the National Library, who said he wanted to paint her, who took her for coffee and talked for hours. David of the dark eyes who was slim and delicate-looking, like a Victorian poet. He had phoned her twice and her mother had said she was not in. 'Plenty of time for boys when you've got your qualifications.' But what her mother didn't know was that she met him anyway outside the College of Art every day after school.

'Who is this boy David?' her mother had asked eventually.

'He's an art student.'

'Oh, one of those. No money and drawing naked hussies, I suppose . . .'

'Yes, I suppose he does,' Joan replied with a laugh. 'I hadn't really thought about it.'

Sometimes when she was tired from studying, and awed at the amount yet to be revised, her father comforted her. 'It'll be worth it; wait and see. Everything yields to effort!'

Sometimes she let the words go round and round in her head. *'Labor omnia vincit.'*

About a hundred and fifty miles away in a small town in the midlands, Jim O'Toole lay awake. He was sixteen and soon would leave home for the building sites of London and Manchester. But now he lay listening to the sounds of his parents fighting and then to the noise he dreaded – the dull whack as the blows fell, the sounds of his mother whimpering and his father's voice raised in angry, drunken complaint. 'Stupid bitch; stupid sow . . .'

He covered his head with the bedclothes. He longed to leave home. There was great money to be had in England, a great life. Plenty of beer and girls and being grown up and doing what he liked. He would be free then, of his father's blows and his

8

mother's whimpering. He pitied her; in a way he loved her, but he also despised her. He hated his father but he did not despise him. He did not despise him because he had power, because he represented some kind of absolute; he understood the rage in him, the need to hit out at the powerless.

Chapter One

The law is a funny business . . . All this insistence on reducing the stuff of living to a set of rules! I know it's necessary, but I wish I knew something substantial about it, something with which I could give Gerry a run for his money.

from *The Horse's Ears*, 1972

November 1989

Joan woke in the dark. She heard the rain against the window, lashing in a cold fury, abating, resuming the onslaught. She flipped the alarm switch on the clock to 'off' and listened for a moment for the sound of David's breathing. She luxuriated in these things she most loved: waking beside him, feeling the warmth of him. His breathing was so quiet that she had to listen for it, as she had done so often during their early days in Ranelagh, when she would wake in the night and tense in the silence, suddenly afraid that he had died. That was even before he became ill, before they'd had Paul. The night was always the time of love, of vulnerability. The day was the time of battle.

She registered a sense of dismay at having to get up, at the thought of the busy day ahead, knowing at the same time that the energy to deal with it would return with activity and daylight. I hate mornings, she thought, especially winter mornings which suck the life out of you.

She huddled a bit deeper under the duvet, put the soles of her feet against David's legs. He moved, put a warm arm around her.

'How are you feeling, darling?' she whispered.

'Couldn't be better.'

'I thought you were asleep.'

11

'I woke up a few minutes ago.'

They lay in silence, warm, together, stealing an extra minute. She put on the bedside light, shivered, went out to the bathroom, opening Paul's door on the way and calling him.

'Come on, get up, get up . . .' She waited for his sleepy rejoinder. 'Oh no! It can't be morning already!'

The door to David's studio was open and she smelt the clean scent of paint, turps, linseed oil. She closed the door to keep the heat in. He would spend most of the day there, lost to the rest of the world in his passion, exploring the universe of his imagination and perceptions.

When she emerged from the shower, David was in the kitchen making breakfast. The smell of toast wafted through the house. She dressed quickly – a grey wool suit, pearl-grey blouse – dabbed on make-up and joined him downstairs. He was in his dressing-gown by the cooker, boiling eggs, putting out the toast on the table, stirring the porridge for Paul.

The welcoming room was very warm, thanks to the heat generated by the solid-fuel cooker, which had been ticking over all night.

The white-walled kitchen overlooked a small garden. The garden had been bigger once, but they had built an extension which made the kitchen into a living space, with room for the old pine dresser they had bought at an auction and subsequently stripped and waxed. There was also room for an old rocking chair which Joan loved to sink into when she came home.

David put her boiled egg on the table. 'Beautifully cooked, beautifully served,' he quipped in a mincing voice, making her laugh. It was an old joke from the days when a slim young David, with a burning zest for life, would read out pieces of culinary advice from magazines.

They had made love incessantly in those days, as though they could never get enough of each other, as though each possessed some element essential to the life of the other.

'You are air and earth and water to me,' he said.

And Joan, overwhelmed by his protestations, doubted them initially. Later she knew that he meant them and, what was worse, she felt exactly the same way about him. She was hooked, addicted, caught up in the whirl of his perceptions, measuring with disbelief the former sedate tenor of her life against the turmoil and excitement he brought her. They had

12

lived together for five years in the little flat in Ranelagh and had married when she became pregnant with Paul.

Her mother had been glum with disappointment, thinking of all the nice men with good jobs that her Joan could have chosen from; her father had been accepting.

'Who are his people?' her mother had asked.

'His mother is dead. His father deserted the family when he was three and he doesn't remember him. He had a brother who was a year younger, but he died in an accident.'

'What kind of accident?'

'I don't know. He won't talk about it.'

It had taken her years to get that story from him. Now, so much had changed: the physical energy had left him, but the fire of his mind burned on.

'You should go back to bed.' She said it gently, aware of his pallor. She knew he hated her harping on anything to do with his illness.

'I'm fine. Never better. What delights are in store for you today?'

'Let's see.' She thought for a moment. 'Appointment at half nine, High Court at eleven – a thing about a Will.'

'Is it interesting?'

'In a way. It's human! Some poor idiot died leaving an ambiguous will and three old biddies of the same name have put in a claim!'

'Will you be doing the same kind of work when you move to Wharton's?'

'Probably not,' Joan said, thinking of her new job offer from one of the big firms. 'They're more compartmentalized. It'll be all conveyancing.'

'Have you told them in the office yet that you're leaving?'

'No. I'll tell them today.'

'Good. It'll give that slave-driver Galligan something to chew on! He'll have to find himself another dogsbody.'

Joan snorted. 'It's not as bad as all that. I like to work hard.'

Paul appeared. He was fourteen, still baby-faced although he was growing quickly. He had his father's hands and his mother's grey-blue eyes. He was dressed for school, still half asleep, moving slowly.

'Good morning,' his father said to him.

'What's good about it?' The boy repressed a grin, glanced from

13

one parent to the other to see if they had appreciated his wit. His parents exchanged looks.

'It's another day and you're still breathing,' Joan said. She made a sudden movement and tickled him along his rib-cage. 'Smile.'

Despite himself, Paul laughed out loud and jumped away from her teasing fingers.

'What would you like for supper?' David asked as he served Paul his breakfast.

'Don't worry about supper,' Joan murmured. 'I'll pick up a cooked chicken on the way home. Why don't you rest?'

'I'm sick of resting.' He said it testily and added, 'I'm sorry. I've a lot of work to do. I want to finish *The Poppies*. The gallery is sending someone around today – a Frenchie – a scout for a Paris gallery.'

Joan stared at David with delight. He was looking into his cup as though the matter were of little moment.

'An art dealer? From Paris? Why didn't you tell me?'

'What difference does it make? He'll probably just make polite noises!'

'No,' Joan said slowly. 'I don't think he will. You know your work is good, and your recent work is haunting. I think he'll be very interested.'

David smiled slowly, breaking the intensity in his face. He leant across the table to take her hand. His own hands were well shaped, the fingers long and sensitive. There were shadows under his dark eyes and his face was drawn; a few grey ribs flecked his hair and beard, but his smile softened everything, suffused his face with life. Joan smiled back at him with love, wondering as she so often did how she had managed to marry such a beautiful man. He studied her for a moment, his eyes suddenly melancholy, his mouth tense.

'I'm sorry for snapping.' He looked away from her with a gesture of sudden dispirited weariness. 'You've a crochety old crock of a husband who hasn't the decency to die.'

Joan looked into her boiled egg. Her eyes filled with tears. She wanted to let them stream down her face, but she stared at her egg and willed them to stop.

'You've upset Mum,' Paul said accusingly.

David got up, went behind her chair, began to massage her shoulders. 'Shh . . . You've a besotted husband who makes silly jokes.'

14

Joan turned her head aside, took her husband's palm and put it against her face. Paul made embarrassed noises. She stood up.

'Come on, young man,' she said to Paul. 'No point in being late for school.' Paul went to get his school bag and his jacket. She kissed David. 'See you this evening. I'll phone you at lunchtime. Good luck with the Frenchie.'

'Bye Dad.'

'Bye Paul.'

Joan started the car, drove down the empty morning road of the small housing estate, turned the corner by Kinsella's still-shuttered shop, and then took the narrow avenue by the river as a short-cut. From there she eased out on to the main road. It was still dark, a grey overcast dawn sneaking up on the city. It was raining slightly and the roads were wet; the traffic lights shone bleakly in the drizzle; the rush-hour traffic had not fully built up. She turned on the heater and the blast of the fan whirred into the car.

'Dad is looking rotten,' Paul said.

'He was up in the night; he's just tired.'

There was silence for a moment and then the boy said in a quiet, tense voice, 'What is wrong with him, Mum?'

She glanced at her son's grim face, which held back the emotion he would not show. Was it because of this that he flogged himself with his studies? He was consistently top of his class, worked until all hours. She would try to get him to go out to a film with a friend: 'Ah no, Mum. I have some Biology I want to do . . .' His teachers enthused over him, but some of them were aware that he was trying to compensate for something he could not control.

She dropped Paul off at the school gates. Her thoughts returned to David. Sometimes she felt that it was her will which was keeping him alive, keeping his mysterious illness at arm's length; she concentrated it on him, wrapped him in a positive force-field. 'There is some spasticity in the gut,' the doctor told her. 'But his blood is fine, he has neither lost nor gained weight. We've run a barrage of tests!' The inference was that it wasn't very serious. But the doctor did not see the scalding early morning baths that David took to keep the pain away.

'Oh God, the country is full of couples who hate each other.

But we don't. Make him better. Let us go forward in peace. Give us that peace.'

David had been unwell for a while, complaining of stomachaches, backaches, vomiting. He put it down to overwork, was reluctant to see a doctor.

The doctor, when he finally saw him, had been reassuring, had taken him into hospital for tests. He had been sent home. All he had wrong, apparently, was a spastic colon.

Her mind switched to the office, to the work confronting her today. She was in court at eleven before the probate judge and had three closings in the afternoon – mortgage work which was straightforward, exacting and boring. Her boss, Gerry Galligan, put more and more of his own conveyancing workload her way, concentrating on the really big ones himself, like the Tunnymore contract which he was dealing with now, a two-million-pound purchase. Larry Ryder, the other partner, did most of the litigation, except for the District Court stuff which he dumped on her; that and any contentious probate matters or other bits and pieces of esoterica. There were two other assistant solicitors besides herself, two young women who did most of the straightforward Land Registry conveyancing, housing estates and road-traffic prosecutions.

Gerry was married to Patricia. Joan had known her from a distance in college. Patricia, an auburn-haired Arts student, had been two years ahead of her, had been more or less engaged to an engineering student called Paddy Johnson. Paddy had been a great heart-throb, a tall, handsome fellow who excelled in debating and who had about him an assured charisma.

Pat had been involved in many of the societies: Hon. Sec. to this and that, very bright and vivacious and pretty. But the engagement had come to grief and the bold Paddy had gone off and married someone else. Patricia had failed her finals, married Gerry Galligan, settled down to instant domesticity and produced two children. Occasionally she came into the office, always beautifully dressed, a little brittle, changed in some way not chargeable to the attrition of the years. It was as though she was putting the whole of her persona into playing the character of Mrs Gerry, and had discovered too late that the role was unending, that there was no respite or remission for good behaviour, that it made demands on the very source of her life and that it had nothing whatever to do with her. This did not surprise Joan.

16

There were few things in life she could imagine more draining than marriage to Gerry, or Larry either, for that matter.

Larry was thirty-five, three years younger than herself. Medium height, dark hair, dark blue eyes, thin, straight nose, flamboyant personality, tiptoeing into her office with his files. 'Oh Joan, pet, here are a couple of District Court files: one's a moneylender's licence; the other's a small breach-of-contract case. No bother to you. Do your usual best.' And she would smile and curse silently.

She didn't like District Court work, which always seemed to her to be much ado about very little. She was not trained in advocacy, but, since they had won the right of audience in the courts, solicitors generally presented District Court cases themselves. It was cheaper for the client, but it was often a great waste of time for the solicitor.

She would have to look up the procedure for moneylenders' licences, study the miserable breach-of-contract case at home so she could present the little case with confidence, and spend an afternoon in court scraping to the justice and honing her wits for the cross-examination. But today she had a surprise for Gerry and Larry. The new job she had been offered was in one of the city's biggest firms – Wharton, Kelly, Phelan & Co. – and she had every intention of taking it.

She drove the car into the car park at the back of the building, let herself into the back hall with her key, smiled at Breda, the receptionist, as she crossed Reception. Breda was speaking in the nasal tones she assumed for clients. 'I'm sorry, Mr Galligan is not in at the moment. I'll have him call you the minute he's in.'

Joan went upstairs, looked into Gerry's office where Larry was opening the post. He put the letters in piles: hers, his and Gerry's, and another two piles for Mary and Sheila, the two other assistants. The drizzle had stopped outside and the sun was brightening through the mist, slanting in through the window, touching the gold lettering in the rows of legal tomes, the *Encyclopaedia of Forms and Precedents*, lingering on the shiny leather binding of *Halesbury's Laws*. In the corner the old scrivener's desk brightened up for a moment as much as to say, 'Here I am. Look at me; look at all the soot-ink spilt on me; look at the marks of real legal toil!' Gerry had been about to get rid of that old desk, but she had told him it lent a certain authenticity to his office, and so it had remained.

17

Larry handed Joan a pile of letters. 'This looks like your lot this morning, Joan.'

Gerry's secretary came into the outer room as Joan was leaving. 'Good morning Mrs de Barra,' she said. Gerry was insistent on formality in the office, at least from the secretarial staff.

'Morning, Prue.'

Joan took the letters to her own office on the next floor. Rita, her secretary, was in her own room, tidying a drawer of her desk where she had a box of man-size tissues. She was snuffling and the end of her nose was red.

'Good morning, Mrs de Barra.'

'Morning, Rita. How's the cold this morning?'

'Much better, thanks.'

'Will you get started on that draft lease I gave you yesterday; I need it as soon as possible so I can check it before I go to court?'

'OK.'

Joan liked Rita very much. She was a petite girl, an excellent secretary, quick, intelligent, and neat. She proceeded into her own office, shut the door. The room was bathed in the glow of the early morning sun. She went to the window and pulled the blind down halfway, glancing out at the sluggish traffic and the damp streets and the river. The file for her first appointment was on her desk. She sat down and began to work.

At home David went into his studio. This was the master bedroom, the bedroom that should have been his and Joan's. But instead they had the back bedroom and Paul had the box-room. It was not an ideal size for a studio, but the window was big and it had soft northern light. Various paintings in various stages of completion were propped against the walls; they were mostly oils, but there were also pastels, mixed-media work, a few watercolours. On the table and the shelves behind it was a collection of cups, jam jars, paint tins, all with brushes sticking out, a forest of brushes interspersed with paint-smeared rags, sketchpads and discarded pallets covered in a riot of paint daubs.

There was an easel in the middle of the floor with a large uncompleted painting resting on it. The picture showed a field of summer flowers and grasses, poppies and daisies and a fierce blue sky. There was no life in the picture, no birds or insects, and no human being except for the figure in black in the right-hand corner. This figure, a man, was at the edge of the field. He was wearing a cloak of sorts and a soft dark hat. His face was in shadow.

David started when he looked at the painting. He felt it each time, the draw of the stranger in black, staring at him there from the edge of the painting, seeing him. While he, David the artist, had no face to give him and was fascinated by his creation. The painting gave the impression that the field of wild grasses and flowers, the world of summer, held its breath; that the dark presence at its perimeter had stripped it of joy, because it represented a dimension so powerful and inescapable that all joy and all summer was only a mirage; as though this dark man could suck in all the field of brightness without himself changing hue; as though he had darkness to spare. The figure addressed the eye, puzzled the imagination.

Once Joan had asked David why he did not just change a painting when he didn't like the way it was going.

'Provided I feel I'm executing it well, whether I like it or not is immaterial. It has its own life; I am merely its servant.'

She had pondered this. 'God, that sounds portentous. Does that go for portraits?'

'Certainly. I look at a face and the face tells me who it is!'

'What do you see in my face?' She had tilted her chin and smirked.

'Vanity.'

She thumped him, laughing, telling him she would never let him paint her.

'I'll paint you all right!' and he had smiled his grim smile. He had painted her; it hung in the sitting room, the picture of a pensive girl with grey eyes and a strong mouth.

'She doesn't look particularly like a vanity box!' Joan observed when she saw the finished article.

'She isn't. She shows strength. It's her principal feature.'

'Yuck. She would much rather have something to be vain about.'

He laughed. 'But she has! And she will endure, this young woman; she is a survivor.' He put his arm around her. 'And she's mine, all mine!'

In Court Number Five, under the dome of the Four Courts, Joan sat in the solicitors' bench watching Nuala O'Byrne on her feet in

19

front of her, addressing the judge. Nuala's horse-hair wig with its little pigtail was worn just over her hairline and the black gown lent her a signorial air, at odds with her youth. She was reading from the affidavit of the applicants, the executors of the Will of Dennis Joseph McCarthy who had died a bachelor. There were sixteen paragraphs, all tending to establish that Brigid Murphy of St Teresa's, Ballsbridge, in the county of Kerry, was the person intended to benefit from the bequest of forty thousand pounds, and showing that the deceased could not have intended the other two putative beneficiaries to benefit. Brigid, who lived in St Teresa's, was cousin to the deceased; they had always been chums. The other two Brigids were hardly known to him, although they had lived in the same town.

Nuala droned on. The judge asked a question when she was finished and then gave the order as applied for.

'May it please your lordship. And costs, my lord?'

The costs would come out of the estate. Dinny Joe, who had been too thrifty to employ someone to draw his Will, would turn in his grave.

When she came back to the office, Breda told Joan that Mr Galligan wanted a word with her. Joan went up to Gerry's office. She knocked, entered. He was standing by the bookcase checking some piece of legislation; the *Acts of the Oireachtas* for 1978 was open in his hand. He motioned her to a chair.

Joan wondered what he wanted to see her for. She had known him from college, had expected in the early days that he would ask her to join him as a partner, but he had brought in Larry instead. 'We need a litigation expert,' he had said.

She had swallowed her disappointment; she had too much to think about: a delicate husband, a young son. She watched him now, his thin, tense presence, his balding head, his dark pinstripe suit, his concentrated air. She tried to read the heading for the Act he was perusing, saw that it was the 'Landlord and Tenant (No. 2) Act, 1978'.

'I have a new landlord and tenant case.' He paused. Does he expect me to take it? Joan wondered. Is that what he wants to see me about?

She was silent. Gerry closed the tome, shut the bookcase and came back to his desk. He looked at her across the mahogany surface, frowning, his glasses and the way the hair sat at the edges of his bald pate giving him an owlish appearance.

'You remember Frank Larkin?'

'Of course.'

'His family have been clients of this office for years and years.'

'I know.'

'You were the last person to deal with him.'

'That's right. It was in connection with his Will.'

'Read the letter.'

Joan read the letter Gerry had given her. It was from a firm of solicitors in Ballybegg, Co. Carlow, saying that they acted for Frank Larkin and asking for his documents of title to be forwarded.

'What did you do to him, Joan? You've managed to lose him on us.'

Joan stared at him. Sometimes she found Gerry so erratic and unpredictable that she wondered why she put up with him. 'I did nothing of the sort. I parted with him on excellent terms.'

'Then why is he taking his business elsewhere? You must have said or done something.' Gerry oozed anger, ill-concealed aggression, contemptuous certainty. He hated to lose a good client, one with plenty of property. His demeanour was accusatory, cold, threatening. Joan shivered inwardly, resentful, at a loss.

'I did nothing. Why don't you phone him, ask him yourself? Ask him why that bunch in Ballybegg want his documents. Suggest it's a security measure.'

'I might do that,' Gerry said coldly. 'But I think it's too bad.' He dropped his voice to indicate that the interview was at an end. And the tone of complaint made it clear that she was in the dog-house, guilty of impropriety. Joan sat still.

'I was going to tell you and Larry later, Gerry, but now is as good a time as any. I'm leaving. I've been offered a job in Wharton's and have decided to accept it.'

Gerry's face registered disbelief. His mouth opened a little; he pushed his pen up and down through his fingers. The phone rang. He picked it up. 'Yes?' he demanded peremptorily. 'All right. Put her through.'

Joan heard the female voice on the line. 'I'm in a meeting.' Every syllable was crisply enunciated. 'I told you not to phone me at the office. I'll talk to you about it this evening.'

He put the phone down, gave a short, dismissive laugh. 'Pat thinks I've nothing else to do except discuss her problems with

21

the children.' He paused. His tone changed. 'You're not serious about this, Joan?'

'I am.'

'Why?'

'More money. A change. I've been here for a long time. It's time I went.'

He continued twiddling the pen, nodded his head in a thoughtful fashion. 'I'm sorry to hear it. Can we make you change your mind?'

'I doubt it.' She rose and left the office.

David worked through the morning. He sat down from time to time on the chair, studying his work, recommencing, sitting down to study it again. He ignored the waves of fatigue, the occasional stab of nausea.

The French art dealer arrived at the door at noon. David heard the doorbell in his studio, came downstairs. He had a pain in his back and every step exhausted him.

'Mr de Barra?'

'Yes. Come in.'

The art dealer introduced himself.

'My studio is upstairs,' David said. 'You go ahead; first right.'

The man stood uncertainly. He saw the way David held the banisters. 'Are you all right?'

'Fine, fine . . . I'm just a bit out of breath. I'll follow you up.'

When David returned to his studio he found the art dealer going through the paintings stacked against the wall. He sat on the chair for a moment.

'Take your time,' he said as the man politely turned to him.

'I'll get on with what I was doing.' He went back to the easel and picked up his brush, put the finishing touches to the grasses in the left-hand corner, touched the sky with cobalt.

'I like your work, Mr de Barra,' the French voice said behind him after a few minutes. 'Your gallerist told me I would find it interesting. When was the last time you exhibited?'

'Last year. I missed this year.'

'I see. And you will be exhibiting next year?'

'Yes. If I can complete enough work.'

The dealer held up a painting. It was like the one on the easel, except that the summer scene was one of moorland, bright and melancholy, with a small, dark figure in the west.

22

'You are, perhaps, creating a series of some kind?' He pointed. 'This figure for example? *L'homme mysterieux*?'

'I don't know,' David said in genuine perplexity, shrugging. 'I'm only doing what's there, what presents itself, what struggles to become . . . And I don't create it, but I try to serve it!'

The man picked up another painting, pointed to it and to the one on the easel, indicating with his finger the dark presence at the perimeter. 'He's getting nearer all the time.'

David turned to look at him, saw the Gallic face, the shrewd, considering eyes, the obvious interest under the politeness.

'Of course he is,' he whispered. 'He has something for me.'

Joan worked through some of her lunch-hour. Then she went out, crossed Capel Street Bridge and found her way to the Church of Adam and Eve on Merchants Quay. This was a daily pilgrimage. Here she prayed for David, begged God to make him better. Her faith was now a mainstay in her life, something she had carried from her childhood, from her devout parents who were strict practising Catholics. In the early days of her independence she had moved away from it, only to return with passionate pleading when David had become ill. But David, however ill he might be, did not share her belief.

Afterwards she bought a sandwich and the *Irish Times* in the little shop a few doors away, and brought them back to the office. She made herself a cup of coffee, sat at her desk, opened the paper, read the lead story, glanced at the foreign news and then the article about the woman living in Cork who was charged with conspiring to murder her husband. The husband had beaten her badly over several years, had caused a miscarriage, had deserted her. When he had tried to return she had sought help 'to frighten him off', but the 'help' had killed him. Joan wondered what kind of sentence they would give her if she was convicted. She had several children.

She completed her two afternoon closings, put the documents aside for stamping and registration, and was ready to see Peter Knight when he arrived for his half four appointment. Peter was a client she enjoyed: he was a small, fat man with a wicked sense of humour. He came to see her about Emily Jane Harper, deceased. Emily Jane had been dead for all of ten years, but her file was still open because it was impossible to ascertain who were her legitimate next-of-kin. The beneficiaries named in her Will had predeceased her. The file had recently landed on Joan's desk.

She had studied the deceased's family tree, seen the question marks. Four nephews, two of them probably illegitimate and therefore ineligible. All of them were dead and had left children. Peter Knight was one of the children. He knew nothing much about his great-uncle except that he had been 'a bit of a lad'.

Peter was a 'bit of a lad' himself, at least so far as his commercial schemes were concerned; he tended towards immodest ambitions and confrontational tactics.

'Gently!' Joan told him, trying to prevent him from browbeating a prospective buyer of a commercial premises he had for sale. The purchaser was taking his time about making up his mind. It was a perfectly fine premises with a good rent-roll, but she was afraid that he would scare away his purchaser.

'I've fought with everyone except you and the Inspector of Taxes,' Peter said, twinkling at her.

When he left, Joan began to draft a long, complicated Will. She concentrated the whole of her mind on it; Wills didn't leave any room for error, as the morning's case had shown all too clearly; it was too late when someone was dead to ask if they wouldn't mind giving clarification.

She was tired when she looked up. The fluorescent light stabbed at her eyes. The dark winter evening was pressing against the window. The small clock on the desk said five. It would soon be time to go home. She thought with pleasure of David and Paul, of the warm kitchen, of the three of them together.

She looked around her office, at the print of the Four Courts, the framed map of Dublin in 1798, the bookcase, the filing cabinets. She wondered wearily if she would be an assistant solicitor for ever.

'*Labor omnia vincit*,' her father used to say. She wondered about that. The Roman Empire in its heyday had been comparable to the Third Reich. The latter had adopted a similar phrase – '*Arbeit Macht Frei*.' Did work make you free? Was it work that conquered everything, or innate genius, or simply luck?

Gerry phoned up from his office. 'Will you call into my office before you go, Joan?'

'OK.'

She worked until a quarter to six, dictated letters, drafted an Assignment. Her mind turned time and again to David. She had phoned him at lunchtime and he'd said he was fine, that the art

24

dealer had come and gone and that he would give her all the news when he saw her.

'Did he like your work?'

'He seemed interested.'

'What did I tell you?'

On her way out, Joan knocked at Gerry's door, opened it. Gerry was sitting back expansively in his big swivel chair. The light caught his shiny bald patch. Larry was in the room too, slim and elegant, lounging by the window and looking out at the darkness and the mercury lights reflected in the river.

'Ah, Joan, there you are!' He indicated a chair. Larry sat down on the other one. Gerry handed her a draft deed. 'What do you think of that?'

She scanned it. 'They've left out the words of limitation. Who drafted it?'

'It was sent to me today for approval; it looks like the work of a student!'

She handed the paper back, aware that they were not in the least concerned with it, that she was here for some other reason.

'Did you find out anything more about Frank Larkin?' she inquired.

Gerry hesitated. 'Yes. I phoned him as you suggested,' he said a little sheepishly. 'He said he only asked Sweeny in Ballybegg to check on a tenancy in one of his business lettings there. He has no intention of changing solicitors. I owe you an apology . . .'

'That's all right' she murmured, embarrassed, starting to rise.

'Joan . . .' Larry said slowly, smiling at her, running his hand through his silky black hair. 'Don't go for a moment, pet. We want to put something to you. We know you've been enticed by Wharton's, but we would like you to reconsider.' He looked at Gerry and then back at her with a boyish smile.

Gerry leaned forward. 'What we want to ask you, Joan, is – what would you say to joining us as a partner?'

Later, as she drove home past the Franciscan friary in the rain, Joan gave God a thumbs-up sign. She was about to leave the ranks of the wage-slaves and join the capitalists.

25

Chapter Two

Gerry has put a deposit on a smashing house – Victorian, with period features intact.
'Here you are!' he said, grinning. 'Now you can nest to your heart's content!'

from *The Horse's Ears*, 1971

December 1989

Patricia was lying on the white bed. Downstairs she could hear Una Foley moving around, putting the finishing touches to the lounge, setting out little dishes of salted peanuts, crisps, cheese sticks.

The light from the lamp threw shadows across the ceiling. There was a fine hair-crack on the white plaster, an irregular etching where a workman who had recently been checking the tank in the attic had half rested his foot. It was not particularly noticeable but, as Patricia stared at it, it became a face, with a pinched nose and witch's chin.

Tonight's dinner party was almost upon her. Gerry was downstairs too, checking glasses and bottles. The party was to celebrate Joan de Barra becoming a partner in the firm. Joan had been with the firm for years.

'Is she a good lawyer?' Pat had asked once, and Gerry had answered immediately. 'Is she a good lawyer? She's lethal! A hard worker. And to look at her you'd think butter wouldn't melt!'

Gerry's other partner, Larry, would be there, and Larry's lovely Virginia who had a slim figure and a mass of red hair which rippled when she moved like a field of ripe corn. Larry and Virginia had recently become engaged.

Her mind wandered to her own engagement, to the solitaire

diamond Gerry had put on her finger.

'It's lovely, Gerry!'

He had kissed her quickly, smiled, glanced frequently at her ring finger during the evening, as if to satisfy himself about the ring – his ring – there on her hand.

'I don't want to marry you,' were the words that came unbidden into her head as he took her home that night. But she did not speak these words. Other thoughts were formulating themselves. 'What happens to me doesn't matter. What does anything matter so long as I don't have to think about Paddy!'

She accepted Gerry's correct goodnight kiss. The nuns would have approved. The nuns, the priests, the system, had drummed it into her so well: sex as evil, sex as sin, sex as tolerable only within the sanctifying confines of marriage, because marriage, being a sacrament, took the harm out of it.

They would definitely have approved of Gerry, she had thought, as she'd watched his car move away down the long, tree-lined avenue of Brierly, her Rathfarnham home. She had turned to walk up the six granite steps to the hall door.

Her mother was still up and she had showed her the ring.

'It's really nice, darling. Are you happy?'

She'd shrugged. 'Of course I'm happy.'

Then she'd gone upstairs to her room, shut the door, got out her photographs of Paddy and tore them into pieces, one by one, smaller and smaller pieces while the tears fell silently. One photograph she kept, a photograph of both of them taken after a dress dance, threw it into the box containing his letters. These she could not destroy.

The wedding had been four months later. Her father had given her away (what on earth do they think women are, she had wondered, to be 'given away'?). Gerry had been very upright at the steps of the altar and stiffly – there in the presence of their families and friends – he had put the plain gold band on her finger in the name of the Father, the Son and the Holy Ghost.

Afterwards, her mother, having partaken liberally of champagne, of which she was very fond, had helped her out of her white wedding dress.

'Make him take it easy!' she had confided conspiratorially, one married woman to another. And then, suppressing laughter, eyes twinkling at the terrible wickedness of her jest, her mother had dropped her voice to a whisper and told her the joke about the ardent bridegroom.

'. . . After three days he went up with the blind . . .!'

'Oh, Mummy!' Pat laughed, tears of mirth in her eyes as she looked at her mother's 'I'm being naughty' expression.

'Oh Mummy, you're incorrigible!'

It was all long ago. She had been determined to make a go of the marriage, had flung herself into it, into the decoration of the house, into the business of having children, into the business of being a good wife and hostess. She went to cookery classes before the children came along, tried out endless recipes. She made the marriage work, made Gerry laugh, pleased him, pleased herself in pleasing him. And as long as she did this the marriage prospered. When she stopped trying to please him, when she became drained, when the demands of the void inside her could no longer be ignored, she waited for his overtures, his confirmation of love, for his emotional support and stimulus. There was none. She stopped herself from rushing back to fill the emptiness from the depths of her own need. It dawned on her, as she stood back and evaluated the relationship to which she had entrusted her life, that there was, in fact, no relationship; that what they had was an illusion created out of his expectations as to what should be his by dint of marriage, and out of her own projection which depended, in turn, on the substance of her will.

Gerry had been very successful. They had had two children. Ostensibly they were a thriving couple, well matched, content. Tonight they were having a dinner party – one of many.

Pat had come to hate these dinner parties. Gerry would announce the day before that he was having some people for dinner. 'I've asked a few people around for dinner tomorrow, Pat.' After that it was her problem; he expected a nice meal, his wife as a hostess who would chat wittily, look beautiful, do him proud. His guests were usually business acquaintances, people who lived and dreamed money, so that the air around them became charged with it. And when the evening was over he would say, 'That was nice, Pat,' with the air of a man remembering to say the right thing, and disappear into his study.

Sometimes, when everyone was gone, she would sit by the dying embers of the fire, longing fruitlessly for a few quiet moments with him, for a tiny interval of supportive conjugal peace. As a dinner guest, Joan would be a welcome respite. She liked her, had known her from a distance in the old days at college, when Joan was a fresher and she was in her final year. She would be smiling, containing delight at her promotion, the brand-new partner in Galligan and Ryder, Solicitors, Commissioners for Oaths. She had put the wind up the pair of them recently when she had threatened to resign. She should have done it sooner. Her husband had been invited too, but had sent his regrets. He was not well. Pat had met him by accident, when she had come face to face with him and Joan one Saturday morning in Easons. He was an artist.

'An utter nutter!' Gerry said of him when Patricia had asked him what he was like. 'They must be the most ill-matched pair! She's Lady Pragmatism in person and he's wired to the moon!' Pat had nodded, aware at the same time that she knew nothing of Joan's marriage.

'You never know what people find in each other. They may be very well matched for all you know!' She glanced at Gerry. 'He's probably a wonderful lover,' she added slyly, but Gerry sniffed. Being a wonderful lover was not something of any consequence.

'How do you know he's an "utter nutter"?' she had demanded then.

'I took one look at him!' Gerry said. 'These bearded fellows are all hiding something!'

Gerry would be so nice to his new partner this evening; Joan wouldn't hear his comments behind her back.

'Good workhorse . . . Plain as a pikestaff . . .'

Gerry measured life in terms of his private sliding scale: wealth, successful business, nice house, nice car, fatherhood, good-looking wife, in that order. It was a list of a kind, and he ticked things off on it. And the more things were ticked off, the more content he was. Life was a geometric progression in acquisition.

She heard her daughter Orla moving about in her room. Pat had refused her permission to go out to a 'sleepover' party at a friend's house. The friend's parents were in London for the weekend.

'It's not fair – you let Simon go out!'

'Simon is not going to a party!'

'What have you got against parties?'

'Nothing, so long as the parents are at home!'

'It's a "girls only" party.'

'Is that a fact?'

Orla was seventeen now and restive, soon to do the Leaving, rooting around for her identity, rebellious. Until recently Orla wanted to be a lawyer, like Daddy, until she had met this boy who seemed to fascinate her.

'Better luck next time; you'll have the son and heir next time,' one of Gerry's friends had said to her at the time Orla was born, as though she had produced a balloon of nothingness, as though she had been puffed up with wind and presumption instead of with this being of will and fire, her daughter. She had seen it all, there on the first day, the will and the fire, and had prayed that nothing – not belief, not love, not the delirium of self-sacrifice – might break it.

Orla was growing up; adult by her own perceptions, her innocence around her like a mist. Almost every other day a boy with a black leather jacket and a motorbike waited for her after school. One night recently she had not come home until after midnight.

'Where were you Orla? I was out of my mind.'

'Oh, just with Mick.' Irritability. Mother being boring and possessive and unreasonable. Young face flushed; clothes dishevelled. Don't overrreact; she is seventeen and knows everything; what she doesn't know she will learn; the process is her own. I hope she isn't pregnant, not to mention the other possibilities. When I tried to mention it to her she freaked. I could kill that fellow. I saw him that night as I waited, saw him from the upstairs window in the light of the street-lamps, all presumption. Kissing my daughter with lordly usage, Orla's body-language supplicating because she thinks it's momentous and she wants it to be special and she wants recognition from him. Does she think herself in love? Does she give herself to him, to a creature like that? All that will and fire gone to the puffed-up little creep in the leather jacket. Talk to her? But I have. I overdid it.

And Simon, my son, is out this evening, staying with a friend. Sixteen, tall now, man's voice, aggressive as hell. Mother is enemy; mother must be mastered. Doesn't take on father. Clever him!

Once I was seventeen; once I finished school and went to college and studied and saw the future ahead of me. And Paddy was there. Beside me in the library, dancing the twist in the Aula Max, kissing in the portico of Newman House under the lugubrious stone lion, kissing in the shadows of the Green across the street. Groping in the sand-dunes in Dollymount; running down the sand to flee myself more than him, to escape both the confusion of wanting the forbidden and the uncertainty of not knowing if I should reach for it anyway. And Glendalough. The night in Glendalough with the song of the water . . .

'I love you, Patricia O'Hehir,' he had said.

'Marry me! Come on, say yes,' he had demanded the next day while they were hitch-hiking home. He had asked it there on the road between Laragh and Annamoe while the countryside smiled around them, the trees white with hawthorn and chestnut candles, the ditches white with cow parsley.

'Maybe,' she had laughed, delighted. 'Definitely maybe!' What had gone wrong? The stupid row. Jealousy; wild jealousy. Susan Carton. Someone told her that he had gone out with her, that he had gone far with her. Susan was an 'occasional student', someone who came to lectures but hadn't registered for a degree course. Susan had a reputation. Pat had been on a weekend visit to her grandparents and when she returned someone had rushed to tell her that Paddy and Susan had been seen together.

'Did you go out with Susan Carton?'

'Oh Christ! Who told you that?'

'Never mind who! Did you?'

'It doesn't matter. It was a party. She asked me. It's not important!'

'Did you sleep with her?'

He didn't meet her eyes. 'Oh, for God's sake, what do you take me for?' But she had felt the quiver in him of something less than the truth.

They hadn't spoken for a week after that. She had been consumed with jealousy, with a sense of betrayal. Although she knew after three days that she couldn't do without him, she still wouldn't take his phone calls, avoided him in college, walked out of the library when she saw him coming.

'How could he? How could he? Go out with that one! Sleep with her! Did he sleep with her? I can't bear it . . .'

When he phoned, her mother had directions to say she wasn't in. He tried to talk to her in the Main Hall and she cut him dead and walked away with Gerry Galligan, a law student whom she knew from one of the societies.

Gerry had been angling after her for months; now she used him as a vehicle for her anger. She had glanced back from the door, saw Paddy's face, vulnerable, upset, and had laughed, more in desperate relief of tension than anything else, as Gerry took her hand and brought her to Bewleys in Grafton Street for coffee. Gerry was out to impress. She had no interest in him, but she accepted his invitation to the pictures. He held her hand as they walked down O'Connell Street to the Savoy and she hadn't seen Paddy until he was straight in front of them. She had paused, suddenly afraid that she had taken things too far, longing to talk to him, to tell him that she was acting out of pique, that she loved him and that nothing else mattered. But he had merely quickened his stride, nodded at Gerry, given her a look of contemptuous reproach, and passed by.

After that he hadn't phoned her any more. She had begun to panic.

She saw him then with Susan. He would ignore her and turn to Susan; he would pass her by in the library and go directly to where Susan was sitting. Susan with the lovely clothes and the perfect pancake make-up and the blue eyes carefully lined and all that mascara. Susan who smiled winsomely, who seduced. Susan who had rich parents. Marry me and all of this is yours. Give me a gold wedding band and look what you will get in return! This feminine body, this feminine mind and, eventually, the bank account!

So, the row escalating, pride unyielding, they had lost each other and he had, in due course, proposed to Susan. Susan had accepted and she, Patricia, had failed her exams.

'You can sit them again in the autumn,' her mother had said, trying to hide the disappointment, comforting her gently.

'Everyone fails something at some point. Life is mainly about persistence.'

'No.'

She did not want to resit. She had gone to their wedding Mass, sat at the back of the neo-Byzantine University Church, while something inside of her seemed to die.

'Do you, Patrick, take this woman to be your lawful wedded wife . . .?'

Gerry had picked up the pieces. She had married him as soon as he had qualified, got his first job. She had thrown the frustrated passion at him; it had bounced back. He knew nothing of passion. It was not a commodity which could be measured in pounds and pence; it had nothing to do with success. It was embarrassing and irrelevant.

Gerry was a cold fish. That was the truth of it. For a long time she had tried to mould the marriage into a real relationship. And after a while she had stopped trying. But it had taken years for the penny to drop, for the realization that this was how it would always be. That he would never be either friend or companion or lover. That she was trapped. He wanted nothing from her except occasional sex, capability as a hostess, children, and a face to impress the world. He gave her a good allowance, she had help with the housework; if she complained he said she was hysterical and absurd, suggested it was her age, suggested she see a doctor. She had refused to see the doctor.

'I don't want Valium!'

'What do you want?'

'I want to know who you are! I want to share life, our lives, what we feel and think. I want a lover; I want the power we could give each other!'

He had left the room, his face registering weary exasperation.

That night she had tried one more time. She had been thinking of the future, of the years ahead of them, the children grown up, no one in the house but the pair of them. And thinking of this she was filled with a forlorn sense of emptiness, as though a shadow moved across her grave.

'Gerry, will you put your arm around me?' She said it diffidently, with great effort because pride was involved. But he moved in the bed and then said in cold, irritated tones, 'Pat, if you think you can get whatever it is you are looking for somewhere else, you're at liberty to try! It just doesn't exist!'

She had gone downstairs and slept on the couch.

That evening she had looked at him as he came in, saw how drawn he was; touched for a moment she had murmured, 'Gerry, you look tired.' But his face had been unyielding; his mind was elsewhere. The Tunnymore contract was giving trouble; the German was having second thoughts. It would have been a big sale, with a fat fee. He had gone into the sitting room and poured himself a drink.

'I'll have one too,' Patricia said.

He did not pour the drink for her. He looked at her for a moment with a pained expression. 'Get dressed, Pat; they'll be here in an hour.'

34

She felt immediately the reduction to status of wife, housewife. 'I am dressed,' she said flippantly.

He had raised his eyes from the newspaper in perfect silence, looked at her in her sweater and skirt. Patricia did not meet his eyes.

She was suddenly afraid. They were so cold that he sent chills down her spine. I would not mind being afraid of a man who excited me, she thought. Strange that. That would be a challenge, even a kind of security. I could grow in that kind of fear. I could translate it into something else.

Sometimes she had looked at the business friends he brought home, men in expensive suits and silk ties, some of whom made surreptitious passes at her, a hand on her knee under the table, a too-friendly arm around her waist. All she needed to do was give a responsive signal. But, studying them, she knew that, like Gerry, they were focused on self and profit; she would merely be plunder. Most of them were married; some were skilled philanderers.

She had retreated upstairs to their room, taking out the little black dress which had served her so well, putting on the make-up with moistened fingers to make the damn stuff spread. A little blue eyeshadow; a touch of mascara; plum-coloured lipstick. She obliterated herself behind the mask she created, became interested in the transformation, the eyes becoming brighter, the lips red and moist. She pouted at her reflection, a Bardot pout. She snorted then, laughing at the mad woman behind the mask. She wasn't bad for forty-one. You need never get old. It was all in the mind. A few lines you wouldn't notice. She brushed her hair, thick and glossy and still auburn, with a few grey ribs which had been coloured in by her hairdresser. She put on the black dress, turned sideways, watching in the mirror this slim self, this sophisticate who was not her, who had nothing in common with a woman echoing with emptiness, a woman who had a successful husband, two children and a bottle of vodka in her underwear drawer.

It was in another drawer that she kept Paddy's letters, a little secret drawer in her Victorian dressing-table which had no knob but yielded to pressure so that the catch sprung. They lay there loosely, unbound, just one on top of the other, notes he had written her during the holidays, small snippets of poems. She seldom looked at them; she didn't need to. She knew them by heart. He had sent her Christmas cards too after his marriage; 'With best wishes from Susan and Paddy.' She had burnt them at first and then, after a few years, had put them on the mantelpiece with everyone else's, had thrown them out after Christmas like all the others.

She had forgotten him. He belonged to the past; he belonged with the life he had made for himself in London and Paris; he belonged with Susan and his family. And yet, sometimes, without any volition at all on her part, he would invade her; words from his letters, words from the poem he sent her after their camping trip to Glendalough:

> . . . And I should find
> Soon in the silence the hidden key
> Of all that had hurt and puzzled me -
> Why you were you and the night was kind,
> And the woods were part of the heart of me.

Words from Rupert Brooke, words from other poets: Wordsworth, Eliot, Auden, Yeats. He had read them for pleasure in those far-off days; they had not featured on the engineering syllabus.

When she had married Gerry she had tried to interest him in poetry and he had laughed and launched into a derisive ditty. ' "A birdie with a yellow bill, Sang upon my window-sill!" You can't be interested in that sort of stuff!'

'I'm not!'

He picked up the poetry book she was reading. 'What's this?'

'It's *The Rubaiyat of Omar Khayyam*.'

He had given a short laugh, had begun to read a few lines aloud, changing his voice to a falsetto, stressing each syllable with mockery.

> 'I sent my soul through the Invisible
> Some letter of that After-life to spell;
> And by and by my Soul returned to me,
> And answer'd "I Myself am Heav'n and Hell".'

He paused, looked at her over his glasses with a superior smirk. 'What sort of old rubbish is that?'

'It's not rubbish,' Patricia cried. 'It's wonderful. Look, this

36

man lived in the twelfth century in Persia . . .'

'A Wop!' Gerry said knowingly, as though all had been explained, and went back to his newspaper.

And in time she had realized that anything, anything, to do with feeling or emotions elicited the same response. Exterminate. Exterminate. Like one of the bloody Daleks! Maintain control. Incinerate the inner life, kill it with derision, heap it with contempt.

She heard the doorbell, the voices in the hall. Panic. Larry and Virginia and Joan Bloody de Barra, the perfect solicitor. She reached into her underwear drawer, rooted among the cotton knickers and found the bottle, took a swig, screwed back the cap, descended the staircase, head high.

Gerry, who was at the door, looked up at her dubiously, narrowing his eyes.

'Larry, how lovely to see you, darling . . . and Virginia, looking as sumptuous as ever.' She kissed them on the cheek, thinking, Christ how I hate you, Pat, you hypocrite. She did not care for Larry. He was cut from the same cloth as Gerry, but he was also touched with a knowing superficiality which grated on Patricia's nerves.

Virginia seemed to start. She could smell the vodka. She took off her coat and handed it to Gerry, who carried it to the cloakroom. She glanced at herself in the mirror, a quick, comparing glance. I'm ten years younger than this woman, Virginia's complacent glance said.

Patricia saw the glance, read it immediately. Have no fears, my dear. Larry will crush the life out of you in jig-time. You may have looks and femininity and life, but you will be caged just the same: exhibit A, possession of Larry Ryder, success story. Mrs Larry, how's that for a handle? And you will grace his life and make his friends envious and your body will produce children for him who will turn on you in fifteen years' time with hatred. Fun times ahead, my girl.

'Has Joan arrived?' Larry asked as Pat ushered them into the lounge.

'Not yet.'

'I've never met her,' Virginia said.

Gerry came back and began to pour the drinks. 'What will you have, Virginia?'

'White wine.'

'Larry?'

'Scotch.'

What's wrong with bloody Jameson? Patricia asked herself.

'I'll have a Jameson,' Patricia said.

Gerry glanced at her coldly, poured her a small whisky. He doesn't like me drinking. I should stick to Ballygowan. It would fit the image better.

'There's the door!'

Gerry went to answer it. There were voices in the hall: Gerry hearty, Joan slightly nervous. Patricia smiled at Larry and Virginia and offered them peanuts, which Virginia declined.

'Hello, Joan.' Larry half rose to his feet when she came in, then settled himself down again. She was dressed in a black skirt and white lace blouse. Patricia introduced her, catching as she did so Virginia's swift assessment of her. Don't worry, my pet. This one is not dangerous. This one believes in the whole shebang: draft contracts, Wills, deeds, separation agreements quicker than you could make up your face. This one does the odd bit of court work, but she's mostly stuck in the office, sitting there day after day, reading titles until it's a wonder her eyes don't fall out from terminal boredom. She's younger than me, but she looks older. After all, she hasn't had all the excitement I've had. She doesn't have a husband perpetually on the make and piranhas for children. She has a sick husband who is an artist and one teenage son. She is not a kept woman. But she is one hell of an exploited one.

'What do you pay Joan?' she had asked Gerry once.

'That's none of your business, Pat.'

'I bet you don't give her more than eighteen grand.'

Gerry had looked at her, then resumed reading in silence. Bull's-eye, Patricia had thought to herself.

'What's your poison, Joan?'

'Sherry, thank you.'

Gerry handed her the amber glassful. Joan sipped. Patricia studied her, saw the way she looked at her two new partners, a certain wariness, saw the lovely legs, the cheap shoes, the cheap everything except the exquisite lace blouse.

'Your blouse is beautiful. Is it Carrickmacross?'

'No. My grandmother made it for my mother.' She smiled at Patricia, fixing grave eyes on her. 'It's more or less indestructible.'

'Congratulations on the new partnership.'

'Thanks.'

'I'm sorry your husband couldn't come.'

'Yes. He would have liked to. He's a bit tired these days.' Pat *was* sorry he couldn't come. She would have been glad to have talked with him.

'How is his work going?'

'Quite well.' Joan paused and Patricia heard the pride in her voice, the way the words slowed. 'A Paris gallery seem to be interested in his work!'

She stared at her. 'Well done! He must be really something!'

Joan smiled, studied her sherry. 'Yes, I think he is.'

Patricia felt the whisky in her brain. She leaned towards Joan and said *sotto voce*, 'The partnership was long overdue; you should have put the skids under that pair long ago.'

Joan raised her eyebrows with a smile and didn't comment. She looked around the room and Patricia suddenly saw it through her eyes: luxurious, overstated; that it should be stated at all was suddenly nauseating. She had always hated that cocktail cabinet thing that Gerry had bought, all flash there in the corner with the bottles of whisky and gin. In the other alcove was the Chippendale cabinet with her porcelain collection, Anysley and Coalport, a collection which had begun with some wedding presents and which had been added to over the years.

'Joan's doing great things for us,' Gerry said heartily. 'Here's to our venture together.' He raised his glass. They all raised their glasses. The Christmas tree shone with tinsel in the firelight. Virginia's long legs stretched and rubbed against Larry's. There was a split in her skirt and you could see her thighs, dark and shapely in the black tights. Joan blushed at the attention.

'How's young Paul?' Patricia asked her, to deflect her embarrassment.

'He's working hard – Christmas exams at the moment.' God, to have a child who worked hard and didn't fight with you! There was silence. Virginia studied her cuticles, arching her back. The turf briquettes in the fireplace settled in a shower of aromatic incandescence.

Patricia rose. 'Excuse me while I check on things. We'll be ready to eat in a minute.'

'Can I help you?' Joan asked.

'Not really, but come down to the kitchen if you like.'

In the kitchen, Una Foley was bending over the cooker.

'I'm ready to serve now, Mrs Galligan.'

Joan looked around the expensive kitchen. 'You have a lovely house.'

'Thanks.'

Joan watched Patricia. She sensed that the defiance, the brittle jocosity, was a mask. Under it, she felt, there was only desperation. She had something to tell Pat and did not want to say it in Gerry's presence.

'By the way, I met an old friend of yours today. He had an appointment with Gerry to discuss a contract. He'll be working in Ireland for a while until his company's new Irish subsidiary is off the ground.'

'Oh . . .?'

'I bumped into him in the hall tonight as I was leaving the office. He asked for you. He sent his regards. He said he'd phone you.'

Patricia turned around, licking the teaspoon she had used to test the sauce. Her face was suddenly wary. 'Oh – who is he?'

'Paddy Johnson.'

Patricia put the spoon down carefully. She did not reply.

Later, when everyone was gone, she said to Gerry, 'Did you have a busy day? Did you have any new clients?' Gerry was in bed, reading an article on commercial law and she was brushing her hair at the dressing-table.

'What . . . new clients? No. Why do you ask?'

'Oh nothing. Just something Joan said . . .'

There was silence.

'So you had no new clients?' Patricia ventured again.

He looked up at her. 'For God's sake, Pat, will you let me concentrate?' Patricia executed a stiff salute to herself in the mirror. She thought longingly of the bottle in her drawer. She looked around the room. The lamplight was mellow on Gerry's periodical, and on the shiny dome of his skull. His glasses reflected a faint blue light. His face was still curiously boyish, although the hair left to him was already quite grey. He was half frowning in concentration, the utter concentration he brought to everything to do with his work. He did not react to her scrutiny; he was not aware of it. She felt the present moment as an intolerable burden of emptiness closing in on her. She felt the silence, the utter silence in all the private spaces of her life. She went to the wardrobe and took out from a shelf a thick student's notepad, sat down at her dressing-table and began to write.

She called her notebook, *The Horse's Ears*, thinking of the story from Irish mythology about a man who found out that the king had horse's ears and, knowing that his life was forfeit if he told anyone the truth, but desperate at the same time to share the secret, told a tree.

Gerry looked up from his reading some time later. 'What are you writing?'

'Letters.'

'Come to bed.'

Patricia closed the notepad, which contained no letters whatever. She put it away and got into bed. Gerry turned off the light. He took off his pyjama bottoms and began to make love, methodically. Patricia thought of what she had written in the notepad and wondered what he would say if he ever read it. That she was mad? Yes. He would say that.

Chapter Three

God, why didn't they tell us what childbirth would be like? It took a day and a half, eighteen hours, and at the end I was seeing double and wanted to die. The doctor came and stood between my legs and discussed a hospital party with the nurses. Once or twice he noticed that I was there and not just a lump of meat.

'Push, Mrs Galligan' – as though I could do anything else! I hated him standing there, staring into my bleeding vulva, talking about hospital trivia to the nurses while my flesh tore and pain became an ecstasy.

'Good girl,' he said.

What would he have felt like, lying there, naked from the waist with his legs up in stirrups? How would he have felt, giving life, to be told, 'Good boy'?

But the experience itself defies description. There's a sudden cry, whistling to begin with as air is sucked into brand-new lungs, and then the new person you have made, all waxen and wet, your blood on its hair, is put on your tummy. You cannot take your eyes off it. You are trembling with exhaustion from head to foot. Inside you feel that you have made a journey to the ends of the world where everything begins anew. But the exercise in humiliation they make of it is unforgivable.

Anyway, it's over and here I am – a mother. The baby is the most beautiful thing I ever saw. We have called her Orla.

from *The Horse's Ears*, 1972

Patricia's notebook, begun about a year after her marriage, added to occasionally, was kept in a cardboard file-cover on the shelf of her wardrobe, under her jumpers. Sometimes, recently, she'd added to it after a few gulps of vodka; other times she read it with embarrassment and barely stopped herself from destroying it. At these times she knew she was in the wrong; at these times she knew she must not think the way she did, knew she must not write the way she did. What if Gerry found it? Read it? She dreaded his reaction, his contempt. Other times she knew that, even if Gerry should chance on it, he would never read it. He wouldn't be interested.

The day after the dinner party was Saturday. Every time the phone rang Patricia let it ring for a moment then picked it up with calculated indifference. And every time it was either one of Gerry's friends, or one of the children's friends. Or Nell, her best friend, who was married to an auctioneer. Nell had one son, Peter, who was friendly with Simon, but today she talked of her nieces, her sister's children, whom she was babysitting.

Gerry went out early. He had a lunch appointment and was to play golf in the afternoon.

Simon came home at lunchtime. Orla was still in bed; she had a cold and Patricia had brought her her breakfast, fixing the pillows behind her, hoping for a moment of conversation with her. She was half in love with her daughter. But Orla was glassy-eyed and unforgiving. She had not dared defy her mother by going out the evening before, and she wanted to punish her for it.

So Pat had retreated into her own room and from there she heard Simon charging into his sister's bedroom.

'Where's my radio? I told you before, you are not to take it!'

Patricia heard the exchange from across the landing. 'Oh, piss off. I'll take your stupid radio any time I want.'

'You're a right little cunt' and he stormed out of her room, clutching the radio.

Patricia met him in the landing. 'Leave your sister alone; she's not well. Don't go into her room again. And don't use that language in this house.'

Simon sensed his mother's love for his sister and decided he didn't care. 'Leave your sister alone; she's not well,' he mimicked her. Patricia stood in his path; he pushed her aside. He was big and strong and he had no trouble pushing her. I am a monster, his gesture said, but I am a monster with power. Under it a smaller, plaintive voice said silently – Love me. Love me even though I am a monster!

Patricia raised her hand and slapped his face. It was the work of

44

an impulsive, angry instant. 'Don't you dare try that again, young man.'

For a moment Simon looked shocked, almost on the verge of tears; then his face twisted and he stared into his mother's eyes with fury and hatred. 'And what are you going to do about it, mother dear? Expel me from the family nest? Deny me nourishment?'

'I will tell your father,' Patricia whispered after a moment in which her impotence struggled with her rage. 'I will tell him of your behaviour.'

'Do,' Simon said. 'Tell him all about nasty me. What do you think he'll say? Do you think he gives a damn? Go running to Dad, do. Or, better still, have another swig of vodka. Do you think Orla and I don't know about your little cache!' Patricia leant against the wall. Her face was white and she was unable to speak.

'How do you know what I keep in my room?' she whispered after a moment, but he was gone downstairs, his face triumphant from having administered the *coup-de-grâce*. If he could not have love he would, at least, have triumph.

For a moment she wanted to follow him; then she thought she had better question Orla, but was subsumed with a sense of weariness and disgust. She was tired of all the postures of power. It was one of them or the other, or if not one of them it was Gerry – it went on all around her, the jostling for domestic preeminence. It was dragging her into a tangle of bleak domestic politics which was changing her into a Gorgon, because it had to do with pride and survival and consequently rubbed against the core of her will.

She went back into her room and shut the door. The sun was shining against the wall by the bed. The brass bedstead was bright. The dressing-table was cheerful with the embroidered runner and her brushes neatly set out. The curtains were looped back with tie-backs from the same material.

I know this is a pretty room; but it is something I know in the same way as I know the world is round. I do not experience it. This room, this house with its expensive furniture, is meaningless.

She was full of pain. She thought of Simon, almost a young man now, embarking on his adult life. She was a woman. He was driven to dominate her, to challenge her space; she must live with

45

dignity only through his indulgence. The situation was desperate precisely because she was his mother. She had authority over him and he could not endure it. He would accept it grudgingly from his father, but not from her. Nothing else, neither their intimately intertwined history, nor the years of her care, reckoned in this contest.

What frightened her most of all was that she no longer had any feelings for him, except dislike and a stubborn sense of endurance. Someday it would end. This monster would some-day become a human being. In the meantime he needed this vampirism to bolster his fragility. If he could hurt his mother with impunity, was he not a god? I cannot order him out; I do not even own the bloody house. And he is a child although he does not know it. But I have had years of this, and I too wish to live.

She reached into the drawer and found the vodka. She tried to remember when she had started to tipple; was it a year ago, was it six months? Just a little, God. Just a swig. I don't want to become dependent on the stuff. But a little drop blunts the boredom and the pain.

Later that afternoon, Patricia steered the shopping trolley through the aisles of a supermarket. She hated shopping – at least shopping for groceries; pushing this steel monster which didn't like corners, loading it up with item after item: meat, vegetables, cheese, fruit, tinned produce, cereals, frozen foods, toilet paper, toothpaste, detergent. Once a week she did the shopping, skated around the aisles, fired the stuff in, waited in a queue, paid for it, dug it out of the boot when she got home, put it in the fridge, deep freeze, cupboards of her state-of-the-art fitted oak kitchen, the perfection of which she had also come to detest. And then she would sit down and have a cup of coffee. Just like the good little housewives in the ads, she thought. All those mindless women. Why do they have to depict women as retards?

So today, because she hated the shopping, she had another swig of vodka before she left; not too much, just enough to take the edge off the ennui, just enough to induce fractional euphoria.

The supermarket was decorated with a huge Christmas tree, baubles, tinsel and the muted strains of 'Jingle Bells' filled the air. Patricia paused and examined different brands, then skidded to the next display, watching herself as though she inhabited a video camera located somewhere above and behind her. Pat is working well today, she hummed to herself. Pat is examining everything, every blasted ingredient. Of course she is. Pat will make sure that His Imperial Importance and the Two Piranhas are not poisoned by E numbers . . .

There was a bump, the impact of colliding trolleys, the dull, self-satisfied crack of breaking glass. 'God, I'm sorry,' she said to the woman in the shiny plastic raincoat who was pushing the other trolley. 'I should look where I'm going. What have I broken?'

There was a child sitting in the trolley seat with ice-cream stains around his mouth. He started to wail.

'Shut up or I'll burst you,' his mother informed him. She looked at Patricia. 'Just a few tumblers. They make them out of thin air anyway. I'll nip back and change them in a minute.' The two women stared at each other.

'Don't I know you from somewhere?' Patricia asked, trying to place the face in front of her, the brown eyes and the lop-sided crinkling smile. The woman frowned, then laughed.

'I know who you are,' she said after a moment. 'Weren't you at St Anne's? Weren't you a prefect in sixth year when I was in first year . . .? Patricia O'Hehir!' she added triumphantly. Pat nodded. 'Of course!' Her mind strained to recall the faces at school, most of them forgotten.

'You nearly ratted on me once!' the woman went on with a lugubrious expression. 'You were supervising our class for Sister Martha and I threw a paper dart and it got stuck in your hair . . .'

Patricia laughed, remembering suddenly the cheeky face of the thirteen-year-old who was regarded as the biggest pest in first year.

'You let me off, but you weren't a bit pleased!'

'I was a prefect!' Patricia said gravely. 'Life was a serious business . . . What's your name?'

'Sarah . . . Dempsey that was. O'Toole now.' She looked at Patricia and added, 'Actually I needed all the straightening out I could get! I thought I could go on taking the mickey for the rest of my life!'

She looked tired. Her dark hair was lank and she pushed her fingers through it in a gesture of fatigue; there were circles under her eyes. On her right jaw was a livid mark. It was covered by make-up, but it was there.

Patricia accompanied her to the kitchenware shelves, helped find the right tumblers, a pack of six in a cardboard box. The broken ones were put back.

'I suppose you wouldn't like a cup of coffee?' Patricia said, indicating the coffee dock with a nod of her head. 'I could do with one.'

Sarah hesitated. 'I'd love one, but I don't think I've got the time. I have to be home for the children. There's no one to let them in.'

'How many children have you got?'

'Three!' Sarah glanced at her watch. 'Well, a quick cup . . .'

Patricia bought the coffees and two slices of Black Forest gâteau. She brought them back to the table. Sarah demurred at the cake at first, and then ate it with relish, complaining about the calories.

'I've an awful sweet tooth.'

Patricia toyed with the other piece and fed morsels of it to the child on a spoon. The little boy grabbed it and shoved lumps of it into his mouth, leaving smears of chocolate on his chin and in between his fingers.

'Dara is greed on wheels,' Sarah said. 'Don't give him any more of that.'

Then they swopped information about how many children they had and where they were living and Sarah trotted out some names; did Pat remember so-and-so from school? Then she mentioned someone who had been killed, someone else who had died from cancer and someone else who was now a television star. 'Do you remember her? She used to be a right little mouse!'

We are like battle troops, Pat thought. Once we were lined up before the battle. Now we begin to see the casualties and the triumphs; and the rest of us simply surrender or soldier on.

'Do you always shop here?' Patricia asked then.

'Not always.'

'What happened to your face?'

Sarah sighed. Her brown eyes focused for a moment in the distance. She gave Patricia a wary look, put a hand to her jaw. 'Is it very obvious?'

'Not very. But maybe you should do something about it.'

48

Sarah's eyes narrowed. 'I walked into a door. And maybe you should go easy on the vodka.'

'Is "that" very obvious?'

Sarah laughed. 'No. But I'm an expert. I can smell it a mile off.'

The two women smiled at each other across the table. Brown eyes met blue in sympathy.

'I have to go,' Sarah said, getting up. 'I'll see you around . . . Pat. Thanks for the coffee.'

Patricia watched her as she pushed the laden trolley away. The child turned his head to look back at her.

That evening, when Gerry and Simon were both out and Orla was still in bed and still in a huff – 'For God's sake Mum, leave me alone' – Patricia decided she would read. She had phoned her friend Nell to ask her if she would come to the pictures, but Nell was still babysitting.

The Agony and the Ecstasy was on her table, all about Michelangelo and his fury of creation. There were a few back-copies of the paper which she had kept for the crossword. Gerry seldom finished the Crosaire and she enjoyed the challenge. She picked them up, tidied them, saw the heading: 'WOMAN GETS THIRTY YEARS.'

It was the sentence in the Cork woman's case, the one who had conspired to kill her husband. Thirty years! And he had been a wife-beater! He had nearly killed her with his beatings, but she had got thirty years! She had instigated this crime out of terror, yet had been sentenced like someone who was involved in cold blood! Patricia threw down the paper. Her mind reverted for a moment to Sarah Dempsey whom she had literally bumped into in the supermarket. She could remember her quite clearly now, a girl with velvet skin and a mischievous grin was was frequently in detention for not having her homework done, or for disrupting class. She would see her sitting there with the other detainees when she, Pat, was on her way home to Brierly.

Sarah had changed. The velvet skin had become sallow, tired, and the mark on her jaw where she had 'walked into a door' was not disguised by the make-up. Patricia looked in the mirror at her own face, trying to compare it with the one which once looked back at her above her school uniform, trying to recall the perspectives she had then, the dreams, the expectation of the

49

future. The drawer with the bottle of Smirnoff was opened quietly, with her mind fixed elsewhere. She poured a measure of the spirit into the plastic cap of her hairspray, deliberately shutting out the thought of what she was doing, as though this would nullify her action. She had begun to fear the vodka. Then Patricia took out Paddy Johnson's letters and read them.

She read them one by one, sipping the vodka slowly from the plastic hairspray cover. Why didn't you phone when you said you would? You told Joan you would. She put them back in the drawer and then she lay back on the bed and stared at the knowing witch's face in the ceiling. She thought of the feel of his hands on her body, imagined what it would have been like to make love with him, what it would have been like to have spent her life with him. But it was all too late. Her mother always said those were the saddest words. Too late!

After a while Omar Kayyam's words began to spin in her head, as poetry always did when she had had a drink or two.

'Heaven but a vision of fulfilled desire
And Hell the shadow from a soul on fire . . .'

The words spun round and round, creating their own measure, and carried her away on their rhythm.

'And Hell the shadow from a soul on fire', repeated over and over while the tears crept hotly down her face.

When Gerry got home he found her still lying there, the empty bottle of vodka on the bedside table.

'Jesus Christ, Pat,' he said in horrified disgust. 'You're drunk!'

She stirred, her words slurred. 'Only . . . Shlightly drunk . . .' She gave a wild giggle and lapsed back to sleep.

He stared at her for a moment, anger gathering, then alarm. His wife, semi-comatose, in a drunken stupor! She stirred and he hissed in her ear. 'You've been tippling for some time! You'll have to shape up or ship out, do you hear me?'

She opened her eyes. They were bloodshot and her breath was acrid with a sweet, sharp smell.

'What?' she demanded thickly. 'What did y'say?'

'You make me sick,' Gerry said. 'When I think of the way I work for this family!'

Simon's face appeared at the door. 'What's wrong with

50

Mum?' His eyes registered a moment's fear, the pupils dilated. 'Is she sick?'

'She's drunk,' Gerry said. 'Your mother's drunk.'

Simon's expression changed to one of amused superiority. He gave a snort halfway between a laugh and a giggle and raised his shoulders. He knew that parents were not supposed to get drunk.

'Should we get a doctor?' he asked uncertainly.

'And let him see this?' Gerry hissed, his voice cold with disdain. Simon looked at his father's face and slowly his own assumed a mirror mask of contempt.

'Stop standing there gawping' Gerry said. 'Go downstairs and bring me up some chocolates. There's a box Joan de Barra brought last night.'

Simon stared at him. 'What do you want chocolates for?'

'Just bring them, and get a basin from the kitchen as well.' Gerry looked at the empty bottle. 'You can take this down to the bin.'

When Simon came back with the chocolates and the plastic basin, Gerry selected a strawberry cream, sat on the bed, and hooked his arm behind Patricia's head. 'Wake up, I've something for you!' He squeezed the chocolate between her teeth. 'Eat that.'

Patricia twisted her head. 'Don't want it.'

Gerry shook her. 'Come on, Pat, it's important. Eat it! *Eat* it!'

Patricia gave the chocolate a few chews and swallowed it. Gerry immediately put another soft centre between her teeth, closed her mouth on it, massaged her cheeks. 'Swallow!'

She obeyed, opening her eyes for a moment, closing them. She made a gesture of submission and ate a third chocolate and then kept on eating them mechanically as he fed them to her. When she felt her stomach lurch, Gerry was waiting with the basin. He pulled her sideways so that she lay on her stomach, and he and Simon supported her head over the edge of the bed. When she was finished vomiting, he gave Simon the basin to dispose of. The boy made a face and picked the basin up gingerly. Gerry held a glass of water so that Patricia might drink. She swallowed the water, slopping some of it down her chin.

'I'll sleep in the guest room!' Gerry said through compressed lips.

51

Patricia woke early the next morning with a raging thirst and a splitting headache. She lay as still as she could; any movement made her feel that her brains were being battered against the side of her skull. Fragments of the night before floated into her mind – drinking the vodka, lying on the bed, being woken by Gerry who had made her get sick. And, Jesus Christ, Simon had been there too! He had let him see it all! He had let her son stand and watch! The bastard! She dozed and woke and dozed again. There was no prospect of being able to get up. Even the dim light from the curtained window was too much. She heard Gerry talking to Orla in the landing, but he did not come.

At ten thirty Orla brought her a pot of tea and some toast. The girl's face was closed and wrathful. She left the tray on the bedside table with only a comment, 'Here's some tea!' and a loud reproachful sigh, her lips parting in disgust. My daughter knows too, Patricia thought. What would I have felt at her age if I had a drunken mother? Am I to become a drunk then? Is that what the future holds?

Later she got up, went to the dressing-table. In the mirror she saw a woman who only barely resembled herself, face drawn and puffy, white, with bloodshot, red-rimmed eyes. She crept back to bed, put her head under the duvet to ease the sense of fear and shame.

When the sense of physical malaise had begun to abate she thought, This is never going to happen again. No matter what! Nothing is worth this. She tried to analyse what was the cause of it, why was she so miserable, why did she drink?

'It's something to do with space,' she murmured aloud. 'I don't have some essential kind of space, so I try to escape!'

She leaned back, examining the ceiling, the silly witch's face. Thoughts came to her. I will not be a drunk. I will stop running away. The witch's face stared back at her non-committally. 'Make your own arrangements,' it seemed to say. 'Don't look at me.'

I have to confront my life and change it. I have a choice in what becomes of me.

She got up and went downstairs to the kitchen. Orla was there, preparing lunch. She turned her head away. Patricia sighed.

'You'll have to forgive me, Orla! You may as well try now! If I can forgive me, so can you!'

Orla registered surprise, looked at her doubtfully for a moment, like someone teetering on the verge of emotional decision. Then her face closed.

'I wish I had a mother who wasn't such a mess!' she announced as she walked from the room in adolescent dignity. Patricia leaned her head on her hand for a moment and then got up and finished peeling the potatoes.

Chapter Four

I've been married for three years. Yesterday was our anniversary and Gerry sent me flowers. They arrived at midday, a huge bouquet with a card in block letters – written by his secretary – 'WITH LOVE FROM GERRY.' No signature.

I spent some time arranging them, put them in the hall. I thanked him when he came home and he looked surprised for a moment, as though he didn't remember sending them. We were supposed to go out for dinner with Nell and Fred but the baby was cranky and I stayed behind. Poor little mite still has colic and I hate leaving him. I walked around with him, whispering his name – 'Simon, Simon', and rubbing his tummy. He loves that. When I got him to sleep Orla woke up, so I took her into bed with me.

When she dropped off I read some of Gerry's book on Family Law. I've been dipping into the textbook here and there out of curiosity. The stuff is incredible, which makes it fascinating. I wish I had done Law. I've often said so to Gerry – it would stop me feeling so bloody helpless and I know I'd be good at it – but he just sighs and tells me not to be absurd.

from *The Horse's Ears*, 1973

'Can I tell you something in confidence?' Patricia said to Nell the next day. Nell had arrived after lunch 'on the off-chance' on her way back from a working lunch to do with one of her charitable activities, a Christmas party being organized for deprived children. Nell had a breathless way with her; her existence was a perpetual rush, as though life were hot on her heels and she had determined to deploy everything at her command to evade it.

Sometimes Pat suspected that she never subjected herself to a moment's solitude.

'Of course!' she said, turning smiling blue eyes on her friend. 'Well, go on . . .'

Pat faltered. '. . . I'm going to make some changes around here!'

Nell laughed. 'Is that what you were going to tell me in confidence? What kind of changes?'

Nell was tall, dressed in trousers and jacket, which suited her. She wore her hair down to her shoulders, thick, dark hair. 'You're looking very peaky, Pat, if you don't mind me saying so. You're pale as death!'

'I know . . .'

'What happened to you?'

'Oh – it's a long story. I'm thinking of leaving Gerry!'

Nell's eyes widened and her jaw dropped. 'What on earth put that into your head?'

Patricia didn't answer for a moment. Then she said, 'It's been in my mind for a long time!'

Nell looked subdued. Her face had become serious, her chin lowered so that the incipient jowls were evident over the top of her black polo-neck.

'My dear girl – how would you live? What about the children?'

'The children are big now. They could come with me if they wanted. I'll get a job!'

'Doing what?'

'I don't know. I must be able to do something. I know I'm qualified for nothing, but I could do secretarial work . . .'

Nell considered this for a moment. 'Can you type?'

'I can learn!'

'What do you know of word-processing?'

'Nothing!'

'Do you know shorthand?'

'They don't use it any more! Gerry only uses the dictaphone.'

'Don't kid yourself. Let's see – how many languages have you got?'

Patricia leaned back in the armchair. 'I've got English,' she said irritably. That should be good enough for anyone. I've also got French . . . well, school French.'

Nell shrugged. 'Look, I hate to sound like the Elder Lemon, but you won't be able to get work without skills. No one is going

56

to give a woman of your age, with your background, a filing job and, even if they did, the sort of salary they'd pay you would be derisory. How would you like to live on eight thousand a year?'

'I'd get something from Gerry.'

'Not if you leave him. That's called desertion. Do you have a stake in the house?'

'No. It's in his name.'

There was silence. A car drew up outside; there was the high-pitched 'beep' as the owner operated the central locking.

Patricia sighed. 'My total assets amount to £1,800 in the bank, my clothes, and my car.'

'You won't get far on that! And you'd die if you had to give up the car.'

Patricia made as if to speak, but changed her mind. Nell was shaking her head.

'Look, you have to keep a cool head in this life,' she went on softly. 'I've been where you are. I never told this to anyone, but five years ago all I wanted was to go, pack up and get out. And then I sat down and thought about it. OK, so Fred was playing the field . . . I know he made a play for you too, Pat, so you needn't look so surprised. OK, so I was bored out of my tree. But what did the big bad world have to offer Nell? Poverty, hardship, a struggle to survive! Fred would never agree to a separation, so there'd be precious little money from that source. Then I realized that all I had to do was not to care so much, not to need anything from him emotionally, to focus elsewhere. Let him philander! As long as he brought in the money, kept the roof over our heads, gave me my allowance. I realized I had freedom of a kind I could never have with a nine-to-five job. So I got involved with my committee work, made a lot of friends. You should do the same. What you need are outside interests. You spend too much time reading and thinking! Get out and meet people; get involved in life! At least your husband isn't hopping in and out of other people's beds! You have a lovely home, everything you could want!'

Patricia began to feel that she was suffering from some kind of myopia, some fractured view of reality where she had failed to connect the pieces. Nell's words made her shiver at the thought of what she might have thrown away. Security. Status. Plenty. She visualized herself at forty-one with eight thousand a year, a bedsitter somewhere, working at some rotten little job.

'Nell, you make me feel like a spoilt child! D'you know what I did the other night? I got drunk! I finished a bottle of vodka and Gerry found me and made me get sick!'

Nell drew her breath in through her teeth, shook her head. 'Second-best plan: keep off the booze. He'll dump you for that!'

Patricia looked out at the well-kept lawn, at Nell's red car in the drive, at the winter sunlight on the branches of the cherry tree. She was aware of her sitting room, the marble mantelpiece with family photographs, the mahogany tallboy with the carved ivory Confucius, the cabinet of her porcelain collection in the corner, and Gerry's awful cocktail cabinet. She raised her hands.

'But Nell . . . if you have to stifle the core of yourself, what good is everything?'

Nell looked at her pityingly. 'My dear girl, if you have to grub for survival, what time do you think you will have for the "core of yourself"?'

Nell left. Patricia watched her from the window, saw her swing down the driveway to her car. Nell had a confident walk, held herself well, wore her tan leather shoulder-bag jauntily. But Pat saw her inner loneliness enveloping her like a thin blue gauze. Nell looked back at the house as she opened the car door, waved cheerily and gave a thumbs-up sign. Patricia drew back the sheer net curtain and waved back. Then the red coupé was gone, purring into the Ballsbridge traffic.

Patricia wondered if she were suffering from schizophrenia. She felt as though she had been saved at the brink. What if she had said to Gerry this evening, 'Gerry, I want to leave you.'? What would he have said?

She knew. He would look up at her with those cold eyes, then back at his paper. 'You're a free agent, Patricia! You know where the door is!'

He would let her go, just like that, without any attempt to stop her. His pride would not permit him to stop her. And then he would be utterly ruthless. She would get nothing from him. All the years of her work in the home, the days and hours of childbearing and rearing, of cooking and hostessing, of running the Galligan residence, of worrying and planning, would count as nothing. No court would recognize the investment of her life as worth a brass farthing. She would be seen as deserting her husband. 'But how can you desert someone who simply is not there?' she asked herself. Could she even explain that? No. She

58

would have to shift for herself. And there was fear in this prospect. Perhaps she should be glad of what she had. She thought of Nell, swinging jauntily down the path. But she knew herself that something in Nell had died. She had felt it years ago, a kind of creeping paralysis of the soul. The fire in her had died. Now she knew why. I don't want to die too, she thought. I don't want to have to scratch for a living like an old hen, not after all these years. But I don't want to die either.

She went upstairs. In an effort to slough off the depression she washed her hair, dried it carefully, blow-drying it up and back off her forehead. She spent some time on her face, put on a face-mask, toned and moisturized her skin so that it glowed. Then she did some exercises on the floor in front of her mirror, trying to shift the malaise left by the events of the weekend, watching her figure: the flat stomach, the still-young breasts, a little fuller than formerly, but what harm was that? Her waist was small and her hips trim. She was proud of her body, was determined not to let it go to rack and ruin. She had developed early, so that even in her early teens men were eyeing her.

Once, on her way home from school, she had stopped to watch a farrier at work and an old man with a greasy peaked cap, who had been hanging around the farrier's workshop, had put his arm around her, walked back part of the way with her, asked her for a kiss. She had been thirteen.

'Please leave me alone.'

She had seen him again a few days later as she walked up the country road from the bus.

'Are ye coming to see the horses again?' he'd said with a leer, and Pat had felt his eyes boring through her uniform, lingering on her breasts.

He moved along beside her, dropped his voice which was thick with longing. 'I'll give ye a fiver . . . come into the lane . . .' He had touched her with a leathery hand and when she turned to look at him she saw the wet incontinence of his lips.

'I'll tell my father if you don't leave me alone!' He had frightened her badly, but she would not let him see that.

Later she had told her mother, who had reacted violently. 'Oh my God . . . You could have been destroyed . . .' and then she had added, 'Don't tell your father . . . he'd kill him!'

But her mother had been there to meet her at the bus stop the next day with her father's shotgun in the back seat. As they were driving back to Brierly, Pat had pointed out the man, who was once again on the road.

Her mother had stopped the car, lifted the shotgun from the back seat and pointed it out of the window.

'Excuse me,' she said to the man in a soft, conversational voice that Pat had never heard her use before, 'but if you touch or bother my daughter ever again I'll shoot you. I'm a very good shot!'

The old peaked cap jerked back. Horror and fear suffused the weak old face as he stared down the twin barrels of the gun.

'I didn't know you could shoot, Mummy!' Patricia said to her mother as they came back to Brierly.

Her mother turned a smiling face to her. 'He doesn't know whether I can or not. Besides, there can't be that much to it . . . Just push a shotgun into his backside and pull the trigger!'

The gun was put back in its place and the man never bothered Pat again. Patricia finished her exercises, glanced at the clock. Almost three. The children were still at school. Orla would be back at half three, Simon fifteen minutes later. Then there would be homework to be done and the supper to be got and bickering to be dealt with.

The phone rang. It was on Gerry's bedside table. She heard it in the landing and turned back to pick up the receiver.

'Hello!'

There was a small silence which was suddenly filled with certainty. In a split second, before she knew who was at the end of the line, she was certain who it was.

'Well, well,' the male voice said. 'It's strangely wonderful to hear you again. I suppose you have no idea at all who this is?'

'Hmmm,' Patricia mused aloud. Suddenly the world was bright and there was room for laughter and all the pieces of her disjointed reality came together.

'It sounds like Paddy Johnson, but of course it can't be . . .'

'You sound exactly the same, Patricia. Young and vibrant as ever. How are you?'

'I'm fine. It's nice to hear from you. Joan told me she had bumped into you!'

'Ah, so that's the reason you recognized my voice!'

'No. I think I would have recognized it anyway!'

Silence.

'Are you doing anything for lunch tomorrow? I would like to take you out for a bite. We could have a chat.'

'That would be lovely!'

'Shall we make it the Shelbourne? Meet you in the foyer at twelve thirty?'

'Great! I'll look forward to that!'

'See you then . . .'

'Paddy!'

'Yes?'

'I suppose you haven't gone bald or anything . . . In case we don't recognize each other!'

His laughter poured down the line. 'No, I still have a few ribs; and my own teeth as well. How about you?'

'I'm in a terrible state. Bald as a coot with one tooth!'

'Well, in that case you'll be easy to identify!'

They laughed together, like children.

'OK. See you then. Bye . . .'

'Bye . . .'

Patricia sat down on the bed, saw her face in the mirror, smiling, glowing. He had sounded just the same, the same voice, the same teasing nuance. The years were gone. She was twenty again, on the road between Laragh and Glendalough.

When she came downstairs she met Orla in the hall, was relieved to see her home early for a change.

'Hello, darling . . . Did you have a good day?'

Orla looked at her mother in open surprise and her closed expression melted. 'You're in good form today, Mum.'

Pat went to the cloakroom for her coat. 'I'm going out for a while, darling. Get the homework done.'

'What time will you be back?'

'About six.'

Patricia went out and bought a new suit, a cream silk blouse, and a small bottle of Armani. The suit had a straight black skirt and a check jacket with black and gold buttons. She had her hair done, trimmed slightly, and a colour rinse. She lay back at the basin, hearing the background music in a blur, her mind full of Paddy. Shampoo bubbles crackled in her ears, the edge of the basin was hard against the nape of her neck; the water was a little too hot, but her mind was far away. Later, she studied her face in the mirror with astonishment. She looked young; there was animation in her face: she could be thirty.

61

It was dark when she left the hairdresser's. A cold wind knifed through Grafton Street, which was overhung with Christmas lights and milling with people; a small choir sang carols and nearby a little waif, a tinker girl, sat in a doorway and played a tin whistle. Pat met her eyes as she passed, eyes without calculation, slightly glazed with the cold and the music. Touched, she placed two pounds in the tin box on the ground in front of her.

'Thanks, missus,' the child's voice said as Pat moved away into the crowd.

It was six thirty when she got home. The house was warm. She drew the curtains on the kitchen window and felt a relief at being home, out of the crowds and the cold. She put down a grill, called Orla and Simon to help with setting the table. They started arguing as to who should do what so she sent Simon to his room. Orla began to complain that she was always the one left to help.

'I'll do it myself, Orla! You needn't bother!' But Orla remained, set the table, glanced at her mother and said after a moment, 'Mum, your hair is very nice. You look really well!' She said it in a flat voice, to indicate that she was merely stating a fact, not capitulating.

Pat smiled at her daughter. 'Thank you, Orla.'

The girl busied herself with the table settings, searched for tomato ketchup to which Simon was partial, and for a couple of minutes the kitchen was filled with the silent, age-old comradeship of women. From the corner of her eye Pat saw her daughter glance at her, as though trying to assess the nature of the change in her, the challenge of the new space she had suddenly come to occupy. Her daughter's approval was patent, albeit unconscious, her interest in this being, her mother, who had ceased to be predictable.

Gerry was late. Pat gave him his supper when he came home and sat with him as he ate. He seemed preoccupied. The children had already eaten and were doing homework upstairs.

'Did you have a good day, Gerry?'

He looked at her. His face did not register that she had had her hair done, but it did register that she was looking well. There was a certain cautious relief. They had hardly spoken since the episode on Saturday. It was never Gerry's form to advert to disagreements, to resolve any problematic or contentious issues between them. Instead he walked away from them and expected them to die.

'Busy day, actually. It's always like this coming up to Christmas. Everyone wants things done the last week! How about you? How was your day?'

For a moment Patricia was about to tell him that Paddy had phoned, but thought better of it. 'I did some shopping, bought myself a new suit!'

He looked at her with approval. His expression registered that she was pulling herself together. 'Good. You haven't bought yourself anything for a while . . .'

Patricia was about to tell him what the suit was like, even put it on if he seemed interested, but she saw that his thoughts were straying.

'I have to read some papers I brought home. I'll be in the study.' He stood up and left the room.

She put the dishes in the dishwasher, her mind dwelling on tomorrow, imagining the moment of recognition.

Patricia pushed through the revolving doors into the foyer of the Shelbourne. Through the glass she saw fire in the hearth, the portrait overhead, the man sitting on the sofa, reading the *Irish Times*.

There were two other people there, a couple engaged in conversation. But the man with the *Times* was alone. He was wearing an open trench coat and a dark grey suit. His hair was still curly, still mousy, but tinged with grey and receding from his forehead. He projected an aura of confidence and suavity. Could this confident, prosperous-looking man in the prime of life be the same Paddy as the slim youth she had slept beside one May night under the stars? He looked up as she came forward, rose to his feet, smiling. The nervousness evaporated. She held out her hand. He caught it warmly.

'Pat!'

'Paddy!'

'You haven't changed!'

'Of course I have!'

He led her into the lounge, to some chairs by the piano. 'You'll have a little aperitif?'

'. . . Ballygowan!'

Paddy ordered a Ballygowan and a dry Martini with ice. He sat back looking at her. He had changed, subtly, definitely. His mouth had vertical lines which used not be there, lines of gravity and ruthlessness. His forehead was lightly scored. The grey in his hair was more pronounced at the temples. His hands were well manicured. He was wearing a wedding ring. He was the same and he was utterly different. The glamour which surrounded him as a youth was there in his maturity, only now it had been transmuted into purpose and power.

'Well, how much have I changed? I can see it in your eyes.'

'You've become mature, maybe even formidable . . . It suits you.'

He smiled. 'Thank you. I find you a little changed too . . . More beautiful if I may say so.'

'Ah,' Patricia said, 'you have become continental! You flatter women!'

'I'm not flattering!' He leant back. 'It's the truth! And to think I was expecting a bald lady with a single tooth!'

Patricia laughed. 'You're looking at her! She got herself a set of dentures and a hair transplant!'

They laughed together a little giddily. Then they asked after each other's family and Patricia inquired politely after Susan.

'She's well. She's done a great job with the kids. They're both at college now: Guy is doing Business Studies in Cambridge, and Michelle is studying History of Art in London.

Patricia smiled politely. 'My two aren't at that stage yet.'

Later, in the Ashling restaurant, they sat by the window. Patricia ordered soup followed by rack of lamb. Paddy ordered roast beef. He perused the wine list, asked her what she would like to drink.

'I'll just have mineral water. It's a little early in the day for me.'

'Are you sure?' He ordered a half-bottle of Burgundy for himself.

The dining room filled quickly, buzzed with conversation, Christmas office laughter.

'Did Gerry tell you that I saw him last week? That he is looking after some contracts for us?'

'No. But Joan de Barra did.'

'She must be the woman I met in the hall.'

'Yes.'

'Would Gerry mind if he knew that we were having lunch together?'

'Why should he?'

'I thought he might be the jealous type!'

'Not Gerry.' She glanced up from her soup. 'He trusts me.' There was silence. Patricia ate her soup. She felt Paddy's eyes, looked up to see in them something both inquisitive and contemplative, something which asked, Who are you now, Patricia; who have you become?

'If you were mine, I would be possessive!' he said, his voice very low. Then he added softly, 'It is very strange to be here with you, Patricia O'Hehir, after all these years . . .!' He reached discreetly across the tablecloth and touched the fingers of her left hand.

Patricia felt the touch. The electricity from it shivered up her arm. Something surged to meet it, recognition, yearning, hope. And then anger. Will you make a play for me now, O Married Man? You could have had me; we could have had each other! It's too late for us! We meet here as brittle acquaintances. Is there enough substance to our history even to dub us as old friends? She kept her eyes on her plate, kept her fingers still and unresponsive, felt the transitory pressure cease.

After that they talked of Dublin and of Richmond where Paddy was living and Paris where he and Susan had an apartment.

'Susan bought it out of her inheritance. It was a very good investment.'

And she told him about her home in Ballsbridge and the two children, chatting as though her world were bright.

'I'm glad you're happy,' he said suddenly, but it was a question, not a statement.

Patricia smiled. 'You must come and dine with us soon. When would suit you?'

'I'll be going back to Richmond on Friday. Christmas Eve.'

'Of course. Your family must miss you!'

'It will be nice to see the children for Christmas.'

'And Susan. You must miss her?'

He looked away. 'Of course!'

'Well,' Patricia said, 'you must have dinner with us the first possible evening you have free. When do you come back after Christmas?'

'I'll be back on Tuesday – this day next week.'

Patricia did some rapid calculations. Tuesday would be the 28th. What the hell was she doing on the 28th? Of course. The bloody party.

'We're giving a drinks party that evening. Will you come?'

65

'I'd love to . . .'

He insisted on driving her home.

'I never drive into town at Christmas,' she said. 'You can't find a parking place.'

'Do I detect an anxious streak in you, Mrs Galligan?' he asked whimsically. 'You used not be anxious!'

'Oh, Paddy . . . you can't possibly remember how I was, anxious or otherwise!'

He turned to glance at her, smiling. 'Can't I? I think you'd be very surprised. Have you forgotten me then? Is that it?'

The question started out on a jocose note and ended on one of resignation. There was silence for a moment, charged with unasked questions, while he waited for her response.

'I never forgot you,' she said. 'Never! There, you wanted the truth! I have your bloody letters – and the poems!'

He took her right hand, changed gear holding it, would not release it. 'Is your time your own?' he asked. 'Do you have to go home now?'

'No.'

'Shall we go for a drive, get out of the city?'

'All right . . . But what about your afternoon – don't you have appointments?'

He turned to her with a grin, the grin belonging to the old Paddy. 'I got my secretary to postpone them! I'm held up!' He squeezed her hand. 'It's nice to be "held up" once in a while.' He turned again to smile at her conspiratorially, and then concentrated on the traffic and the road to Rathfarnham and the mountains.

Chapter Five

Legally, it seems, Gerry is entitled to my services (my domestic services!), to my body, to rape me, if such is his inclination, with impunity (it's not a crime to do it to the wife!). This gives him the right to have as many children by me as I am capable of bearing. In this just and careful manner, the Law weighs male sexual desire against a woman's bodily integrity, the agony of labour, maternal exhaustion, hypertension, haemorrhage or death!

He can sue any man who seduces me, or who offers me shelter or who entices me away, notwithstanding my complicity in all or any of these activities. (The wife's wishes don't count.) There are no reciprocal rights for me, except the right of support, and he can decide the level of that. All this carefully balanced wisdom and equity is overwhelming.

from *The Horse's Ears*, 1973

Paddy drove to Scholarstown Road, negotiated the bends, changed down gear, turned into Stocking Lane and, without dropping Patricia's hand, eventually brought the car to a halt in the viewing spot above Kilakee overlooking the city and the bay. It was three o'clock. The December light was beginning to fade. Down below them the city twinkled, already fogbound, lights beginning to show through the dark mist, the lonely expanse of the bay blue-grey in the distance.

He pushed a button and the window on her side opened. The cold winter air flooded in, bringing the silence of the countryside, the forlorn chirp of one or two birds, the cry of the wind.

The road beyond them forked – to the mountains and the Sally Gap – or back towards the city via Lamb Doyles.

They sat in the silence, looking down at the city and the bay.

'What happened to us, Patricia O'Hehir?' Paddy demanded after a while. 'I thought we had something good going for us.'

Patricia felt the constriction in her throat. 'You met Susan,' she said as airily as she could.

'And you met Gerry!'

'Yes.'

'Any regrets?'

Patricia was silent. She scanned the contours of coastline. There was the Howth Peninsula and Ireland's Eye, and there were the twin Pigeon House chimneys and the two piers of Dun Laoghaire. The yellow sodium lights were starting up, an orange-red necklace along the coast road.

'Do you expect me to regret my life because you have shown up again?'

Paddy turned to look at her. He filled the car with his certainty, his melancholy. 'Not because I have, as you put it, "shown up again". I am well aware that it's none of my business and that I have no right to ask. But being here with you, side by side with you, makes me feel that time is an illusion. Shall I tell you that I never forgot you, that you were often on my mind . . .?'

Patricia did not reply. She looked away. His voice was seductive; it had a timbre which addressed itself to her secret self, which went to the trouble of addressing this secret self. Women are turned on by men's voices, she remembered reading, and knew it was true. He was enormously attractive, this new Paddy with the fruits of success around him, radiating purpose; the Paddy of the old days had been a callow youth in comparison. But she also sensed the years in him, his toughness, the ploys he had learnt to achieve what he wanted; and she sensed the old contact, effortlessly there, but strangely uncharted. He was foreign now and he was familiar. Above all she sensed in his stillness, in his concentrated gaze, the unmistakable pressure of his desire. Paddy leaned over, kissed her suddenly on the mouth. She felt the rasp of his chin, the subtle hint of his aftershave, the touch and scent of his clothes, and she felt the reaction in herself, powerful and involuntary.

'I shouldn't do that either; but we have less time,' he whispered when he let her go and, in releasing her, his hand brushed almost accidentally across the front of her blouse, under her open coat.

68

Patricia felt this gossamer touch on her breast, tensed, closed her eyes and opened them to find him watching her.

Desire. They tried to tell us it was dirty. The wish to possess and be possessed, so powerful that it seems to have all the meaning there is to life.

Patricia let him hold her hand again on the way back to the city. They spoke of the past, student days; sometimes banal, sometimes personal. She was still cautious; he was not. He was like a man who had some unfinished business to deal with, important business, and not too much time left him, and who had therefore dispensed with usual formalities.

'I wanted to see you again. I volunteered for this job here, you know, so that I could! And when the plane carried me over Dublin Bay and I looked down and saw the city, all I could think of was that you were down there somewhere, a happy wife and mother, someone I would meet again, be glad to see again. That was all! But you are not happy, Patricia. I can feel it. And I feel something else too, an empathy between us that I had forgotten and which I don't want to lose again. And I'm not happy either so you needn't tell me how mistaken I am!'

'What about Susan?' Patricia asked after a moment. 'Is she happy?'

'Probably. She seems to be. Her requirements for contentment are not the same as mine!'

'What are your requirements for contentment?'

He laughed. 'Ah . . . I can't identify them like so many pounds of spuds, but I know them when I find them!'

'Have you found them often?'

'No. I thought I would. The world is a big place and has an awful lot of people. They dig some kind of a trench into us in this country, score right down to the core, and we spend our lives aching and trying to find the appropriate grout . . . to make us feel whole, to make us capable of happiness!'

He waited, expecting a revealing response, expecting her to divulge, if only by innuendo, the real state and condition of her life. But Pat merely asked, 'What's grout?'

'It's a fluid mortar for filling interstices.'

'You're talking like an engineer!'

He laughed. 'Sorry. I'm basically inarticulate.'

'Am I some kind of grout?'

He laughed again. 'You are the most direct woman I've ever

69

met. No, but maybe we could grout each other . . .' he ended with a laugh. 'Christ, I'd better shut up!'

'Yes, I think you should!'

The car filled with laughter.

After a while he said, 'What are you thinking of?'

Patricia was watching the glare of the headlights, the rushing darkness on either side, the grass verge, the dark branches reaching over the road.

'I was wondering . . .' she answered softly. 'There's a verse of an old poem – I was wondering if you would remember it . . .'.

'What is it? Say it!'

Patricia cleared her throat.

> '. . . And I should find
> Soon in the silence the hidden key,
> Of all that had hurt and troubled me,
> Why you were you and the night was kind,
> And the woods were part of the heart of me.'

'That's vaguely familiar. Who wrote it?'

'No one,' Patricia murmured, deflated. 'No one at all!'

He glanced at her. 'Is that right? Well now – I think it was written by a young English poet by the name of Rupert Brooke,' he said in a teasing voice. 'And I sent it to a girl I loved! Once, long ago . . .' He did not turn his head again to look at her. 'Would that fit the bill?'

Patricia smiled in the darkness. 'It would fit the bill!'

As they approached Scholarstown Road he said softly, 'Will I drive over to Brierly?'

'No. It's sold now. It's gone. Mummy's moved into a flat.'

His hand reached again for hers and did not release it.

When he left her home he turned up her hand and slowly kissed the palm. It was half past four and already dark. Paddy made to accompany her to the door.

'It's all right . . . There's no need. Thank you, Paddy!'

I am alive, Patricia thought as she went up the steps to her front door. I am alive. Why do I feel so alive and whole? And healed? She fumbled for her key, inserted it into the lock. Behind her she heard Paddy drive away.

The house was silent. She went into the kitchen, turned on the light, saw that Orla's school bag was on a chair. Where was she? She must have gone out again. But then, on the hallstand in the back hall, she saw Orla's jacket.

She went upstairs, heard the sounds of muted rock music, saw the light under Orla's door and, as she approached the door, heard the loud urgent whispers, heard Orla say, 'No . . . Mick. *Stop*! I don't *want* to,' in a voice which rose in angry irritation laced with fear.

'Ah, come on . . . Don't be such a tease . . .' A young man's voice answered, quite loudly, quite dismissively, urgently, in a tone which indicated that 'No' was not an acceptable answer, that he had needs which she existed to satisfy.

Patricia crossed the landing, threw open the door to her daughter's room. Orla was lying on the bed, her dark blue gymslip up to her thighs, her blouse open, her face flushed, her hair tousled. Beside her on the bed was the same youth Patricia had seen one night in the light of the street-lamp. His back was to the door and he was attempting to pull Orla's gymslip up, while she pushed it down with one hand and pushed him away with the other. His leather jacket was on the chair, a sleeve with its steel zip dangling down to the floor.

'Get out!' Patricia said.

The youth jumped, turned his face to her. 'Jesus!'

Orla rapidly adjusted her clothes, stared at her mother in mortification. 'We were just listening to some tapes, Mum!' she said lamely, her voice trailing away.

Patricia ignored her. 'Get out,' she repeated to the youth. 'And don't let me see you in this house again!'

The boy moved with impertinent body language, put on his boots, picked up his jacket and sauntered past her. He was stockily built; he wore his hair in a crew-cut; his face was handsome after a set fashion, but without the grace or diffidence of youth. She saw that his pupils were dilated. He radiated maleness, raw strength.

Patricia went down the stairs after him. He shut the front door behind him with a clap.

She went back to Orla, shut the door and sat down on the bed. Orla had tidied herself a little, her blouse was buttoned again, gymslip restored, and she was standing by the cassette player on her desk, her auburn head bent. She switched off the music. Silence filled the room. She did not meet her mother's eyes.

71

'We weren't doing anything,' she said defensively after a moment.

'Why did you bring him up to your room?'

'We weren't doing any harm! We wanted to play some tapes.'

'Did he meet you after school?'

'No. I don't meet him any more. I go home straight now!'

'So he came to the house?'

'Yes!'

'Coming up here was his idea?'

'Yes . . .' Orla's voice teetered on the verge of tears. 'He said "Let's go to your room and play some music." He went up himself.'

'That was after you told him I was out?'

Orla didn't answer the question.

'I don't like him any more . . .' she said through her tears. 'I thought he was nice at the beginning . . .'

Patricia watched her daughter cry. She wanted to take her head and cradle it, hold her, but she knew that Orla's pride, fierce because she had not yet learnt the vulnerability of everything that lived, would reject her with fury. The blotched, tearful face had the same expression as the one Orla the baby had worn at six months, when her green rubber hedgehog had fallen out of the pram. But she couldn't remember herself at six months, had no recollection of a green rubber hedgehog, and did not understand the expression in her mother's eyes.

'For God's sake, Mum, go away and leave me alone.'

Patricia stood her ground. If she dared not be maternal, she could at least be pragmatic. 'All right. But if you carry on like this you will get yourself pregnant. Or you will get Aids. Or both . . .'

'Carry on! I'm not carrying on,' Orla howled. 'I didn't mean him to try anything. I thought it might be romantic . . . just some music . . . Leave me alone!'

Patricia fought with a mélange of feelings: compassion, tenderness, anger at her child's invincible touchiness, anger at her own inability to deal with it.

'Where's Simon?' she asked, by way of introducing a neutral question.

'How should I know?' Orla replied through her sobs.

Patricia went to her room. She took off her new suit and

72

hung it up. She looked at her face in the mirror, sat down before her dressing-table, her mind in a turmoil. The afternoon with Paddy, the interview with Orla, the evening ahead *en famille* – Gerry incommunicado, Simon aggressive, Orla sulking.

That was how it would be for years to come. Paddy would go back to England to his family; the short while with him would form part of the indelible fantasy about him. 'It is fantasy! Make-believe!'

And yet, despite her self-exhortations, the glow of the afternoon suffused her still, brightened the room, quickened her pulse. So short a time with him and so intense an effect! But he was probably playing with her. After twenty years what else could it be? Orla had mentioned romance; she had projected romance on to the encounter in her bedroom, at least initially. Wasn't she doing exactly the same thing herself? And this was what women did; they reached for something higher and finer; they hungered for some kind of transcendence.

The drawer with Paddy's letters was in front of her hand, and she flipped the catch, pulled out the letters. The writing on the pages, slightly crabbed, brought back the sense of him. She took a pencil out of a drawer and, in a sudden certainty of futility, wrote on the back of one of the sheets.

> Women weave their own romance
> From scraps, little bits and pieces,
> Gild them with the shining blood of the soul . . .

She heard Simon come in downstairs. Gerry would be back soon. She put the letters back into the drawer and went down to the kitchen.

After supper that evening Patricia said to Gerry, 'I met someone from the old days today!'

Gerry looked up from his paper. 'Oh – who?'

'Paddy Johnson!'

'Where did you meet him?'

Patricia found herself unable to say that she had lunched with him, had spent the afternoon with him. 'I met him in Stephen's Green. He told me that he has retained you in connection with some corporate contracts.'

'That's right.'

Gerry was silent then. He did the Simplex crossword, then attacked the Crosaire, sighed in defeat and stood up.

'Where are you going?'

'I'll be in the study.'

When he was at the door Patricia said, 'Gerry.'

He turned. 'Yes?'

'What did you think of him?'

'Who?'

'Paddy Johnson!'

He stared at her for a moment, ostensibly in perplexity, although she knew perfectly well that he remembered her relationship with Paddy, that he had done everything in his power to prevent them from healing the rift. Then he said in a dismissive, matter-of-fact voice, 'He's a chancer. Why do you ask?'

'No reason. I invited him to our party on the 28th.'

Gerry nodded uninterestedly and left the room.

'If he's a chancer,' Patricia said angrily to herself, 'he'll be in the best of company!'

Pat's mother phoned later to ask what the children would like for Christmas. For a moment Patricia thought of Christmas at Brierly when she was a child: log fires, Christmas tree with a silver angel at the top, and the view of the mountains through the drawing-room window. The light would fade at three and the mountains would become misty, purple, and darkly mysterious. She had loved to look at them from the window and listen to 'Carols from the Vienna Boys' Choir' – 'Silent Night', 'Adeste Fidelis' – while the logs crackled in the hearth and her father puffed his pipe and read. She had spent only one Christmas in her old home after her marriage. Her father had died suddenly during the following year from a heart attack, and her mother had sold up and moved into a rented flat not far from where Pat and Gerry lived.

'You could get them jumpers!'

There was silence for a moment. 'Pat, you didn't care for jumpers as presents at their age. I was thinking of getting Simon a "ghetto blaster" – isn't that what they call them? And Orla might like a make-up kit and some nice perfume. She's a young lady now!'

'Mummy, they don't have "young ladies" any more. The breed has died out!'

Mrs O'Hehir laughed in her 'don't be ridiculous' voice. 'What has replaced them?' she inquired. 'Sabre-toothed tigresses?'

'Women, Mummy. Girls grow up and become women.'

Her mother sighed. 'They have no fun any more! Everything has become so serious. It's a shame!'

Chapter Six

Nell is into religion. She finds solace in it. But what does she trade for this solace? What do women get from religion? I remember going to a women's retreat in the parish church when I was a teenager. I heard the priest warning the women about refusing their husbands, warning them about obedience. The women would kneel, row after row of them, in headscarves, while the priest told them about his God's plan for them, from which there was no appeal. They drank humiliation, knelt to it; it was the word of God.

'How many mothers have produced a fine son to have him ruined by a bad girl?' Stern stuff.

The confessionals were choked with guilt-ridden women, desperately seeking honorary membership of the male hut, begging for the right to prop up a group of men who taught women to hate themselves.

from *The Horse's Ears*, 1978

January 1990

Sarah wondered how she would tell Jim that she was pregnant again.

She knew she was, although no pregnancy test had been undergone. She knew from the tenderness in her breasts and the incipient nausea which would get worse for the next few months. He might be raging; or he might take it well, depending on the mood he was in. She had been filled with despair when she recognized the old symptoms but, now that the pregnancy had progressed a little, she had become attached to the baby, as she always did, imagining it there inside her, curled up, waiting to be born. As always the sense of the miraculous subsumed her. A new person, someone who might yet set the world on fire; someone who belonged to her . . . And then again, she would be resentful; all these children at her expense, while all he could do was rant and rave and hit her and father more.

Sometimes she wondered why she stayed. There was no one reason. She had invested so much already in this marriage – hope, pride, the daily momentum of her life, her face before the world. And motherhood had trapped her; it had forced her to concentrate on the pluses, the occasional nugget of domestic harmony. So much energy went into this search, so much was extracted from each small find, that there was no emotional energy left to plan any kind of alternative existence. Her will drove her to make her marriage work; it was something she wanted so badly that she was prepared to pay almost any personal price. She knew her man had his good side: was he not always distraught after he had given her a going-over; wasn't he generous to a fault? She blocked the recognition of the truth – she feared what it would demand of her; she was cursed with resilience and hope.

But Christmas had been good this year, Jim in a benign mood and not drinking. He had gone on a binge before Christmas and had been contrite.

'I'm making an effort,' he had said. 'It won't happen again,' he said.

The children were up early on Christmas morning, looking for what Santa had left them: a doll for Lorraine, train set for Liam, and Junior Lego and a teddy for Dara. They charged into their parents' bedroom.

'Look, Mammy, Daddy, look what Santy brought me . . .' Sarah held up the fluffy teddy bear.

'What are you going to call your teddy?' she asked Dara, and he turned round blue eyes on her before reaching out for his toy. 'Dee-Dee,' he said gravely.

Jim had got a good Christmas bonus. He was generous with money, talked of the new kitchen he would build her. 'What would you like, kitten? Oak is popular but very dark; ash is nice!' Sarah looked through his firm's brochure, their new line in kitchens.

'I think I like the blond ash the best,' she said. 'It would not cut down the light.'

'I'll start it for you after Christmas. I'll get some of the lads to help.' And while they discussed the kitchen, while the bruises from the last beating faded, she began to hope again.

He started the new kitchen as promised in the second week of January. Two of his mates from work came around and got it under way, set up the carpenter's bench in the middle of the floor, and almost completed it by the Monday, but needed the rest of the week to put the finishing touches, working in the evenings. Fiona from next door came around to see it.

'It's gorgeous. I wish Charlie would do the same for me!'

Jim stayed off the booze for several weeks. He did all the jobs around the house that Sarah wanted, asked her repeatedly if she liked the kitchen, was delighted when she said it was wonderful.

'Thank you, Jim; it's really nice. Even Fiona said it was the nicest she had seen!'

'Gave it the green eye? I bet she did! There's no way Charlie would build one for her. He doesn't know a nail from a spanner. And of course the price of getting one done is astronomical! Not everyone can get this stuff at cost.'

Jim knew that he had absolved himself from the crime of beating and hurting his wife. He had paid for it with labour and money. He had given her a new kitchen and that made it all right. He felt good, better than he had felt for a long time. He did not feel so small compared to her now, compared to the maddening infinity of her patience. He hated this patience, because he had no right to it, because there was something perverse about it in the face of what he did to her. And he hated it more because he knew it was for the children and not for him. But because he had built her the kitchen, and because she loved it, he was feeling better; he had a new self-image – which he liked – of the strong, indulgent provider.

So when the lads invited him down to the pub he looked at Sarah and declined. 'Not tonight. I'm taking herself out tonight!'

Sarah asked Donna, Fiona's fourteen-year-old, to babysit, and they went to see *Amadeus* in the local cinema.

'Right mad berk that Mozart,' Jim said after the film was over and they were on their way home.

'The other fellow – Salieri – was even madder!'

'The fellow who's supposed to have killed him? Do you blame him?'

'The music was lovely,' Sarah said. 'I really liked the music!'

'It was all right' Jim said, 'but I thought your man was a pain in

79

the bum, farting around and being so bloody clever, and not able
to hang on to a penny!'

Sarah was silent. She detected the tone in Jim's voice, recognized it like a sailor who knew, from the taste of the wind when it
shifted, that a storm threatened. So, like a sailor, she pulled in
her canvas by retreating into silence. Her withdrawal irritated her
husband.

'You're very quiet. Did you not like the film?'

'I did!'

'Then why haven't you a word to throw to a dog? I tried to give
you a nice evening.'

'I enjoyed it very much. It was great!'

'If it was great you'd think you'd say so, without me having to
drag it out of you! I wanted to give you a good time. I'm sorry if
I've failed! I'm really sorry if I've failed!'

Sarah turned to look at him. 'Don't spoil it, Jim. I said it was
lovely! It was good of you . . . I hope Donna had no trouble with
the children . . .' she added in an attempt to change the subject,
and also because the children were on her mind and she wanted
to get home to them.

'Jesus! Do you ever think of anything except those children?'

'I do,' Sarah said with sudden spirit. 'I think of you, actually! In
fact, I think of you quite a lot!'

Jim turned to glance at her, met her eye and lapsed into
silence. Sarah tensed, waiting to see if he would confront her on
what she thought about him. But after a while he began to
whistle, and when he did Sarah felt the tension leave her.

'You're as good as Roger Whittaker,' she ventured after a
moment, and he gave a short laugh.

' "The Mexican Whistler"? Maybe. But I haven't got his
money!'

'Penny for them, Mrs de Barra!'

Joan looked up from the piece of tapestry – a Christmas
present from her sister Delia – and stared at David across the
studio. They had moved an armchair into a corner of this room,
and she sat there in the evenings as much as possible in order to
be with David while he worked; silent for the most part, so as not
to impede his concentration. She enjoyed his company, albeit
worldless, because she never felt apart from him, felt rather that
she was part of whatever artistic journey he was embarked on, as

though he brought her with him through solitude. So she would change into an old black tracksuit and sit in the corner on the chintz armchair and answer when he spoke. Sometimes she brought some legal work in here, papers which she had to read, but mostly she set aside this time for thinking, or trying her hand at tapestry, as now, half aware of the slapping and scraping of the palate knife, the whisper of the brush, the sharp, clean smell of paint and linseed oil, and the controlled tense breathing of the artist.

'They're not worth it!'

'You must have been thinking of something!'

'I was wondering when you would hear from the art dealer!'

David shrugged. She looked over at him, his face partly hidden by the easel, at the black hair, the wiry black beard. Since the French dealer had come and gone, promising that he would be in touch in the New Year, the change in him was patent. He worked harder than ever, with less fever but greater certainty. He seemed better; colour had come back to his face.

The man in black had disappeared from his painting. His latest picture, a four-foot-square canvas, was an outpouring of excitement; joy spurted through the colours, through the whirl of movement, the suggested human forms rioting in an exhilaration of life, fragile dancing forms, possessed by a dynamic of impossible human bliss. Or so it seemed to Joan.

'The happiness is super-human,' she commented when he let her see it.

The remark displeased him. 'Nothing is super-human. Man is the measure of all things; what is expressed is there because – if *I* can envisage it – Man possesses it . . .!'

'How about Woman?' she asked softly.

He kissed the nape of her neck with a chuckle. 'Woman is included; the term "Man" is generic, as you well know. No one – man or woman – knows their own power!'

'That's what artists are for, to show it to them?'

He sighed. 'Oh Joan . . . do you think that presumptuous? The most I can do is raise a few echoes!'

Sitting there in the armchair, listening to the tenor of his soul, Joan thought that the swings from joy to melancholy, so furiously expressed with paint, had to do with the frustration of a spirit which was too finely honed to endure the confines of ailing flesh. She could feel the way his spirit surged and ebbed and surged

81

again in a passion of creativity, the driving desire to express what he regarded as the miracle around him, and then, emptied, frustrated, he would sink down exhausted on the chair. But she suspected too that his choice of métier, his fury of effort, was an attempt to screen out the past, the events of his childhood, the loss of his brother. She had asked him how he had died, had met with a curt explanation; it had been a drowning accident. What he hadn't told her for a long time, not until a picture of a drowned child appeared one night on television, when he had reacted violently, were the circumstances of his brother's death.

His brother Damion had been a year younger. One summer, when Damion was ten, they had gone swimming in the pool belonging to a nearby secondary school. The pool was closed, but David had discovered a faulty catch on a dressing-room window. He and Damion had got into the dressing room through this window one summer evening, and from thence into the pool.

It was a small pool. It lay there, the water very still and a little scummy. The boys stripped and walked around the edge. Neither of them could swim. They had never been to a swimming pool. They had paddled among the rocks at Sandymount and along the frothy edge of the waves. They had got into the shallow tide while their mother looked on, but they had never been taught the rudiments of survival in water.

'Which end is the deep end?' Damion inquired of his brother, and David indicated the far end. He did not know which was the deep end, but he was used to sounding knowledgeable to his younger brother, and did not want to confess his ignorance.

Damion immediately jumped in, found himself in over six feet of water, went to the bottom, came up, thrashed around, while David jumped in and held the rail, tried to reach for his brother, tried to swim and found he couldn't, got out and ran screaming for help. But by the time help arrived Damion was floating face down in the water and was beyond human succour.

David wept as he told Joan this, buried his face in his hands, refused to be comforted.

'I am a murderer! You are married to a murderer!'

'It was an accident. You were a child!'

When he had composed himself, David said, 'We were like twins; we went everywhere together. He would be thirty-nine this September. He had more courage than anyone I knew and, even

82

though he was a child, more compassion . . . You would have liked him, Joan!'

And then he had shown her a photograph of Damion dressed for a part in a school play, with a black cloak and a tri-cornered black hat, under which a grave child's face stared back into the camera.

' "The Scarlet Pimpernel." He was very good in the part. I can't help thinking the part of Chauvelin was thrust on me . . . I killed my mother through this. She never forgave me . . .'

'You tried to save him,' Joan said. 'You did what you could.'

David was silent. Then he said, 'I tried to swim, to grab him. But I couldn't. I went down to the bottom and there was a vast roaring in my ears. The water was greeny and opaque. I panicked, aware of this other world I had never known which would not support me, which was quite merciless, aware of a shadow moving towards me through the water, longing suddenly to reach out to it.'

'What kind of shadow? You mean Damion . . .'

David looked at her, shook his head. 'No!'

Joan shivered.

'Afterwards I dreamed for a long time of Damion in the water, his hair swept up, his eyes staring, staring, and his hands raised for help . . .'

'How did you get out?'

'When I came up I was near enough to the edge to grab the rail. Then I ran off howling for help.'

Joan was about to change the subject but David added musingly, 'Damion and I had a pact that, no matter where we were, we would meet on my fortieth birthday.' He smiled. 'We thought we would be so old then that it would be nearly time to croak anyway!'

'You'll be forty in June!'

He glanced at Joan. 'If he can come back he will come.'

Joan stared at her husband, bit back the words which sprang to her lips. David's face was perfectly serious. He's dead, Joan said to herself. Damion is dead.

It was after the drowning programme on television, after this conversation, that David's pain had started. Joan never spoke to him of Damion after that, did everything to keep his mind away from his childhood. But she knew that in a corner of the studio facing the wall was a painting of a drowning child, dark eyes open and staring fixedly through the water as though they looked calmly into dimensions beyond time and space.

But this evening David was calm; he had put away the painting of *The Dance* and had begun another one, and he worked on it, glancing over at her from time to time. She was curled into the chair, bent over the tapestry, but put it down and stretched in a sudden movement, angling her neck and head back over one arm, and her knees over the other, so that she saw the room upside down, felt her hair sweep the floor, felt the pressure of blood in her face. When she sat up she saw that David was watching her. 'Do that again!'

'Do what?'

'Do that stretch again, back over the arm of the chair; give it the same abandon; let everything go!'

Joan laughed and obeyed, threw back her arms, let one dangle down towards the floor. She heard the scratch of charcoal on canvas.

'Are you doing a picture of me?'

'You've given me an idea. Stay like that!'

'I'll suffocate!'

'Just for a minute!'

David, the room, looked funny upside down, as though she had never seen him or it before. She saw that her husband's face was too thin, the bones sharp under the skin. But the blood was singing in her head and roaring in her ears.

'I'm sitting up; I'm not going to die for art's sake!'

He laughed. 'All right.'

Later, as she undressed for bed, she asked him, 'Did you ever feel violent towards me?'

David was in bed, lying back, dark eyes watching her. 'All the time. Violent and tender and flayed with desire.'

'I don't mean it in that sense . . . It's just that today a woman who came to see me told me her husband beats her. She doesn't know what to do. He's a teacher. I told her she should get a Barring Order, but I know she won't. I told her she could leave him, go to the women's refuge! She probably won't do that either! He's the breadwinner.'

David made a gesture of disgust. 'They should be put down, these little creeps . . . She should do it herself!'

Joan sighed. 'If she did, God help her . . . You saw how the courts deal with women who defend themselves.'

84

David regarded her in silence. Then he said, 'The male system assumes primacy as of right, bases it on its own parochialism, insists its parochialism is an objective, universal measure. The male system reacts savagely to statements of individual worth from women.'

'Why?'

'It makes them afraid!'

'Afraid of women?'

'Of life, of whatever they can't control! The separate culture of women is intolerable. It means that the male experience is only half of the human equation, that there is human territory out there which they don't begin to understand!' He smiled teasingly. 'We can't have that!'

Joan ignored the provocation. 'I think a lot of men are just scared of shelving shibboleths,' she said. 'There's too much at stake for them. But I like men,' she added. 'Because of you I'm a hopeless romantic. And because of you I believe well of men. As long as there are men like you there will be happiness for women in the world!'

David lowered his head. 'You honour me . . .' After a moment he added, 'There is a great faith in you. I want you to have everything that life can give. When I first knew you, all I wanted to do was to wrap you up and carry you away! I had a dream once that I built a cottage for us in the country, with roses and everything, and that your breasts grew so big you couldn't fit out the door!'

Joan laughed. 'Male fantasy if ever I heard it!'

She got into bed. David's hand lifted her nightdress, caressed her, and she took the nightgown off, switched off the light and turned to him, burying his head between her breasts.

'Are they too small for you? I have to tell you, I can still make it through the door!'

Patricia dressed for the evening out, dinner with Paddy. He had come back to Dublin after Christmas, come to their party on the 28th. The house had filled with the sounds of laughter and animated conversation, and Patricia waited for the only person she wanted to see. He arrived when the party was in full swing, deposited a bottle in Christmas wrapping on the hall table.

'Ah, hello there, Paddy,' Gerry greeted him politely. 'Pat told me she had invited you. I should have thought of it myself!' He brought Paddy off and introduced him to various people. Patricia mingled with her guests, spoke to Paddy as cheerfully as became a hostess, exchanged a brief few words with him by the fireplace while the people around were talking in fragmented groups. The room was merry with voices, rising, laughing voices, and the scent of wine and spirits.

'How was your Christmas?'

'Christmas is for children!' Paddy said.

'I agree!'

'You're looking wonderful!' he whispered.

'Flatterer!'

He grinned. 'We've had this conversation before . . .' Patricia smiled.

'Can I phone you again?' he asked *sotto voce*.

'Do you need permission?'

Then Nell had come up and been introduced and Paddy had drifted away while Nell questioned Patricia about the boy who was bothering Orla. There had been problems with him during the holiday; he would wait outside on his motorbike and watch the house. Hour after hour he kept up this vigil, until Gerry found out about it and told him to clear off.

'His name is Mick Clancy. She tried to break it off with him and he won't take no for an answer! Sits outside the house on his motorbike so that she doesn't want to go out. Gerry got the police today and they warned him off.'

'He's probably in love, the poor young fellow!' Nell said. 'I feel sorry for him.'

'You didn't see him!' Patricia said. 'To tell you the truth, I feel a bit afraid of him.'

'Why?'

'Just a feeling. The look on his face, all that determination! As though he had rights which were being denied him!'

Nell laughed. 'He's only got a touch of glandular fever. He'll get over it!' She took a sip of her drink, added after a moment, 'I see you decided to take the saner course . . .'

Pat thought of their conversation before Christmas, smiled ruefully. 'Oh Nell – what is sanity?'

Paddy left early and Patricia and Gerry saw him to the door. 'Nice of you to come!'

'Nice of you to have me.' His voice was modulated and polite.

His eyes were impassive but, as she stood there at the hall door saying goodbye, Patricia felt as though she were wired to him, as though there passed between them whatever life had to offer that was warm and meaningful and alive. And it seemed to her that he took this life and warmth away with him down the front steps.

But now she was going out to dinner with him. He had phoned again, voice conspiratorial. 'Are you free for a bite this evening? I would like to drive up the mountains. We could take dinner in somewhere.'

Patricia hesitated purely out of form. Gerry would not be home until late. She would leave him a note. The children could have pizzas. There was no reason why she shouldn't go. It was only for dinner, after all. There was no harm in that.

'What time?'

'Seven thirty?'

'I'll be ready!'

Chapter Seven

'The State recognizes that by her life within the home, woman gives to the State a support without which the common good cannot be achieved.' (Article 41.2 of the Constitution.)

Isn't that nice? Doesn't it make it all worthwhile? But if women are merely the support system, whose *is the 'common good'?*

from *The Horse's Ears*, 1980

January 1990

Sarah was crying. Her head ached. The small of her back hurt. Her arms were bruised; her left elbow throbbed where she had come down on the floor on it. The children were in bed. The house had the unnatural listening silence it always had once Jim got going; there would be no arguments or scuffling from the children tonight. Dara would be fast asleep, his plump cheeks damp from frightened tears. He always fell asleep quickly when his father got going.

She sat on a chair, nursed her swollen elbow, felt the rage, felt the fear ebbing. She was drained. Jim had gone up to bed. She would sleep on the couch tonight and in the morning would pretend nothing. The children would pretend nothing either, except for what they were unable to hide – Liam's white face and Lorraine's anxious eyes. They would eat their porridge in virtual silence and go to school. And Jim would come down, quiet, morose, making a pot of tea for her in silence. That would be in the morning. He would be so nice to her in the morning.

Right now she was in pain. Was her elbow broken? Was her back damaged? Would she lose the baby?

'Oh God almighty, what kind of a sow are you? Do you think

I'm made of money, that I've nothing better to do than support you and your litter?'

He had beaten her during her other pregnancies, too, just as he did whenever the devil that drove him was riding high and wild and lashed out. The frustration of his life was vented in this way, and she was the convenient focus. She was his wife and this gave him the right. Sometimes he wanted sex immediately afterwards, couldn't wait, hitching her skirt up, entering her there against the kitchen wall, grunting and puffing like one of those elephant seals she had seen on TV. Three conceptions had resulted from that, including the present one.

Tonight he had simply gone up to bed, slamming the kitchen door so violently that he had loosened a hinge and a screw had dropped on to the floor. She gazed at it there on the floor. 'A loose screw . . . like himself!' A cup which had been knocked off the table lay in fractured bits by the table leg.

Sarah was used to the conflicting emotions she always experienced after a beating. First was humiliation; that anyone could do such a thing to her, could do it with such impunity! Then there was guilt. Had she deserved it in some way? Maybe she should have broken the news of her pregnancy more gently. Yes, she could have done it more subtly . . . It was partly her fault because she hadn't been perfect in her approach. She should be perfect in everything she did. Then came the knowledge that, for the moment, she had the upper hand; after beating her he was always chastened, a bit downcast, as though fearful that this time he had taken things too far. This brought a queer, momentary triumph. And lastly came the anger, the slow simmering fury, the desire to go up to that room where he lay, sleeping off the exhaustion of having beaten and violated his wife, sleeping off the drink, go up with the poker and knock his head off. But there were the children to think of; there was tomorrow to think of; no matter which way she turned there was devastation. To take on someone like Jim you needed to have your alternatives settled and sure, be ready to act on them. But she was pregnant; she had children; she was as proud as Caesar. And surely, surely, surely, he would realize now – he *had* to realize this time – that it couldn't go on. Had she seen it in his face as he stumbled away, the seed of self-disgust?

And with all the conflict raging within her, the absence of any one clear avenue of resolution, came the encroaching paralysis of her will.

She got up from the chair, found the dustpan and brush and knelt to sweep up the pieces of broken delph. Her back hurt as she bent, and she moved gingerly. She picked up the screw and put it in a drawer. Then she automatically set out the breakfast dishes; she didn't want the children to come down to a kitchen bearing the signs of a struggle.

There was a knock on the back door. Sarah pulled the curtain aside and saw Fiona's face looking in at her. For a moment she wanted to tell her to go away, but that would be an admission of her own turmoil, an admission of the seriousness of what had happened. She unlocked the door and let her in. Fiona studied her for an instant in silence. Then, in silence, she helped to set the table, dried the dishes which were stacked on the draining board, wiped the surfaces, put the milk back in the fridge.

'I'd break his head,' she hissed after a moment. 'If Charlie lifted a finger to me I'd break his head!'

Sarah put a wet dishcloth to her cheekbone. 'It's easy for you to say,' she replied angrily. 'He never has! And you'd be surprised what you'd put up with for the sake of the children!'

'I wanted to get the Guards when I heard him at you tonight; next time I'll get them.'

'What's the point?' Sarah said wearily. 'I told you before. They're not interested. You remember yourself the time Maura D'Arcy took her auld fellow to court, and all the justice could say to him was that he was a decent man if it wasn't for the drink and would he go and get help from that Sister Genevieve who does counselling work with the alcoholics?

' "Is that all right, ma'am?" he said to poor Maura, and what could she say but yes? After taking her courage in her two hands and making them prosecute him! And she was left to go back home with him and the hands and face of him sweating like new putty. He walloped hell out of her that night! . . . No, getting the Guards wouldn't do any good, except make him worse!'

'Do you need a doctor? Fiona asked, watching the way Sarah winced as she applied gentle pressure to her face with the wet cloth.

'I don't think so. I don't think anything's broken. I can't afford doctors.'

Fiona made tea. Sarah hoped that Fiona would keep her mouth

shut. She was a dreadful gossip; kind hearted but unable to resist the conversational starring role. While she put the tea and the cups on the table, she launched into a story about a friend of hers who had started an affair, gone to London with the man for a passionate weekend, a man who said he loved her, a man who had told his wife he was going on a business trip.

'She spent part of the time trailing around the shops with him while he filled his wife's shopping list; and his wife even phoned their hotel because she wanted something added to the list! Can you imagine? "Hello, darling. Of course, yes, yes . . . See you on Sunday . . . Love you too!" Can you imagine that, while she lay there in bed waiting for him? Can you imagine that as an aphrodisiac?'

Sarah laughed. 'Christ!'

'She's still seeing him!'

'Women are looking for something,' Sarah said. 'They're digging for treasure. They keep looking and digging. They're so sure that if they keep digging they'll find it. And they forgive everything while they're excavating, while they still have hope.'

'Do you forgive Jim?' Fiona demanded.

'I used to,' Sarah responded after a moment. 'Still do in a way, when I feel he can't help it. But sometimes I am so angry I'm afraid that I will kill him. Sometimes I am afraid that he will kill me.'

Fiona went home and Sarah got a duvet and pillow from the wardrobe in the boys' room. She went softly past the door of her bedroom. She went downstairs and put the bedclothes on the couch, shut the door and started to undress.

The mirror over the mantelpiece reflected her body, her movements, the gingerly way she moved to take off her jumper because raising her arms over her head was an agony, the grimace of pain. She touched her left breast tentatively, wincing. It was sore and seemed to be swollen. Her arms had red marks from the grip of his fingers.

When she had her nightie on she turned out the light and drew back the curtains a little, enough to show her the shadow of the little willow tree in the front garden. The street-light illumined this garden, showed the thin spears of the daffs waiting to burst out soon, the small purple crocuses. A car went by, headlights like beacons. The bare, newly budding branches of the willow stirred a little in the wind. It would be a nice tree some day, but the lawn would then be too small for it. She thought of the day they had gone to the nursery gardens to get it – not long after they had bought the house. She had visualized herself sitting under its lovely drooping branches in the summer evenings with a book. She had loved to read, but now there was no time. Children aged eight, six, and two and a half – and another on the way – didn't leave you much time. She had been on the pill for a while after Lorraine was born, but it had disagreed with her and the doctor had advised her to give it up. So they used the safe period and condoms. That was when Jim was sober. When he wasn't sober it was another matter. When he wasn't sober he screwed her against the kitchen table or up against the wall. And then she had to pretend to everyone the next day that nothing had happened, larding on a thick layer of make-up to cover facial bruises, trying not to wince when she moved. The only thing worse than what was happening was the fear that people would know, that she would meet morbid curiosity in their eyes, or pity.

Once things had been different. Once she had had money of her own, a job, dental nurse-cum-secretary. She had attended typing and secretarial classes and Mr Ward had taught her all there was to know about how to mix amalgams, keep charts, send out accounts, do the bookkeeping. Mr Ward, her employer, had kept her busy, doing messages in her lunch-hour, expecting her to stay on after hours when occasion demanded. He never offered extra pay for this. But she didn't mind, took pride in her work; although sometimes she had been sorry for the patients who couldn't afford proper treatment, like the poor widow who was on social welfare and needed a crown. Mr Ward had extracted the whole tooth instead, a front tooth. 'I'm not a charitable organization.'

Jim had come into her life through her work. He had arrived at the surgery one morning, without appointment.

'I'm in pain. Will you ask the dentist to see me, miss?' Mr Ward had seen him; the X-ray revealed decay under a filling in the left upper canine, and that this was the source of the pain. The old filling was removed and a temporary filling installed. On his next visit he had been charming.

'Thanks for what you did for me last week. I was half out of my mind with the pain.'

'It wasn't me.'

'Would you like a bite of lunch? I don't have to be back at the yard until half two.'

'Where do you work?'

'O'Connor's Builders' Suppliers. I'm a supervisor.'

'Oh.'

'What's your name?'

'Sarah.'

'Mine's Jim, Jim O'Toole.'

They had had lunch at Kennedy's pub around the corner. They talked about taxes; 'Jesus there's no living on PAYE; I bet Mr Ward doesn't return every penny to our friends in the tax office!'

'How should I know?' Sarah said, knowing a great deal more than she was going to pretend.

He had smiled at her, a personal winning smile, his pale blue eyes crinkling, his interest flattering her. He looked at her as though there were no one else in the place, as though she filled up the sum total of the world.

'You have a nice mouth . . . You don't mind me saying so, Sarah, you're one of the prettiest girls I've seen in a long while. I mean that.'

She had blushed. This had been the start of the courtship. He would come to the flat she shared with Myra and Jenny to take her out; to the pictures, to a meal, for a walk, for a drive, for a long necking session in Howth. 'Stop Jim, don't,' hands up her skirt, hands at her breasts. But she hadn't really wanted him to stop, not completely stop, and he had no intention of doing so. The excitement had made her come, just the feel of his hand on her thigh, the knowledge of his erection, the touch on her breast. There was power too in being so desired. Power was heady.

'I love you, kitten, I love you.'

She was sure he loved her; she felt she was being swept away on some kind of tide which did not wait to ask her if she wanted to sail.

'What do you think of him, Myra?' she asked her flatmate.

'He's . . . good looking . . .'

Jenny hadn't been forthcoming, crinkling her forehead. 'If you ask me – I think he's out for number one.'

'So what else is new?' Myra had rejoined.

The flat was small, tiny kitchen, one bedroom with twin beds, a sitting room with a single bed which doubled as a couch. This was Sarah's bed and she refused to let Jim share it, no matter how much he coaxed, no matter how cross he got.

Sarah could sense his perspective. His needs were paramount. Men needed sex. He told her so himself. Whatever men needed was an automatic apologia for what they took. I need it therefore I am entitled to it. Whatever women needed was irrelevant.

'Jesus, anyone would think you were a princess in an ivory tower,' Jim had muttered one night. 'I've a good mind to rape you and get you pregnant.'

Sarah had frozen. 'I'd never speak to you again . . . I'd have the Guards on you!' she had whispered, aware even as she spoke of the utter insufficiency of this rejoinder; he had spoken of her violation with the same flippancy as if he were referring to some inconsequential liberty, some small personal trespass with a funny side to it. But she had not been able to think. No one had ever spoken to her like that in her life.

Later, having mulled it over, she told him, 'If you ever try to rape me, I'll kill you. I'll kill you if it's the last thing I do. I'm telling you now so that there will be no misunderstanding. I don't even care if I go to jail.' This statement was so coldly delivered that Jim, who had been driving in silence, started visibly.

'And I don't want to see you again.'

Jim had pulled over on to the side of the street. 'Christ, what's wrong? What's the matter?'

'Nothing's the matter. Not after what you said.'

'Jesus, what did I say?'

'About raping me, about getting me pregnant!'

He breathed out loudly in sorrow and exasperation. 'Kitten . . . I was only joking. Can't you even take a joke?' His arm was around her, her face tilted up with his right hand so that his pale eyes looked into hers.

'Come on now, Sarah; we know each other better than that! You're not going to get all cross over a silly thing like that! You know how I love you, kitten.'

'It wasn't silly,' Sarah said sulkily. But she was mollified. It was just his way, she told herself. He would never hurt her. Maybe she shouldn't have taken offence.

She had brought him home to see her parents. He had been all out to charm; a box of Black Magic for her mother. But she knew that her father was not impressed, knew it from the flexing of his eyebrows, the tension around his mouth. Later this impression was confirmed by what she overheard, her father in the kitchen being pacified by her mother.

'For God's sake, Michael, he's only here for the day. Will you pretend, at least, for Sarah's sake?'

'That fellow isn't a man and never will be one,' her father had said in a low voice, adding, 'I hope she's not serious about him!'

'Of course she isn't; she's too young. Give her a chance.'

At that time Sarah had had a dream, a romantic dream of recognition by a man whose recognition would really matter. This recognition was more important to her than becoming the president – even if that were possible – or making a great career for herself. And this recognition would never come her way if she gave in to Jim, if she went the whole hog. You were 'damaged goods' if you were not a virgin. And she was not at all sure that she wanted to marry Jim – not since the day she had tried to make a lamb stew for him in the flat and he had gone half wild. 'You stupid woman . . . how can anyone eat that?' There was fat swimming around at the surface; how was he expected to eat that!

'I can strain off the fat . . .' but he was not persuaded. She knew he was exercising his right to rant and rave because he thought she was property, because he was hungry and impatient, because he was afraid that his dinner would be disappointing, because he had been looking forward to a delicious stew and it might be greasy, because everything was all about him. So what would it be like if they were married?

She had not spoken to him for the rest of the day and he had come to apologize. 'I'm sorry, kitten; don't be cross with your old Jim,' and he had brought her a box of chocolates.

'He's really a very generous fellow,' Myra said to her, sampling the sweets. 'If you don't want him, can I have him?' But Sarah did want him. He was better than loneliness. She was afraid of loneliness because, being insecure in her self-image, she suspected it would be her lot. She had never regarded herself as particularly pretty; she was convinced she was a bit thick, someone who couldn't even get a good Leaving Cert. She did not know if she was attractive enough to find another man. With all her spirit she did not know how to value herself. She wanted the romantic dream of what she could share with a man who loved her. This was the only dream that life had to offer her. She was sure that if Jim loved her she would be able to change him; with her love and joy she would be able to change him, make him join forces with her to face the world.

And he had been careful after that. He gave her just enough love to make her want more, to make her overlook his occasional testiness, to make allowances. She was hungry for love, for the possibilities it offered of rapture and peace.

Sarah slept. She woke when the light began in the sky, tried to turn and found that she was stiff. There was a sharp pain in the small of her back.

She rolled sideways, got on to the floor, dressed with difficulty, and then went to inspect her face in the mirror. There was a small red and blue swelling on her cheekbone, still tender to the touch. Anger came suddenly. God blast the bastard, she thought. I'll have to plaster something on this. She went to the kitchen to start the breakfast.

Lorraine appeared, looking distraught. Usually she came down already fully dressed, hair done, tie knotted, but this morning her blouse was open, her tie in her hand.

'Sit down, pet. Porridge is ready,' Sarah said, turning to fill the child's bowl. As she did so she felt the arms around her hips and the face of her daughter was buried in her stomach.

'What's the matter, darling?' Sarah whispered.

'I had an awful dream,' Lorraine sobbed. 'And I went into your room, but there was only Daddy in the bed . . . and I thought you were gone away . . .' The sobs intensified. The grip tightened.

'Where did you get such an idea?' Sarah asked her, sitting down and taking her on her knee. 'Ooh, you are a heavy lump; what made you think that Mammy would go away? How do you think she could manage without you? Whist, whist . . .'

'I hate Daddy,' Lorraine said then, looking up at her mother with her runny nose and tearstained face. 'I will take the big knife from the drawer and kill him if he hits you again.'

Sarah caressed her daughter's wet cheeks, looked into the blue eyes. 'Look, darling – Daddy doesn't mean to hurt Mammy; only he takes too much to drink . . . and then he doesn't know what he's doing.'

'I don't care,' Lorraine said, wiping her eyes and gazing at her mother with intense eyes. 'He should never hit you.'

'Look, he won't hit me any more,' Sarah said. 'He's probably sorry himself. He won't do it any more. So smile! Let me see my big girl smiling!'

97

She got a cloth and wiped her daughter's face and plaited the long fair hair, tying the ends with two butterfly elastics which she took out of the drawer.

'Eat your breakfast now. You don't want to be late for school!'

She got Liam up then, told him to hurry. The eldest of her children, he had his father's pale eyes and mouth. He looked at his mother with something like pity, examined her silently for bruises.

'Are you all right, Mammy? Did Daddy hurt you?'

Sarah felt that Liam secretly had no respect for her, because it was possible for a man to treat her as his father did.

'Come on now, love, you'll be late,' she whispered. But she didn't answer his question, because she was suddenly ashamed of her vulnerability. She indicated Dara, who was still asleep in the cot. 'Shh, you'll wake him . . .'

Liam came down for his breakfast. While the children were eating, she put make-up on her face, put on her coat, and when they were ready she took them to the corner to wait for the school bus. She met two women she knew.

'God it's cold this morning,' one of them said, and Sarah fixed her thick woollen scarf so that it hid the side of her face.

She went back to the house. Dara had woken up and had let himself out of the cot and he was halfway down the stairs. He chirped when he saw her. 'Mamee,' and Sarah's heart turned over as it always did when she saw his little fat legs. his nappy was soggy and smelt to high heaven, so she changed him and fed him and put him on the bright yellow potty in the kitchen while she cleared up after Liam and Lorraine's breakfast. Then she put a towel on the table, lay him back on it while she put a fresh nappy on him, kissing his fat tummy and making him laugh. But as she bent over him, as she laughed at him, something happened to her back, because she found she couldn't straighten, couldn't stand up. It was as though her torso had become disconnected from her legs. The baby thought for a moment that this was all part of the game, and he gurgled with delight as his mother lurched sideways, until she grasped a chair and supported herself and howled through the open door.

'Jim – get out of that bed and come and help me!'

Dara started to wail.

'Do you hear me? Get out of that fucking bed,' Sarah continued at the top of her voice. 'Jim!'

He appeared in his pyjamas, looking annoyed, then sheepish, staring at her there on the floor. 'Take Dara off the table.'

He put the child on the floor and then he grabbed Sarah and tried to pull her into a standing position.

'Something's wrong with my back. I need to lie down. Help me to the couch in the sitting room.'

Jim's face registered defensiveness, then alarm. His pale eyes washed over Sarah, sleep still in the corners, his breath reeking from last night's drink, his body smelling of stale sweat. He half carried her to the sitting room and deposited her on the couch.

'Lie there for a while,' he said gruffly. 'You'll be all right if you lie there for a while.'

He brought Dara in and put him in the playpen, threw in some toys and a cardboard box. Dara seized on the cardboard box, searched it, put things into it, put it on his head.

Jim made coffee in the kitchen and came back to her with a cup, milked, one sugar, the way she liked it. He got a small table, positioned it beside the couch, put the coffee on it. Then he got his own cup and perched on the edge of the couch.

'Jesus, Sarah, I'm sorry,' he said after a moment, his voice very low. 'I didn't mean to hurt you. I don't know what got into me.' He didn't meet her eyes. 'I'll make it up to you, love, I really will. We could go to the pictures tonight if you like,' he added eagerly.

'In this state? I can't go to the pictures. I can't get off the blasted couch. You'll have to take the day off. You'll have to get the doctor!'

Jim looked hunted. 'You'll be all right, kitten. You'll be fine. I'll take the day off. Just rest there for a while and you'll be fine.'

Sarah didn't answer. She tried to move. She tried to use her legs. They moved, but did not seem to be part of her body. There was a dull ache in the small of her back.

'Get the doctor, Jim. I need the doctor.'

'I can't get the doctor. Not with you in that state!' he said eventually. 'He might think it was my fault!'

'Yes,' Sarah said. 'He might think you had hit me. Wouldn't that be awful? Don't worry. The whole cul-de-sac knows that you hit me. They're not deaf and blind! But I'll tell the doctor I fell down the stairs. He won't know you hit me.'

Jim put his hand to his face, bent his head. 'You have to be so goddam snide about it, Sarah. I said I was sorry.'

'Just phone for the doctor,' Sarah said carefully, suddenly

afraid that he might start up again. 'Otherwise I may be like this for ever!'

Jim phoned the yard to take the day off and then he phoned the doctor. 'He'll be here about midday,' he said.

'Don't worry,' Sarah said, 'I won't tell him. I have some pride too!'

The doctor came punctually at midday. Jim had helped his wife to bed in the meantime, and he admitted Dr Roche with a certain sheepishness.

'She's hurt her back.'

The doctor shut the bedroom door behind him, turned to Sarah who was lying against the pillow Jim had plumped up for her.

'What happened to your back?'

'I fell downstairs,' Sarah said.

'I see. Is that where you got the bruise on your face as well?'

'Yes.'

He examined her, drawing in his breath sharply, touching her spine, pressing lightly on the small of her back while she stifled cries of pain.

He listened to her heart, took her blood pressure. 'I don't suppose you play rugby, Mrs O'Toole?'

She turned at him, assuming he was joking, but his face was grim. 'Of course not. What put that into your head?'

'Because you are presenting like someone who has been in a particularly vicious scrum.'

'Never mind the scrum,' Sarah said tartly, aware that he suspected the truth. 'What's wrong with me?'

'Inflammation of the sacroiliac. Bruising. I would like to send you in for X-rays.'

Sarah thought rapidly. If she went in for X-rays the radiographer would see the bruising, the nurses would see it; every nosy little creep of a student would see it.

'No way! Who'd look after the children?'

'Your husband could manage.'

'No!'

The doctor glared out of the door, sighed and gave her a prescription. 'Anti-inflammatory tablets and Ponston for the pain. Stay in bed for at least three days.'

He shut his black case. 'You ought to do something about those stairs. This isn't good enough at all!' He looked at her meaningfully.

Jim met him in the hall and paid his bill with a cheque. The doctor was curt with him and did not speak to him except to state the amount he owed him.

Upstairs Sarah stared at the hieroglyphics on the prescription before she tore it up. She patted her belly.

'I'm taking no chances with you, little bird. Maybe I should have told the doctor about you, but it'll wait. We can't have you on bloody Ponston!'

She thought of the doctor's caustic comment. But, in spite of herself, a part of her mind was bright with hope, the part which latched on to the possibility of a sea-change; the part which knew that Jim realized the horror of his behaviour and would therefore, surely, alter it. She always experienced this spear of hope on the day afterwards, when Jim was nice to her.

Chapter Eight

It's just that nothing is personal. He gives me a present, but it's not personal. He makes love, but it's nothing personal; we have conversations, sometimes quite intense ones about 'legal' problems that I concoct, but they are never personal. If I say, 'Do you love me?' he says, 'Of course I love you!' but there is no change in tone except, perhaps, exasperation, or he might turn it into a joke. If I say, 'I love you', he takes it as his due, but it certainly does not trigger any moment of disclosure. It's not that he abhors the personal in any deliberate way; he just doesn't know it exists.

from *The Horse's Ears*, 1978

Paddy got lost. Patricia had been too busy savouring the fact that they were alone together that she had not bothered to watch their route. When she saw the signpost for Enniskerry she began to suspect that they were off course.

'Do you want to go to Enniskerry?'

'Not particularly!' He laughed, turned to glance at her. 'Are you worried? Did you think I would abduct you?'

'I wish you would,' was on the tip of Patricia's tongue, but she commented merely on the fact that she thought he had been going around in circles.

'I can't believe I have forgotten my way!' he said. 'I used to know the Dublin outskirts.'

'The "Dublin outskirts", as you call them, have changed, Paddy. There are houses where once there were fields; people sit and watch television and eat their dinners where the wind once blew unimpeded.'

'Are we waxing poetic?'

Patricia laughed. 'No, just garrulous!'

But the drive was nice. The rain spattered the windscreen,

headlights from other cars came and went, and the darkness swallowed them at intervals. Laughter spilled over, sparkled, died. He put the radio on. Classical music wafted through the car, the lights on the dashboard were muted with intimacy, the radio presenter's voice came softly and went away again, the motor droned through the night. She was alone with Paddy. The silence between them was full.

The restaurant was in the foothills – Kildoran House – an old house with turf fires and a French menu. They sat in armchairs by the hearth and when the waitress gave them the menus and asked them if they wanted a drink while they were waiting, Patricia hesitated. She had not had a drink of any kind since that awful night when Gerry had found her with the empty vodka bottle, and she felt that she would love a drink, if only a glass of wine. But it was too dangerous. She didn't trust herself with drink any more.

'Mineral water,' she said to Paddy. 'I don't drink.'

'Not even wine?' he asked. 'Not even wine with your meal?'

'No.'

They placed their orders. The waitress asked if they wanted help with the French and Paddy, who spent quite a lot of time in France in connection with his work, and was fluent in French, smiled and allowed her to explain the menu. While they waited they sat staring into the fire, watching the brilliant orange in the heart of the blaze, feeling the heat on their faces. His hand touched hers and then grasped it and they sat in muted conversation, watching the dance of the flames.

Patricia felt the peace. It came out of the air and the smell of turf smoke and the black night outside. It came from the touch of Paddy's hand and it surrounded her, muffled her against the world. It was as though she suddenly had found the door in the circular wall around which she had been groping her way for an eternity. She was inside the charmed circle at last: wise, discovered, and profoundly happy.

Why do I feel like this? This simplicity of being, this sense that everything important in life is within reach? It's like being a child again. Or like being old, with a fulfilled life behind me.

The dining room was of medium size, half empty. A fire burned in a hearth and a young man in evening dress played the piano. The walls were decorated with hunting prints and a pair of antlers. Candlelight flickered. The scents of good food filled the air. Paddy smiled at her across the table.

'You look superb; you have a great colour from the fire!'

'What makes you think it's the fire?' she said in low voice.

He smiled. 'Are you telling me it's something else?'

After a while he said, leaning towards her but without changing the level of his voice, 'There are hotels in France where we could have a fire like that, with logs, in our room . . . A room with a big bed and a fire and a dinner brought by room service . . . Would that appeal to you?' Paddy said this with such calm aplomb that Patricia thought for a moment that she had misheard. She blushed to her hairline.

'You're blushing,' he murmured.

'I thought I had forgotten how!' But she did not answer the question.

Afterwards, as the rain had stopped, he suggested that they take a short walk, 'To stretch our legs before we head back.'

He took her arm and led her down a lane which was just visible from the moonlight, and there in the boreen he turned her to him, lifted her chin and kissed her very slowly. Patricia, responding in a haze of pleasure, put her arms around his neck.

But even as she kissed him she realized how much had changed: the kiss was too expert; the erection she felt against her was too expectant; the suggestion made over the dinner table had been too ready. Paddy had lost his innocence. She felt very young compared to him. She had never ventured even into the shallows of the waters he was obviously at home in. She felt out of place, and suddenly ill at ease.

She was filled with sadness. How could she possibly have expected it to be different, expected the freshness of the old, awkward contact, expected him to have remained unchanged? He had become a man of the world, whatever that meant. His hands moved to unbutton her blouse and she pulled away from him. He made an immediate apologetic gesture of acceptance.

'I am intruding and I don't want to intrude!'

They drove home in desultory conversation, lapsing into long silences. The earlier calm was gone for Patricia. She felt charged with a tension which made her nerve-endings tingle, her skin alive, her mind confused.

He left her at the door. 'Will you dine with me again?' he asked.

Patricia looked into his eyes, the same eyes, except for the lines around them, but behind them was hidden the life he had lived, a life she knew nothing of. She could say something to fob him off; he would understand.

She could refuse and go back to her life with Gerry and the children and fight the longing for escape.

I'm not turning my back on this! she thought. I don't care where it leads.

'I will,' she said. 'Thank you, Paddy, for the evening!'

Upstairs Gerry was in bed. He was reading, his glasses reflecting the light from the bedside lamp. He looked up at her.

'Where were you?'

'I left you a note!'

'To say you had gone out with Nell; but she phoned while you were out and seemed to know nothing of any such arrangement!' Patricia grasped at straws.

'I meant to phone Nell, but an old schoolfriend rang me out of the blue and I spent the evening with her.'

'Oh? Who was that?'

Patricia mentally scanned her old class at school. 'Monica Dwyer . . . you don't know her.'

'What did you do?'

'We had a drink and a meal at Ferdia's.'

She felt the pressure of her husband's gaze. He was looking for signs of drink.

'Did you enjoy yourself?'

'Yes. We had a good chat!'

Gerry went back to his reading. What a good liar you have become, Patricia, she told herself. Why are you in a position that you have to tell lies?

'By the way, that fellow who is so fond of Orla was around again. Called to the door. I sent him packing.'

Pat experienced a combination of alarm and distaste. She had not told Gerry about finding the youth in Orla's room. She felt angry that he had dared to defy her.

'Good! He has a nerve coming around again. You'd think she was property! What did she say about it?'

'I didn't tell her!' Gerry said coldly. 'I haven't worked all these years for this family to have buckoos like that calling at my door!'

Patricia went to the bathroom, checking en route that Orla and Simon were in bed. The light was off in both rooms; she could make out each of their heads sunk into the pillows and remembered the nights when she would sit with them and read stories, embrace them, kiss them, feel their small, plump hands.

'Read the story about the beakers,' Simon would ask. The 'beakers' were a family of beavers who lived in a river and whose lodge had been damaged by flood waters. So the little beaver, the youngest of the family, sneaked off and built a new lodge downstream and was the hero of the hour.

Simon identified with this little 'beaker'. Orla, on the other hand, had loved the story of Thumbelina and would stare for a long time at the colour illustration showing her nude in a tulip. But the 'beakers' and Thumbelina were no more. No more maternal goodnight kisses. They were above and beyond all that!

Nell phoned Patricia the next day.

'Pat . . . I hope I didn't stick my foot in it last night! I rang and Gerry said you were out meeting me. I didn't know what to say! I must have sounded like a right idiot.'

'Don't worry about that! I was meeting an old friend . . . who is visiting Ireland. Gerry got his wires crossed!'

'That makes a change! Not like our Gerry!'

Nell waited for Patricia's description of her evening; where she had gone, how her friend was, who she was married to. But Patricia changed the subject.

Joan put her witness in the stand. The case concerned a consignment of custom-made packing cases which were the subject of a dispute. The recipient had refused to pay for them; they were the wrong size, he said. His company had ordered a different size.

Joan's witness produced the order form, which gave the size as per the delivery. Joan handed a copy to the court clerk, who gave it to the justice. The courtroom was warm, carpeted, one of the comfortable new appointments in Dolphin House. Beside her the barrister retained by the defence was reading through his notes.

'I haven't seen this order form,' he said.

Joan bent down and gave him a copy. 'Your eyes are gorgeous!' he said.

Joan ignored him. 'Is this the order signed by the defendant?' she asked the witness.

'It is.'

'Did the delivery fill the order?'

107

'It did!'

'Thank you.' She turned to defence counsel. 'Your witness.'

Joan sat down and listened to the defence. Oh God, nine hundred quids' worth of bloody packing cases and the afternoon spent on it! She thought of David at home, putting paint on canvas; thought of the glimpse she had had of the latest picture, a room with a huge window and a vast night-time sky. And in the room a woman leaning backwards, hair falling down to the floor, hands limp, a gesture of abandonment. What she had not liked about the painting was the emerging figure in the corner which overshadowed the woman, the dark head turned towards her, looking down on her, the face shadowed. The picture had three different strands: the great vacant sky, the woman who looked like she was drowning in the confined space of the room, and the imponderable dark figure which was susceptible to any interpretation. Every time she saw him, Joan felt that this figure represented Man as he would have been if left to himself, if untrammelled by the strictures of any kind of dogma, if left to his own power. She felt disturbed by his re-emergence in David's work.

The barrister sat down. He had just conducted his examination of the defence witness, who claimed that he had varied the order over the phone and had followed this up in writing. He produced a copy of the letter he had written.

'Did you post this letter?' Joan asked him.

'No. My secretary posted it.'

'Is she going to give evidence?'

'She left. She doesn't work for me any more.'

'Was she the person who made the phone call to allegedly vary the order?'

'She was.'

'What evidence have you got that the phone call was made or that this letter was posted?'

'I know it was posted. It went out with all the other letters.'

'You heard my client say he did not receive it. Have you got a certificate of posting?'

'No.'

'Would you concede that it is possible that it might not have been posted; that there was some kind of oversight?'

The witness sighed. 'I suppose it's possible, but . . .'

'Thank you,' Joan said. 'No further questions.' She sat down.

The witness was about to leave the box, but the justice intervened. He wanted to get through his list as quickly as possible, and the case was boring him to death.

'You signed an order; you say you varied it but you have no proof. Isn't that the position?'

'I'm afraid so, Justice.'

'In that case,' the justice said, 'I have no alternative but to find for the plaintiff. But I'm making no order as to costs!'

The barrister and Joan stood up and murmured, 'May it please you, Justice.'

The barrister looked at Joan and raised his eyebrows, collected his papers and, after bowing to the bench, left the courtroom. Joan followed him.

'Well – how did you get on?' Larry asked when Joan returned. He met her in the hall.

'We won! But there was no order as to costs.'

'Was Mr Stapleton pleased?'

'Of course he was. I think he was nurturing doubts.'

'I know it was a bore, Joan, but he is a good client and we couldn't let him down!'

'We'll have to get someone else to do this sort of stuff,' Joan said. 'I have much better things to be doing!'

Larry stared at her, taken aback. His expression indicated that it was unlike Joan to complain about anything, that she was getting uppity because she had been made a partner.

'By the way, pet, I understand your husband phoned for you earlier. I think it might be urgent!'

Joan almost ran up the stairs to her office. When she had shut the door behind her, she dropped her briefcase and reached for the phone.

David answered after a moment. His voice was bright and jovial. Joan felt the tension leave her, felt the flooding relief.

'You phoned while I was in court?'

'I just wanted to tell you, darling, that we're off to Paris in June.' His voice became very calm. 'The Paris gallery have offered me a contract! There'll be an exhibition in September and they'll be flying the pictures out quite soon!'

Joan took a deep breath. For a moment she had a sensation of the horizons surrounding her life being pulled back, so that the vistas were immeasurable. For an instant she felt that David was

109

moving beyond her in some way, slipping out of the familiar cocoon sustained by her efforts and anxiety.

'Well?' David demanded. 'Aren't you pleased?'

'I'm over the moon,' Joan said heartily. 'Congratulations!'

When Joan got home that evening, David was still in his studio. Buoyed up with adrenalin, he was still working with a frenzy. Joan put on the supper and brought him up a glass of wine.

'We're celebrating!'

Paul left his homework, came up to the studio, and the little family sat talking together among the paint pots and brushes and the stacked canvases.

Wouldn't it be strange, Joan wondered, looking at her husband and her son, if this family stopped depending on me! What would I feel like if David were well and successful and I were no longer the lynchpin?

It would be wonderful, she answered herself honestly. It would be absolutely wonderful to have this weight lifted from me. But all the same she recognized the tiny frisson of fear. If she were no longer the mainstay, would she know the new David who was? He smiled at her now, his teeth white, his eyes teasing, came to put an arm around her, clinked his glass against hers.

'Here's to us, who's like us?' he intoned.

'Damn few,' Joan answered. 'And they're all dead!'

It was an old joke, but now it seemed horribly incongruous. Paul tensed and the smile died in David's eyes.

Chapter Nine

If a woman (a member of a class which has never been responsible for mass destruction) needs an abortion, even for a reason as compelling as rape, there's no question of her obtaining one in our righteous land. There never was. So why this abortion referendum? And even though an abortion is indicated for the mother's mental survival, she is not entitled to that much self-determination. They talk about equality of rights; they talk about the destruction of the innocent. But the thing is unequal from the start – one party builds the other in her own body at her own colossal cost. If the embryo is a person enjoying legal rights, it must be subject also to legal restraints (a 'person' can't legally tap into your blood supply, push your body out of any recognizable shape and cause you great pain and bodily harm!); and if a woman is a person, why should she be forced to submit to any kind of plunder?

The truth is that pregnancy is the province only of the pregnant, and the rhetoric is misplaced. Turning the country into a police state and women into second-class citizens will change only our place in the history of civilization. A campaign to address the reasons for abortion – a campaign to educate – why can't we have that instead of this sinister referendum? You'd think we had nothing but immaculate conceptions and women vying for happy holidays in abortion clinics!

from *The Horse's Ears*, 1983

March 1990

Pregnancy, after four children, was murder; each one harder than the last: tummy muscles gone to hell, the weight of the sixth

111

month, the bulge big and sagging. Sarah felt the baby moving, turning inside her; she put her hand on the bulge. Is that your head I feel, my little bird? Who are you? Who will you be? Are you girl or boy? I don't care. Just be all right, whole, with ten fingers and ten toes.

Christ, I'm so tired. I'm not having any more after this one. You're the last! Make him tie a knot in it, Fiona had whispered to her. She laughed at the absurdity. Jim's dong in a knot! Fiona was funny; she was kind too: she had taken Dara for the morning.

The baby moved again. Right little footballer I've got here. Sarah visualized the child in her womb, tucked up, knees against chin, translucent skin, face full of unearthly peace like the photograph of the unborn child she had seen.

She finished washing the dishes and began to dry them, stacking them in the cupboard. Then she began to wipe down the surfaces, digging at the egg yolk on the kitchen table with her nail. God I'm becoming a slut, she thought, looking at her uneven nails with the bit of yellow yolk stuck under one of them. For a moment the vision of the sofa, tidy room, fire lit, nail file and varnish at the ready, floated into her mind. Hand cream, bottle of perfume, hair freshly washed and blow-dried, Sarah as she used to be, Sarah expecting a lover. Jim had been a lover of sorts in those days, had even become careful of what he said and did, anxious to please.

But there were the nappies still to do and then the beds. And the kitchen floor was a mess. Jim had promised to lay the new vinyl two weeks before, but it was still like this, the bare concrete underfoot. She visualized the new vinyl: the roll was in the garage, small octagonal tiles, yellow, to go with the walls. It would suit the new kitchen. She was glad she had a decent kitchen at last. She had been going on about it for a good while, whenever she thought his mood benign.

She sat for a moment, looked into the garden still wet with winter dew.

How had she felt when he asked her to marry him, when he told her how much he loved her? Did he love her still; maybe in his own way he loved her still? But if only he would say it sometimes, would hold her when the shadows crossed her soul, the fears she woke with in the night. It had occurred to her that she might die in childbirth. Nonsense, the doctor had said; no one dies in childbirth any more. Anyway, half the time Jim either

112

wasn't there at night, or came to bed so late that it was almost morning. But still she felt the foreboding there, like a clairvoyant searching for the future in a crystal ball and finding only darkness.

She cleared the sink, poured the nappies into it from the plastic bucket, nauseated from the combined smell of Nappisan and urine, but they worked out cheaper than the disposable ones. She rinsed them under running water, wrung them out and put them into the washing machine to await the rest of the load. Upstairs she made the beds, cleaned the lavatory, washed out Dara's potty, holding down the nausea from the smell, gathered up the shirts, socks and underclothes which were lying here and there; the boys' room was the worst, Liam's socks thrown in a corner, but even Lorraine wasn't much better with her knickers under the bed. How many times had she told them – bring down your dirty clothes; don't leave them upstairs for me to pick up.

'OK, Mum.'

OK was cheap. Bending was the problem. The weight of her pregnancy tugged at her spine, making her back ache. The bulge got physically in the way; already she had to bend sideways. She caught sight of herself in the mirror: face tired, body swollen. It was all ahead of her again, the pain beginning in the small of the back, the agony spearing its way through every part of her, while she pushed and laboured and tore and the blood flowed. A new person howling, the waxen umbilicus thick and twisted, the baby's head narrowed from the birth canal, blood on its hair. The terrible surge of joy. Is s/he all right? Yes. The sense of absolute, godlike achievement. The sudden, perfect peace. But the doctor would be there, standing between her legs. She hated his professional remove, his pleasure in his power. After all, he would never have to go through this. He was safe. He was blind to this experience, yet he would name it. But he would not name it as it was. He did not know the surge of joy, the absolute, authentic moment of achievement.

It was ahead of her again. The corridors in the Rotunda with limping women the day after, and young, smug men – students, housemen. Titillated by their power. Titillated by the semi-sexual access, the bodies of women open and in pain, open there before their eyes, bleeding, naked. Young men who read *Penthouse* and *Playboy* examining the bodies of women in the process of parturition, women helpless with pain. While the women hated it and pretended to themselves that it was all right because these smooth-faced men examining them with half-concealed prurience were 'doctors'; because if they admitted the truth it would not be bearable to live. Why can't I have the baby at home? I could be free of all those white-coated little pricks. Christ, why can't they share the burden of being human?

Sarah brought the dirty clothes down to the washing machine – the new automatic Jim had bought for her. 'For her.' He had bought it in a fit of remorse after the last time he had belted her around. 'I'm sorry, Sarah; I don't know what got into me.'

'There are six people in this house,' she had told him. 'Six lots of dirty linen. Why do you say the thing is for me; am I a slave?' She had laughed then because he was in a good mood; he hadn't understood.

She pushed the load in, put in the powder, pushed the button. The motor started, water rushed into the drum. Thank God for that. The old machine had been on its last legs. Once she had washed the sheets in the bath – pounding them up and down, wringing them; that had been in the early days.

Jim liked to buy 'her' household gadgets. He meant well. Except that he did whatever he liked. She was just the domestic back-up.

I starve, Sarah thought. I must be content with the washing machine and the fitted kitchen. And children. I love the children. But I love my life too, or would if I had one. Guilt. Mustn't think like this. It will make me mad.

The doorbell rang. It was Fiona, Dara in her arms.

'I don't think he's too well, Sarah. He's been crying and moping, wants to lie down. He's hot, too.'

Sarah took her child from Fiona's arms, carried him into the sitting room. Dara was white, listless.

'What's the matter, sweetheart?'

She put her hand on his forehead, felt down the side of cheek and neck, felt the alarm gathering in her, the knot of fear, the quickening of her heart.

'He's got a high temperature!'

Dara began to cry. Sarah rocked him, felt the baby inside her lurch in a sudden, spasmodic movement.

'I'd better get the doctor.'

'Stay where you are; I'll phone him.'

Fiona went into the hall. Sarah heard her lifting the receiver, press the buttons. Dara had closed his eyes, tears glinting on his soft cheeks.

'Mammy will put you to bed. Will you go to bed . . .?'

'No,' Dara whined.

'Whist, darling, whist. The doctor is coming. He'll make you better.'

The child indicated his eyes, sniffed jerkily. The eyes closed again. Sarah held him on her knee, head against her breast and the child curved his body over her belly, his hands clinging to her clothes, although his neck seemed strangely stiff. His hands were plump, dimpled at the knuckles; his lashes were luxuriant; the fair hair curled at his forehead. I made this, Sarah thought, this person, this child of mine. The whole of her will surged behind his life. She was no longer tired, but she was trembling inside with fear. This baby with dimpled fists and blue, long-lashed eyes whom she loved with such ferocity, was very ill. It needed no doctor to tell her that.

Fiona's voice came from the hall, speaking into the phone. 'He seems very sick. He has a high temperature, a pain in his head.' And then her voice added, 'All right, I'll tell his mother.'

Sarah heard the receiver being replaced and Fiona's cushioned step.

'Dr Roche was gone on his rounds,' Fiona said, standing in the doorway. 'He'll call at lunchtime. Is there anything I can do?'

'Thanks, Fiona. I'll just put him to bed.'

'If you want me, you know where I am.' She went back into the hall and the front door opened and clicked shut behind her.

Sarah glanced at the clock on the mantelpiece. It was a carriage clock, a wedding present, still miraculously working despite the children. The mechanism had broken once but Jim had had it repaired and had threatened to skin any of them who touched it again.

Eleven o'clock, the carriage clock said. There were at least two hours to wait. Dara seemed to drowse. Her mind scanned the money situation. Had she enough for the doctor? There was ten pounds in her purse. And Jim had left her a couple of blank signed cheques in case there was ever an emergency. They might bounce, Sarah thought, but that isn't my problem. Now I have to get you to bed, young man.

Gently she lifted him, cradling him, and he came out of his half sleep and cried out, whingeing, lapsing back into sniffles. Her back wobbled for a moment; she felt the strain in her stomach, felt the foetus move, felt its pressure against the walls of the womb, against the mouth of the cervix.

Oh Christ, don't you start giving me problems. For a moment she wanted to cry. Why was Jim never there when she needed him? Years of children's illnesses, measles, mumps, jaundice, worry. He was always down in the yard and could seldom be contacted. But maybe it was better to cope without him. He couldn't stand domestic pressure; if one of the children were ill he did not see what it had to do with him.

The stairs were hell. One step at a time, carefully. Dara felt like a ton, two feet six of solid concrete. How do children get so heavy? She panted, moved slowly, feeling the agitated movements in her womb.

Upstairs she put Dara into his cot and sat for a moment on the edge of Liam's bed. Her eyes rested on the wallpaper, yellow with little red Noddies driving little red cars. She put her hand on her stomach to quiet the flutter within.

'Peace . . . peace . . . peace . . .' she said to the baby in her womb. It was a mantra she had adopted. 'Peace; it's all right.'

The movement inside her settled. Dara shifted in the cot, opened his eyes, screamed.

She went to him, knelt beside the cot, put her hand on his forehead, gently, gently willing away the pain.

'Would you like a drink?' she whispered. 'Mammy will get you a drink.'

Downstairs she got out the junior aspirin, crushed one into powder and put it on a spoon. Then she got the bottle of orange out of the fridge, relieved that there was still a drop left, and poured some into a cup.

Dara's crying came down to her, thick, trapped with pain. 'Mam-ee, Mam-ee . . .'

She rushed up the stairs. He was shielding his eyes. The sunlight was bright against the primrose-yellow wallpaper, where Noddy in his little red pixie cap drove his little red convertible, an eternity of Noddies. Dara's face was screwed up, lines of pain across his small forehead, flushed now. Sarah ran to the window and drew the curtains; shadows swept the room.

'Is that better, sweetheart?'

He moaned. Sarah went back downstairs, got the orange and the junior aspirin and brought it up, raised Dara's head and gave

116

him the drink with the aspirin. She prayed all the time, 'Let him be all right, God. I'll never complain again if he's all right.'

She put her hand on his forehead; the heat burned upwards into her palm; his cheek and neck were so hot that she could feel the radiated energy without touching. She got the thermometer and put it in his armpit, gently so as to disturb him as little as possible, brought his arm down to secure it in place. She counted out the three minutes – one two three four five – second by second. Don't say them too fast; a full three minutes or you won't know.

The thermometer was warm when she pulled it out. The silver line of mercury thrust itself down the glass tube. One hundred and four degrees.

'Oh God, oh Jesus.' Her heart started to wallop again. The child in her belly moved. She rushed downstairs for the phone. Try Dr Moore. He might be in.

'It's urgent,' she said to the cool female voice. 'It's my little boy; he's very ill.'

'The doctor is at the clinic,' the voice said, now suddenly gentle. 'Has he a temperature?'

'It's a hundred and four!'

Silence, then a muted ooh. 'You can't allow it to go any higher; you'll have to sponge him. Get some warm water and sponge him all over. The doctor will call when he gets back.'

Sarah rushed back to the kitchen, got a bowl of hot water and a J-cloth and brought them up to Dara. As she ran the water rushed against the side of the bowl and slopped on to the stair carpet.

Dara was lying quite still, breathing in shallow, rapid breaths. She began to take his clothes off, but he cried louder when she moved him. He screamed while she took his clothes off, while she wrung out the J-cloth and wet his body all over, and Sarah cried too, silently. Dara vomited, spewing orange and porridge over the duvet, filling the air with the acrid scent of puke. She cleaned him up and noticed the red blotchy rash which had appeared on his body.

Dr Moore called shortly after one o'clock, took one look at Dara, shone a torch into his eyes. Dara was cooler now because of the sponging, although his temperature had begun to rise again and he was drowsy. Sarah was on the verge of tears herself from fear and emotional exhaustion.

'We'll have to get him into hospital,' the doctor said gently, turning to look into Sarah's face. 'It looks like meningitis. I'll send for an ambulance.'

Sarah's mind went cold, suddenly calculating. The children would be back from school at half three. She'd have to ask Fiona to keep an eye on them.

'OK,' she said.

When the doctor had gone Sarah phoned the yard. Jim was on his lunch-break. They paged the canteen. No response. She left a message. Then she went next door to ask Fiona to take the children when they came home. But Fiona was out; she went from door to door until she found someone at home – Marian Keely; she didn't like asking her. Marian said, 'Yes, all right so.'

Sarah went back home and phoned the school, gave the message. Then she packed a little bag for Dara and waited for the ambulance. Before it came she tried the factory once again and was told that Jim was on an outside job that afternoon. Dr Roche called just before the ambulance arrived. She had forgotten to cancel him. She got flustered explaining.

In Crumlin Hospital they examined Dara, did a lumbar puncture, confirmed Dr Moore's diagnosis. It was meningococcal meningitis. They put him into a cot in a small room and fixed a drip into his arm. He seemed drowsy to the point of unconsciousness. Sarah stayed with him, murmuring words of comfort, held his little fat hand, whispering to him. A young nurse brought her a cup of tea and a biscuit.

'Don't worry. He'll be all right. You got him in time!' Sarah drank the tea. There were drawn curtains on the window. They had a design with Mickey Mouse and Donald Duck. She pulled one of the curtains back a chink and looked into the ward on the other side of the glass at the children in bright pyjamas, some playing with toys, some sleeping, some lying listlessly.

'Have you other children?' the nurse asked as she picked up the cup later on.

'Two.'

'And when's the next one due?'

'June.'

'You need to rest. You look done in. Did you have a lunch?'

'No. I'm not hungry.'

Jim arrived in the hospital that evening at about eight.

118

'I got home to find the house empty. I didn't know what had happened, no dinner and the place smelling of puke! Then Marian Keely sent Tim over to tell me.' His voice was low, on the verge of complaint.

'I left a message for you.'

'I was out on a job.'

'Where were you?'

'Just out!'

'He could have died!'

Jim looked into the cot at the sleeping Dara. His colour had improved. His face was no longer crumpled in pain. The drip cascaded in sudden small shivers down the long tube to his vein.

'He doesn't look too bad! Can you come home now?'

'No.'

'What are the children going to do?'

Sarah leaned back in the chair. 'You're going to have to mind them.'

He was silent for a moment. 'I'll ask Marian Keely to mind them for another while; I have to go out.'

Sarah did not move. 'Marian Keely doesn't want them,' she said slowly. 'She took them as a great favour. You're going to fucking mind them yourself. That's what fucking fathers are for.'

The words came through her teeth. She was filled with hatred. She wanted to cry. The exhaustion she had staved off all day had arrived, and with it hunger both physical and emotional. He turned to her, eyes hard, lips thin and drawn back, the longing to belt her written all over him.

'You watch your foul mouth,' he hissed back. 'You think you can treat me anyway you like. And you're good for nothing except breeding, like a sow!' He indicated her pregnancy with a disgusted sweep of his hand.

'Is it that floozie?' Sarah asked quietly. 'The one Fiona saw you with last Saturday?'

Jim did not reply. He looked out into the adjoining ward, avoiding Sarah's eyes, then looked back, raised his arm.

'If you hit me here they'll get the police.'

'I told you to watch your mouth.' But he dropped his arm and reached for the door handle.

'I don't have to listen to this.' He opened the door, turned back to her, face twisted angrily, hissed, 'And I'll break your effin' face one of these days if you don't learn to shut your trap.'

119

Sarah watched him go. She expected him to slam the door, but he shut it quietly enough. She watched him through the open chink of curtain, saw his profile for a moment as he crossed the children's ward, saw the smile he gave to the nurse on duty. A different Jim already.

He hates me, she thought. He hates me because I am trapped and dependent on him. He hates me because we have so many children and they make him feel tied. He hates me because he thinks he will have to look at me for the rest of his life. He wants challenge and newness. He wants to be a boy for ever. But he needs me to be his punchbag; it makes him feel like Cassius Clay.

Dara stirred. She put out her hand to the sleeping child, gently stroked his head, wiped the small beads of perspiration from his forehead. He opened his eyes and smiled sleepily at her.

Chapter Ten

I tried to talk to Gerry, really talk. Not just superficial stuff; if he would let me see who he is it would be something to build on. I asked him about his childhood. He became irritated, said that he had been blamed for everything in his family and that no one was going to pin things on him again.

Then he walked out of the room.

from *The Horse's Ears*, 1976

March 1990

The daffodils were out, drifting down the length of the garden wall. Some were white and some yellow, heads drooping shyly. Scattered among them were jonquils and a few crocuses. It was Sunday. Patricia was standing by the cooker in her dressing-gown, getting breakfast and enjoying the view of the garden. From where she stood she saw that the two magpies who lived in the elm tree next door were stalking the cat. Poor Muffy had been trying to sunbathe on the garage roof. One of the birds would approach the cat from the front, and while she was concentrating on him, crouching down, tensing for the spring that would dispatch him, the other one had stalked up and pecked her behind.

The cat eventually gave up and went off in a huff, pretending that she hadn't noticed them anyway. Muffy was Simon's cat, seven years old now, prone to dust-baths, keen on eating and sleeping. Patricia watched the charade on the garage roof with amusement, struck by the arrogant strutting of the magpies and their deliberate bullying. Aggressive brutes, she thought.

The kitchen was bright with spring sunshine. Patricia hummed softly, an old Irish lament she had learnt at school, letting the rich words roll softly in her mouth, savouring the sense of their

121

antiquity. It was a song which mourned the exile of a lover, an Irish soldier, one of the so-called Wild Geese, who had fled to France after the siege of Limerick in 1690. They're right to hold on to the language, she thought; it's strange and wonderful. And it's ours!

'What are you singing in the "nyaa"?' Gerry asked with jovial derision, looking up from his paper. He had it folded in front of him while he ate his bacon and eggs. She stifled the irritation. It was his language too.

'It's an old song about the flight of the Wild Geese!' She said it mildly. Gerry had recently begun to extend to her occasional jollity. Instead of silence and weary exasperation, he sometimes now invited her participation in his dismissive view of the world. She knew he was aware that she had not touched a drink since that night in December, and that he was relieved, pleased. She also knew that he sensed in her a new distance, one he could neither identify nor bridge. She had thrown him a subliminal challenge by this distance; he felt it and, because he could not control it, was uneasy.

Patricia turned the rashers on the grill; the fat dribbled into the pan and the smell of bacon filled the air.

'Would you shout for the children? Their food is ready!'

Gerry muttered, 'Some children!' and went to the kitchen door, yelled, 'Orla, Simon, your breakfast is ready!', and returned to his chair.

Patricia put her own breakfast on the table and sat down. Gerry looked at her plate. 'Why don't you eat a proper breakfast?'

'This is a proper breakfast!'

'A poached egg?'

'I'm watching my figure.'

'Your figure is fine.' After a moment he added, 'You're in good form!'

'It's a lovely day,' Patricia said, wondering why she felt she had to explain herself. 'As a matter of fact, if the weather continues so nice, I'm thinking of going away for a weekend in the near future.'

'On your own?'

'Why not? I had thought of asking Nell to come, but she talks non-stop!'

'What about the children?'

'Mummy said she'd stay here – to give me a break. You wouldn't mind that, would you?'

'No.' His eyes dwelt on her for a moment, the blue of them very cold.

'Where are you thinking of going?'

Patricia gestured. 'Wherever the fancy takes me. I might go to the west, Connemara . . .' She blushed as she said this, lowered her gaze and put the remains of the egg into her mouth with a morsel of toast. Her back was to the window and she hoped he wouldn't notice her heightened colour.

It had taken only moderate persuasion on Paddy Johnson's part to bring things between them to this point. He had hinted about it in the beginning; then, as they saw more of each other – Gerry had even invited him home to dinner once to discuss business – he had asked straight out, 'Patricia, what are we going to do about us? We need some time together.'

This Patricia knew. He had come back into her life as though he had never left, as though their separate histories for the past twenty years were dreams. At night she lay awake thinking of what it would be like to sleep with him, to feel his body beside her, to lie in his arms, to make love, proper love, not the stolen kisses in his car, the groping like adolescents; to be able to say to him with her body the things that only the body could say. He was renting a flat in a new block of apartments in Ballsbridge and had asked her back several times, but she had refused.

'I'm not being prudish, Paddy, just cautious. This is a small, spiteful city.'

'Come away with me so . . . for a weekend; for a night – whatever you would like.'

Something in her leapt at the prospect. The old fears she knew were shibboleths; she would not live for ever; she wanted this man. Why should she not take what she wanted?

'As a matter of fact,' Gerry said, breaking her reverie, 'I thought we might go off for a bit of a dander ourselves. I mean, just the two of us. A real break . . . Egypt or somewhere like that! Easter might be a good time.'

He glanced up at her over his glasses while he said this.

Patricia stood up to put her plate in the dishwasher. 'I didn't know you were interested in Egypt!'

'Well, it would be interesting; to see the Sphinx and the temples and all that . . .'

Patricia had a mental picture of her husband looking up at the Sphinx, unawed, derision in his gaze, muttering, 'So this is what all the fuss was about . . .'

She imagined him in the temple of Karnak, glancing at his watch, indicating the guide and whispering caustically, 'Bloody wop's been waffling on for hours . . .'

'It sounds nice,' she said. 'But I think I'll take the break anyway. You don't mind?'

'No,' he said, thinking it was part of her rehabilitation, incapable of alluding to it as such, incapable of ever discussing any personal topic. 'Have your break!'

Orla appeared in the kitchen, Simon hot on her heels. 'Is Mum going away somewhere?'

Patricia smiled at her children, saw Orla brighten momentarily, felt Simon relax. He is tense around me, she thought. Is it my fault? She watched his face, saw the way he glanced sideways at her, his rapid assessment as to what his demeanour should be, hostile and defensive or basically human.

'Just for a day or two . . . sometime soon . . .'

'Oh – where are you going?'

'I don't know yet.'

Gerry turned the page of his paper, made a sudden exclamation of disgust.

'What is it, Daddy?' Orla asked.

He sighed. 'A twelve-year-old was raped by seven louts. The abuse continued and she had a baby at fourteen. Two of the seven charged pleaded guilty, but they all walked out of court free men!' He clicked his tongue.

His daughter got up, stood behind him, and read the paper over his shoulder. 'It's disgusting!' Orla cried. 'She was only a child! And *look* – they went home to a hero's welcome!'

'At least the two who pleaded guilty got suspended sentences,' Gerry said, already tired of the topic and wishing to turn over the page.

'What kind of justice was that?' Orla demanded. 'What earthly use was that?' She was suddenly stiff with adolescent fury. She went back to her chair and added, with just the hint of a glance at her mother, 'I think women who put up with crap deserve what they get!'

'Yeah,' Simon agreed, 'she was probably asking for it anway.'

Orla gave a loud, exasperated sigh. 'What would you know about it, you dweeb?' she demanded.

Patricia said she was going to have a shower and left the room, hearing the raised voices behind her, Gerry's eventual sharp command and the ensuing silence.

'You're taking today off,' Joan announced. 'It's Sunday, and it's fine!'

David, sitting at his easel, smiled into his beard. 'Yes, sir!' he said meekly, turning to look at his wife who was standing sleepily in the doorway in her old blue bathrobe. He had risen at dawn, and had come into the studio to look 'for a moment' at his latest work, but had become involved at once. He felt well today, full of joy in being alive.

Joan laughed. 'Don't dare call me "sir".'

He raised innocent eyebrows. 'I was just trying to be respectful!'

Joan crossed the room to put her arms around him and nuzzled him on the neck. David jumped.

'Help! She's got teeth!'

'At least you managed to get the gender right this time!' Joan said, her voice muffled against his skin. 'With a bit of application, you might really go places . . .!'

He grinned. 'What kind of application? What kind of places?' He put down his brush, stood up, opened her robe, put his mouth to the base of her neck. 'A little application here for example . . .' He moved his mouth. 'Or here?' He bent down. 'Or even here? Mnn,' he said dreamily as Joan drew her breath in sharply. 'Yes, I think here is a good spot for "application".'

Joan gasped. She closed her eyes and felt the unexpected sense of dissolution steal up on her. David steered her against the door, shut it, leaned her against it, knelt and continued with what he was doing.

'God . . . take me back to bed!'

'You can call me David.'

Joan opened her eyes and made a mock swipe at her husband, giggled. He took her hand and drew her back to their bedroom, humming a little threateningly under his breath.

In the next room, the box-room, Paul woke and listened for a while to the restless sounds coming from his parents' bedroom. He heard muted gasps and then, a little later, a thin high cry, his mother's cry. He stared at the ceiling, his expression changing from one of perplexity to one of awe. Then, slowly, he smiled. He waited another few moments and, when the sounds from his parents' room ceased, he pulled on his clothes and tiptoed to the kitchen.

'I want to do it again and again and again,' David whispered in his wife's ear as they lay wrapped in each other's arms, 'but your man down there is insubordinate.'

Joan pulled his head down to her and cradled him in her arms. 'Leave a girl to purr in peace, you sex maniac.'

They dozed and only woke when the knock came on the door. It was Paul, with breakfast on a tray. He left it discreetly on David's bedside table, grinned at his father in a male 'I know what you've been up to' glance, and left the room without a word. His parents looked at each other. David sat up and inspected the tray.

'There's something scrambled . . . they might even be eggs!' Joan laughed until the tears came.

'What's wrong with you at all?' David demanded, cup in hand. 'The best efforts of your men folk . . .'

'Give me the tea before you spill it,' Joan ordered, drying her eyes. Then she added in an embarrassed whisper, 'Do you think he knew?'

David looked lugubrious. 'Oh, he knew. And why shouldn't he?' He peered into the white dish, stirred the contents with a fork. 'You see how he even tries to celebrate us with his amazing vulcanized eggs . . .'

Paul wore a secret smile when his parents came down to the kitchen. 'Thank you for the breakfast, darling,' Joan said. 'It was very nice of you to think of it!' She looked straight into her son's eyes and added as his expression wavered with a diffidence new to him, 'I'm a very lucky woman . . . A wonderful husband and a wonderful son!'

Paul's face relaxed. 'Ah, it was nothing. Did you like the eggs?'

'They were delicious,' she assured him, avoiding David's eye.

They drove to Greystones for lunch and, afterwards, walked for a while along the beach. David talked about the future; how things were going to happen for them at last . . . they would even

126

be able to buy a decent house . . . what kind of a house would Joan like . . .? She could even get out from under Gerry Galligan and that other barracuda, start her own business.

Paul raced along the sand like a child, stopping now and then to scoop up flat, rounded stones and fling them far out into the breakers. Joan challenged her son to a race and ran, shrieking with laughter, through the soft, wet sand, leaving crisp footprints. Paul won. 'Ah, Mum, you can do better than that!' Joan turned to look for David, but he was sitting on a rock, and was bent in such a way that she hurried back to him. 'Are you all right?'

He looked up. 'Of course. I'm just having a cogitate,' but something in the slow response, something in the careful way he organized his breathing, made her heart stand still.

When the day came, Patricia still didn't know where Paddy was going to take her, except that it was somewhere in Ireland. This was a little dangerous, but she didn't want to go to London or Paris which were his other suggestions. Some other time, perhaps. *I don't want to be stuck with him in London or Paris, only to find it doesn't work.*

She went to the bathroom, brushed her teeth and showered, studying her body, white, reasonably taut, tracery of blue veins on the breasts, nipples erect from under the falling water. Excitement shivered in her. The water cascaded on to her skin, dripped in bright beads and rivulets on to her feet. She scrubbed them carefully, scrubbed all of her body. Redness rose on her arms and legs from the heat. The steam filled the shower cubicle; water spat out through the join of the doors. She used a scented soap – hydrangea – smelt its perfume, soaped herself all over, carefully over the breasts. She emerged from the shower, towelled herself briskly, put on her bathrobe, looked at her shining face in the mirror. Her eyes were bright, the whites very white, the grey-blue rather dark, the pupils a little enlarged.

'Bloom,' she told her reflection, her still young body. 'Bloom, blossom – for now; later you can grow old! I need you to be young now!'

'You can't go off without something in your stomach,' her mother said. Her mother had arrived the evening before, looking well, her grey hair newly permed. She seemed pleased at the prospect of being with Orla and Simon for the weekend. But she looked at her daughter critically over the breakfast table.

'I don't know why you want to take off like this! You will drive carefully, won't you?'

'It's just for a break, Mummy. It gets claustrophobic in Dublin. And don't worry. Gerry put petrol in my car and even checked the tyres.'

Mrs O'Hehir lowered her voice. 'Where is he this morning?'

'Gone golfing.'

'Is he gone every Saturday?'

'Yes.'

'He ought to spend some time with you,' Mrs O'Hehir said, frowning. 'It's not good enough.'

Patricia knew that her mother did not like Gerry; that she was a little awed at his continuing success, but that she did not like him.

'I meet him in bed!'

Patricia laughed at the expression on her mother's face. 'It's all part of the thirst for the top. He works terribly hard all week and spends the weekend meeting the right people . . . or working!'

'He's a great doer,' her mother said. 'But there's more to life than work and socializing. Home and family are very important.'

'He figures he has them nailed down,' Patricia said, 'so he doesn't have to worry about them!'

Her mother looked troubled. 'Do you remember that nice young man you used to be so fond of . . .? Paddy someone or other? Have you ever had any regrets about him?'

Patricia almost choked. Tea went down the wrong way and she wheezed.

'God Mummy, you're a real romantic!' For a moment she longed to tell her mother the truth. Instead she said; 'Actually I have met him since. He's been here twice – to a party and also to dinner! He's back in Ireland now, at least for a while.'

Her mother looked at her carefully. 'That's nice, darling. Old friends are precious. I hope you don't lose sight of each other again!' Pat was surprised. Her mother's voice was very quiet. 'Perhaps you're still fond of him?' her mother continued. 'It happens – even in marriage – that you can be fond of someone else!'

Pat studied the table, aware of her parent's gentle questioning gaze. I need him, need him, need him, she wanted to say. But she glanced at her mother's face, felt her innocence, felt how she would be shocked.

'I'm fond of him,' she said. 'Of course I'm fond of him. He reminds me of long ago.' She paused. 'And now, Mummy darling, I have to get going if I'm to make the most of my break!'

'I hope the weather holds for you.' Her mother stood up, put a few dishes into the sink.

'I think you're right to get away if you feel like it,' she said after a moment in a musing voice. 'I have become terribly aware of the folly of living in the future!' Pat turned to stare at her mother, touched with premonition, but her mother smiled and the moment passed.

Patricia glanced at the clock. Paddy would be waiting. It was time to go.

'When do you expect to be back?' her mother asked as Pat took her coat from the stand in the hall.

'About seven tomorrow evening,' she said casually, schooling her voice. Inside her head was the voice of reason, sudden, questioning: you don't have to go; you could phone him and make an excuse. Suddenly her feet were cold. The course she was embarked on seemed suicidal. She could tell him something had come up, that she couldn't go. She weighed this suggestion for a second, refused it. 'Don't live in the future,' her mother had said.

'Where can I reach you if I need to?'

'I'll phone.'

Her mother sighed, looked at her doubtfully. 'Well, be careful!'

She carried her weekend case out to the car, put it in the boot. She picked up her jacket, draped it over a shoulder, slipped on her shoulder-bag.

'Bye, Mummy. Thank you for coming. I know the children are big, but it's nice to know someone is here to keep an eye on them.'

'Bye, darling. Have a good trip.'

Patricia kissed her mother, glanced up at the upstairs windows where the curtains on Orla's windows were still drawn. Then the door was shut with a smack, seatbelt on. She waved briefly and then she was gone, out the driveway, down the road, around the corner, a three-mile journey to where Paddy waited in a car park.

Afterwards Patricia tried to etch the moment of this meeting succinctly into her memory: she even wrote it down, although she subsequently destroyed the account.

I get out carefully, smiling, aware of his eyes. He gets out quickly, comes to help me with my little case, puts it in the boot of his white BMW.

We do not kiss or touch. I lock my own car, sit in beside him. He is dressed in a suit and striped shirt. He wears a Rolex watch; his wrists are hairy. There is a wedding ring on his left hand. Susan put it there one fine September morning many years ago. I was at the wedding; I saw her, her head bent under the white veil, slip it on his finger. I am nervous, excited. Am I in love? I don't know. It is surely too late for that. But I am full of hunger.

'Lovely to see you. You look wonderful.' His eyes are soft. He clasps my hand. His fingers are warm and strong. My hand is cold, as always.

'Your hands are freezing!'

'Sign of a warm heart!'

'Ah . . .' He looks at me sideways, a male look, raw desire quickly cloaked.

Key is turned in the ignition, motor springs to life, car moves out of the car park and into the mainstream. I have left the straight and narrow of my life behind me.

Paddy Johnson stretched his long frame as he waited behind the wheel. Company executive, corporate animal, married, two children, boy and a girl grown up and at college now. Married to Susan who socialized well, who was something of an heiress. House in Richmond, five bedrooms, two bathrooms, big garden, charlady twice a week, Indian gardener once a week, apartment in Paris (owned by Susan), cosmopolitan lifestyle and, except for his work, bored out of his skull.

Paddy remembered meeting Patricia a hundred years ago in 1968 – Earlsfort Terrace – pursuing her, dancing with her in the Aula in 86 St Stephen's Green, kissing her in the starlit, lamplit footpath of the Green. She had been nineteen then, he twenty.

'Oh, woman,' he had said knowledgeably. 'So near yet so far!' She had been wearing a cream wool dress which had caressed her, as he had wanted to. She had laughed, drawn back from him a fraction, suddenly reserved. Later, powerfully, as though it had

130

been Jove's thunderbolt, they had fallen for each other. The delirious days and months – one whole year – of young love had followed: unrequited love.

Why had nobody told them about the attrition of the years, the encroaching cynicism, the spectre of mortality, the emptiness of all that moral certitude, John Charles, the puritan archbishop of Dublin, and the rest of them laying down the rules.

'Bless me Father for I have sinned.'

God, they must have been joking! All that religious hocus-pocus! It didn't matter now; it hadn't mattered for years.

As for women! He needed what they gave him, what he did not find with his wife, the deliciousness of intimacy, the sense of his stature, his maleness; they refurbished him and kept away the shadows of the future. He would be chairman of the parent company's board someday; he would continue the upwards curve of success. But although he believed utterly in his corporate identity and the pre-eminent importance of his continued upward mobility, he felt sometimes the draughts of uncertainty, cold little shivers of meaninglessness.

Pat had been a discovery. Years without seeing her. Years of having forgotten her except for the unbidden, momentary stabs of memory when her face would surface among all the urgencies, stresses, problems in his mind.

Romantically? In a way. Sentimentally would be more accurate. In meeting her again he found that she renewed his life; she made him feel that he was twenty again in the pavement lamplight with the watching shadows of St Stephen's Green behind them in the night. The world was ahead and worth the effort, and they were invincible. And he was innocent again, revisiting the days when a kiss, soft lips, thrust of breast, gentle hands, were breathtaking. Nights when he would leave her at her door at Brierly and drive the motorbike back to Sutton along by Dollymount and the yellow necklace of sodium lights around the bay; parents still alive, concerned; father in same tired suit, mother smoking Gold Flake.

'Buckle down to work now, Paddy . . .' Father an employee of Arthur Guinness Son and Company Limited. If only he could go home to the Sutton bungalow now and find them there and Claire, his sister, studying for her secretarial exams in the college run by the Loreto Nuns in the Green. Claire was plump now, mother of three children, failed husband, partial to gins and tonic, the Family Rosary when she could get them to say it. She had given up on this world for the one without end.

Whenever he saw her, which was infrequently because her refusal of her own potential irritated him, he sought for the girl in her that he remembered, bubbling and laughing and teasing. When people die they should have funerals.

Patricia hadn't changed that much in looks: small lines around the eyes, jawline a little dropped, expression changed from open surprise at life to something of cynicism. He would not have recognized that once. Or maybe she didn't have it once. But there was also a certain kind of power in her face that hadn't been there once. The power intrigued him.

'What will you do when you graduate?' she had asked.

'Sell myself to the highest bidder.'

'Christ. You're very organized.'

So long ago. Newman House across the street, lion couchant over the door, Byzantine University Church next door, down at the corner the Russell Hotel still standing in discreet, expensive elegance. Yesterday.

Paddy saw her coming. White Ford Escort. Neat coiffure of auburn hair. Cream-coloured suit with pearl earrings. Even behind the windscreen, he thought, she looked good. She had a good body. He visualized it now in ways he would have felt guilty about once: top to toe; shoulders, breasts, soft white, impertinent brown nipples, round, full hips, curve of the mons veneris, crinkle of pubic hair.

He thought of how he would rub the tips of his fingers along her back, down her sides and let his mouth and tongue go where they would go. Discovery, my Patricia. Belated, but better late than never.

He remembered the dunes in Dollymount on an overcast summer's day – a Tuesday – nobody about – tide out, so far out that you could hardly see the water – just the eternal stretches of wet sand, the sad, raucous cry of the gulls and the wet sandy spirals from the lugworms; away to the left the promontory of Howth and the smell of the sea. Patricia beside him, hands on her white breasts, she pushing him away.

'Paddy – no . . .'

'Stop playing hard to get.'

'I'm not playing hard to get; I'm not playing at all.'

She had been angry. Pat angered easily, a short fuse, an

idealist's outlook. She had not wanted to be second-hand goods. She was saving herself for the marriage bed, for the one and only who would make sense of her life. He had stifled the urgency. One could always try again.

'I'm sorry . . .'

Bending over, kissing her lips, the salty grit of sand suddenly between his teeth, her thick curling hair smelling of shampoo. Her eyes were made up, fashionable then, eyeliner curving upwards at the corners; she was wearing liquid make-up – sheen on the skin – and pale pink lipstick. Blouse still open; goose bumps on her breasts. She pulled away, buttoned herself up, panting slightly, flushed, glanced at him as she raised herself up, wind whipping strands of hair as she left the shelter of the dune.

'Race you to the old wreck.' She was gone, laughing, ploughing through the sand and the tough wisps of marram grass, and he had followed. And now – across the reach of twenty years – she was here beside him as they entered the Naas road, talking and laughing very calmly. He felt both relaxed with her and excited. More excited than at Dollymount with all its adolescent confusion. She was a woman now: there was something real here now; sensuality untrammelled by John Charles, the Ten Commandments, the perspective of parents, fear, terror of being second-hand goods, formed by control, deepened by experience.

Paddy glanced at her, saw how her knees were primly together, mink-coloured tights – presumably tights – but he mourned her suspenders and the tight elastic roll-on, yesteryear's damned chastity belt. She had always had good legs. He felt the anticipatory tremor, the urgency stirring in the crotch. She does not notice that, he thought. But she will notice it soon enough. We shall have our consummation after all, my Patricia. We should have had it that night in Glendalough; I remember it like yesterday. But I was gauche and you were afraid. And then we lost each other.

Patricia lit a cigarette, drew on it, sat back into the seat, conscious of the speed, the powerful car. Mélange of emotions: he was Paddy from the old days, and yet there in the dashboard was an envelope addressed to Mr and Mrs Paddy Johnson, and a pair of ladies' black kid gloves. Susan had recently visited him in Dublin. She sighed to herself. He was borrowed.

Patricia stifled self-disgust. It doesn't matter, she told herself. I can be strong. I am not going to turn my back on this. I am stealing a little time. I feel so young again, not an hour older than the day in Dollymount when I wanted everything and ran away down the strand instead. It's all right; it will hurt no one. Just this once. Susan need never know; if she understood she would forgive. Well, she might forgive. To understand all is to forgive all.

Her head ached. The headache had started after saying goodbye to her mother, a dull throbbing in her temples which now extended to the whole of her skull. She had never been unfaithful. She had idealized chastity. It was a safety net; it satisfied the idealism in her; it pre-empted the possibility of destruction at the hands of men; it answered the utter disgust for the casual and the meaningless. Yet here she was, applying for membership to the human race, vaginal muscles contracted with desire, tension like electricity on her skin.

'I am alive, alive, alive . . .'

Paddy glanced at her from time to time. She smiled back at him, showing white teeth, a rueful smile, showing a confidence she did not feel, designed to hide the excitement she did feel, but the tremor of her heart showed in her eyes. Paddy saw it, smiled to himself, was suddenly touched.

'Sing to me,' he said after a while. 'That old Beatles number you were fond of once – the one called "Yesterday".' And Patricia began to croon – about yesterday, when troubles seemed so far away.

She stopped suddenly, feeling ridiculous. The song seemed absurd, too evocative. She looked out at the busy motorway, the warm green fields, the cattle, the telegraph poles flying across the countryside, the juggernaut ahead of them, pulling in a little to let them pass.

'Go on,' Paddy said, and when she smiled and was silent, he continued the song in a light baritone. When he was finished, he glanced at her, and she looked back at him without comment.

'What happened to us?' he asked after a moment, having overtaken the long vehicle, changing up to overdrive.

'You've asked that before! Don't you remember?'

Silence. 'Yes. I remember . . .'

'You met Susan!'

'Ah . . .'

'And I met Gerry.'

134

'Was it that simple?'

She laughed out loud. How can you even ask it, she wondered? Don't you remember anything? Don't you remember Glendalough? Have you forgotten what must have been written all over my face when you walked by me in O'Connell Street that first night I went out with Gerry?

'We had a fight,' Patricia said. 'Don't you remember?'

'I do. I remember it all. Life rushes along from significant moment to significant moment, as though there was nothing in between. I can remember the events of twenty years ago better than what happened five years or even two years back . . . Funny, isn't it? Do you remember us with the same clarity, Pat?'

Patricia, for whom the summer of 1969 and the following year of torment were etched into her soul, did not want to talk about it.

'You are as presumptuous as ever!' she said lightly.

'Really . . . I didn't know I was presumptuous!'

'You know now . . .!'

An oncoming car flashed lights. 'Speed trap,' Paddy murmured, slowing to sixty mph. 'I'll get a fuzz-buster the next time I'm in the States.'

'Do you find it very strange to be back?'

He glanced at her. 'Yes. Very strange to be here with Patricia O'Hehir! Very strange indeed to be going away with her. Very strange to find her so changed and unchanged. Is she here because I am presumptuous?'

'You're at it again!'

He laughed. 'What should I do to please you, my dear madam?'

'You could try humility!'

They both laughed.

'Very well then! Why are you coming away with me, Patricia? Perhaps I am arrogant to ask it, but I ask it humbly!'

'God! I suppose you want the truth?'

'If it flatters! . . . No, seriously . . .'

Patricia saw her reflection in the wing mirror. Her colour had mounted, her face was laughing, animated. She thought for a moment, fixed her gaze on the road ahead.

'I am here with you because I desire you, because I want to sleep with you! Because there were things left unsaid between us. Because neither of us is going to live for ever. Because you represent, at least for me, some part of the truth.'

She spoke quietly. She did not look at him. He changed down to overtake. Then he took her hand and raised it to his lips.

'Thank you.'

The room was bright, carpeted in blue, with floral curtains looped back. There was a double bed, covered in a bedspread made of the same material as the curtains, but quilted and finished with a deep flounce. There was a white Victorian dressing-table with funny carved curlicues. The house itself was old – Georgian – converted to a hotel some thirty years previously.

She put her bag on the suitcase-stand, stood looking out of the window at the view, the hills in the distance, the fields, the cattle; trying to will away the thumping in her head. She was so nervous she felt as though her arms and legs had weakened. Paddy took off his jacket and sat on the bed. She looked back at him and he patted the bedspread, then rose and took her gently by the arm, sat her beside him on the bed, began to kiss her, began to undo her blouse. The pain in her head crescendoed, waves of pain pressing against her skull, beating against her forehead.

'Not yet,' she whispered. 'Wait until tonight.'

'All right. There's no hurry, you know. We needn't do anything, if you would prefer it . . . The last thing I want you to feel is some kind of obligation.'

Patricia felt annoyed. Obligation! What did he take her for?

'We could go for a walk,' she suggested.

'We could. The possibilities are inexhaustible.'

She laughed, looked into his smiling face.

'I'm serious,' he said, some time later, when they were walking through the hotel shrubbery, 'I don't want you to do anything you don't want to do.'

'Tonight can look after itself,' Patricia said, beginning to be afraid that if he kept up this kind of talk she would simply want to go home. He was making her aware of why they had come – aware in an objective way which was death to desire. 'Meanwhile, let's just enjoy the walk.'

He stopped, held her, and suddenly kissed her lips, and she felt the sensation of free fall, gravity and solid ground had disappeared; there was only merger, lips and breath, and the spell he threw over everything, like a wizard she had once seen on TV throwing out some kind of enchanted net to capture the stars.

136

She longed for a drink after dinner, a vodka, whisky, or gin or anything. The panic had risen again, the headache which had ebbed and flowed all day reasserted itself. She needed a vodka to kill the panic. It was a queer thing to be full of panic and desire at the same time. But she conquered the urge. You're a big girl now, Patricia; you are old enough to abide by the decision you have made. You will not drink. Not now. Not ever again.

After dinner he said, 'Shall we retire, Pat, or would you prefer to watch television? I believe there's a good knitting programme on RTE.'

She turned to him, laughing, embarrassed, eyes shining. 'I'm not that keen on television.'

He undressed her slowly in their room. The curtains were open to the gathering night, deep blue shadows over everything. She heard a cow lowing in the distance. She heard the music from the hotel annex where there was a party going on; pounding nostalgia – 'Do you miss me tonight?'

The dress fell from her shoulders; her bra, tights, and the little black lace panties she had bought in honour of the occasion, followed it to the floor.

He took off his clothes and lay beside her, touched her naked body gently, unhurriedly, travelled over it with his hands and lips, turned her over, kissed the curved length of her spine.

Because he was so slow with her, Patricia felt the tension leave her, the headache ebbed, her flesh tingled; she allowed herself the latitude to get lost, knowing that he was kneeling, that his lips were against her pubic hair, his tongue tentative, his hands caressing. She gasped. 'Oh, don't.'

But he did not heed her. He tugged back the bedclothes, pulled them over both their heads, encapsulating them in a kind of tent, in a warm and private darkness.

I am falling endlessly, down tunnels and caverns and dark, intricate whorls of sensation. I am in an enchanted cave and I am at home, belonging. And I am awake too, conscious, in a half-acute kind of way, aware of the moment of penetration, an instant of pain because I am still not fully ready, and then, at last, the rhythm of two bodies knowing each other, as though they had known each other for every instant of some obscure eternity.

Chapter Eleven

'The most dangerous place in the world for a child is a woman's womb.' It took a bishop to articulate this profundity. Evil, hate-filled words from the representative of an institution still reeking with the blood of the millions of women it burnt as witches. It is women who have always championed children. But who has ever championed women?

When I saw the wording of the amendment – 'With due regard to the equal right to life of the mother', I wanted to cry. They give the mother's life 'due regard'. The generosity of it! The life of a woman has to jostle for legal equality alongside that of her own fertilized ovum!

Why? It wouldn't have anything to do with power, would it? Don't tell us it's love for little foetuses! Not in a world where the men so obsessed with love of little foetuses live out of the pockets of the poor, ignore the billions spent on instruments of mass destruction, and colonize the human psyche with dogmas obsessed with death.

Where is your proof for fantastic claims? I ask these bishops. For your Heaven and your Hell and the iniquity of women. And if you have none, what right have you to speak?

from *The Horse's Ears*, 1983

April 1990

Patricia drove to the supermarket. It was Holy Thursday, 12 April. She wanted to get the Easter shopping over, had asked Orla to come. She wanted a chance to talk to her alone and the drive was the ideal solution. Orla was still being bothered by Mick; sometimes he came around at night and threw pebbles at

139

her window. Only a week before, Patricia, lying awake in the next room, had heard the small sharp sounds against the glass. She had got up, looked out of the window, seen the youth standing on the lawn. She had rapped on the pane and he had started, stared at her, shrugged dismissively and slowly moved away towards the gate. She had waited until she heard the sounds of his motorbike starting up and dying away. She had spoken to Orla about it the next day.

'It's not my fault, Mum; I don't want him coming around!' Was it fear she saw in her daughter's face? She had said little more about it, afraid of precipitating the sort of confrontation which would be counter-productive. But now that the episode was almost a week behind them, she felt she could broach the subject, try to find out what precisely was going on.

'All right,' Orla said truculently, when Patricia called up to her to ask her would she come to the supermarket. 'I'll be down in a minute.' Orla was in her room a lot these days: studying, she said. But any time her mother had ventured into her room when the girl was there, she had found her lying on the bed with a book, her eyes vacant and 'far away'.

'I'm worried about Orla,' she said to Gerry. 'That fellow was around again last night, throwing pebbles at her window!'

'I didn't hear anything.'

Patricia knew at once that she should not have broached the subject. Gerry was in a bad mood and had never been able for domestic pressures at the best of times. Simon's school report for Easter had been poor, and his father had reacted typically. He never concerned himself to the same extent with Orla's reports, although she usually did well.

'Of course I'm sure. I got out of bed and saw him in the garden.'

'I hope she's not whoring,' Gerry said testily, his forehead gathering up into storm clouds. 'I won't stand for any of that in this house!'

'God, Gerry . . . how can you say things like that! She's a child and she's being bothered and you put the blame on her!'

'Well, what do you think would bring that fellow around here? She must have given him some encouragement. He told the police she was his girlfriend. She's probably seeing him after school. She probably does her whoring then! They're all at it, you know, the kids these days; a shower of spineless layabouts without a moral between them. You should hear some of the stories I hear!'

Patricia let him fulminate. She was relieved that he had not pursued the proposed trip to Egypt; but in another way altogether she was sorry he had not. Anything which would have marked some turning point in their relationship would have been welcome; she would have gone more than halfway to meet him along the road of conciliation. She was frightened by her relationship with Paddy, by the speed with which they had got to where they were, by the power of what was between them. Her relationship with him elicited from her feelings she had not known she possessed, presented her with a vulnerability which was terrifying. He was the door into summer, the space where she could live and grow, the place, the only place, where she found pleasure and peace. Away from him she mistrusted all of this; with him it made perfect sense.

He had talked to her of Paris, of a little flat in Paris – not his, but one he could get for her – where they could see each other in September. He was going to Paris in September; he would be working there in the company's Paris office.

'Make an excuse and be with me in Paris. We could see so much of each other, have our own little place.'

He was going back to Richmond now for Easter, and she had space to think. The thought of being with him for a few weeks in Paris took her breath away. But she saw that he controlled the relationship. He said he loved her, he had told her so that night in Kilneary as they lay entwined, torpid, watching the night sky deepen through the window. Yes, he loved her, but he controlled everything to do with them: when they would meet, when they would talk on the phone, when they might snatch time for a quick lunch together.

'I can't let it go on,' Patricia told herself. 'Somehow I will have to find the strength to end it. Or present him with an ultimatum. If I presented him with an ultimatum, what would he do? Accept it? Choose his wife over me? He is proud and stubborn and almost certainly used to playing with women, so he is bound to choose his wife! Could I cope with the pain of that?'

Occasionally she divined in him an obdurate toughness which was irreconcilable with any passion. It was a cold, precise place in him where he watched over his life. Within the parameters of its perspective, Patricia guessed, she was no more to him than a

141

way-station. She was certainly not someone to whom he would disclose his soul. He had been careful about avowing anything to the contrary. His protestations of love never went that far. He has been spoilt by women, she thought. An amenable wife; amenable other women. How many I don't know. But there have been others. And she had to recognize in herself that her own desire for him was ambivalent. On the one hand, now that she had found someone with whom such contact was possible, she wanted the sharing and disclosure of it as an escape from the prison of her own being and for the discovery of her self.

But on the other hand she sought it as power. The status of powerlessness appalled her; she wanted him to recognize who she was, to lose the male perspective that the relationship was his possession. In this he was a challenge. Why do I even think in terms of power? I have no power! But she knew that if this were true, she had no existence either.

'Orla, I want to talk to you, darling!'

'Oh God . . . Is that why you asked me to come shopping?'

'Look, I need to know a few things. I love you and I worry about you.'

'What do you need to know, Mummy? If I am seeing Mick? The answer is no. If I am pregnant? The answer is no. I have a great deal more self-respect than you evidently credit me with.' Orla sniffed. There was silence. Patricia glanced at her daughter, saw the tense set of her face, the belligerent cast to the mouth. She drove carefully approaching the supermarket. There were so many cars, edging and pushing themselves forward, dodging into the car-park queue.

So that's what's bugging her; she is still mad with me for telling her she could get pregnant. Oh God, I have forgotten so much.

'I wasn't going to ask you that – to ask you if you were pregnant! Don't put words into my mouth, Orla!'

'Well, you asked me already, weeks and weeks ago. I don't see Mick any more. He follows me around a bit, but I don't see him and I'm still a virgin and is there anything else you want to know?'

'Yes.'

'What?'

'I want to know how serious a nuisance this Mick fellow is; I want to know if he is frightening you?'

'Oh God! How could he frighten me? Do you think I am a total wimp? Just because he hangs around.'

142

'I don't like the way he hangs around, Orla. I don't like his attitude to either of us.'

'Well, I'm not going to get my knickers in a twist about that!'

'Listen to me. Just stop being cross for a moment and listen to me. There are men in this world who see women only as prey, as scores, as challenges. A lot of them think nothing of violence against women, trivialize things like rape. I'm not saying Mick is like that, but I don't like the way I see him skulking around. He seems to be somewhere in the locality all the time. Where does he live?'

'I'm not sure. He doesn't live around here. And you needn't think that anyone, anyone, would dare to rape me . . . I'd kill him!'

Patricia sighed. Orla's face was flushed. Oh God, the dignity was all up in arms. Was she even listening?

'What I am trying to say to you,' Patricia continued in a low voice, 'is that you do not have to suffer any hassle from him. He told the police you were his girlfriend. He indicated you had an hysterical mother who overreacted if her daughter was out late. He gave them to understand that he called at the house by appointment with you. He made me out to be a fool. Now, that being so, I would like you to talk to the Guards yourself. That way they'll move him on and you won't have any further trouble from him.'

'And I'd look like a right scaredy-cat, wouldn't I? Just because you have a chip on your shoulder about men!'

Patricia did not reply. She got out of the car and locked the door. She did not speak to Orla except, when they were inside the supermarket, to direct her to get a few groceries from the cereal shelves. The weight of her impotence oppressed her. All she had tried to say translated only as a chip on her shoulder about men!

Orla was looking a bit sheepish now, but ready to rear up again in a moment and defend her perspectives.

'You can go home if you like,' Patricia said when Orla put the few cartons into the shopping trolley with bad grace. 'You can get the bus. It would be better if you did!' She handed her a pound for the bus fare.

Orla drew back, stiffened. 'All right!' She took the money and disappeared into the crowd.

As Patricia placed her order at the meat counter, she was jostled out of her reverie by a voice saying, 'Hello.'

She turned to see who had addressed her and saw that it was the same woman, Sarah Dempsey, or rather O'Toole, now very large with her pregnancy, who had had coffee with her before Christmas. She had a small girl with her, who hung back shyly.

'Hello, Sarah. How are you?'

Sarah smiled, brown eyes crinkling at the corners, the dimple by her mouth deepening. 'Not so bad. How's yourself? You're looking very well.'

'Thanks. Is this your daughter?'

'Yes. This is Lorraine.'

Patricia smiled at the child, who lowered her head and smiled back.

'She's a great girl,' Sarah said. 'A great help to her Mam.'

'I see you're well on the way,' Patricia said sympathetically, indicating the bulge of Sarah's pregnancy with her eyes. 'When are you due?'

'June. It will be a girl!'

'You'll have your hands full. How is your little boy – the one you had with you the last time?'

A shadow crossed Sarah's face. 'Dara? He was very sick recently. I had to get him into hospital'.

'You poor thing. What was the matter?'

'Meningitis!'

Patricia drew her breath in sharply. 'Is he all right now?'

'Yes,' Sarah said. 'Thank God! We have him home again, but he has to be minded. His father is minding him today.'

She paused, seemed to hesitate. 'Would you like a cup of coffee when we finish this lot?' she asked diffidently. 'My turn to ask you! This is my only time out for ages,' she added, as though she should explain herself.

'I would love one!'

'See you at the coffee dock in half an hour?'

'OK.'

When Sarah had gone, Pat tossed over in her mind the conversation she had had with Joan de Barra just a week earlier when she had called to the office to leave some papers which Gerry needed and had forgotten to bring with him. He had phoned and she had said she would drop them in when she was in town. She had met Joan on the office stairs and had followed her into her room for a brief chat.

'Don't look either to right or left,' Joan had said in a jocose apology. 'My office is like a tip at the moment!'

Pat had looked at the files laid out on the floor, the laden desk, the bookshelves, the bundles of documents tied in pink ribbon or held together with thick rubber bands. She felt the tenor of Joan's workday and its weight.

'God, what a busy woman you must be!'

Joan pulled back a chair. 'Sit down. All that stuff,' she indicated the files on the floor, 'is for a High Court case next week. There are so many papers that it's simplest to sort them all out on the floor!'

'You're involved in something useful, worthwhile. I envy you . . .'

Joan looked at her, hunched her shoulders. 'Am I? Sometimes I wonder; so much effort, and eventually it's all like froth on the river. But if you envy me, why don't you do something yourself? Study . . . get a job?'

'I'd really like to do law, be a solicitor like you . . . be part of the world!'

Joan smiled. 'So! What's keeping you?'

'Gerry . . . he thinks it's a joke.'

Joan sighed. She looked as though she were about to say something, and then thought better of it.

'You're looking well,' Pat said after a moment's silence, in which she had searched for something with which to change the subject, something to restore her to impersonal urbanity. 'I'm delighted to hear about David's success. You must be looking forward to his Paris exhibition!'

'I am, although I don't believe it yet.'

'Is he over the moon?'

Joan's gaze directed itself out of the window, to the clouds. 'He's very pleased, very excited, very busy. I find I practically have to sue for some time with him!' She glanced back at Patricia. 'Can you imagine it? Sometimes I'm even jealous of his work!'

Pat looked back at her and smiled. 'I can understand that, you know. For some men, work is everything.' Then she asked a little diffidently, 'How is his health now?'

Joan's eyes darkened. 'For a while he was a lot better; but now I'm not so sure. Sometimes I feel he is hiding things from me . . . sometimes I think he's in some kind of distress and won't pretend . . .' She shook her head. 'Never mind, I shouldn't burden you with all of this.'

145

'What do the doctors say?'

'He won't go near them now. They sent him home from Vincent's with a spastic colon. He's taking something for that, but if I suggest he should go back to the specialist, or seek a second opinion, he takes no heed.'

Pat had no answer. She looked around the office again. 'Do you do any family law?' she asked on sudden impulse.

Joan shrugged. 'Bits here and there . . . why do you ask?'

'I know someone who's in a bit of a mess. Would you take on her case? Her husband beats her, she's pregnant and has three children . . . I think he even raped her!'

'Well he can't do that any more with impunity! Send her along by all means, although it's not really my cup of tea. But I'll certainly do whatever I can if she would like to make an appointment.'

Pat had gone on to tell Joan what she knew of Sarah's story. 'I've only bumped into her in the supermarket, so I'm not really much use to her.'

Joan had listened in silence, and when Pat had finished she said simply, 'The best thing is for her to get out. She won't change him. She can go through the hoops and look for a prevention order and a barring order, but if the husband defies them there's only prison, and a breadwinner in prison is not much use to anyone!'

'But how can she get out? She has no money, no job.'

'There're the women's refuges. They're often the first step in breaking the cycle.'

Now, staring at the tins of Ambrosia creamed rice, Pat remembered what Joan had said. She would say something to Sarah over coffee. People who were in an intolerable situation should withdraw from it. If something could not be redeemed, you had to let it go. Otherwise you were throwing away your life, the only life you knew you would ever have, for something absolutely worthless.

When she met Sarah at the coffee dock twenty minutes later they had a long conversation, much longer than either of them had intended. Sarah thought of Jim at home with Dara, thought of his disapproval. But somehow she didn't care. The conversation was necessary to her and she figured Jim was able to do a bit of babysitting for once in his life. Lorraine was restive, but too withdrawn to do more than fidget. In the end Sarah said, 'I don't know; I'll see . . .'

★ ★ ★

When Sarah returned home she heard Dara crying, felt the tension in the house. Instantly a pall of silent accusation descended on her; she had been away longer than was necessary. Jim was smoking in the kitchen, sitting at the table, several dead cigarette butts already ground into a saucer.

Dara was in the playpen, wailing angrily. She picked him up and sat down, rocking him. His crying subsided into sniffles. He leant his head against her breast.

Lorraine disappeared silently upstairs, as she tended to do when her father was in bad form.

'Well, well,' Jim said. 'So you eventually decided to come home. What kept you?'

'I met an old schoolfriend,' Sarah said. 'We had coffee.'

Jim's face darkened with suspicion. 'Nice of you to remember you have a husband and child . . . I suppose we should be grateful you decided to come back at all. After all, you could spend all eternity yapping with every silly hen you meet.' He glared at her as the full extent of the liberty she had taken, the affront she had offered him, sunk in. 'If you do that again – leave me here with a whining baby while you spend the afternoon yapping – I'm telling you now . . .'

Sarah did not look at him; she kept her head bent. Inside she was telling herself that she wished he would go to hell; inside she wondered where he thought he got all the power he laid claim to; but she did not evince by word or gesture the tenor of her thought.

'Dara's very cross,' she murmured instead, ignoring the threats and wondering why the child had been in such a state. Jim breathed out in noisy exasperation. His face was tight with fury. He pointed at the corner unit, the last one, which he had been fitting. His tools were on the floor.

'Oh good,' Sarah said with as much coolness as she could muster. 'You were great to finish that. It looks nice.'

'Nice! It looks nice, does it? Can't you see the bollox I've made of it?' and he stood up and put his finger on the wooden cornice which was a half-inch too short. 'I cut the bloody thing short because –' he pointed at Dara – 'His majesty started whingeing. How can a man work with a child whingeing? Will you tell me that? How can a man work with a child whingeing?'

'Did you feed him?' Sarah asked in a low voice.

147

Jim's face registered a moment's surprise. 'Feed him? Christ! Was I supposed to feed him too?'

'I told you,' Sarah whispered. 'I told you he was asleep before I went out and that I was leaving his lunch to be reheated. He's hungry. That's why he's so cross!'

She went to the fridge, indicated the covered bowl with the minced meat and mashed potatoes. 'It's all right! I'll heat it now!' She put Dara back in the playpen, took the bowl and began to heat it over a saucepan of boiling water.

'In the name of Jesus Almighty God . . .' Jim began, the words hissing and tumbling over each other as his ire gathered force, 'What do you think I am? You piss off to do a bit of shopping and practically go on holiday, leaving me here to mind and feed the child and do skilled work at the same time! It's skilled work fitting bloody kitchens. Skilled work! And look at that!' and he took the lump hammer from the box and hit the offending corner unit, so that the door splintered with a crack of tearing wood. Sarah was silent, watching the hammer in her husband's hand. The thick fear she lived with was there again in her stomach, deadening everything; even the baby in her womb was still, as though listening like some small woodland creature to the steps of a predator.

Dara was silent in the playpen, curled up, his head on the old foam cushion, his thumb in his mouth.

Jim swung again with the lump hammer, and the door cracked again as the frame smashed. He turned to Sarah, his face tight with a mixture of righteous rage and grief at the destruction of his handiwork. She backed against the wall.

'If you hit me with that thing you'll kill me!' she said. Jim glanced at the lump hammer in his hand. He was breathing heavily. His thick eyebrows met in the middle as he frowned.

'I'm going out, you bitch,' he shouted. He dropped the hammer and turned to the door. 'And when I come back I want to see this place like a new pin, do you understand? A new pin!' And he kicked Dee-Dee, Dara's teddy, which was lying in the hall. 'Place is like a fucking slum . . . and the stink!'

Sarah smelt the pong too. Dara, lying in the playpen with his eyes closed, had reacted to his fear. She picked him out of the playpen when the front door had shut and began to change him. She fished Dee-Dee from the hall and put him sitting up at the table. Then she fed her son, giving him all her attention, trying to make him smile. 'A little spoon for Dara and a little spoon for Dee-Dee,' until the child began to laugh. She wondered about Lorraine, called her but there was no response. She was probably asleep. Like Dara she escaped her father's tantrums through sleep; she would creep away like a wraith and be found curled up in bed. Sarah was glad that Liam was with his cousins and would not be back until tomorrow.

When Dara had finished his meal she brought him upstairs for his nap. Lorraine was, as anticipated, in bed, but she was not asleep. She was lying with her eyes closed, but answered when Sarah spoke to her. 'Is Daddy gone out?'

'Yes, love. Do you want to go out to play?'

'Not yet; I'll do my homework.'

While Dara slept and Lorraine did her homework, Sarah started the housework, cleaning the kitchen, mopping the floor. She started hoovering the sitting room, picking up the toys. All the time her mind veered between Jim and the state he would be in when he came home and what Patricia had said to her at the supermarket. Patricia had said that women who were victims of domestic violence should leave if they possibly could; that nothing would change the man. She had spoken to a solicitor about this. There were legal remedies, but she knew herself that nothing of that kind would stop Jim for long. Somehow or other she would have to find the courage to leave him.

Patricia had not been drinking; she had been looking very well, and she was obviously well off, married to a rich solicitor, and she had no business trying to tell her what to do. But still – the blessed relief it would be if she had a place where she and the children would be safe, where she didn't live from one minute to the next on tenterhooks. She knew that if she went she would never come back.

But it was easy to think and talk, and so hard to act. If she left, everyone would know; she would have nothing. She would have to leave the things she treasured: the Chinese hearth-rug, the set of good glasses; the set of Newbridge plated cutlery they had got as wedding presents; the whole pretence of family life and normality. She would be on the margin of things, a pregnant woman alone with three children. Not even the women's refuge, if she got a place, would keep them for ever. And she hated the thought of charity anyway. She would need a job, but where would she get that?

149

It would be so much easier if Jim was always like this. But sometimes he was lovely. Sometimes he bought her chocolates, took her out.

Tonight, however, he would come home drunk. She knew that. And he would find fault with everything, look for dust, check to see if she had done the ironing, knock her around. He would be full of hate. She dreaded the evening, tasted the defeat.

Suddenly, almost without conscious effort, she walked into the hall and picked up the phone, took the envelope with Patricia's phone number out of her bag. She listened, heard the phone ring at the other end. It gave about four tones before it was picked up.

'Hello?'

Sarah did not recognize the voice; it was young and a bit petulant. This must be Patricia's daughter.

'May I speak to Patricia, please?'

'Hold on . . .'

Sarah heard the girl's voice call, 'Mummy, it's for you,' and then the sound of footsteps on a tiled floor.'

'Hello?'

'Pat, it's me . . . Sarah. Will you give me the number of that solicitor you were talking about. I've made up my mind . . . I'll make an appointment to see her on Monday.'

Sarah wondered why she was whispering, why her heart was beating faster, as though she were doing something daring or forbidden. Jesus Christ, she told herself, you're a grown woman, an adult, someone who's supposed to be in charge of her own life!

'Good girl,' Pat said. 'Have you a pen handy?' She reeled off the office number. 'Her name is Mrs Joan de Barra. Tell her who sent you.'

Chapter Twelve

I looked through those soft-porn mags someone had given Gerry. I admit I reacted violently, to the pictures because no woman could see them and not react, but more so to the covert 'look how we have debased these women; now who's important?'

I saw Gerry examining them, smirking. I hated his smirk. The women were beautiful and young. They pouted and posed and pushed out their breasts and buttocks. They pretended they didn't think. They smiled with white teeth, coyly. Their poses assured the reader as to usage, violation, by any man at all. And underlying it the thrill of plunder of the innocent, crossed with a violent hate.

If I were a man would I be terribly turned-on, reassured, made to feel powerful? But the turn-on is not in the nudity; it is in the degradation.

from *The Horse's Ears*, 1990

While Pat was driving home she thought of Sarah, of their conversation over coffee, of the way she felt able to talk to her. Not even with Nell had she felt she could open up, yet with Sarah she had even been on the verge of discussing her problematic relationship with Paddy. There was a quality to Sarah's listening which was old and non-judgemental. There was also the fact that they hardly knew each other; this made it easier in some way to unburden the problems neither of them was supposed to have.

They had lost themselves in an intense, empathic conversation, so much so that neither had noticed how the time had flown, how the coffee dock had begun to empty, the child begun to grow restive. The little girl had sat there patiently, looking at the children's book Patricia had bought for her, occasionally glancing up with shy brown eyes. When Patricia smiled at her she leaned towards her mother, touching her with her thin shoulder. Sarah was looking haggard.

'You're looking tired,' Patricia told her. 'Are you taking your vitamins?'

Sarah smiled, narrowed her eyes. 'You sound like my poor mother, God rest her.' She sighed, the fatigue evident in her gestures, in the way she leaned back in the chair. Her dark eyes were tired and under them were deep shadows, tiny purple veins just under the skin.

'How's everything?' Patricia ventured after a moment.

'Could be worse.' Sarah lowered her voice to a whisper. 'He doesn't like me being pregnant.'

'Has he hit you . . . since the pregnancy?'

Sarah hesitated. 'Four weeks ago. It was my own fault. I miscalculated his mood!'

'He'll cause a miscarriage if he goes on like that!' Patricia said, keeping her voice very low so that the little girl would not hear.

'I know. He already has . . . a few years ago.'

Pat was silent, feeling suddenly that she had no right to so much confidence, aware of the real horror in Sarah's world.

'I was two and a half months pregnant,' Sarah added, her eyes on her cup, glancing up to meet Patricia's eyes. 'There was a lot of bleeding.'

'Did you see a doctor?'

Sarah smiled ruefully. 'I was too ashamed.'

'Did your husband know?'

'I told him, but he wouldn't believe me! He said I hadn't been pregnant to begin with!'

The couple at the next table stood up to go. Lorraine moved her chair to give them plenty of room. A waitress cleared some empty tables, wiped them. Nearby a child in a buggy ate an ice-cream, mashing it into his face and down his front. The air was full of the smell of coffee and the clatter of crockery and cutlery.

Why is she telling me all of this? Pat wondered, touched by so much trust.

After a moment, Sarah asked diffidently: 'Your husband is a solicitor, isn't he?'

Patricia had a mental image of Gerry confronting Sarah's problem, imagined his basic indifference. He had been apprenticed to an elderly solicitor who had told a client consulting him about a marital separation to go home like a good woman and get her husband's tea. Gerry had overheard the exchange, the weeping woman and the testy old lawyer, and had found it amusing; but he was not likely himself to be any more sympathetic.

'Yes, and that's what you need, a good solicitor. Gerry doesn't do family law. But his partner does. She's a woman; she's very nice!'

Sarah seemed to consider this. Then she said, 'I can't afford solicitors!'

'There'd be no charge for a consultation for a friend of mine!' Patricia said. If necessary, she thought, she would pay the firm's charges herself.

Sarah smiled. 'You're very good. Do you mind if I think about it? But even if I got a Barring Order or whatever – he'd never stay away. He'd be back. But the first step is a Protection Order and then you have to live with him in the same house!' She shook her head, smiled ruefully.

'I know a bit about it,' Sarah continued. 'I know someone who has the same problem. She got a Protection Order and after that he used to follow her around; she never had a moment's privacy – not even in the bathroom! He hit her again, but the police wouldn't do anything. They were not prepared to take him out of the house, even when he broke the Protection Order. And the husband got very cunning because he knew that if there were no obvious signs of beating, the police would do nothing at all.'

She paused, shook her head. 'I'm not prepared to go down that road only to fail!'

'But what if he doesn't change? I was talking to the solicitor friend of mine and she said anyone with your kind of problem should get out, go to one of the women's refuges. Are you going to put up with this for the rest of your life?'

'No. If the children were "done for", I'd clear out. I could go back to my work.' She glanced at Pat. 'I used to be a dental nurse, you know!'

Pat nodded. More than I ever managed to do, she thought.

'He's doing a bit of work in the kitchen today,' Sarah added. 'He volunteered to mind Dara – he's not all bad, you know . . . It would be much easier if he was. It's the jar, and something else: he has a need to do this!'

Patricia finished her coffee. 'We all have needs,' she said.

'That's why the world is the way it is!'

Sarah leaned towards her, her eyes suddenly sly with humour. 'Are you on the wagon yourself?'

Patricia started. 'I am,' she said humbly. 'I'm on the wagon!'

'You look all the better for it!'

But then Sarah's thoughts reverted to what was uppermost in her mind. 'Did you see the English case recently they reported in the news – where the wife killed her husband? She killed him with the carving knife!'

Patricia remembered it. The woman had been beaten over umpteen years and had finally turned on her tormentor. She had got a suspended sentence.

'But she didn't get a jail sentence,' Sarah said, 'not like your woman in Cork.'

'You have to kill them while they're at it,' Patricia said dryly. 'That way it's self-defence!'

'I don't know why Jim goes on the way he does,' Sarah said, her eyes suddenly filling with tears. 'I'm at my wits' end. He can be so nice, you know; and then again he's like the devil. He enjoys hitting me so much; when he's at it he needs it so much; he feels very powerful and like God when he's belting me, when he's finding something I didn't do, like not ironing his collar properly and using it as an excuse. I tried so hard to understand, I even began to feel what he was feeling and blame myself! God, the way I tried to iron his shirts, spent ages on them! And when he was sorry I always felt so sorry for him! I felt important then – when he was sorry. I felt it was nearly worth it! Does that sound sick?'

'Victims always think it's their fault,' Patricia said. 'At least that's what I read.'

'And now there's all this porn, the stuff on video. What happens when they start copying all that, I ask you? Have you heard about the snuff films?'

Patricia lied. She knew about pornography, but she had never heard of snuff films. But she was reluctant to appear innocent. 'Yes,' she said.

'Jim and a couple of his pals actually viewed one at home one night. It was in the early days, before we had the children,' Sarah added hastily, responding to the expression on Patricia's face.

'I was over with Mam. It was a few weeks before she died and she was very poorly and I came back to pick up some things and to tell Jim that I would be staying with her. But when I let myself in I heard the clapping and the cheering and there they were, the three of them, drinking beer and watching something which made me sick.'

'What was it?'

Sarah clicked with her tongue, glanced at her daughter and lowered her voice. 'You don't want to know . . . A gang rape! There were close ups of her vagina and her anus and then they stuck knives into her and sliced off one of her breasts and she lay there dying and covered in blood. They loved it, grunting and hooting! They didn't see me standing there at the door of the sitting room, they were so delighted with themselves. Yet I know Jim and Dan and Bill. They would go mad if that was done to a dog! But because it was a woman they loved it.'

'What did you do?'

Sarah took a deep breath. 'I don't know where it came from, but I felt so crazy . . . it took me over . . . A red haze came into my eyes. I didn't care what happened. I grabbed the poker and turned on the three boyos who were sitting there like statues. Not even Jim seemed able to move and I told them to get out before I killed them.' She looked at Patricia.

'The funny thing is – they went. Jim and all! He was a bit sheepish after that for a while and said nothing about it. We never discussed the incident. He felt ashamed, I think. He never belted me over it either, or at least he never used it as an excuse. Of course, in those days he was a bit more careful; he was afraid that I might leave.'

Patricia was silent.

'I shouldn't be shocking you like this,' Sarah said. 'I know by your face that I've shocked you. Didn't you know about all this stuff?'

'I knew about pornography. But I never dreamed it was anything as bad as what you've described. They must have got the video from England. You can't get that sort of thing in Ireland!'

Sarah sighed, pursed her lips. 'Not only can you get it, but they gorge themselves on it. They can't get enough of it. It's a colossal industry. Teenagers, young men, older men. I know because I hear about it from local women. Even your own son is possibly watching it! You would want to be careful about where he is and what videos he's watching. He'll think that hurting and destroying women is what it means to be a man. He won't realize he's having his monkey button pressed to make fat cats rich!'

155

'Something should be done about it,' Patricia said, while she strove with panic and a sudden desire to cry out with the surge of pain and rage. 'We are like deer baited by dogs. No matter which way we turn they're waiting for us with dripping fangs! If it's not the Church or the Law or people like your husband, it's the so-called entertainment industry!'

She thought of Simon and his aggression, especially towards her. He had often told her he was watching a video at his friend's house. She had never inquired as to what kind of video. Was her little Simon who had loved the 'beakers' watching pornography?

Sarah rested her chin on her hand and gazed for a moment at her daughter. 'What kind of a world is it going to be for her?' she asked softly. 'With men watching films showing women as trash, as blood sports, as something to be degraded and murdered and even eaten – cannibalized – for their entertainment, so that they can have a power trip. Just because they're women! It makes me laugh when I see the hullabaloo about vivisection and the tins of dolphin-friendly tuna. Why can't we have a "woman-friendly" world? Why can't we have "woman-friendly" films? Why don't they realize that our bodies are designed the way they are so that we can continue the race.' She shrugged. 'Anyone would think we planned the business ourselves deliberately to provoke them. It's so unfair.'

She stared around the coffee dock with her hollow eyes. 'God made the whole mess,' she added. 'Why don't they blame God?'

'There's legislation,' Patricia whispered.

'How far does it go?' Sarah demanded bitterly. 'We should have more women in the Dáil?' She looked at Patricia with scorn. 'If you imagine for one moment that something effective will be done about the stuff – all I can say is, don't hold your breath!'

Patricia was silent. 'Look, Sarah,' she said after a moment. 'If you're being belted around you have to do something. If you won't take legal action, you could leave. There are women's refuges in Dublin, four of them, with accommodation for sixteen families. You would be safe there! In fact, the solicitor I told you about said anyone in your situation should simply get out!'

Sarah shook her head. 'Easy to say! I don't know. It would be a kind of defeat . . . How do you know so much about them anyway? What makes you think I could even get a place?'

156

'I have a friend who is involved with various charitable organizations,' Pat said reluctantly, aware that she was beginning to sound like Madame Bountiful, when her own helplessness was stark.

'I don't want charity,' Sarah said stiffly. She looked away, glanced at her daughter, put her hand down to find her shoulder bag. 'Why are we the ones from whom so much courage is always demanded?' she hissed. 'I'm scared to death; but my second greatest problem is hope. Secretly, I'm dogged by hope!'

Pat thought of her own life, of Paddy, of the future. 'So am I,' she whispered. 'So am I!'

When Patricia turned the corner into her road she saw Mick Clancy on his motorbike outside the house and Orla talking to him. They saw the car approaching and moved away, and Patricia drove into the driveway. She waited for a moment before leaving the car. Orla had given no indication that the conversation was in any way against her will.

She got out of the car, opened the boot, began to unload the shopping. After a few moments Orla appeared and wordlessly began to help her carry the bags into the house. It was the nearest thing to an apology she could manage.

'Is he bothering you?' Patricia asked.

'For God's sake, Mum. You can see for yourself we were just having a conversation. I'm able to look after myself!'

I'm getting old, Patricia thought. Full of unnecessary chagrins, waffling knowledgeably in supermarkets to semi-strangers who could tell me a thing or two. Maybe my perspective is distorted. Maybe I'm the one who needs divine intervention. Maybe the world is on course and Patricia is mad.

Simon was not at home.

'Where's your brother?'

'How should I know?'

'I think you should do a bit of study. Your exams are only around the corner!'

Orla breathed in noisily through her nose and raised her eyes to heaven.

Later, Patricia phoned Nell. 'Are you doing anything this evening?'

'I'm stuck! One of Fred's brothers is coming home from England!'

157

'Oh . . . well, have a nice evening!' Patricia was about to replace the receiver, when a thought struck her. 'Nell . . .'

'Yes?'

'Have you seen Simon?'

'He was here when I came in. Peter had a few friends around to watch a video.'

Patricia felt herself tense. 'What was the video?'

'I don't know. It was brought by one of the pals.'

'Will you try to find out?'

'Why? You don't think they were watching something unsuitable?'

'It's always a possibility.'

Nell sighed. 'I'll ask Peter, but I'm sure he wouldn't watch anything like that!'

When the phone rang about an hour later, Patricia was preparing dinner, chopping up a cooked chicken to make a curry. She picked up the extension in the kitchen, said hello. For a second there was silence, a kind of hum on the line, and then the voice came.

'Hello, my darling!'

Patricia edged towards the door and closed it with her foot. 'Hello. Where are you phoning from?'

'Richmond.'

'The line is good!'

'How are you?'

'Fine. How are you?'

'Bored. I miss you terribly.'

Paddy's voice was full of longing. 'I'm bored and fed up and want to be back in Ireland with you. Life simply doesn't make sense without you.'

Patricia felt the glow rise inside her, warm and comforting. Paddy had a strong voice. His words of love were gentle, muted, full of passion. The whole world came back into focus. Life resumed its point. Her earlier reservations about their relationship were squeezed out of existence. He couldn't sound like that unless he meant it.

'I miss you too.'

'I want you, Patricia. I want us to be together.' There was a pause. 'Darling, have you thought about Paris?'

'I have!'

'Will you come? It would be wonderful. We could see so much

of each other. I could show you the city, even take you away for a weekend to some quiet little French town with a good hotel. It's keeping me going, the thought of us having some real time together.'

There was silence; the line hummed discreetly. 'Darling!'

'Yes?'

'Will you come?' There was desire in the voice. Patricia felt the longing in herself, the aliveness.

'I'll come,' she said. 'I'll come.'

In the hall, Orla, who had just picked up the phone to make a call, replaced the receiver very softly. Her eyes were dilated with shock. Her mother heard the soft click and said to Paddy, 'Hold on a moment.' She rushed out to find the hall empty.

'Sorry,' she said to Paddy when she came back. 'I had to check on something. I thought one of the children was listening!'

'Were they?'

'No.'

Simon came in at six.

'Where were you?'

'In Peter's house; we were watching a video.'

'What was it about?'

'It was a war film, U-boats and stuff.'

Patricia sighed with silent relief and felt guilty for having entertained any doubts.

'Are you hungry? Supper will be ready in a few minutes!'

Simon nodded. 'Yeah, I'm starving.'

He reached into the cutlery drawer and rooted around.

'What are you doing?'

'Just looking for Excalibur!'

He took out the fork with the bent prong and put it down at his place at the table, removing the other one. Patricia laughed. Sometimes Simon was funny. He grinned, glanced at her. His colour was a little high and his eyes bright.

'Will you stir the sauce for a moment while I nip upstairs?'

'OK.'

The phone rang as Pat was returning to the kitchen. Orla, who had preceded her mother down the stairs, picked it up in the hall.

'It's for you, Mum.'

'Who is it?'

Orla shrugged, dropped her voice. 'Dunno. Some woman.'

159

Then she added, under her breath, but so low that Pat could not be sure she had heard her, 'At least it's not that man again!'

Patricia picked up the receiver on the hall table, started in surprise to hear Sarah's voice, and gave her the office number so she could phone Joan on Monday.

Chapter Thirteen

Spent the afternoon in the garden with the children. Orla was interested in the story of Cinderella which we read together from a Ladybird book. She was riveted by the fairy godmother and the coach and glass slippers and the wonderful prince who wore satin trousers and worshipped her because she was beautiful. In the end was the splendid wedding and the happy-ever-after.

'Did she really live happily ever after, Mummy?' Orla asked.

'Of course she did, darling,' I said, to make her happy. 'Of course she did.'

from *The Horse's Ears*, 1982

Lorraine came downstairs and helped her mother with the housework. Sarah tried to joke, 'Look at the mess; wouldn't you think the place was a zoo?', but Lorraine's watchful eyes remained grave. Sarah was puffing with exertion and Lorraine asked her to sit down. 'I'll finish the hoovering, Mammy.'

Sarah complied, deposited her weight on the couch, lay back to ease the discomfort of the bulge under her diaphragm. In her mind she was rehearsing what she would say when she met the solicitor, Mrs de Barra. She closed her eyes for a moment, but when she opened them the room was empty and Lorraine's steps could be heard on the stairs. She came back into the room with a pillow, approached her mother, put the pillow on the couch. 'Lie back on that, Mammy.'

Sarah, touched by her little daughter's thoughtfulness, obeyed. She fixed the pillow on top of some cushions, and watched her child do the hoovering, saw the way she glanced over at her from time to time, watching her, smiling to herself with the pleasure of having made her comfortable.

161

'Come here to me, cushla!'

Lorraine went to her mother's outstretched arms, lay her cheek against hers, submitted to the caresses, returned them eagerly.

'If I never had anything else good in my life – it is all worth it to have you,' Sarah whispered. 'I want you to know that. I love you and am so proud of you, my little princess!'

Lorraine smiled her secret, diffident smile. 'I'd better finish the hoovering before Daddy gets back!' But as she started up the machine again the doorbell rang.

'It's Jennifer,' Sarah said. From where she lay on the couch she had seen her coming up the path. Jennifer was Lorraine's best friend who lived around the corner. Lorraine admitted her and she trooped into the room full of smiles to ask if Lorraine could come for tea and to stay the night.

Sarah saw the delight in her daughter's eyes and the chagrin as she looked at the hoover and the floor and the unfinished housework.

'Is this your idea, Jennifer – or your Mam's?'

'It's my Mam's. Well, I asked her and she said all right!'

Sarah looked at her daughter. 'Well, what are you waiting for?'

'I'll do the hoovering first,' the child said doubtfully.

'No you won't. Get your pyjamas and toothbrush and be off with you!'

Lorraine laughed, ran upstairs with Jennifer in tow.

That makes only Jim and me and Dara tonight, Sarah thought. Maybe it's just as well.

When the two little girls had gone, Sarah went back to the hoovering. Then she made the beds, leaving the boys' room until last so as not to disturb Dara's nap. His illness had really taken it out of him; he slept half the day still.

When Sarah had finished the hoovering, she tiptoed into his room and stood looking into the cot. The child lay on his back, both hands thrown up to lie, palm upwards, on either side of his head. His face was flushed and for a moment Sarah was afraid he was feverish, but when she touched his neck she knew it was just the heat from sleep. He opened his eyes, smiled at his mother.

'Mamee . . . Uppy daisy,' and he raised his arms to be lifted. Sarah kissed him, put him down on Liam's bed while she changed him. She felt half elated; she had telephoned Patricia O'Hehir – Galligan – and now had in her possession a phone number which could change the course of her life. The line between action and inaction was so thin, but the outcome could be so momentous. Well, she would see.

'You're like a little fat ball,' she told her baby, kissing his tummy in a sudden rush of passion, and the child gurgled with laughter and peed, a long warm stream arching up and catching his mother on the nose.

'Little savage; you always know when to let go!'

Dara toddled around the kitchen. The pots and pans, which Sarah kept in a cupboard near the sink, were soon out on the floor, and Dara became immersed in the business of banging lids and fitting smaller pots into bigger ones. Sarah gave him a couple of dessert spoons, a rubber spatula, a plastic cup and a piece of string from the drawer. She fetched Dee-Dee and put him sitting beside the playpen to oversee operations. Then she scoured the sink, wondering should she cook Jim a supper; would he be back? If she cooked him something nice it might put him in a good humour. The broken door of the corner unit hung drunkenly on its hinges and she regarded it with sorrow. It spoilt the kitchen and he would be all a dander putting in a new one. She would have to tell him how wonderful it was when it was in; she would have to sound exactly right; not too enthusiastic or he would say she was putting it on, not under-enthusiastic or he would say she didn't care. Dara soon became fascinated by the broken door and began banging it, putting his fat fist through the broken piece, swinging it back and forwards.

'No darling, don't do that,' Sarah said. 'Daddy will fix that. You'll make it worse and Daddy will be cross!' But the child's fist was caught in the gap between the frame and the panel and was being squeezed. He began to scream. Sarah rushed to the rescue, pushed back the panel to release the hand, but in so doing there was a further crack and the panel, already splintered, and made of thin wood in any case, broke in two and fell on to the floor.

'Whist, whist.' Sarah kissed the small hand while she stared with dismay at her handiwork. She picked up the pieces of the broken panel and put them on top of the fridge. She felt stiff with fear. He would be bound to blame her. Her earlier sense of elation evaporated. What was the use of making an appointment to see a solicitor on Monday? Monday was two days away. Today was Saturday. For a moment she thought of what Patricia had said to her; maybe she should make another phone call, and if

163

they could have her in the refuge pack a bag, leave. But there were Lorraine and Liam to think of. She would have to get them home, spoil their fun. And if she did go she would spend the rest of her life in fear of Jim tracing her. She knew that he would make a crusade of it. He would find her in the end. But still the thought gathered momentum. She saw herself walking down the path, going down to the bus, Dara in the buggy, Lorraine and Liam beside her. She imagined herself waiting for the bus. What if he came along while she was waiting and saw them? He would drag them home.

But if she made it to the refuge she would be safe. At least for the time being. She would be able to draw breath, get her bearings. Then the baby would be due and where would she go then? No job! Nothing! I'd better feed Dara now, she thought, shelving the problem. At least I can talk to the solicitor about all of this.

She put down two eggs to boil and when she looked around she saw that he had wandered into the hall. Sarah went out after him. He had found the felt pen she had left on the windowsill earlier and forgotten about. He had scrawled on the wall with it. She dragged him back to the kitchen, put him into the playpen, got a wet cloth and tried to remove the purple stain from the wall. But the stuff had penetrated the paper, and if she rubbed any harder she was afraid she would take part of the paper away. She went back to the kitchen and sat at the table, unable to stem the sudden tears. Dara, watching from the playpen, began to howl.

'Oh shut up,' Sarah told him, wiping her eyes. 'You're nothing but trouble!' She surveyed the mess in the kitchen that had been so clean half an hour before, the pots and pans, saucepan lids, general detritus on the floor, the broken pieces of the unit panel on top of the fridge. She would have to clean it up all over again. Dara was standing in the playpen, leaning against the mesh, screaming to get out, tears pouring down his face.

'All right, all right; wait a minute, will you?' and she threw Dee-Dee in to keep him company while she fished the eggs out of the saucepan, put them in egg cups, cracked them and put them on the table with a few slices of brown bread. She made a pot of tea. 'We have to eat; but I'm not hungry!'

She sat Dara at the table and spooned egg into his mouth. Dara made an uninterested face, turned his head sideways, and Sarah played the old game with Dee-Dee. While she was thus engaged she heard the key turn in the hall door and in a moment Jim filled the kitchen doorway. Sarah tried to smile. She saw from the tense set to his shoulders that his mood was very bad. She saw from the slick moistness to his face and the redness of it that he had been drinking. He was holding something in his hand and Sarah stared at it, recognizing it as the crook-lock from the car. What did he bring that in for?

She stood up and lifted Dara back into the playpen. The child stared at his father and sat down silently. Sarah threw the teddy in after him. Jim looked around the kitchen in evident disgust.

'The mess! All I ever have is a dirty, filthy mess to come home to.' He kicked a saucepan lid that Dara had been playing with and it skidded under the table.

'I'll tidy it up in a minute,' Sarah murmured. 'What would you like for your tea?'

'What would I like for my tea? As if you gave a damn. The breadwinner of this family comes home to a slum; other men come home to their tea on the table! But I come home to a slum! Anything is good enough for me!'

'What do you want the crook-lock for?' Sarah asked, while she rapidly took the saucepans and lids off the floor. 'Is something wrong with it?'

'It won't work, that's what's wrong with it!' He put it down on the work surface. 'It's like everything else . . .!'

Sarah bent sideways to get rashers and eggs from the fridge. A lock of her hair escaped from the clip and fell sideways over her face. She glanced at her husband, saw the disgust on his face, the hatred.

'Look at yourself! Do you know what you look like . . .? You look like a big fat whale . . . or a bloody hippopotamus. You look as though you're ready to burst! It's disgusting! And the house is fucking disgusting. Didn't I tell you to clean up this place before I left? But no. You have to loll around, spoiling that brat!' He directed a half kick to the mesh of the playpen and Dara backed away, lay down beside his teddy and sucked his thumb.

Sarah was silent. She started to fry eggs, put some rashers under the grill. Her silence infuriated Jim. He sensed its censure and its fear.

'Don't make anything for me! I'm going out.'

And as he turned at the door he saw the missing door panel,

saw his tools scattered on the floor on the other side of the playpen.

'Oh God! What have you done, you brainless slut? You've fucking ruined the door!'

He turned to his wife, glaring like a madman, ready to lash out. 'You and these fucking children . . .' and he kicked Dara's playpen again – 'it never ends!' Dara looked up at his father from his crouched position, held on to his teddy, afraid to give vent to his tears.

Sarah felt something snap within her, felt something reckless rise up inside her as she saw Jim prepare to deliver a kick more savage than the last.

'Don't touch that child!' she hissed. 'That child has been very sick and I'm trying to build him up. And I'm not a brainless slut. There isn't a woman in Ireland would put up with you and the carry-on of you. But I've put up with as much as I can take!' and she slammed the frying pan to one side.

Jim's eyes brightened with relish at the legitimate confrontation. She was challenging him; he would have to show her who was boss.

'I'm going to leave you,' Sarah continued softly, keeping her voice low so as not to frighten Dara any worse. 'If it's the last thing I do. I'm arranging to see a solicitor on Monday. I'm going to leave you and I'm taking the children! You're not a man. My father said it the first time he saw you. You're not a man and never will be one!'

Jim's face darkened; his eyes paled, bulged insanely; he lifted the crook-lock from the unit beside him, took two paces forward and brought it down on Sarah's skull. There was a crack as though someone had dropped a clay pot to the floor, a dull moan and then silence. Jim brought the crook-lock up again and hit her a second time as she slumped on to the floor, a concave dent in the side of her head where the blood seeped. He continued to hit her. Splatters of blood hit the floor and the wall. In the playpen Dara shivered, his face very white, his eyes glassy and trancelike, his mouth open in the scream that wouldn't come.

Jim bent over his wife's body, his fury spent, his alcoholic frenzy abated.

'Oh holy shit!' He tried to move her, but she lay inert and heavy. Under her maternity smock something trembled and then was still. He knelt down.

166

'Sarah . . . Sarah love . . . Don't do this to me, kitten!' He took her wrist – there was no pulse.

Jim ransacked the kitchen, opened the drawers and emptied them, raced around the house and did the same. Then he phoned the police.

'I've just got home . . . My wife's been attacked; I think they've killed her. I don't know, I don't know . . .' He burst into tears.

When the police came they took a statement; examined the house. An ambulance took Sarah's body away. The police removed the crook-lock in a plastic bag. Dara had been given to Fiona to mind. The police interviewed her and asked her if she had heard anything.

'It wasn't burglars,' she told them. 'He's been beating her for years. The poor child is in a bad way. I had to get the doctor for him. He's in shock.'

'Did you hear anything?'

'No. I just got back before you came. But I'm telling you. He did it . . . And I bet you anything the child saw him do it!'

Chapter Fourteen

I passed Joanna Hayes near the Ormond Hotel today at lunchtime. A small woman, young, the focus of so much prurient probing. It has become so bad, so offensive, this questioning by the legal people, that every morning well-wishers deluge her with roses.

She had a baby out of wedlock. It died. How did it die? There is a welter of confusion. But one thing is clear – the orgy of triumphalism indulged in by the men questioning her, the bullying and the gratuitous insults. She is not on trial after all: she is only a witness at an inquiry. Yet every detail of her private life, every detail of the childbirth – her blood, her womb, her vulva – is poured over with hideous voyeurism.

Where is the relevance of all of this? This 'Kerry's Babies Tribunal' is more than just an eye-opener; it is a kind of terrorism.

from *The Horse's Ears*, 1984

Patricia saw the headlines, searched for some change, grabbed the evening paper. The dead woman's picture stared back at her – Mrs Sarah O'Toole who was found beaten to death and whose husband was helping police with their inquiries.

'Jesus Christ! I know her . . . I know that woman.'

Paddy leaned towards her in sudden solicitousness, took her hand.

'She used to shop at the same supermarket; sometimes we had coffee . . . I was talking to her only the other day. Oh God!'

Pat had been walking with Paddy by the newsvendor's stand in Nassau Street. Behind her the rush-hour traffic surged towards Lincoln Place and Merrion Square. The summer evening was fine, full of promise. Paddy had met her by arrangement for a brief rendezvous. They were planning to meet again later for a drive into the mountains.

The tears welled in Patricia's eyes. 'She was pregnant. She was really nice, you know. A really nice person . . . I knew her at school. I told her she should leave him.' Patricia realized that she was shaking and felt Paddy's grasp on her hand.

'Darling, you're ashen; you need a drink. Come back to the flat.' He glanced at her face. 'Please! I could look after you in the flat!'

Paddy's flat was on the first floor of a Ballsbridge apartment block. They went up by the thickly carpeted stairs to the white door with a spy-hole. He opened the door and Patricia found herself in a small hallway with a coat-stand, a mirror and a small table with a telephone. It was warm and close in the flat. The windows were closed and the evening sun shone into the living room. The place was carpeted in olive green. There was a leather suite with cushions, a small table beside the hearth with a pink lamp, several large pictures awash with colour. The coffee table was piled with newspapers and Paddy shifted them to one side, went to a small table between the two windows where there were some bottles and poured Patricia a stiff gin and tonic. She took it with a shaking hand and placed it in front of her on the glass top of the coffee table. She stared at the photograph in the paper, a picture of Sarah, smiling, a younger Sarah with her daughter in her arms. She read the caption twice:

Mrs Sarah O'Toole, whose body was discovered by her husband on Saturday in their home at 42 St Teresa's Crescent, Dundrum.

Mrs O'Toole, who was the mother of three children and expecting her fourth child in June, had sustained head injuries. Her husband, James O'Toole, 40, a foreman at O'Connor's Builders' Suppliers, is helping the Gardai with their inquiries.

Paddy sat beside her on the couch, put an arm around her.

'You're trembling, sweetheart. You should have your drink.' Patricia picked up the G and T, took a slug, felt the bitter fizz of it slide down her throat. She let the tears flow as she drank, snuffled, blew her nose in Paddy's proffered handkerchief.

'The poor thing; the poor, poor thing . . . I can't believe it. I was talking to her on Saturday. She was going to make an appointment to see Joan – because she was afraid of her husband. Oh Paddy . . . She was a decent person, funny, and crazy about her kids.'

'Did you know her well?'

'Not very well. She was in school with me, but several classes behind. We met in Supersales a couple of times and had coffee and chatted the way people sometimes do with strangers. She told me things about her life; we were able to talk to each other. Although we met only the odd time, we got to know each other quite well. There was a kind of sympathy between us, if you can understand that?'

Paddy nodded. Patricia's eyes were red, the blue irises washed out, the whites pink. Her eyelashes were wet and spiky and some eye make-up had streaked on to her lower lids. She ran her hand through her hair.

'How could anyone hurt her? She was six months pregnant too . . .'

Paddy put a cushion on his lap and pulled Patricia's head down on to it, began to gently massage her temples.

'Let it go, my darling. There's nothing you can do. The only thing we have power over is our own lives . . .'

Patricia closed her eyes. She felt the gin in her brain, the expanding emotional space, the contracting judgement. What was it he had said? Power over one's own life. Is it a mirage? Does Paddy have it? Do I?

Paddy picked up her glass. 'Will you have another drink?'

Patricia hesitated, opened her eyes to study Paddy's face. Behind him a shaft of evening light touched the wall, brightened his hair, gave him a kind of nimbus, like a medieval saint.

'Oh Christ, I'd love one. But I shouldn't drink, you know. I gave it up. I had a drink problem and I gave it up. I was becoming a mess!'

Paddy's face was inscrutable. He placed the glass back on the coffee table. The lines around his mouth tightened.

'How bad a problem?'

'Stupid really. I drank vodka. I kept a bottle in my bedside drawer.' She sat up, wiped her face. 'So you see what a hopeless case I am, or was?' She reached up to touch his face. 'But I can stay off the stuff; so long as I have you I can do anything!'

171

Patricia could have kicked herself. She saw the alarm in Paddy's eyes, the sudden shift of perception. From being the love object, the object of tenderness and desire, she had become a possible threat; from being someone with her own autonomy she had become a potential emotional dependant. She laughed shakily.

'I'm joking. Bad joke!' He looked at her carefully and she smiled into his eyes.

'I'd better go and wash my face. I must look a sight!' She made her way to the bathroom off the hall. There was a huge mirror over the washbasin which reflected her blotched face. She bathed it in cold water, and she got out her hairbrush and lipstick, cursing herself all the time.

He wasn't ready for that, she thought. He wasn't able for it; you should keep your big mouth shut.

Paddy was in the kitchen when she came out of the bathroom.

'I'm making us some tea.'

'Good. I'd love some. Then I have to go.'

Paddy turned on the switch by the electric kettle, moved towards her, took her in his arms.

'Do you have to go? You could phone and say you'll be back later. We could do something, have dinner somewhere nice – somewhere small!'

His breath was warm above her ear. She smelt the faint remnants of his aftershave. His chin rasped against her cheek. She felt the body warmth, the hand moving down her spine. A space opened before her into which she could hurl her life and senses and find peace.

Paddy took her hand and led her to the bedroom. The kettle came to the boil and turned itself off. Patricia took her skirt off, folded it over and placed it on the chair and then huddled under the duvet in Paddy's bed. He joined her immediately: naked, erect, eager. He tugged her tights and panties off, pulled at the brooch fastening at her throat, opened the buttons of her silk blouse, unhitched the fastening of her bra. Then he buried his face in her breasts. The world receded. And as it did so the universe of spirit and senses beneath the duvet filled and unfolded.

'You're beautiful; I love you and need you . . .'

'I love you too, Paddy. I always have.'

172

Later, Patricia heard the doorbell, pushed Paddy who was half asleep.

'There's someone at the door.'

'I am not available!' he said dryly, sleepily.

She laughed, snuggled down again into the curve of his back, nibbled at the hairs along his spine; the ringing at the door ceased.

'It's as though I have no choice, she thought. If I can be with you I have no other choice. To be with you is to be alive and warm and whole. To be without you is desolation, loneliness, death. She sighed inwardly. Which means, I suppose, that I am really in a lot of trouble.

Half an hour later she was dressed and ready to leave.

'I have to go home. I don't want Gerry getting suspicious.'

'Have you told him about Paris yet?' Paddy was sitting at the edge of the bed putting on his socks.

'Not yet. Every time I mention about going away he talks of the two of us going to Egypt.'

'You'd better tell him soon. I have to book that flat for September.'

'When you first spoke of it, I thought it was yours.'

'No. Our apartment is a different one altogether. Susan uses it a lot. She likes Paris.'

'I see.'

'But she won't be there in September. And it's safer and more discreet the other way!'

Patricia was silent. 'Ours,' he had said, referring to what was his and his wife's. The word conjured up matrimony, commitment, the paraphernalia of a joint life and experience. She felt suddenly on the outside, peripheral, plundered, used. She was still warm, still vibrant from his lovemaking, and he talked of his wife and what was theirs. He was like some sort of hunter who was on a marauding spree, but would return to his hut. She, Patricia, was the prey or, maybe, the entertainment. Susan was his life. That was how it felt.

She made for the door.

'Wait a minute. I'll see you to the car.'

He pulled on a pullover. His face was sleepy from lovemaking. He looked wonderful – lovable, masculine, desirable, unattainable. Sorrow filled all of Patricia's spirit. She went in silence through the door and down to the hallway and out the front door to the car park. Paddy followed her.

As she unlocked the car she heard a shout. A middle-aged man in a business suit got out of a car parked nearby and approached them.

'Hello, Paddy. I thought you were out.' He leered at Patricia, smiled at Paddy a conspiratorial 'we're all lads together' smile. 'But I see you were busy.'

'This is Mrs Galligan,' Paddy said. 'Pat, this is John Millar, my accountant.'

The burly man shook her hand. His face was a study of knowing, prurient disrespect. She felt at once his perspective. Paddy was being a bit of a boyo. Nice little bit of skirt. Paddy was on to a freebie. Good old Paddy. His glance, his leering eyes, even the way he leaned towards her in impertinent familiarity, all spoke of his power to name what he had identified, a power untrammelled by any understanding. Patricia froze, said, 'How do you do' icily, and shut the door, driving out of the car park without looking back.

Oh God, if there is a God, why are they so presumptuous and prurient? And if they have to be like that – why must they have so much clout?

As she drove she felt the numb despair. It was over with Paddy. It had to be over. She could not run any further risks for a man who made passionate love to her and then spoke of his wife in terms of 'us'.

And she was running too many risks. That she did not know the man Millar, that he was not one of Gerry's acquaintances, was just good fortune. Next time she might not be so lucky.

'Where were you?' Gerry demanded irritably when she got home. He had a fry of bacon and eggs in front of him on the kitchen table. He radiated reproof that his dinner had not been there waiting for him, that she had left no message. Orla and Simon were also in the kitchen; they had evidently made the fry for their father and were eating grilled hamburgers dripping with tomato ketchup. The air was full of the smells of hot bacon and beef fat.

'I met someone.'

'Whom did you meet?'

'A friend! I got an awful shock today, Gerry. A woman I used to meet at the supermarket was murdered.'

Patricia sat down and saw the three pairs of eyes boring into her. She felt the tears she had tried to check all the way home

174

assert themselves, spilling down her face. Gerry went on eating. The children exchanged embarrassed glances and then Orla got up, took her jacket from an empty chair so that her mother could sit down.

'Who was this woman?' Gerry asked.

'Sarah O'Toole.'

'I saw it on the news,' Orla said. 'They think her husband did it.' She stared at her mother, at her tears, in dismay. Simon gave a croaky laugh. 'Hey, the guy who mashed his wife with a crook-lock . . . And you knew her, Mum! That's cool! Wait till I tell the gang at school.'

Patricia wiped away the tears and glared at her son.

'Have you been drinking?' Gerry asked conversationally, keeping his voice low, but the children heard him and looked up at her accusingly.

'Oh for God's sake leave me alone,' Patricia said. She rose and left the room, closing the door behind her. Behind her she heard Simon's comment, heard the half laugh in his voice which played to his father and sister. 'Good old Mum, rat-arse drunk again!'

'You can be as crude as you like with the long-haired louts you associate with,' came his father's cold voice, 'but not in this house!'

Upstairs, Pat changed into an old tracksuit and began to sort through her clothes. The house became quiet; the muted voices from the kitchen ceased.

She heard Gerry step on the stairs. He appeared in the doorway, took a fresh shirt from a drawer, put it on.

'How much did you drink?'

'I had one G and T.'

'I thought you had given it up!'

'I have. I have given everything up; life, fulfilment, happiness!'

Gerry did not react to the bitterness of her voice, except to glance at her coldly while he put on his tie. Suddenly it occurred to her that he enjoyed her unhappiness, that the power of it flattered him, even sustained him, because she continued to endure it.

'I'm going out for a while.'

He put on a sports jacket and left the room. Patricia heard his departing steps in the hall, heard the front door close behind him.

Patricia heard the television being turned on downstairs; that

175

would be Simon. He watched far too much of it.

The phone rang. She picked it up, said 'Hello', heard the voice. It was very low and anxious, tinged with humour in which she was tacitly invited to participate.

'I'm sorry, darling, about this evening.'

Patricia took a deep breath.

'It's my own fault, Paddy. I shouldn't have gone back to your flat. There is no space or peace for us in this country – or anywhere!'

'I didn't expect John Millar,' Paddy went on. 'But it seems he has to go away on Monday and there was something he wanted to check with me first. I know you were embarrassed. I told him you had come with some papers for signing. I think he believed me. Am I forgiven?'

What's in a voice? Why did the timbre of his voice bring the world back into focus? Patricia battled with the instinctive prompt which would have extended instant understanding, which would have responded to the cajoling tenderness, which would have done things his way, which would have said it didn't matter. But it did matter.

'It won't happen again!' His voice was coaxing.

There was silence.

'It can't go on, Paddy. There's too much pain and all of it is mine!'

'Darling, I never meant to cause you pain. You know that!' There was sudden real distress in his voice, realization that the situation had changed, had slipped from his control. 'I love you.'

'Thank you, Paddy, for loving me. Maybe if there is reincarnation things will work out for us!' She tried to sound witty, to end on a bright note. 'I have to go now, so thank you for everything . . . I hope everything works out for you.'

'Pat! Wait a minute! Are you saying that this is it – that you won't see me again – that you won't be coming to Paris?'

'Yes. Precisely that. I love you more than you could imagine, but I am saying precisely that!'

She put the phone down, sat and stared at it for several minutes. It lay there on its cradle, stupid and unfeeling, as though it inhabited a different universe. The day was fading outside; the birds were doing their thing, shrieking in the trees. The world was full of emptiness. Nothing in all its wonder had anything to satisfy.

When the phone rang again she had to stop herself jumping to pick it up, then felt her heart sinking when she realized it was Nell.

'Pat, do you know what I've just discovered? The video the boys were watching the other day . . .'

'What about it?'

'It was . . . unspeakable!'

Patricia was silent.

'Oh – you wouldn't believe it. Men doing terrible things to young women – not just sex – but torture and slashing them with knives and shoving things into them. Oh, I'm still sick. Peter was able to take a copy of it because we have two videos. I watched it today out of curiosity to see what they had been looking at. I thought it would be some sort of war thing.' She went on to describe in some detail the content of the video which their teenage sons had watched earlier that day for entertainment.

'It's war all right' Patricia said in a low voice, 'except that women didn't declare it.'

'What are we going to do?' Nell demanded. 'I cannot bear the thought that my son should have watched such material. The humiliation of it is crawling up my spine!'

'We can talk to the boys,' Pat said dryly. 'Other than that, there's not much we can do except bomb video shops or start a new political party. Are you interested?'

'Patricia,' Nell said, 'you're getting fiercer as you get older. And I'm not sure that video shops are the only culprits; the stuff can be had through the post. I'm going to talk to Peter and you'd better talk to Simon.'

When Nell rang off, Patricia went downstairs to talk to Simon. He was watching a soap opera and when his mother spoke to him he said 'Shh' and concentrated on the screen. Patricia picked up the remote and turned off the television.

Simon turned on her aggressively. 'What did you have to do that for?'

'I want to talk to you, Simon.'

'About what?'

Simon's hair was slicked back and his check shirt was opened at the neck. He was lying back on the couch. He had taken off his boot runners and left them on the floor. He tensed himself so that his demeanour was one of confrontation. His long body was graceful and beautiful. His face was sprinkled liberally with what

177

he called 'zits'. His expression was closed and resentful.

'About the kind of videos you've been watching in Peter's house. I've just been talking to his mother. She looked at one of them today. It seems that Peter made a copy and left it lying around.'

'Holy shit!'

The expletive came from under his breath. He did not meet his mother's eyes, but he clicked with his tongue.

'They were only rubbish; they don't matter,' he muttered. It took Pat a moment to realize that he was talking about the young women who had provided his afternoon's entertainment.

Patricia felt her eyes sting with tears. He was her son and he was blind. He offered her the same insult these videos offered all women.

'You've been watching material for which women have paid horribly; maybe with their lives. Innocent women. I know there must be fundamental psychological anxieties which fuel the demand for this kind of stuff, but if you hire such videos, watch them, you are accessory to what is in them. I can't stop you watching them; I can only tell you that your sexuality and latent cruelty are being played upon, and that you are being depraved and dehumanized. The material also infers things about men with which you might not care to be associated!'

'They were just sluts,' Simon said hotly. 'The girls in those pictures were just sluts!'

' "Slut" is only a word. They were born brand-new like everyone else. No matter how you try to rationalize it or explain it away, they were, at the very least, used and hurt. No one bargains for being rubbished, mutilated, humiliated and turned into blood sports!'

'There's no need to get into such a tizzy,' Simon said with a sniff. 'Everyone watches the stuff.'

'Do they indeed! Pretend for a moment, just pretend, that men are physically weaker and poorer than women and that women make these kind of films about men. That they cut off real penises, balls, fingers: that they cut open male bellies with hunting knives, that they stuff explosive material into real male anuses, that they film the torture and the result – the bleeding, castrated, degraded result – for entertainment. That it is a billion-dollar industry, watched by countless millions of women who also happen to have almost all the political and economic

178

power. That it informs their attitudes towards men and that it is dismissed by them as fun, as rubbish, as unimportant. That vast numbers of women are addicted to it all the same and that they grunt and cheer when they watch it. That every single day thousands of men all over the world are raped and murdered by women, their half-clothed bodies found in alleyways and ditches, and that there is little justice even if the perpetrators are caught. Imagine that! Imagine it all being done to men! How would you feel about such films then?'

Simon shrugged, but did not reply.

After a while, Patricia added: 'And it's time you did some work. If you want to spend your life cleaning lavatories, at least try and be in a position where you do it out of choice! Because cleaning lavatories is where you're heading!'

As she left the room, Patricia glanced back. 'And another thing, young man – I am not "rat-arsed drunk".'

Simon did not reply. His head was bent, his profile suddenly vulnerable. For a heartrending moment she saw the little boy she had so loved.

When she came into the hall, Orla was standing there, wearing an expression halfway between shock and anxiety. Pat looked at her and snapped, 'What do you want, Miss Know-it-all?'

Orla said in a quiet voice, 'I just wanted to tell you, Mum, that I've made you a pot of tea and some sandwiches. I thought you might be hungry!' Then she walked upstairs to her room.

Pat put her hand to her head. 'Thank you,' she called after her daughter, but the bedroom door had already shut.

She went to the kitchen, saw that the scullery window had been left open and that Muffy, the cat, was scuttling over the sill. Muffy, who knew when she had broken house rules, threw a guilty feline glance back over her shoulder and Pat soon saw why. The chicken sandwiches, which Orla had made for her mother, were in disarray, some half eaten, and the butter dish on the table sported paw prints.

Chapter Fifteen

*I saw Joan de Barra this evening while I was waiting in the
car for Gerry. She came out of the office, looked around
expectantly, brightened when she saw her husband. He got
out of his car to wave to her. I've never met him so I had a
good look. Gerry says he is a nutcase, but he struck me as
merely intense, maybe a little volatile. He took her hand
when she approached and she leant towards him like a tree
in the wind.*

from *The Horse's Ears*, 1985

June 1990

Joan and David strolled around Montmartre, visited the Sacré
Coeur, sat in a back pew. It was late evening and the church was
dark, lit only by masses of white votive candles. The air was full
of the smell of candlewax and of the private, intense atmosphere
generated by prayer. A black woman in a pew in front of them
knelt stiffly, every atom intent on the prayer she offered, her
head bent forward and leaning on her hands. On the altar the
monstrance glittered, exhibiting the Host, golden spikes sticking
out around it like rays of the sun.

David looked around him in silence. He watched the people with
grave faces move in the side aisles like spirits of the dead, watched
them light their white tapers and then kneel or sit in the gloom. He
watched his wife's profile outlined against the tongues of flame as
she knelt and prayed. Her prayers were for David. She besought
God earnestly, hiding from the Divine gaze the fear in her heart.
Fear was not good enough, because fear evinced doubt.

How many times had David said to her, 'Can't you see – it's in
you, darling; the miracle – life – is in you! Everything on the altar
is dead!'

But he was silent now, sitting beside her, respecting her belief. She finished her prayer, sat back, touched him. The semi-darkness seemed to close about them, held them in a capsule of peace. He sought her hand. She felt as though the boundaries of her own life were lifted and that she flowed effortlessly into his, merged with him in a sense of subdued ecstasy.

They came out of the Sacré Coeur to the sight of night-time Paris stretched below them, and to a faint breeze which wafted a few sweet wrappers past the portico. About thirty feet away from them the famous steps of the basilica cascaded down towards the jungle of lights. The metropolis extended out below them, mile upon mile; the smothering heat of the day still over it, except here on the hill where the air was relatively cool.

'It is a great, inhuman city,' David said after a moment. 'Beautiful, but inhuman.'

'Don't you like Paris?'

'Of course. But I recognize its cruel complacency.'

'You don't mean you're missing little Dublin?'

'Good God, no . . . I belong where I happen to be and, of course, wherever you are.' He squeezed her hand, was silent for a moment before he added in a low, tight voice, 'I am rooted in you. Without you there is nothing!'

'The same goes for me,' Joan whispered. 'You know that!'

They stood, looking over the city.

'Are you hungry?' she asked innocently. Their last decent meal had been the day before. Then there had been the night. She was still vibrant with his lovemaking, the first abandon for weeks. She thought about it during the day, remembering her own ferocity, responding to every touch and kiss, to his mouth on her neck, to his mouth at her nipples, to his fingers down her spine, as though her skin were on fire.

'These are the sacred rites,' he had whispered passionately in her ear; 'there are no other!'

Thinking of it made her realize how much she missed this communication between them, which was so infrequent now because of David's health. She had kissed him everywhere, lips gentle on sensitive places, laid her face against him to feel the pulsing of his life, used lips and hands in rediscovery.

Afterwards, in the peace, they smiled at each other like conspirators.

'You were always implacable,' she whispered.

'Hold on to your hat from now on,' he answered, his smile a little wicked, but his eyes had been melancholy and she felt an exhaustion in him that the toll of requited desire alone could not account for.

'My hat?'

'Well, maybe a few other vestimentary details, superfluous in certain circumstances . . .'

Breakfast had been coffee and a croissant; lunch a salad with David's gallerist in the Rue Dauphine while they discussed the exhibition of David's work scheduled for September. The art dealer had asked her what she thought of her husband's work, had waited carefully for her response.

'I think he's a fine artist!' she said, aware even as she said it that it was something to which she had never given much thought. Her mind was always so concentrated on his health, on their relationship, that she had never tried to evaluate seriously the quality of his work. Few artists made it, she knew, and she did not expect that he would either. She had seen a programme on TV about artwork as an investment alternative to the stock market. The advice had been to buy only the works of dead artists. It was enough for her to be with him, to be married to him, to surround him with strength. She knew little about art, but was stirred sometimes by his work, recognized its unorthodoxy. Now she looked into the speculative pale blue eyes of the Frenchman, who seemed so curiously interested in her evaluation, offered him a smile in sudden inadequacy.

'What did you think of *The Night*, for example?' the man pressed on, and Joan remembered the painting referred to. It was a strange picture, she knew, nothing but a great black raven on a dead tree, its head thrown back, beak open, screaming up at a leaden sky. The picture was otherwise empty of life; the tree was blasted as though struck at some time by lightning and the heath around it was covered in the shadows of night.

'It has power,' she said, wondering why she had never realized it before.

The man smiled, looked at David who winked at his wife. And Joan sat quietly, disguising her relief, her unease at the moment of inadequacy, at the sense of being out of her depth.

Joan knew the waistband of her skirt was looser. She pulled at it with her thumb. 'I'm losing weight. You're certainly good for the figure!'

David laughed, breaking the tension, squeezed her hand. 'I am neglecting you, sweetheart, while I indulge my imbecile imagination.'

'There's nothing imbecile about your imagination,' Joan said indignantly. 'You saw for yourself today the reception you got in the Rue Dauphine.'

David laughed dryly, ran his index finger along his beard. 'That's because I'm exotic – a wild Irishman. In Dublin, where I am merely a fellow sufferer among all the other poor eejits, I am fair game for the true genius of the Irish.'

'What's that?'

'Derision.'

Joan laughed. 'You're a terrible cynic and you have a starving wife.'

He kissed the nape of her neck. 'Point taken.'

The restaurant had red gingham tablecloths. A young man with a dicky bow played softly on a black upright piano. The place was half empty, the door opening on the cobbles of Montmartre. The pianist sat up very straight.

He was slender and youngish, about thirty, with the jaded air of one who has sampled life's decadence and come away weary. His long fingers caressed the keys, a French tune redolent of Paris, of art, of *joie de vivre*. And then, without warning, he started to play 'Galway Bay'.

The contrast between the two pieces of music was startling. One was bright, sophisticated, whispered of love, of wine, of pavement cafés; the other wept with yearning, metaphysical longing that nothing could assuage, not even the place it reached for.

'Bloody Irish – no discipline – neither of the heart nor the soul,' David muttered, and Joan saw that he was moved, that he kept his eyes down on the check tablecloth where he traced the edge of a red square with his index finger.

'We have some mysterious penchant for suffering – as though we knew that at the quick of experience we find life at last . . .' Joan saw the shadows under his eyes and was afraid. He had seemed well that morning. But he had insisted on a gruelling walkabout and now it was taking its toll. He looked suddenly tired, intense, worn.

The waiter took their order. Veau aux champignons for Joan. Sole bonne femme for David, green salads, a bottle of white wine. Joan ate quickly, aware that David barely picked at his food. He seemed listless, the fatigue he had seemed impervious to all day finally defeating him. His thin shoulders were hunched a little and his speech came with an effort and with some sort of subliminal apology.

'I'm sorry,' the effort in his voice seemed to say. 'Something is really wrong; Joan, my darling, I have ruined everything for you!'

But what he actually did talk about was impersonal: the visit to the Louvre, the Italian room, the Mona Lisa's 'marvellous smirk', while Joan thought of the painting of the Florentine on the adjacent wall, an inscrutable man with face in shadow occupying the whole of the foreground, while behind him a sunny piazza was bright with colour and light.

'He reminds me of that queer fellow in your work; you know – the Shadow!' she said to David as they stood before the picture.

David had laughed. 'Nonsense. Your man there is just your typical medieval gobshite! When I was a student and here for the summer,' he added, 'I spent the weekends in the Louvre, glutting myself. . . .Tell me, where would you like to go tomorrow?'

'I think we could take it easy tomorrow,' Joan said lightly. She glanced at his plate. 'Are you not hungry? You're making heavy weather of your dinner?'

'It's delicious. I'm just savouring it!'

Joan finished the veal, said she didn't want dessert or coffee. 'I'd like to go back when you're ready.'

They took a taxi to the hotel.

Although it was still relatively early, David went to bed. He gave up the attempt at talk and slept. Joan sat up, trying to read, watching his face sunk in the pillow. She phoned Dublin, spoke to Paul. Yes, she told him, they were having a nice time. They had lunched with the gallerist. Paris was wonderful, but they both missed their Paul. She hoped he wasn't studying too hard for the exams.

'Can I talk to Dad?' Paul asked, and Joan said he was very tired and had gone to sleep.

'I just wanted to say happy birthday to him in case I didn't get the chance to talk to him before Thursday.'

'Don't worry darling; we'll talk to you tomorrow. And we'll talk to you again on Thursday!'

185

After a moment's hesitation Paul asked, 'Is he all right?'

'Of course. He's just a bit tired, which is understandable! Why do you ask?'

'I have a queer feeling about him,' Paul said in a very quiet voice, his words dropping like stones in the pool of long-distance silence.

Joan made reassuring noises, tried to hide the anxiety, asked then to have a word with Auntie Lil. Her sister came on the phone, said everything was great, Paul was in good form, if a little quiet in himself.

When she rang off, Joan watched David's face for a long time. He slept deeply, silently, his breath very shallow, the dark shadows still around the eyes. His wiry black beard seemed the most robust thing about him. But he was soundly asleep and she turned off the bedside lamp and lay awake for a while, listening to the sounds of Paris pursuing its nighttime revelries outside the window; heard the occasional voices in the hotel corridor, the sound of bathwater being run. She felt subsumed with loneliness. A sense of resentment came to tug at the edges of her mind.

David had not been well for so long; why couldn't she have a husband who was healthy, a husband with whom she could discover life and love and the world? It seemed to her that years and years of her life had been drained in minding him, in chasing Fate away from him. Her strength had been squandered, poured without reckoning into his sustaining. What would happen if she took it back, all that strength that she had honed so carefully to make sure that he lived, the support that he took so completely, and sometimes testily, as his due? For the first time it occurred to her starkly that so much of her love for David was based on her own will, on the projection of her own expectations, the passion to weave a magical web to encompass him, because she needed it, needed the magic. For the first time it occurred to her that David's physical debility might be due in part to some subliminal choice of his own. All this business about his drowned brother, about his drowned brother coming back to him on his fortieth birthday. All his interminable guilt and ill-health thrown on canvas, and subtly thrown at her, binding her, causing the focus of her energy to centre on him to the utter exclusion of anything else that might take her away from him and fulfil her life. Yes! He had wrapped her in chains!

'I'm sick to death of it!' she whispered suddenly to the night air;

186

'I'm sick to death of it,' she whispered to the romantic City of Light outside her window.

'I'm sick of being a support system. I too have a right to live!'

Instant and furious remorse followed these promptings. She put out a hand and felt him beside her, put her arm around him as if in apology, tried to undo, to obliterate the thoughts she hadn't meant to think. She recognized the force of these thoughts, but knew there was a certain injustice in them, because she suspected, but was unable to measure, the extent of her own complicity. David felt almost rigid under her arm and the thought suddenly came to her with terror that he was awake and had heard everything.

'David,' she whispered. But he made no response and finally she slept.

David got up during the night, went to the bathroom and almost collapsed as he returned to bed. She was awake immediately. His left leg was swollen and he seemed to be in pain and she rang the porter immediately to ask for a doctor.

He arrived in the morning, a small dapper man with a black case, examined David, listened to his heart and lungs, looked at the swollen leg with a sharp intake of breath. David told him in halting French about his problems, but the doctor spoke English reasonably well and suggested that he should either be admitted to a French hospital or go home at once.

'You should be in hospital, monsieur,' he said. 'I will get you an ambulance! I do not like this leg . . .'

'Over my dead body!' David said. 'I'm going home!'

The doctor looked at Joan. She nodded. 'I'll arrange it.'

'He must stay in bed,' the doctor told Joan as he left, giving her some tablets for David. 'He must not get up for any reason, except his journey! And even that is so dangerous . . .'

'Why?'

The doctor sighed and looked her in the eye. 'Because he could die, madame!'

Joan phoned Dublin, spoke to David's doctor, told him what had happened, explained that David's leg had swollen and that she was taking him home that evening. The doctor said he would arrange for an ambulance to be standing by to take him immediately to Beaumont Hospital.

Joan lay down beside David. Her mind scanned the possibilities. There was his exhibition in September which might have to be cancelled. There was the possibility that he was indeed seriously ill, as the grave face of the French doctor had indicated and that he would die.

'I'm sorry,' David's voice murmured coldly beside her. 'You have no life because of me. You would be far better off if I died. You could marry again, have a life, have a real marriage!'

Joan rounded on him. 'You're going to live whether you like it or not! I haven't put up with all those years to lose you now. So shut up. I won't listen to defeatist talk.' She burst into tears, threw herself back down on the bed. But David did not move to comfort her.

'I saw it in the Sacré Coeur,' he said after a moment. 'I should have painted you as Fire, my lady.'

'Fire, my arse' Joan hissed at him. 'Just cut the crap and get better.'

David looked at her expressionlessly. Then he laughed coldly. 'Well, I won't die of sympathy anyway!'

Joan turned to stare into his eyes. 'You've had a lifetime's worth of sympathy already! If you want me, if you want life . . . come and get us!'

David looked angry, made as if to get up. 'You heard what the doctor said. You stay put. There is something seriously wrong with a leg that is swollen and turning blue!'

David lay back without further comment and closed his eyes. After a moment he said icily, 'I heard you last night when you thought I was asleep. You're quite right, of course. I am a terrible burden, but one way or another it won't continue much longer.'

Joan felt too tired to remonstrate.

There was an ambulance waiting in Dublin airport. It was rush-hour and raining. The ambulance tore down the dual carriageway, siren screaming, and swerved left at Collins Avenue. They're hitting the road in spots, Joan thought, and her eyes filled with tears at the human solidarity of it. David seemed feverish. She took his hand, but he did not return the pressure. He had his eyes closed but she knew that he was not asleep.

What would it be like to die? The thought came to her on a wave of defeat. Would it be a gradual seduction, a slipping away, or would the body fight with the last ounce of its strength? And if there was life afterwards, would he remember? Or would he forget, be oblivious of what they had meant to each other, know nothing of the bitter passion of their grief?

And what of her? She saw the years ahead of her, middle-age, loneliness; she saw the years behind, the struggle and the unremitting toil. It did not fit with the lifeplan she had once made, with the vista of the future she had had with David on their wedding day.

Some things did not yield to effort. Her father had been wrong. Some things broke you. Some things tested you to destruction.

In Beaumont they sent for a consultant, Mr O'Neill, who examined David at length.

Afterwards he said to Joan, 'Your husband has acute venous thrombosis of the left leg and I have absolutely no idea as to what is causing it. He will be given anticoagulants and we'll probably take him to theatre tomorrow for exploratory surgery. That's if the scans don't reveal the problem, although I gather he's already been put through the mill in St Vincent's!'

Joan nodded. 'He spent a few days in the private hospital. They said he had a spastic colon!'

The doctor looked at her impassively and didn't comment.

They wheeled David to a ward. Joan phoned her sister's number, spoke to Paul.

'Will he be all right?' the boy asked in an unnaturally quiet voice.

'Of course he'll be all right! You know your father!'

Next day they operated. She waited in the hospital, had a cup of coffee, tried to read a magazine. The minutes dripped by, became hours. She closed her eyes, but the tension kept her poised, waiting for the sound of footsteps, hearing other people's voices like background blur.

The ward sister spoke to her when David came back from theatre.

'Mr O'Neill would like to see you, Mrs de Barra. He'll see you at five thirty in his office!'

'What did he find?' Joan cried in anguish. 'What's the matter with my husband?'

The ward sister looked at her in compassion, lowered her voice. 'It's cancer,' she said. 'It's mesenteric cancer, always difficult to diagnose! But it's treatable' she added hastily, reacting to the expression on Joan's face.

189

'What are his chances?' Joan whispered.

'I don't know, Mrs de Barra – Mr O'Neill will discuss them with you. But say a little prayer and God will be with you and him!'

'I'm an expert at prayer,' Joan said bitterly. 'I've spent years besieging the God-Who-Does-Not-Really-Exist! I've sat at his gates beseeching him, like Lazarus at the gates of Dives – you remember the poor bugger in the Bible who was so miserable that even the dogs had pity on him. But He or She or It, or whoever is responsible for moving this continuum, doesn't give a damn!'

The ward sister raised her hands in a forgiving, priestlike gesture, shook her head and moved away.

'Right, God,' Joan said to herself, 'you'd better get your act together. This time you'd better get on your skates. Because I'm not grovelling to You any more. Because it's the least You can do. Because if You don't I'll never speak to You, not ever again! And if poor idiots like me stop talking to You – even You will die!'

She sat beside David. He was still asleep. He looked diminished, shrunken into the pillow. She took his hand and he opened his eyes for a moment, looked at her. Then he went back to sleep.

'You'd better go home and get some rest,' the ward sister said kindly. 'He won't really be out from under the anaesthetic for hours.'

Joan nodded and walked back along the shining rubber corridor to ask the porter to get her a taxi.

Chapter Sixteen

I should look for a job! But I'm qualified for nothing and I hate to leave the children.

Why do I hate being married to Gerry? I know why, but the reason is not respectable.

He is a good provider. He has bought a lovely house, expensive furniture. He seems to be faithful. So what's wrong with him? Men would say that there is nothing wrong with him, but that there is something wrong with me; that I am sick; that the hunger I have is deviant. Maybe they're right!

from *The Horse's Ears*, 1977

Paddy phoned day after day. Patricia did not answer. She kept the answerphone on. The phone rang again in the evening, each evening. Gerry answered it once. Orla answered it twice.

'Whoever it was hung up. That's the second time. I suppose it was a wrong number again,' Orla said in a voice full of innuendo. She was alone in the kitchen with her mother. After what she regarded as her rebuffed attempt at improved relations with her mother, she had reverted to careful cynicism.

'It was probably your lover!' she added, watching her mother's face.

Patricia started. 'My who?'

'Your lover. Don't you have a lover?'

'Don't be absurd.'

'Isn't there someone who is going to take you away from all this: from your husband, your family?' Orla asked in a tight voice.

'Where did you get such an idea?'

'It doesn't matter. But it makes me feel very insecure!'

Patricia did not answer for a moment. Then she turned to look

191

at her daughter standing by the table, pretending to examine the evening paper, her daughter who had changed and grown and challenged her.

The girl's hair was held back by a black velvet hairband which showed up the bright auburn strands. She was slim and graceful, still in her navy uniform, her slender legs elegant even in the black school shoes.

'Sit down, Orla.'

Orla gave her mother a careful look and sat down.

'Let me tell you a story,' Patricia said.

Orla was silent, her eyes on the table on the open evening paper.

'Once there was a girl of your age. She was seventeen and when she went to college she met and fell in love with a boy.' Patricia paused. Orla pretended to suppress a yawn.

'Standard stuff, you might say, except that it created expectations for her of what a living relationship could be, and these standards obtained, consciously or unconsciously, ever afterwards.'

Orla toyed with the newspaper. 'What happened to this paragon with the expectations?' she asked sweetly.

Patricia felt the irritation rise in her. What was the use of trying to talk to anyone in this house?

'She threw her life away; that's what happened to her,' she said coldly. 'One should always confront pain and not try to escape it. She tried to escape it. That was her mistake.'

'What happened to the fellow she was in love with?'

'He married someone else.'

'Did she have an affair with him when he came back?' Orla's voice was very low.

'How do you mean?'

'When he came back twenty years down the line, or whenever. I presume that's the next instalment!'

Pat held down her temper. Orla might as well know, she thought, that changes were in the wind.

'She saw him from time to time.'

Orla looked aghast. Her dismissive demeanour changed to one of outrage. 'Mummy, you don't seriously mean that you would even consider leaving us for this man. My God, it was a long time ago; it was simply ages. You can't turn around and dump everything for something that happened twenty years ago!' She

192

sounded like a headmistress reproaching a foolish child.

Patricia felt cold. She was a fool; a hundred times a fool. How could Orla be expected to understand that Time was an illusion, that sometimes maps drawn early in life remained the only maps; that you could meet a kind of destiny and walk away from it, only to have it dog you down the years.

'Who said anything about leaving? Who said anything about me? For goodness' sake will you have sense! It's only a story,' she said briskly. 'What sort of notions do you have in your head? Lay the table; your father will be home soon!'

Orla complied. Her demeanour, her glances at her mother, suggested questioning uncertainty.

'Can I go to a disco in Lulu's on Saturday?' she asked after a moment as she put the cloth on the table. 'Katie and Helen and the gang are going.'

'I suppose so. Do you think Mick will be there?'

'I don't care whether he is or not,' Orla said defensively. 'Anyway, he's not as bad as you make him out to be. He's got a lot nicer . . .'

'People are seldom as good or as bad as other people make them out to be. But sometimes they are driven and, occasionally, they are dangerous.'

Orla pointed to the article in the paper about a recent rape trial. He had raped and buggered her all night and put a kitchen knife up her vagina. He said she wanted it. This seemed eminently reasonable to judge and jury and he had been acquitted.

'The courts in this country make dirt of women,' the complainant had said afterwards. 'What happens if I get a gun and kill him because I have been denied justice?'

Orla was shaking her head with distaste. 'There's heaps of articles about these rapes. Every day there's one in the paper. It's disgusting.'

Her mother looked at her. 'Rapists don't wear labels!' she said. 'It's usually someone the victim knows!'

Orla sighed. 'Well if you're thinking of Mick – he's not dangerous. He's just a bloke!'

Patricia raised her hands in a gesture of acquiescence. 'OK. OK! You know him, after all. I don't.'

Patricia mourned for Sarah. It was two weeks later and still the thought of the dead woman would intrude; sometimes she dreamt of her.

'When is the trial likely to be?' she asked Gerry.

'I don't know. You should watch the papers. It could take up to a year. They have to prepare the Book of Evidence.'

Gerry had been watching her closely since her admission of having had a G and T, as though he expected her to break out in feverish alcoholism. But that drink had proved something to Patricia. When she found that the episode had not filled her with any uncontrollable desire to binge, she realized that she was not chemically dependent on drink. That she had a problem, yes, but nothing that she could not cope with. She knew the only way to cope with it was by keeping away from it. Sometimes this needed all of her willpower; she thought of Paddy all day, most days, and when the longing for him became unbearable she yearned for the surcease lurking in the bottom of a glass of vodka. She got involved with Nell on various charitable activities, which took her out for most of the day and gave her a lot to think about.

But Paddy wouldn't go away. She carried the memory of his warmth, the bliss of their communion, with her, like a charm to ward away fear and cynicism. Once she took up the phone to ring him and hung up as soon as he answered. Sure that it was her, he had phoned back immediately, only to get the answerphone. He had hung up.

He must think I'm playing adolescent games, she thought. How long can I keep this up – trying to pretend that I can distance myself from the one thing that could, that might, make me happy?

The next day his letter was in the post. The envelope was typed and Gerry glanced at it for a moment when he picked up the post from the mat before he left the house. He made no comment. Patricia brought the letter back to the kitchen which was empty, warm and bright with early summer sunshine. She put the end of a knife under the flap and tore it open, removed the folded sheet of paper. She wondered who the letter was from and so she read the signature first, started with pleasure.

My darling,

All right! I can't bear it without you. You must know that!

Everything seems cold and pointless; all the work and effort is meaningless.

I went home to Richmond for the weekend. Nothing made sense. We had dinner with friends; I thought of you all the time.

You are the only person I want to talk to. You are the only person visible on any horizon. Come back to me. We can talk about everything; surely we can work out the problems?

There are things I know I don't understand, but I need to see you, Patricia. I hate your damned answerphone.

Come back. I love you.

Paddy

When the phone rang at ten she answered it.

'Thank God' the beloved, familiar voice said. 'I am desperate.'

'So am I!' Patricia whispered.

'I love you!'

'I love you too!'

The words sighed softly down the line. The words came back, breathed in the same muted desperation, tones of hope, recognition, relief. 'It's been terrible.'

'I know!' She laughed, breaking the tension, relegating the intervening weeks of famine to the realm of the bad dream. It was astonishing how easily this was done, the dismissal of so much torment.

'What about lunchtime?'

'All right!'

At lunchtime she lay in Paddy's bed and they fell on each other like the starving at a banquet.

Afterwards as he dressed for the office he asked, 'You will come to Paris? I need some time with you on our own.'

'I will come to Paris,' Patricia said. 'I have begun to recognize the limitations of free will! I will do whatever you want, for as long as I can bear it. And I will do this because, essentially, I have no other choice.'

'We will have Paris at least,' Paddy said in a grave voice. 'We can talk then; we will have space to discuss things, space for ourselves.'

That night Patricia heard the sound of pebbles against Orla's window and she heard the whispered words as she got out of bed to investigate.

'Piss off, Mick, and don't be coming around here in the middle of the night. No . . . I won't come down!'

She watched behind the curtain while the youth left the garden, saw him glance back at Orla's window, saw the smouldering resentment.

I can't bear that fellow, Patricia thought with a shiver. He's too full of some kind of inverted rectitude, projecting resentment at being wronged if he doesn't get his own way. But she was pleased that Orla had no interest in him, that she had told him to clear off.

She should ignore him altogether, she thought. If she ignored him altogether she could leave her father to deal with him.

Next day she told Gerry she was going to take a break in September, that she was going to Paris for a few weeks.

'You're not thinking of going on your own?'

'Why not! It has to do with some space for myself, Gerry. I might learn some French, see the sights, take a train to Lyon maybe and see a bit of France.'

Gerry's expression suggested incomprehension. Why would anyone want to learn French when English was the accepted international language – even the French were learning it? Why should she need 'space for herself,' it seemed to say. Glimmering at the edges of his reaction was uncertainty at the idea of his wife as a separate entity with separate requirements.

'I thought we were going to go to Egypt.'

'We should have done that in April. It would be very hot in Egypt in September. I couldn't bear the heat.'

'How much is your Paris expedition going to cost?'

'I don't know yet. It won't be too dear. I have enough saved for it!'

'What about the children?'

'The children are old enough to look after themselves for a couple of weeks!'

Gerry's expression was disapproving, inclined to be outright rejecting, but wary at the same time. He could not help finding this wife more interesting than the one he had been used to. She had acquired instant attraction the moment she expressed an autonomous thought process which was independent of him, which did not demand his judgement, which did not hover around the edges of any kind of complaint.

'You've never wanted to go away on your own before. Why now?'

'Because it's time I did! You don't mind Gerry, do you?' she asked almost coquettishly, noting the half smile the moment of coquetry brought to his mouth. He shrugged.

'Suit yourself. So long as you don't run up huge credit-card bills.'

'I won't.'

'Where will you stay?'

Pat felt the panic rise in her.

'In a hotel, I suppose.'

'Good hotels in Paris cost the earth!'

'Or . . . I might be able to borrow a flat from one of Nell's friends. Her daughter has a flat in Paris, and it may be vacant in September . . .'

Gerry wasn't really listening. Otherwise he might have sensed his wife's trepidation.

That night Gerry made possessive love. His wife had edged away from the claustrophobic position of being flesh of his flesh, and he found her very desirable and individual. He did not work out why he felt the way he did, but his response was unmistakable. Patricia read it and sighed. Once she would have mistaken it for something else.

Patricia's mother died on the 8 June. She had been hale and hearty the day before when she had phoned, asking for all the family, speaking to Orla and questioning her about her boy-friends . . .

'I don't have any, Granny.'

'Always remember,' the old woman's voice came down the line with a characteristic note of wickedness, 'love is blind, but the neighbours ain't!'

Orla, half exasperated, half laughing, gave the phone back to her mother. 'Granny's in great form!'

When Pat put down the phone she had called to Orla, 'I'm going to see Granny. Do you want to come?'

Orla was very fond of her grandmother and always seemed to enjoy having tea in a threesome with her and her mother.

'Here we are, all the women in the family!' the old lady would say, and Orla would glow a little, like someone who had been admitted to a select society. She was always relaxed on these occasions, reverting to childlike delight, listening to stories about her mother's childhood with open interest.

So Orla had accompanied Pat again on this occasion and the

197

three generations of women had had tea together, while Mrs O'Hehir questioned Orla about her school 'Debs' dance and who she was going to invite. Orla blossomed, described the dress she wanted and glanced at her mother for approval, forgetting, for the moment, the imperative to be either defensive or challenging.

'Purple is a bit unusual for a Debs dance' the old lady mused, 'But I don't see why you shouldn't wear purple if you want to.' She examined her granddaughter critically. 'You'll be able for it; only the finest complexions can cope with it! If you've got it, flaunt it, as I used to say to your mother!' She glanced at Pat over her bifocals. 'But your mother was always a bit older in her thinking than I was!'

Orla and Pat laughed.

'Why was Mummy older than you in her thinking, Granny?'

'The poor girl was brainy: took after her father. Brainy people always take life seriously.' She had twinkled at Pat and added in a graver note, as though of warning, 'They tend to expect, to need, what may not be obtainable!'

And now Mrs O'Hehir was dead; heart failure in the middle of the night. She had been found by a neighbour who had a key and who kept an eye on her.

Patricia went to her at once and, when she was alone in the flat with her, she washed her mother's body, brushed her lovely silver hair, laid her out in her pale pink dress with the tracery of satin at the collar. She had often thought with dread of this last service she would do for her mother, who had always evinced a horror of being touched by undertakers; but she found that it was neither macabre, as she had expected it to be, nor did it fill her with despair.

Something in us understands these things, she thought. Something in us knows all about death and birth. Deep inside us there is a profound recognition of the great tides of life!

The real wrench came as the coffin was being lowered into the grave: the knowledge that the reference point for so much of her life, the unconditional love, the bubbly, sometimes caustic, always loving, presence was gone. She looked at Gerry in his dark suit who had not been able to comfort his wife, who had not even tried because he could not bear emotion. She saw her two children, handsome and tall, weeping quietly together. Behind her was the world of her childhood, her young adulthood; before her was the second portion of her life, the time of harvesting what had been sown, before she and Gerry and the rest of their generation were gathered in themselves. There was panic in the thought. How could so much time have passed? And why, she wondered, given that so much time had gone, did she feel no different at the core of her heart to the young girl who had sat in her mother's kitchen and dreamed romantic dreams, arching her head to catch a glimpse of herself in a mirror with the word PADDY written across it. Was life a joke, or a cruel test, to leave you with a young heart and to change almost every single marker and parameter, remove the support system, leave you standing alone?

Almost as though she had read her mother's thoughts, Orla moved silently and came to stand beside her.

Paddy phoned her from America where he was gone on business. There was a pause after Patricia picked up the phone before his voice came clearly down the line.

'Mummy died,' Pat said when he asked her how she was. 'We had her funeral yesterday.'

'My poor darling! You must feel so empty and rotten. I wish I were there to comfort you!'

Patricia burst into tears. 'When are you coming back?'

'Friday, darling. Plane gets in at four. Can we meet in the evening?' He sounded desperate, frustrated at being so far away, anxious to give comfort.

'I'll meet you at the airport.'

'I hoped you'd say that.'

'Who has your mother's Will?' Gerry asked her that evening. It had always been a source of surprise to him that she had never consulted him.

'It's presumably in the Wills' safe in your office. Joan drew the Will for her – you remember she acted when Mummy sold Brierly ten years ago and took a lease of the flat in order to be near us.'

Gerry thought for a moment. 'I'll check tomorrow. I'll get the thing moving.'

Patricia sighed. 'I think she made Joan her executrix. Why not let her look after it?'

Gerry looked at her coldly. 'Have it your own way!'

'I'll go to see her in a few days. I have to go through Mummy's things.'

Patricia spent the next day clearing out various effects from her mother's flat. There was a cardboard box of papers in the top drawer of her wardrobe and she put these aside to bring to Joan. On her mother's bedside table was a framed picture of Patricia, taken on the lawn in Brierly when she was fifteen. Her father had his arm around her and was smiling. She shook her head, fighting the lump in her throat, remembering how Daddy used to read from the paper, discuss current affairs with her, asking for her opinion and listening as though it mattered.

She cleared some of her mother's clothes, put them into plastic sacks for the St Vincent de Paul Society, keeping a few of her blouses for herself.

'Some of my things are good and will fit you, Pat; if you throw them all out I'll come back and haunt you!' her mother had once said to her.

I wouldn't mind a bit, Patricia thought. I wish you would haunt me, Mummy. I wish you would.

Her mother's funeral had been on Monday. On Friday Patricia met Paddy at the airport. She saw at once that he was very tired and when he explained how he had shortened his American trip and come post-haste from California by means of different flights, she understood why.

'You must have terrible jet-lag.'

'Divil a bit!' He bent over her, his eyes creasing in sympathy. 'How are you, my poor darling?'

'All the better for seeing you!'

Paddy threw his bag in the boot and they drove out of the airport and turned north towards Balbriggan; Paddy had asked that they just find a country place to park the car and be alone. Eventually, having driven down a quiet side road for a mile or two, Patricia pulled into a wide margin by a ditch. She turned off the ignition and turned to look at her lover. He leaned over, took her in his arms, drew her head against his chest, put his lips against her hair.

'Tell me about it.'

Patricia told him. The tears she had been withholding came in a scalding torrent and soaked his shirt. He rocked her like a child.

When she could cry no more, Patricia wiped her eyes with the proffered handkerchief. 'I've put mascara on your shirt!'

He looked down at the dark smudges on his shirt front. 'Do it all the good in the world.'

He asked her then to have dinner, but she saw the exhaustion in his face.

'No. I'm going to drop you off. You look done in and I have to go home.'

'See you tomorrow then?'

'Yes. Tomorrow.'

On the following day, Paddy told her that he would be leaving Ireland at the end of the month.

'The work I came for is done. The company here can manage without me. I can't justify my existence here any longer.' Patricia stared at him, dry eyed, aware that this had been coming but, now that it had, feeling like someone who had had the carpet pulled out from under them.

'I see.'

'Trust me. We'll be together often, here or, if you can get away, in London or wherever. Anyway we'll have Paris in September . . . That's still on, isn't it?'

'Yes . . . What choice do I have but to see you if I can?' she said in a low voice. 'I'm not free where you're concerned. You know that!'

A shadow crossed his face; his eyes registered silent disquiet. He's afraid that love will burden him, she thought wearily. God, do we have to play games for ever?

'I'm joking, Paddy. There's forty-five men all expiring for love of me. You'll be bloody lucky if I go to Paris! If you're not careful I'll clear off with one of Gerry's cronies to some love nest or other in the South Seas!'

'Think he'd have you – the crony?'

She laughed. 'Think I'd have him?'

A few days later she dropped the box of papers into Joan at the office. She had gone through them, found a bank deposit book and a building-society book, each containing a little over four thousand pounds.

Joan produced the Will and told her she was the sole beneficiary and that she, Joan, was executrix.

'That's the way she wanted it,' Joan said, half apologetically. 'I suggested that she make you executrix, but she said that if she did, Gerry would insist on acting for you!'

Patricia nodded. 'She didn't want Gerry involved in her affairs! She never took to him.'

When she went home she told Gerry that she had been to see Joan.

'How much is in the estate?'

'About eight thousand.'

'What! Is that all?'

'I think so. Being of sane mind she must have spent it all while she was alive!'

Gerry did not smile at the attempted levity. He looked thunderstruck. 'But the money from the sale of Brierly . . . what happened to it?'

Patricia shrugged. 'It could have been anything . . . Fast men and slow horses, for all I know! There's no sign of it among her papers! Maybe she gave it to charity,' she added slyly. 'She knew, after all, that I had married well, that I was well settled!'

Gerry looked furious. Privately Patricia did wonder what had happened to the money. Her mother liked to travel and lived comfortably on the pension her father had provided, but that did not explain the missing thousands. Lurking beneath her surprise was a sense of let-down, a sense that whatever half-formed plans she had made for the future would have to be shelved.

Joan sat with David. He was semi-comatose as he had been since morning.

The little room was impersonal, half dark, with green and white curtains and a view across a bare and soggy stretch of ground to another wing of the new hospital. The faceless bulk of the modern building seen through the window reminded her of photographs of apartment blocks in Siberia: functional, austere, inhuman. The evening was drawing in and it was raining. The rain collected in little pools and the ripples from the raindrops opened in perfect circles, widened and died. The drops pattered against the window on the sudden bluster of wind.

Paul stared out the window in silence. The boy's face was pale; he had got thin, his upper arms losing flesh, his shoulder-blades becoming prominent.

The Intermediate was in progress and he had a day off between exams, but had insisted on being with his father. It was difficult to get him to eat.

'I don't care any more, Mum. I don't give a frig about the

202

exam.' His voice broke. 'I just want my Dad!'

Joan held David's hand, felt with her index finger the fluttering of his pulse. The drip shivered as another drop was released into the tube and slunk silently down to his vein.

David stirred, opened his eyes, looked at his family and smiled.

'Happy Birthday, Dad!' Paul said, and rushed to hand him a card showing a picture of three bears and some ribald verse.

'Happy Birthday, darling,' Joan said.

'How are you feeling?'

'I'm right as rain,' he said in an unexpectedly coherent voice. 'That damned anaesthetic knocked the stuffing out of me! Can you tell me what's wrong? Will I survive or should you just dig a hole?'

Joan looked at her son. She thought of the interview with the surgeon.

'Why didn't they discover this in St Vincent's?' she had asked him.

'Quite honestly, Mrs de Barra – I haven't the faintest idea!'

'What are his chances?'

'He has a good chance. We'll start his X-ray treatment on Monday.'

Now David narrowed his eyes as he watched his wife's face. 'It's all right Joan . . . I know. I know I have cancer.'

He reached for her hand and Paul's. 'And I know something else . . . I'll make it!'

Joan sought his face for evidence of fear or bluster. There was none.

David lay back and looked at the ceiling. 'I had the oddest dream . . .'

Joan's face closed. She turned to her son who was sobbing, held him in her arms. 'It's all right! The surgeon says Dad has a very good chance of complete recovery.'

David met her eyes. 'He didn't say that, Joan, but it's true all the same. And it isn't a chance, it's a certainty!'

Paul's sobbing became uncontrollable. He pushed his mother away and turned back to the window. Joan sat rigidly, holding on to the torrent of her own tears.

'Paul,' David's voice said sternly, 'your mother has carried all of this alone. Have you no comfort for her, or is everything about how you feel?'

Paul's sobs quietened. He approached his mother and embraced her gently.

'Damion came to me early this morning!' David whispered. 'He told me about the cancer; he told me I'd make it!'

He looked into his wife's face, saw the horror and disbelief. 'He has forgiven me!'

Joan turned from him. I can't stand any more of this, she thought. Aloud she said: 'Will you excuse me for a minute?' She turned to her son. 'Look after your father.'

Joan walked down the corridor, around the hospital, looked in at wards and rooms, saw the trolleys being taken to theatre, smelt the hospital smell of order and disinfectant and peril. Her mind was almost a blank, the movement of her feet on the rubber corridors a therapy. In a half-formed kind of way she wondered if David were mad. It dawned on her that she had never really known, much less understood, the mystical side of him; that in some ways he inhabited a set of perspectives as foreign to her as the dark side of the moon.

When she returned to his room she met the ward sister in the corridor. The sister drew her aside.

'Mrs de Barra,' she said in a reproving voice. 'I know you're very concerned about your husband, but it's not a good idea to be with him at night. It's against regulations and besides, he needs his sleep!'

Joan stared at her. 'What do you mean?'

'I'm talking about last night!'

Joan scanned the night before, remembered collecting Paul and taking him home, comforting him. 'Who was with my husband last night?'

The sister looked surprised, as though to say – wasn't it you? She raised her shoulders. 'Well, early this morning. Someone left his room just before dawn.'

'Did you see his face?' Joan whispered after a moment.

'It was one of the night nurses who saw this person. The visitor was wearing a dark cloak. The nurse followed – but when she turned the corner, the individual concerned was gone!'

Joan came back and sat by David. He had been talking to Paul and the latter looked more cheerful, his face stained where he had wiped away the tears and he was now laughing jerkily at something his father had said.

204

David closed his eyes. But Joan was upset and unable to contain her turmoil. 'Who was he?' she demanded. 'Your night-time visitor?'

David opened his eyes and looked at her. Her eyes were starting and her face was set. Gradually his own assumed a mask of irritation. 'For heaven's sake, Joan!' he whispered almost contemptuously, 'don't be so bloody bourgeois in your thought processes; why not step back a bit from the morons who populate the planet! Alternatively, you can always rush off and pray about it. Or – seeing that it's your favourite time for important disclosures – talk to me again when you think I am asleep.'

Joan stared at him, met dark, objective, unforgiving eyes. She looked away and when she glanced at him again he seemed to have slipped into sleep.

He will live, she thought, feeling the recumbent power in him. He will live, but everything will change. She felt a kind of terror; the landscape she thought she knew so well was alien; the one human being in the whole world for whom she would have sold her soul was becoming a stranger.

He will live, and I will fade. The law, the years of unremitting toil, have desiccated the heart and soul in me. He feels the emptiness in me. What else can he do but move away? Why should he be wasted on someone without vision or artistry? We have made the mistake of finally discovering each other.

Chapter Seventeen

What is love? A leap of generosity? Thank you, Paddy, for the generosity!

from *The Horse's Ears*, 1990

September 1990

Paris! Patricia saw it down below her as the plane swooped over Charles de Gaulle. The Boeing 707 landed with a bump and a roar of reversing engines and, in ten minutes, having followed the crowd down several escalators, she was standing by the baggage reclaim, waiting for the conveyor belt to disgorge her suitcase. She put it on her trolley with her overcoat and steered it towards the exit. Through the glass barrier she saw Paddy waiting, smiling in at her with his quizzical smile, his hands clasped behind his back.

They barely kissed; the slightest peck and then he had taken her case and steered her outside to where he had parked his car. Once seated within he hugged her to him.

'I was afraid for a while that there had been a hitch!'

'The flight was delayed for half an hour in Dublin,' Patricia said with a chuckle of relief, touched by the passion of her reception, by the unfeigned delight. What a half-wit she would have felt if there had been no Paddy! It had been churning in her mind during the flight. What if he couldn't come or had forgotten or had changed his mind? She smiled, caressed his face.

'You look wonderful.'

'And you look beautiful.' He leaned back to look at her. 'Elegant, as always!'

'Thank you.'

Paddy gave a deep, happy sigh. 'It's there again!'

'What is?'

207

'The feeling that everything essential is within reach!' He lifted her hand to his lips. He started the car and they moved into the mainstream of traffic.

Patricia looked around her at suburbia, struck by the atmosphere, by the advertisements, strained to translate the French on signposts and billboards as she passed them by. She was happy, hoarding the bliss. She was seduced by the sense that she was where she belonged, that she belonged with Paddy and he with her; she built a personal fantasy, rested in it, blocked any intrusive hint of a reckoning.

Paddy concentrated on driving. As they drove they passed a semi-derelict building on the opposite side of a railway track; he said in a dead-pan voice: 'Your flat is over there . . . No windows – I'm sure you don't mind!'

She glanced at him, saw the effort to keep his face straight, pinched his thigh. ''Course I don't; I love the fresh air.'

'Ouch . . .'

They came into the city centre, crossed the river. Paddy drove with careful panache, at home with left-hand drive. The traffic flowed quickly, despite the busy day. She saw Notre-Dame looming ahead of them – flying buttresses, gargoyles like petrified evil spells; the stone bridge, the Quai d'Orsay with its booksellers. It was warm and sunny; the tall buildings with shutters and attic windows were redolent of perspectives foreign to the ones she had been used to, whispered of values to do with passion and privacy.

'We're nearly there,' Paddy said. He turned left, drove a few hundred yards and parked the car. Then he pointed back down the street to a window on the second floor of a building.

'There it is. Your little apartment on the Left Bank!' Patricia stared up at the window with the open dusty shutters and the off-white curtains.

'Jesus, I don't believe any of this,' she told herself as she got out of the car.

The city sang with traffic. On the other side of the street a woman with a baguette, wrapped around its middle with a piece of paper, stood in conversation with a man. They parted with cheery goodbyes.

'*A bientôt, madame*' the man said, and the woman answered him with unselfconscious flirtatiousness, turning to glance at Patricia as she crossed the street, Patricia met her eyes, realized that she was looking at her suit, the navy linen suit with the red belt, and that she approved. She followed Paddy, who had collected her case from the boot and who was heading across the street towards a dark green door.

Paddy pressed a button. There was a loud, raucous buzz; the heavy door opened into the narrow hallway. She followed him up a semi-spiral staircase, wooden steps worn in the middle, to a small landing and another dark green door which he opened with a set of keys. She found herself in a tiled living room, furnished with a couch and two easy chairs, a round table and four dining chairs, a television, a small desk in the corner, a bookshelf containing an assortment of items including some books and a potted plant. There were two windows and she went to one immediately and looked out at the street below, at the buildings opposite with their shutters and wrought-iron balaconies. This was Paris; she had a flat in Paris! It was like something out of a novel, the scarlet woman with the love nest. Part of her wanted to laugh out loud at such nonsense; part of her was high on the romance of it all.

'It's charming,' she said, turning to him and raising her hands, turning up the palms. 'It's just that I simply don't believe it!'

He dropped her case, seized her, kissed her. 'I can't believe it either.'

His lips were strong and warm; she was surrounded by his breath, by the taste of his mouth, by the sudden surge of desire. When he released her he said, 'I have to go. I thought I would take the afternoon off, but there's a meeting I have to attend. I'll be back around four and we'll have the rest of the day. I'm sorry for going like this on your first day, but it can't be helped! Am I forgiven?'

He had his head slightly to one side, eyes questioning, sure of her response.

'I forgive you,' Patricia said, concealing the disappointment which had suddenly dissipated the high sense of romance. He moved past her to open the windows and the noise of the city came flooding in.

At the doorway he smiled back at her, pouted his lips in a kiss, and then the door shut. She heard him speak to someone he met on the stairs.

'Bonjour, madame . . .', 'Bonjour, monsieur', and then his footsteps receded rapidly down until she heard the street door clunk to behind him. She watched him from the window cross the street to the car, and he looked back, waved up at her like a boy, and was gone.

Patricia looked around the flat. The kitchen was off the sitting room. It overlooked a small interior courtyard where a woman with short grey hair was seated in a sunny corner with a book. Patricia opened the window and leaned forward to get a better look into the courtyard, and the woman glanced up, saw her. Patricia smiled down. After a moment's hesitation, the woman smiled back, a smile full of charm and humour.

To the left was the bedroom, a room with raffia-covered walls, old nineteenth-century prints, calendar, bamboo table, double bed, steps to narrow bathroom. Geraniums were blazing on the windowsill. The ceiling throughout was white, the floor covered in cardinal red tiles.

She unpacked her case, hung up her clothes in the built-in wardrobe. The bed had already been made; Paddy had come to do it the evening before, something she found touching. She took the keys from the table where he had left them and let herself out, locking the door. The autumn heat of the city met her as she left the building, wrapped her up in it. She walked around the block and down the Rue d'Ecole, past the brasseries and cafés. She saw the way the men looked at her as she passed, their glances washing over her with a curious, impersonal vigour.

She stopped for a coffee, sat alone at a small round table, looking out on the busy street where the traffic flowed without snarling. She thought of Dublin only briefly; they would manage without her. There was an extraordinary sense of freedom, of release in being away from the family; a sense that she had become a person instead of a domestic appendage, that she had walked into some real, personal identity.

Her thoughts reverted to her flat with the red tiles. Paddy would come at four and they would spend the rest of the day together, spend the night together, make love several times. He had told her that Susan was in London, that she would not be coming to Paris until Monday. They would have the whole weekend together.

I have embraced this interlude, Patricia thought; there is no point in being coy. I have spent my life trying to cope with either half measures or no measures at all. I am harming no one. This time, this little bit of space, belongs to me.

210

She came back to the flat at three. It was good to reach the safety of the cool hall downstairs, to let herself in. She had been lost briefly, without a map, couldn't even remember the name of the street where she now lived, had found it because she remembered an unusual signpost over a vintner's shop, had berated herself, as the panic subsided, for her idiocy.

As she entered the building she met the woman she had earlier seen in the courtyard, who was on her way out.

'*Bonjour, madame,*' the woman said to her.

'*Bonjour,*' Patricia returned awkwardly.

'You are English?' the woman asked with a smile.

'No, Irish.'

'I hope you have a happy stay in Paris!'

'Thank you.'

The woman went out, the door shut behind her with a clap. Patricia went upstairs to the flat, struggled with the key, slipped off her shoes to feel the welcome coolness of the tiles. Then she went to the bathroom and showered, sprayed herself with Armani, and went back to the bedroom. She put on the negligée she had bought in London the year before, a black lace affair which showed off her breasts, white translucent skin against the dark lace. She had bought in fit of romanticism and never worn it. What would Gerry have said, after all? He might have raised his eyebrows for an instant and then she would have reverted to invisibility. Or he might have been inflamed by sudden desire and quickly gone about assuaging it. Either way he would not have paused to indulge in the delicacy of courtship, to acknowledge in any way the power of her womanhood. Any of that would be weakness. It would take from him, it would do her too much honour; and it might upset, for a moment, the balance of power.

She glanced at the books in the shelf, took out the last one because of its strange title – *Requiem pour la Vie* – lay back with it on the bed, leafing through the pages, unable to concentrate properly, tense with anticipation, high with excitement.

I have arrived, Patricia thought. I have taken possession of this little flat, have tasted the city. It is quite hot out there but here it is cool and dim and I am alone. She threw her arm back against the pillows; the black lacy sleeve rode up; the flesh was white, the skin on the underside very soft. She brought her wrist to her nose to inhale the Armani, lay back luxuriously. She heard voices in the flat above, French, terrible speed, child complaining, angry, stressed mother. In an attempt to ape some kind of normality, she went to look for her English-French dictionary, brought it back to the bed and began to read. She looked up the occasional key word when she was stuck; but mostly she soldiered on, letting the sense of the story inform her, calling on what she remembered of her school French. But her mind wandered, to the bed, the dark brown bedspread, to her legs, white and bare. She wriggled her toes. The toenails were painted in pale pink varnish.

She ran her hand through her hair, felt the silken texture of the freshly washed strands, thousands of them, curling stubbornly. There was pleasure in the feel of them.

This is the new Patricia, she thought, who is waiting for her lover, who has given herself up to sensuality. He'll be here soon. I know him, the old Paddy, and the new, the owner of so much acquired ruthlessness and inexorable work ethic. His hair is still thick, although now it is tinged with grey; his smile is the same although there are lines around his eyes. I know his body. I know many things about him and me. I know the springs of our life, the roots, back to the roots.

The doorbell rang at ten to four; she called out happily 'Who is it?', heard his voice, hopped out of bed and opened the door to him. She knew he had a key, was pleased at his delicacy in not using it.

He stared at her; his eyes, which took in her negligée, her décolletage, her bare feet, were full of surprised desire. He shut the door behind him.

Does he think me a strap, Patricia wondered, experiencing a sudden stab of insecurity, to greet him like this?

'I had a shower,' she said in explanation.

'I'm going to have one too before I touch you.'

He came to her from the bathroom, naked, his bare feet leaving damp patches on the tiles. She lay still, watching him. He paused at the window, drew the curtains; the heavy buff-coloured cloth muted the sunlight, made the room dim and secret. Neither of them spoke, but they smiled diffidently at each other as he lifted the sheet and got in beside her. The bed creaked; he was cool and still damp from the shower. He undid the black satin belt of her negligée, pulled it back. His hands moved over her, down her back, over her belly, over her breasts.

212

'Beautiful, beautiful. Christ, Patricia, you were always beautiful.'

Outside the roar of traffic went on. There was the non-stop tooting of horns, the roar of a motorbike as it turned the corner.

Patricia felt the tension leave her. He moved his head to her breast, his mouth to her nipples, blindly, like a child. She felt the thrust of his penis against her legs, warm and erect, possessing its own life. After a moment she pushed him away, sat up, threw back the sheet.

'Lie still,' she whispered, 'I want to look at you.'

He lay on his back. She squatted over his body, studying it, loving it with her eyes and her touch. She pushed the arms he moved to caress her to his sides.

'Lie still. Close your eyes.'

He smiled behind his closed eyes, was still.

His stomach was full from good living; below it his penis stood proud and eager, blue veined, silken to the touch. It moved under her fingers in salute.

'Don't move!' she whispered, letting her lips touch him slowly.

My body knows what to do, knows how to love this man. It has always known; I do not even have to think. I will love him so that he never forgets; so that he will remember for ever. Every inch of him will remember.

Eventually, afraid of losing control, he pulled her to him suddenly, kissed her, here, there, wildly. She saw, through her lashes, the dazed expression at his eyes and mouth, saw him bend his head over her. Then his weight descended, pinning her. She felt the release, the pleasure at penetration, the serenity in the midst of desire.

The day faded. There was silence everywhere, as though the city had vanished and Time had died and then, after a little while, a man cried out in guttural joy as though he too had died and been reborn.

'Is he, or was he, a good lover?' Paddy asked her later, a little diffidently. He still had the washed, startled look of one who had been awakened from trance.

'Who?'

'Gerry. Your husband.'

'Dear God – what a question!'

She gave a half laugh, threw back her hair. She was high with euphoria, with the high-powered sense of well-being and knowledge of self that Paddy had brought her. They had left the flat some two hours earlier, had gone for a walk by the river, wandered hand in hand through the Ile Saint-Louis and the Ile de la Cité, enjoying the river and the floodlit Notre-Dame. Now they were back on the Left Bank in a pavement café.

Her eyes followed the crowds going by on the Boulevard Saint-Germain; droves of people, mostly young, students from the Sorbonne. They streamed down the street, down the Boulevard Saint-Michel, children almost, arm in arm, laughing, kissing. Across the street, behind its railings and among a few trees, were the floodlit ruins of Cluny.

'We don't have lovers in Ireland!' Patricia said primly.

'Don't be silly'.

Patricia sighed. Paris was a foil. Measured against Paris, Ireland was full of fear; fear and denial of the power between women and men.

Her eyes clouded. 'I'm not being silly. Ireland is full of some kind of male triumphalism; women can't compete against it. I know that sounds awful, but it's true and it doesn't leave much room for lovers. How can you love a minus quantity? In Ireland men think women owe them something! Rapists walk free from courts; religious fundamentalism informs the institutions of state. Misogyny and presumption are ruling precepts . . .'

She lit a cigarette, a Gauloise; she seldom smoked, but she wanted one now. The razor-harsh smoke burned her throat, calming her with its astringency.

Paddy was silent. It can't be that bad, his silence seemed to say. Patricia wondered if she had shocked him. After all, he was an émigré, with romantic notions of the homeland. But it was his exile that had made him a romantic. If she shocked him would he turn from her? If she spoke of the things that burned her, would he turn away? Was she about to ruin everything by being serious?

'And it's different here?' he asked after a moment.

'I feel it is. Maybe it has something to do with France having escaped puritanism. I get the feeling that here men and women know they belong to the same species!' She shrugged, smiled. 'They seem happier here, at all events.'

He gave a sudden, short laugh. 'On the contrary – the French know that happiness does not exist. They opt instead for pleasure, which does!'

214

She blew smoke delicately, watched it curl in the light from the café, glanced at his face, interpreting his remark. Cynicism? Bitterness?

'I'm sorry,' she whispered when she saw his expression. 'I shouldn't preach at you. I love you desperately and I hate the vulnerability of it. But I am neither cold nor cynical nor embittered in any cause.'

He smiled, took her hand, looked into her eyes. 'I know you're not, Patricia. It's my fault; I shouldn't have asked. It's none of my business.'

'You can ask what you like; you're my first lover. Does that answer the question?'

She could see from his face that he doubted this intelligence. He gave a small, indulgent smile. 'But you have been married for years. You must have got something from it . . . You have children; it takes two to make them . . .'

'I could have forty children for all the difference it would make. All you need to make babies is a mate. And a mate,' she added slowly, with a sudden arch laugh, 'is not the same thing as a lover. I know whereof I speak!'

He smiled, sat back, raised silent eyebrows. Then he said, 'And you are very angry.'

'Probably. At me more than events. It's my own fault, the "haughty spirit that goeth before destruction", and all that sort of thing. When you and I split up, when you married Susan, I clutched like the drowning person at straws. Gerry was a straw. He is a solid, hard-working man and might have made someone else a good husband, someone who had no personal or emotional requirements. But as for me . . .'

'Ah; but I'm sure he loves you all the same,' he responded with uneasy raillery in an attempt to divert the trend of the conversation, which he found uncomfortable. 'Men love spirit. And you have plenty of that!'

'Do they?' Patricia mused for a moment on the response. Was he saying that everything was all right if Gerry loved her? 'I suppose it depends on the man. In Gerry's case he has stationed an angel with a fiery sword to stand guard over his emotions. It is his one religion; he must never betray anything that could be construed as a human feeling; tenderness or love would annihilate him. So he remains inviolate, unfit for life, and so, perforce, do I.'

215

'Not perforce.'

Patricia looked at him for a long moment, smiled. 'No,' she said softly. 'Not perforce.'

'Are you hungry?' he asked, leaning towards her with a conspiratorial air. 'We could go somewhere nice. I know a superb restaurant in the Avenue de la Bourdonnais.'

'No. I'm not hungry.'

'Are you tired then?' he asked after a moment while the corners of his mouth smiled. 'Would you like to lie down and rest?'

'I would very much like to lie down,' Patricia said gravely. 'But I am not really interested in having a rest.'

He laughed, signalled to the waiter for the bill. She ground out the half-smoked Gauloise in her saucer.

They made love. The flat was half dark, the light coming from the street, the sound of French voices wafting on the air; laughter, animated snippets of conversation.

I have never known such happiness, Patricia thought. Remember this, remember the quality of this, the contact, the heightened awareness of the whole persona, the sense of being set free. It does not even require sexual climax, though that would be perfect. And it will come. It will come.

Afterwards they dozed and talked and cuddled up.

Towards midnight, Paddy reached for his watch, turned on the small bedside light. He sighed, leaned over, kissed her cheek. 'Forgive me sweetheart. I have to go.'

Patricia, who had been half in and half out of sleep in a state of delicious languor, stared at him, sat up, pulled the sheet up under her chin.

'I thought you said Susan was in England.'

'She is. But she may phone.'

Patricia did not reply. She gave him a small smile, nodded. 'Of course!'

Paddy dressed quickly. 'I'll see you tomorrow. You are formidable . . . I wish things were otherwise; I love you – you know that?'

Patricia smiled again, picked up the book she had been reading earlier.

'Don't forget to lock the door,' he said as he blew a kiss at her from the bedroom door.

'I won't,' Patricia answered quietly. 'Of course I won't.' When he was gone she said to herself out loud:

'He leaves our warm bed, where we have shared what we have shared, because a woman he does not love might phone! If I can understand that, perhaps I will succeed in understanding men.' Inside her head a voice, coldly dismissive, whispered that love was action, but that words were cheap.

But next morning, Saturday, when she visited Notre-Dame and walked in the quiet, candlelit atmosphere, she was seized by a sudden impulse and, turning at a candle-stand to face the flickering mini-flames, put ten francs into the box and selected a tall white taper.

'This,' she said silently and defiantly to the statue of the Virgin as she lit it, 'is for Paddy and me.'

She returned to the apartment in buoyant mood, only to meet the woman of yesterday in the hall.

'Hello.'

'Good morning. I love your city.'

The woman laughed, a startled tinkle of surprise, answered in perfect English, 'You don't have to live here!'

Patricia launched into her impression of Paris; the French woman smiled indulgently at the compliments. 'Have you not been here before?'

'Years and years ago for a few days. But I never really savoured it. I love having my own little place!'

'Come and have a cup of coffee with me and I'll tell you where to shop. You can pay a fortune on clothes here if you're not careful!'

Patricia followed the woman to her apartment, which was on the ground floor on the other side of the courtyard. Like her own, the floor was tiled, but it had an old oriental carpet and the white walls were covered in paintings. There were books everywhere.

'Where did you learn your perfect English?' Patricia asked from the depths of a tapestry-covered armchair.

'You're being kind! It's not perfect. But I used to teach French in London once. I was there for three years.'

Patricia looked around. There were potted plants and trailing greeneries and a huge gilt-framed mirror over the fireplace. The smell of fresh coffee wafted from the kitchen and her hostess emerged with a tray, placed it on the coffee table. She smiled at her guest.

217

'We should introduce ourselves. My name is Jeanine Remion.'

'Patricia Galligan.'

They talked about Ireland while they drank the coffee. Jeanine had been to Connemara, which she had loved. She was divorced and had a daughter who was married and living in Lyon. She hunched up her shoulders, spread out her palms. 'It's better to be divorced than fighting! Don't you agree?'

Patricia told her about life in Dublin, about her own husband and two children and then Jeanine asked, 'Is your husband going to join you?'

Patricia blushed to the roots of her hair. 'No. I'm on my own!'

'I see . . .' Jeanine smiled slowly, like someone who finally understood. 'Paris is a good place for lovers!' She laughed kindly, watching her guest's embarrassment. 'You blush like a girl.'

Patricia gave an embarrassed laugh, changed the subject, spoke of her desire to learn French properly. After a few minutes she looked at her watch. 'I'd better go. I'm expecting someone!'

Jeanine smiled, rose and went with her to the door. 'I hope your lover deserves you!' she said gravely, eyes twinkling.

Paddy came at midday.

'Come on. I'm taking you to Versailles, young woman.' He breezed in the door, filling the flat with his size and his life.

'Oh, Paddy . . . I went for a great walk, visited Notre-Dame, and when I came back I had coffee with a neighbour, Jeanine something or other.'

'Where does she live?'

'Just there, across the courtyard,' and she drew him to the kitchen window to show him. 'She said she hopes my lover deserves me!'

Paddy laughed. 'He doesn't deserve you,' he said, looking down at her. 'And if I find him I'll break his head!'

'Oh Paddy!'

They drove to Versailles; walked around the gardens, visited the two Trianons, kissed fiercely by the little Temple of Love, joined a group and were shown around the château. Patricia looked at herself in the Hall of Mirrors, thought of the luckless Marie-Antoinette gazing back at her sixteen-year-old reflection; thought of the Sun King getting up and going to bed and never a moment

218

of privacy, except those he stole; and he must have stolen plenty, she mused, as she gazed at his portrait and saw the dissipation and depravity in his face. Poor little Antoinette was long after him, the victim of politics, caught in the grinding machinery of court etiquette and intrique. And there would have been the jealousies and hatreds and politicking, while beyond the walls of Versailles the whole country seethed with the resentment and suffering so soon to explode.

Paddy watched her reactions, seemed delighted in her pleasure.

'You have a vivid imagination!' he told her, when she tried to get him to join in her reconstruction.

'Indeed I don't. But I do love history.'

They had lunch in the town of Versailles and then went back to Paris where they visited the Musée d'Orsay. Afterwards Paddy took her on a trip in a *bateau-mouche*. They dined on board while they were swept around the islands on the Seine, looking up at bridges and great floodlit buildings. A harpist played throughout the journey, soft melodies on a huge Irish harp.

Patricia refused wine, found the food delicious, gave herself to the pleasure of this cruise in this company. Paddy leaned over to kiss her several times. He drank a little too much.

'You are the woman I want. I can go anywhere, do anything with you.'

Patricia leaned towards him and asked suddenly, dropping her voice, 'How did we manage to lose each other? Were you so very angry with me for being angry with you?' Her eyes filled with sudden tears at the sense of the irredeemable loss. 'I think we would have made a go of things, Paddy!'

Paddy was silent for a moment. He looked straight ahead. 'I had to marry her, Pat. She was pregnant!' He put down his fork and took her hand in silent apology.

'Did she phone you last night?' Patricia asked after a moment, steeling her voice into nonchalance.

'No.'

When they were disembarking, Patricia walked up the carpeted gangplank behind Paddy; as she turned for a moment to look back into the boat, she saw a face she knew, recognizing it with a start and a horrible sense of foreboding. It was John Millar, and he had seen her, was nodding at her and at Paddy's back, his face creased in a half-suppressed smirk.

When they were outside she said to Paddy, 'Take me home immediately.'

Paddy, thinking she was feeling ill, hurried her to the car, opened the door. When they were en route she said, 'I saw that John Millar on the boat . . . he must have been sitting at the back. He knows Gerry, you know. He invited him home once, some weeks after you left Ireland. I was so embarrassed. But he didn't say anything, although he was insultingly familiar when Gerry was out of the room, asking me about you and grinning. I was afraid he would come and talk to us just now, that's why I made you hurry!'

Paddy was silent for a moment. 'He did tell me once that he would be visiting Paris with his wife in September. Did he recognize you?'

'Of course he did.'

'You're not worried about it, are you? He won't say anything. Men are discreet about these things!'

'Are they indeed?'

She lapsed back into silence. Inside her head she still heard his words – 'I had to marry her, Pat; she was pregnant.' While in her mind's eye she saw only the knowing leer of John Millar. She felt like someone who had undertaken a brave swim, but found the water colder and more treacherous than she had ever imagined. Paddy escorted her upstairs to the flat.

'I need to be alone tonight, Paddy. I hope you don't mind!' He nodded, sighed, looked at her with troubled eyes. He moved to kiss her, but she turned aside. He raised his hands in acceptance. She closed the door behind him and heard his steps retreating down the wooden stairs.

From the window she watched his tall form cross the road to the car. He looked up at the window but she stood behind the curtain and he could not see her.

She sat in a chair in the dark. 'Stop caring so much!' she whispered to herself. 'It's gone; it's in the past; it was another life! What matters is now. Enjoy the now!'

But she knew that 'the now' could be divorced neither from the past nor from the future. It depended on both for its meaning and its life.

She went into the kitchen, glanced out the window. There was a light on in Jeanine's flat. The curtains were not drawn and she saw that she was entertaining. She imagined Paddy in his car, halfway home to his wife's apartment in the shadow of the golden dome of Les Invalides. She thought of Gerry and the children in Dublin, who almost certainly hardly gave her a thought. She thought of herself, alone and foolishly vulnerable in a strange city where she didn't know a soul.

An intensity of loneliness overwhelmed her. She felt like a small misplaced marine creature, peering from under a rock on the ocean floor, while around her the sea boiled with purpose. She was outside that purpose. Since the day she married she had tried to fill a role she had not invented; one to which she was not even suited. And by coming to Paris to be with Paddy, she had precipitated herself into a situation which was really only viable for a strong woman with an independent base. The strong independent woman would be identified as a free moral agent who seized some time to be with her lover. The dependent woman, without economic clout of her own, would be identified as the mistress, the whore, the slut.

Resentment gathered in her. I could go home tomorrow, she thought. All I have to do is phone the airport and change the reservation. And then she thought of her reversion to invisibility, to her status as domestic football. She thought of Gerry's sarcasm, Simon's aggression, Orla's touchiness.

'But I don't want to go home!' she whispered out loud.

'I want to live and I want to be free!'

Paddy drove home, parked the car and let himself into the spacious tiled foyer of the apartment block. His mind was full of Patricia, of her face as she said goodnight, as she turned from his kiss. The day which had started out so well had ended in a taste of ashes. The day before had been incredible, soared to heights he had seldom known.

He was uneasy about her. She did not fit the usual pattern of an affair. Although she was the mother of two children, she possessed a pristine quality, as though she had never been touched. 'You're my first lover,' she had said. Could such a thing be possible, in this day and age? What kind of a fool was she married to? He knew that in her he had found his youth, where he had left it twenty-one years before. The exhilaration of it was novel, but there could be no future, not now. He would not tell her that. He knew what she hoped; he could feel the undertow of it.

He was halfway through his life and he was weary. He felt that he had lived too hard to have anything left of passionate speculation, that in the realm of love as elsewhere he knew the score, the relish of the first contact, the gradual ennui, the eventual reluctant claustrophobia. For years he had taken pleasure where he could, easily. He was good at love; women felt his sensuality, his audacity. It addressed their own. What he loved about women was their difference, the promise of the new and the deliciously secret. What he hated about women was their vulnerability, their humanity, their mortality. He wanted a woman who would pose a perpetual challenge, who would maintain the mystery, the freshness of her difference, the delicious piquancy of her initial, impersonal curiosity.

And before she had given of herself, there was always the even more delicious challenge of the chase.

With Pat it was different. At first he had just wanted to prove something, to revisit his youth, to see if she was still as he remembered, to find out if she found him attractive, to lay the shade of her memory. And if the renewed relationship were to lead somewhere – well and good. Provided it didn't become heavy or difficult or demanding.

But it wasn't working out the way he had planned. He thought of her more and more in a way which troubled him; he had lost his peace as he had lost it long before. He struggled with the unwelcome reality. It was just an interlude, he told himself. She would be going home soon and they would seldom see each other again.

He let himself into the empty apartment. The family photographs stared back at him from the mantelpiece in the salon, Susan with Guy, their eldest child. Guy and his sister Michelle. He and Susan by the fountain in the Place de la Concorde on their fifth wedding anniversary.

He drank a glass of water in the pristine kitchen. He tried to focus on the problems facing him on Monday: the board meeting, the preparation he had done for it. But the only thing he could think of was Pat's face, the curve of her body, the contained sense of pain. He shouldn't have told her that he had got Susan pregnant. He was a fool to have told her; he had put salt in old wounds. The sense of Pat's vitality, the force she carried under so much effort to contain it, to make it decent, the intensity of their lovemaking, came to him in a mélange of emotions. He wanted to be free of it, so that he could indeed be free; but he wanted also

222

to be with her and talk to her and make love with her until he died. In her he found the gateway to himself. The prospect of the night without her suddenly seemed intolerable.

He reached for the phone.

She jumped when the telephone bleeped and she moved across the half-dark apartment in stockinged feet to pick up the receiver.

'Hello?'

She heard his intake of breath before he spoke. 'I'm sorry, darling; I love you. I hate to hurt you!'

Patricia hesitated before she spoke. 'What's past is past,' she said, knowing that she did not believe it.

'I miss you . . .' he whispered, his voice full of longing. 'Shall I come back? May I come back?'

'Yes,' Patricia whispered. 'Come back; I'm waiting!'

Paddy spent the night. The phone in his apartment shrilled in the early morning, but there was no one there to answer it.

Chapter Eighteen

We are beings of violent emotional power trapped in bodies; exhausted with issues of survival, sold dreams by countless religions.

It is only through life – through love, passion, through sex as their celebration, that women and men find their common humanity, the polarity and power that holds the race together.

It is through sex and love and the compassion born of them that we discover who we are, find our limits, push them back and grow. I know that in this love I would find myself and freedom.

But where will I find this love? Will it come to me, because Fate knows where I am and will not waste me, or should I trawl the world and be misunderstood?

from *The Horse's Ears*, 1988

Wind on the Pont Neuf. End September; 6 p.m. The evening was drawing in; on the pavements and streets the desiccated leaves swirled in lonely spirals. Alcoholics huddled in the bays of the bridge. The city lights shone in the water. The Eiffel Tower, golden in floodlights, was away to the right, and to the left was the ancient Conciergerie with its cruel turrets, more than one hundred and fifty years since it had imprisoned Marie Antoinette. The river was choppy; the *vedettes* – pleasure cruisers by the bridge – seemed scarcely patronized. The city was homeward bound; it had begun to rain.

Patricia walked back from La Samaritaine where she had bought herself a new sweater. On the way she dropped in for a take-away – pork chops for two in a mushroom sauce with a salad to go with it, in a charcuterie in the Rue Dauphine. Earlier she had been in a nearby gallery where they were exhibiting David de

Barra's work. It struck her as bizarre that she should view his work in Paris.

I will buy some of his paintings, she thought, inspecting the strange landscapes, identifying the shadowy figure at the perimeter of some of them as a kind of nemesis, but I will buy from him in Dublin. The prices here are for the birds! Then, with a sense of shock, she saw the picture of Joan, leaning back while a shadowed figure, half phantom, half reality, stooped towards her. She stared at the picture fascinated. It was like seeing someone you knew well transformed on stage, so that you realized you had never known them; that they possessed reaches of energy and purpose you could not have guessed at. Joan looked strangely compelling with the fierceness in her face. This was presumably how David saw her, this woman with her tensile strength, looking up at the looming shadow with a sturdy challenge, like someone pushed against the limits of endurance and holding fast. The power changed her face, made it beautiful. The light caught her hair, danced along it in sparks of fire. Behind her in the painting there was a vast night sky, as though the artist had deliberately measured his subject against some kind of infinity.

He needs and admires her, Patricia thought, touched to the quick. She is the power in the painting and not the strange dark figure. And then she found herself wondering why Joan's face registered so much desperate purpose; what was there in her life with David to provoke it? Or did he provoke it in order to paint it?

She wondered what it meant for him that he was being exhibited in Paris; it must mean that his career was really taking off. And, knowing how Joan loved him, she was glad.

She was about to leave the gallery when she saw David himself. He was standing near the door, deep in conversation with a man whom Patricia assumed was the owner of the gallery. She recognized him with a start; she was sure it was him, although she had only seen him twice. She looked around, wondering if Joan were with him, but there was no sign of her.

What would she say to Joan if she were to suddenly materialize? Tell her she was spending some time in Paris, invite her and David back to the flat? What if they came and Paddy turned up? No, the best thing to do was scuttle away without making contact.

Joan was very much in her mind as she walked back along the Boulevard Saint-Germain to her flat in the Latin Quarter. The crowds had begun to thin already, beckoned by the French family evening, the meal, the television news, friends in for a chat or to share the repast, then an early night.

She compared it with Dublin. There would be rain, sure, and plenty of it. But the day would be beginning. The work over, the evening ahead; the pubs filling. While here in glamorous Paris, even the cafés had begun to lose their pizazz; people sitting behind the windows, the pavement tables empty.

She walked under trees where possible to dodge the rain. In the doorway of the Sorbonne medical school lay an old woman, alcoholic, bottle at the ready, barely out of the wet. Patricia shivered, tried to imagine the woman as a child, running and skipping through summer days. What would she have said then had she been shown the future? How had she come to this?

She turned up the collar of her jacket. She had neither scarf nor umbrella. She could shelter in a doorway and wait for the rain to ease; she could run and get home a bit quicker. But she walked instead, a smart pace, while the rain trickled to the roots of her hair and rolled off on to her shoulders. She imagined the pleasure of the hot bath, the warm bathwrap.

She joined the short queue at the boulangerie near the flat.

'*Une baguette, s'il vous plaît.*'

Why did she buy this bread? Long crisp stick, delightful for that evening, but if you tried to keep some for breakfast it would break your teeth.

Paddy's flight from Marseilles would be getting in to Orly at seven that evening. He would be at the flat by eight. She would be ready, bathed, perfumed. He would take her in his arms; his touch instant chemistry. She would laugh and tell him about her invented triumphs – how she spoke to the *vendeuse* in La Samaritaine and almost understood her when she rattled off the price. She would not show loneliness. She must remain a challenge, conceal vulnerability. They would have a few hours and then he would probably go home.

The interlude in Paris had not been what she had anticipated. The bliss of having time and space to be with Paddy had degenerated into having time and space to be by herself. She was now almost four weeks into her 'holiday', and Paddy seemed to vacillate from an intense contact to a hurtful flippancy, as though he were riding an emotional yo-yo, as though he were struggling with how he should categorize their relationship. She had more or

227

less come to terms with what he had told her on the *bateau-mouche*, that Susan had been pregnant when they married.

Paddy, with diffidence and hesitancy, had explained the circumstances on the evening following their trip on the river. He had, he told her, met Susan at a party given by a mutual friend, another engineering student, while Patricia was away visiting her grandparents in the country. The fruit punch had been well laced with spirits and they had both drunk too much. Afterwards, when· he had taken her home, she had invited him in and there, in her flat, on the couch, they had engendered their eldest child.

'She seduced me. I'm not blaming her. I was . . . vulnerable to seduction at the time, Patricia. Can you understand that?'

Patricia thought of Glendalough with a wild stab of regret. 'If I had been any use I'd have seduced you. But I was scared . . . brainwashed.'

'Our whole generation was brainwashed,' Paddy said. 'Have you any idea what I felt when I realized not only what I had done, but the consequences?'

He ran his hand through his hair in a gesture of fatigue. 'How could I tell you? You were the princess in the ivory tower! You would have been so full of contempt!'

'No I wouldn't,' Patricia whispered. But she knew he spoke the truth.

'Anyway,' Paddy went on, 'the die was cast after that. In a way I blamed you, you know . . .'

'Why?'

'I don't know. I blamed you for being so bloody virginal. I blamed you for clinging like a limpet to Gerry and with such amazing alacrity. I blamed you for not giving me a chance to try to tell you, to make you understand that it made no difference to the way I loved you. But no . . . you were gone. I was dumped, just like that! I heard you laugh as you took Gerry's arm in the main hall in Earlsfort Terrace one day after I had tried to talk to you.'

'There was no mirth in the laugh,' Patricia whispered, remembering the old hurt and anger. 'You hated me!' she added, aghast.

'In a way. When I heard you had married him I did not wish you well. I wished you miserable. I was like the Bad Fairy at the christening, albeit from a distance. I wished you a life of yearning for me, so that you would know what we had lost!' He stared at her, stared her down, ignored her tears.

'There,' he said brutally. 'Now you know the truth!'

After a moment Patricia said, 'You're so unjust! You got married first. I see now that you came back to Dublin for revenge! But you already had it. Years and years of it. Your letters and poems thumbed out of existence. Your face in my dreams! What more do you want from me?' She gestured around at the flat.

'Is this revenge too? To have me here, on your territory, on your terms, as some kind of whore?' She paused, breathing rapidly. 'Is that it? Well, enjoy it; if revenge is sweet, enjoy it! But it is not what I would have expected from you!'

She turned away, made for the door, but Paddy caught her in his arms and took her, struggling, to the bedroom. He pulled her down on the bed forcibly, pinned her with his weight. She tasted his tears in her mouth.

'I'm sorry, I'm sorry . . . It was my fault, Pat, and I can't bear it. That's really what's wrong with me. I can't bear to have made such a dog's dinner of my life!'

Patricia's struggles subsided. 'Are you that miserable?' she asked after a while.

'Sometimes! Sometimes I am that miserable! It's not Susan's fault, it's just that we're such utterly different people with different needs!'

Then she asked a question which she had not meant to ask. 'In that case, why are you so committed to her?'

He rolled over and looked at the ceiling. 'Because I gave my word.' He sighed. 'I gave my word and built a life upon it . . . I abide by my commitments!'

'Was it a life you built on it, or a lie?' Pat demanded with mounting ire. 'And if you abide by your commitments, what the hell are you doing in my bed, in any other woman's bed? Or is it the case that what you are really committed to is appearances, sustaining a sham because your pride is at stake? Because you are attractive and can use other women to prop up your unbearable marriage for you?'

He started angrily. She felt the coldness in him, the withdrawal to his private, internal space. For a moment she thought he would get up and leave.

'I'm sorry,' she said miserably. He did not answer, but after a while he put his hand out in the half darkness and stroked her wet cheek.

229

They did not make love that evening. They stayed side by side, in each other's arms until sleep came. When she woke in the morning Paddy was gone.

After that, Paddy was terribly busy with his work. And Susan came to stay with him in Paris and was installed in their apartment near the Invalides.

Sometimes, on the pretext that he was away for a business meeting, he stayed the night with Patricia in the flat, but he never again alluded to the past. In the main he gave priority to his domestic life, as though he knew he had made his point. Patricia had to admit that this too, lonely as it was, was useful in its way. She toyed with the idea of going home, but was too immersed in the sense of new-found sovereignty to be quick to lose it. The space, the solitude, allowed her to see her own life in focus. She knew she had to make profound changes, but was unable to target what was necessary or to commit herself to any one plan.

She had kept in touch with Dublin, phoned home from time to time, and had spoken to Orla, who asked her questions about Paris and said Daddy was working hard. Orla expressed pleasure at the prospect of going to college. She had been offered a Science place in Belfield, her second choice. She had not got enough points for Law.

'Is Mick still bothering you?'

She could hear Orla's sigh at the other end. 'No, Mummy.'

Simon spoke to her once, Gerry twice. The latter seemed preoccupied, said that everything was all right but asked her with muted sarcasm if she was enjoying herself, indicating that he was overloaded with work and that she had a wonderful life in comparison.

'I'm going on a fishing trip when you come back.'

'Oh – where?'

'Galway!'

'I think that's a good idea! You need a break.'

'Have you had enough of Paris?' Gerry asked sententiously.

'The real question is – has Paris had enough of me!'

But she found herself unable to completely jettison what she had hoped from her relationship with Paddy. Stubbornly she believed in it, despite everything her reason and her common sense could throw at her. It is a reality with a depth I have never known. How can I throw that away? Don't ask me to throw that away! I can't and I won't! The perfect moments are worth the pain!

And yet, in cooler moments, she reminded herself that she was still relatively young and that avenues of endeavour and love were still open to her, that the only power Paddy had over her was the power she gave him herself.

She saw him most evenings for a couple of hours before he went home. This evening, this wet Friday evening in late September, her second last evening, he would be coming to her from the airport; he was in Marseilles on business and his flight would be getting in at seven.

She reached the dark green hall door, keyed in the combination, pressed the button – buzz – pushed the door. The tiled hall was in darkness and she fumbled for the light, then went up the queer wooden stairs with the worn steps. She heard voices, television, in other flats, smells of cooking; someone was making an omelette.

She let herself in, taking off her wet shoes immediately. She had learnt to be very tidy, very fastidious. No one now to 'do' for her.

Her wet jacket was put on the back of a chair. She went into the kitchen, looked out at the dark courtyard, saw the light on in Jeanine's apartment.

She had come to know her quite well; they often had coffee together and had even gone shopping together. She had met her daughter and grandson who had come up from Lyon for a couple of days.

Then she drew the curtains, went to the tube-like bathroom, so small that the bath fitted it exactly and you had to get into it from one end, turned on the taps. While the bath filled she lay on the bed, feeling the tension ooze away from her. It was good to be back, out of the rain, into a safe place like a womb. The phone rang.

'Hello there, darling,' the beloved voice said.

'Hello, Paddy.'

'The bloody flight is delayed. Won't get in until nine. But I'll see you at ten – if that's all right.' She could hear above his voice the noise of people, the hum of other voices, the blurring sound of a public-address system.

'Yes. All right.'

'I'm sorry. I won't be able to make dinner.'

'Pity. Pork chops. They'll keep.'

'Do you still love me?'

'Silly question!'

'See you at ten . . . Have to rush now. Bye.'

She replaced the receiver. Silence. She turned on the transistor radio; 'A Whiter Shade of Pale' filled the room and then the announcer in rapid French introduced the next song. She got into the bath and closed her eyes, stemming the angry sense of let-down. It wasn't his fault. It wasn't his fault. He would be there at ten.

Somewhere above her a woman's voice rose, shrill with stress and anger. She could barely make out the other voice, a male voice, muted. She had never seen this woman but had often heard her, the same shrill, desperate tones filling the evening for a moment.

I will not make love this evening, Patricia promised herself. It's too bloody convenient for him; he comes here for a couple of hours – tonight it will be for only one hour – and then it's back to his wife and I am left feeling like a convenience. Tonight I shall be inscrutable, elusive.

Towards ten she put the door on the latch, put on some music, sat back on the couch with a book. He came, knocking first as he always did, then let himself in. She looked up at him from the couch, smiled, did not move, except to extend her hand.

He bent down, squatted beside her. 'You look beautiful. I'm sorry. It was so frustrating. All I could think of was you, looking just as you do with your hair like that.' He bent his head towards her, buried his face in her hair.

'Would you like some tea?'

'No.'

She moved to let him sit beside her. He looked tired, a little drawn. She felt sudden pity for the endless effort of his life, for the endless meetings, the scurrying between airports. His arms surrounded her, drawing her tightly against him. 'I love you,' he said into her ear. His fingers fumbled for the buttons on her blouse, his hands for the fastening of her bra.

The chemistry was instant; the desire surged from nipple to groin. She forgot all resolutions. He got up, took her by the hand and led her into the bedroom, pulled her on to the bed, undressed her. The lovemaking was feverish; he entered her quickly, ejaculated quickly, and she, her body frustrated and feeling cheated, contained the disappointment.

When she got up to visit the bathroom, he looked at his watch and dressed quickly. 'I have to rush; Susan will be wondering . . .'

Patricia did not reply. When she came out of the bathroom he was putting on his watch. He kissed her.

'I'll see you tomorrow. Three thirty? I'm sorry, but you do understand . . . don't you, darling? Don't forget to lock the door,' he added as he let himself out.

When he was gone, Patricia turned off the music and the lights, locked the door. She turned the pages of a magazine for a while, but without concentration.

Madness, madness, madness.

The anger and sadness blazed, sought some outlet. She knew there was a bottle of wine in the fridge. Paddy had brought two bottles with him a week before when she had cooked him a meal and he had drunk most of one of them. The other was still there. She saw its ruby glow in her mind's eye, could feel it sliding down, the glow, the release, the anaesthesia, the postponed frustration. She went to the fridge, took out the bottle, removed the cork. As she was about to pour she suddenly saw herself, as though she were watching from the corner, a woman hell-bent on self-destruction. Like a child who could not have what it wanted and who held its breath until it turned blue. Rather than face the pain of living she sought any possible escape. How many years would it take her before she too ended up on the steps of some public building, bottle by the neck, a plastic sack to keep off the rain, like the old woman at the Sorbonne?

'Frig this,' she said aloud, and she held up the bottle and brought it down on the edge of the enamelled stone sink with all her strength. The bottle shattered, the enamel was chipped, the wine poured down the sink.

The neck of the bottle split and gashed her hand between thumb and index finger. The blood dripped silently along the side of the sink and down the plug-hole. She smarted at the pain, sucked at the cut, looked around wildly for something to bandage it with, ended up doing the job with lavatory paper.

Paddy drove home. He parked the car and let himself into the apartment. Susan had left the hall light on and he padded quietly to the bedroom, undressed and got into bed. Susan did not move

233

although she muttered sleepily, 'Is that you, Woofie?' He felt the irritation surge in him and he suppressed it. He hated being called 'Woofie'. But the bed was warm and after a few moments he was asleep.

Patricia lay awake for hours; she could hear the non-stop traffic in the Rue d'Ecole. Some students went by singing. Someone moved in the flat above; there was rhythmic pressure on the joists above her head. These old buildings gave everything away. Was it the stressed woman? Was she with her husband or her lover? It was all right to have a lover in Paris.

But for me! she thought. Strange beyond the bizarre! I am driven into this. All those lofty ideals they gave us at school; all the 'don'ts'; they fail the human requirements of life. I want to live; and if living means pain, I will take pain.

She leaned over from the bed and pulled back the curtains, let in the light from the street. Her hand throbbed as she moved the thumb and index finger. The window was open; she wanted to shut it, but it was stiff and she was afraid she would start her hand bleeding again. On the building opposite, which caught the sun all day, the louvred shutters were closed.

How many people lay behind those shutters in sleep, in lovemaking, in conversation, each one in his or her own world?

Her mind dwelt obsessively on Paddy. The pendulum of her emotions had swung down, examining him. She felt that, within the context of his perspective, life was centred on him, and everything else, including her, was marginal.

Was he a trap? If she believed in him, believed in the love he offered, allowed herself to rest in it, was it only a matter of time before he was restless, scanning the horizon for something new?

Patricia thought of all this. But against this assessment was the prospect of emotional solitude which she dreaded above everything. Surely she could change the prognosis? She could maintain a bright gaiety which would charm without giving her away. So long as she had mystery, he would be the courtier; she needed him as courtier; she needed the homage.

She recognized that the pain of this relationship was a kind of masochism. Am I indulging in perversity? she wondered. It is just that the crumbs of life are better than no life at all. If it is a toss-up between dishonour and death, I must take dishonour. At least for the time being. I have never been allowed to live; I do not want to die before I know who I am.

Anyway, she thought after a moment, there is a splinter of ice at the heart of me, and this will save me in the end.

Paddy got up late the next day. The room was dim; the shutters still closed. The bed was empty. He lay still, remembering it was Saturday, luxuriating, then his mind began to churn over yesterday's problems, alighting with pleasure on the thought of Patricia. She thought herself inscrutable and this touched him. He was surprised by her continued capacity to reach into the relationship, to extract so much from it, to show so much emotional resilience. He was sorry the night before had been so rushed; it wasn't fair to her. At the back of it all she was a strong woman. Certainly Sue would never be able to do anything like that, but then Sue would never have an affair. The very thought of her in another man's arms was ludicrous.

He got up, threw on a dressing-gown and went to the kitchen. Susan was there. It was a nice room, with a small pine table and every possible gadget, beige and dark-brown tiles, ivory walls. Her head was bent over the list she had been making, long strands of fair hair loose from the clips. She was smoking and spirals of smoke rose from the cigarette, followed by a small cloud as she exhaled. He stood at the kitchen door and watched her for a moment, and she raised her head and looked at him, smiled, put down her pen. She was almost as slim as she had been twenty years before, although her smile had lost its arch gaiety and little dry lines, hastened by cigarette smoking, had come around her mouth and eyes.

'Hello, darling,' she said. 'Did you have a good sleep?' She left the cigarette in the ashtray, stood up, moved to fill the electric kettle. The table was already set for his breakfast and he sat down in his accustomed place. She pecked his cheek without personal contact. He smelt the mixture of eau-de-toilette and cigarette smoke. She was fulfilling her role of wife, reaching for the kettle, putting out the fresh croissants she had bought earlier.

'Yes, slept like a log.' He smiled at her from still sleepy eyes. His hair was rough and tousled, the neck of his bathrobe open over his chest.

Susan smiled back. 'Did you have a good trip? You got back late.'

'Yes . . . It's all right,' Paddy said, 'you can go back to whatever you were doing, Sue. I'll make the tea.'

She looked at him doubtfully.

'I don't want you to feel you have to make me tea,' he went on. 'I want you to be you, to do what you want, to seize your own life . . .'

Her frown deepened, shadows in her eyes. 'But I always do what I want. I am your wife; I'm just getting you your breakfast.'

Paddy sighed. 'You're not my servant,' he said irritably. 'I don't want you to be my servant.'

'Just because I try to make you some tea! Really, darling!' She clicked her tongue and stared at him reproachfully. He kissed her cheek. But for all the manifest emotion, he knew she was still at one remove, suiting herself for the most part, preoccupied with her own concerns, her hectic social life, the romantic novels she read, her anxiety over the absent children. After more than twenty years she was still unsure where he was concerned, still didn't really know who he was. As a result she was incapable of any action concerning him that was not vetted in advance, that was not tailored to his mood. When all he wanted was a woman who would challenge and devour him; so that he could feel his blood flow in his veins, know he was alive; so that he could release the erotic turmoil in his heart. I don't want much, he told himself; and I certainly don't want this burden of gratitude you make for me.

'Thank you, sweetheart,' he said.

She made the tea. 'Tell me about your trip.' She said it sweetly, sitting at the table. Paddy told her about the Marseilles meeting, became animated about it for a moment, glad to be able to discuss it because it was so important and so much in his mind; but when he looked at her he saw that her eyes were glazed, that she sat uneasily, like someone longing to be elsewhere, that she was not interested in a word he was saying. But she smiled encouragingly and nodded her head.

'What do you think I should do?' he asked suddenly. 'Do you think we should go ahead with the proposed contract notwithstanding these conditions?'

She started. 'Em . . . well, whatever you think best, Woofie darling.'

Paddy drank his tea, buttered a golden wedge of croissant. 'I have to go out this afternoon,' he said after a moment's silence.

Her expression changed. 'Where are you going? Is it about the Marseilles thing?'

'Yes. I have to meet someone.'

'What time will you be back? Remember we're having dinner with Patrick Rouvier and the Martins, won't you, darling?'

'Of course! I'll be back at seven.'

She waited for him to finish his tea, then, when he indicated he wanted no more, took the cup and saucer and washed them at the sink, dried them and put them away. She began to hum; she was thinking of the dinner party, what she would wear, the other guests, particularly Patrick Rouvier who always made her feel wonderful. Patrick, widowed for several months, had been making a play for her for years; he found her wonderfully feminine and desirable on several fronts, or so he had given her to understand. While Paddy seemed past it; over the hill. Particularly so in the last nine months. They still made love, but not often, and she usually had to initiate it. She was tired of being taken for granted by this husband who did not begin to understand her, who was impatient with the things she hungered for: society, gaiety, admiration.

She thought of the new jade-green silk dress with pleasure. She would wear pearls with it.

Paddy, aware that his wife was no longer concerned with him, left the kitchen and went to his study. He felt curiously forlorn, curiously lonely. Susan, relieved that she did not have to discuss the Marseilles thing, went to her bedroom to check on her wardrobe.

Patricia went out. It was a nice morning, Paris was warm, smelt of freshly baked bread. She bought some croissants at the local boulangerie; delicious but hell for the figure. Did it matter? She had lost a lot of weight anyway with her long walks and she was going home tomorrow. She went for a walk, down to the river, along by Notre-Dame, doubled back and found her way to the Pantheon. The city breathed majesty, civilization.

The river pleasure-cruisers plied the water by the cathedral, bringing the children of the twentieth century around the island where Abelard had preached eight centuries earlier. Eloise and Abelard. They had castrated him. She had become a nun.

The atmosphere by the Pantheon was different; great looming sense of history, gigantic building brooding over the Sorbonne.

She found the entrance and paid for a ticket, wandered into the crypt where Victor Hugo's ashes rested in the company of other great literati, a silent place of stone, iron-latticed doors to vaults where someone had placed single red roses on the tombs; beautiful, blood-red roses trapped in the great stony silence beneath the earth and the light. Her footsteps echoed, ringing off the limestone. Greatness; fame; remembrance. In the end it all came down to this – dying roses on stone sarcophagi and a silence vast and cold as the sea.

Ten minutes later, glad to be back in the warmth and the daylight, she stood on the roof below the dome and looked out at the city. In the distance, through the grey-blue city haze, was the basilica of the Sacré-Coeur. The horizon was shrouded. Below her were the rooftops, the tall buildings with their apartments, geraniums at many windows; what was it like to live six storeys up without a lift? She craned her head and looked down into the street below. Vertigo. She made her way back down the stone spiral stairs. Her hand was paining her where last night's cut was beginning to heal. She had bought some sticking plasters and kept the hand, as much as possible, in her pocket.

Paddy would be coming at half three. The prospect of seeing him surged with a joy of its own. She felt like a girl again, the deliberations of the night before forgotten in the anticipation, in the renewed energy and optimism. She could cope with it. She could cope with it all, the whole vista she had examined in detail in the dead of the previous night. She could take from the relationship the crumbs that were on offer and forget about its potential. She knew its potential. She knew the potential was vast. But it was not on offer and the crumbs were.

Back in the flat she made coffee and ate the croissants with apricot jam, savouring the mouthfuls. The radio blasted out songs in French and English.

Paddy came at three thirty punctually. He brought her a box of handmade chocolates. She put on the Chieftains tape she had brought from Dublin and they listened to the haunting strains of 'An Cualainn'. She lay back on the couch in his arms. He stroked her hair.

'What happened to your hand?'

'Nothing much. I dropped a bottle and the hand got a bit of a cut. I'm sorry,' she added, looking up at him, 'it was your Burgundy!'

'The wine doesn't matter. Can I see the cut?'

'Ah no. It's all right, really.'

After a few moments he whispered, bending over her face, kissing her forehead and down her nose with small, tentative kisses, aware of the emptiness at the bottom of his heart which had been there since morning and which was fuelled by the knowledge that the next day she would be going home.

'I love you. I love you and need you.'

Patricia answered him with love. 'I love you too.' She had not meant to say the words, fearful that they might sound clinging, but they rose up of their own volition, the emotion behind them so powerful that she could no longer be sure she was the same person as the midnight insomniac who had sought, and found, frost in her soul. He reached for her breasts, put his mouth to her nipples through the blouse, leaving little wet stains.

'Come to bed,' he whispered, pulling her to her feet, drawing her into the bedroom, so small a room that the bed filled it almost completely.

They made love silently. He did not come for a long time, trying to give her pleasure, waiting for her orgasm, which almost came, but didn't, because her body, for its own reasons, would not release itself to him, never had fully, although he had given her intense pleasure. She had tried to find out why, why this physical recalcitrance, thinking about it on her own, tracing the memory of his touch. Climax had happened with Gerry several times, mostly because he was not aware of her reactions and no self-disclosure was therefore involved. But with Paddy, whom she knew was extremely aware of her, she wondered why it always eluded her; and thinking about it, searching for the reasons, she found the fear.

They put the fear so deep in me long ago, she thought, that it will take time and time and time to undo it, to find the perfect trust in him that would undo it. I do not have perfect trust in him.

Then they got up and dressed and had tea and ate the little cakes she had bought in the boulangerie. He looked at his watch.

'I must go, Pat. It is nearly half six.'

She did not raise her head to look at him, but she felt the sensation in her chest of a void, a pit of darkness deep enough to drown in.

'But I thought we would be going out.'

239

'I'm sorry. Susan and I have been invited to a dinner party.'

'I see!'

'I'm sorry, darling; you do understand, don't you?'

He said it miserably. Patricia narrowed her eyes. My God, to be so secondary, to permit it. It was Saturday evening, her last evening, and she was to be alone. It seemed to her that his first priority was to please his wife. After that he pleased himself. Whether she was pleased or not was immaterial.

'Oh, just bugger off!'

'I can't hurt her, Pat!'

'You're hurting me!'

There was silence. Hard cheese, Patricia said to herself. What does he care for your pain? It does not come endorsed in ink, supported by statute, so it doesn't count.

'But you are married too,' he said after a moment. 'I don't really believe that you would want to hurt your marriage either.' She stared at him.

'Don't talk to me of my marriage. It sucks the life out of me. The more I try to make sense of it the more it eludes me. My marriage is a disaster. Don't talk to me of it. I did not come to Paris to be told how great my marriage was, Paddy. I came here to be with you!'

He shifted uneasily. 'But don't you think what we have is better than nothing?' he went on after a moment. 'It's either this or nothing . . . Life is lived on a myriad of levels. Some levels are never achieved. We have found ours, our plateau, together. That doesn't make everything that exists on other levels disappear.'

He looked at her as he spoke, his face wretched for a moment, his voice soft and pleading, his hands turned up to stress the obvious. Then he glanced at his watch.

'Darling,' he said on a note of firm apology, 'We can talk about it tomorrow on the way to the airport. I have to go now.'

Patricia turned her face away from him. 'Suit yourself!' She heard the door click behind him, heard in her mind the echo of his words: 'It's either this or nothing!'

When the doorbell rang some minutes later, she assumed that Paddy had returned, and her heart sank with disappointment when she heard Jeanine's voice. She opened the door.

'I saw your lover leaving and I thought you might like to have tea with me,' said the voice with the rich French accent, speaking of Patricia's lover as though he was an entirely natural and respectable entity.

Jeanine's voice trailed off as she looked at the set face before her. 'I'm sorry,' she said. 'I didn't mean to intrude – but I knew it was your last day!'

Patricia opened the door wide. 'Come in.'

Jeanine closed the door behind her and followed Patricia to the sitting room.

'Sit down,' Patricia said miserably, searching for urbanity, turning to go to the kitchen to put the kettle on the little gas stove. Jeanine was beside her in a moment, silently getting out the teapot and the mugs.

'What happened to your hand?' she asked, indicating the bandage.

'Nothing much!'

'I got a taste for tea when I was teaching in England,' Jeanine resumed after a moment.

'Is that right?' Patricia said politely, her voice suddenly breaking.

Jeanine put a motherly arm about her, took her by the arm and sat her down. 'You should cry if you feel like crying. I will not preach or tell you to listen to *la voix de la raison* as I would my daughter. I know only too well the crown of thorns worn by the mistress of a married man.' She paused. 'That's what Lorca called it,' she added. 'And he was right!'

'I'm not a mistress!' Patricia said indignantly.

Jeanine smiled, raised her eyebrows, pursed her lips in a Gallic expression. 'Well, the name doesn't matter!' She sighed. 'What matters is that he has little or nothing to offer you, except, of course, some exquisite suffering.' She sighed. 'I can talk about it because I tried it myself once, loving a married man . . .'

Patricia turned red eyes on her. Jeanine shrugged. 'It was in England. It nearly broke me. I was newly divorced and very vulnerable.'

'What happened?' Patricia asked.

'You mean how did it end? I came back to France. I stood up for me!' She patted Patricia's shoulder, put a mug of tea in her hands. 'And in the end, *ma chère*, you will stand up for you!'

When Jeanine was gone, Patricia phoned the airport. Yes, there was a morning flight. Ten thirty. Yes, they would change the reservation. She packed her suitcase, tidied the flat. Then she sat down with her head in her hands and after a long time began a letter. Her hand hurt as she wrote.

My dearest love,
There are things I long to say to you. I could talk to you of love, which I don't understand because it consumes me and I have lost objectivity.
I could speak to you of the empathy between us.
I could try to find the words to describe the intensity of our private reality which (for me at least) makes sense of life.
I would like to make you understand why a proud and private woman came to share some time with you in circumstances which did her little credit.
But you would not understand. In your perspective I think this is some kind of norm; it is something plenty of people do. In my perspective this is the one exceptional journey of my life.
And there are things I must say to you which I fear. I'm afraid to tell you that if there is a choice between nothing and something, (the something being the occasional secret meeting where I cannot hold up my head), I must choose nothing. And how can I tell you that I must choose nothing when the whole thrust of my will and self is towards you? But if I do not tell you this how can I live with myself? And if I do say all this to you, and we are lost to each other, how can I live?
But I must endure myself; anything else is a descent into madness, formlessness, despair.
I believe what you say you feel for me. I have seen it in your face, felt it, known it in your touch. To be able to rest in it is to be free, alive, powerful, to be creative, to be at peace. It is discovery of myself and the world, like some kind of miraculous regained childhood.
But I also know that within the ambit of your requirements our relationship has a secondary place; it is secondary to your domestic life.
I sense the defence mechanism in you which betrays what we have together in your terror of betraying Susan. You have honed this mechanism well and have used it many times before, I think, not just with me.
I love you. I love us. I love both of us enough to end it before resentment destroys what we have, closes up our

space. I would not be able to help the resentment. I have chosen between the two positions you postulated in the only way I can.

Ultimately, I suppose, I refuse to be less than I am.

Patricia

She set the alarm for seven thirty. By the time he called in the morning she would be airborne.

She had a bath and when she came out of it she went to the sitting room to re-read the letter.

'Bloody female earnestness! What's the point?' she muttered. She folded the sheet of paper and tore it into pieces.

Instead she left a short note.

Dear Paddy,
This is the best way.
Pat

She had not packed the black lace negligée. It hung from the back of the bedroom door and she unhooked it, folded it carefully and put it in the kitchen rubbish bin. Then she took up the book she had never managed to finish, looked at it with unseeing eyes. The title swam across the page, its four words in capital letters: *Requiem pour la Vie*.

In the morning Paddy called and, when there was no answer, let himself in. The apartment was empty, the bed linen folded, the sink scoured. His feet echoed a little on the tiles. He picked up the note on the table and read it, stared at it for a moment before crushing it in his hand. The wardrobe was open in the bedroom and he saw the forlorn clothes-hangers. The bright day outside seemed to dim, become unbearably ordinary. The void he felt inside him intensified into pain. He glanced one last time into the kitchen and saw a loop of a satin belt sticking out of the rubbish bin. He pulled out the negligée, shook it out, smelt its perfume and buried his face in it.

Chapter Nineteen

The ability to let things go is the secret of sanity.
from *The Horse's Ears*, 1990

Joan watched the clock. It would soon be time for David's return. His plane from Paris was due in thirty minutes. Allow an hour after that for his arrival in the door.

'I'll pick you up,' she had said, but he had politely declined. 'I'll get a taxi.'

He had not asked her to come with him to Paris for the opening of his exhibition. It hurt her so much that she shied away from asking why. She knew why. So, to keep it light, she had murmured that she had a lot of work on hand at the moment anyway, while secretly she felt his rejection of her as a blow to her very life. He had become someone else; but she loved him as always, more perhaps, as the challenge of his newness, his recovered strength, was like discovery, offering new vistas, fresh horizons.

The six weeks of radiotherapy had been hell; in the mornings she would drive him to St Luke's Hospital for his session, and then drive him home, stopping the car when the nausea overwhelmed him, and he would open the door and vomit. She worked late in the evening to compensate for the time lost to the office, although Gerry and Larry had both indicated that they would help where they could.

But, once the treatment was over, David had started, little by little, to improve. He had recovered his appetite, walked to the local shop and then as far as the supermarket; brought home French cheeses, garlic bread, strange sausages; all kinds of food which he had not looked at for years. He began to fill out; his shoulders became firm; the thin hollows in his cheeks disappeared. He applied himself to his work with renewed, relentless vigour, preparing for his exhibition.

But as he improved, so did he increasingly distance himself from Joan. On the basis that it would be more convenient, and less disturbing for her when he was working long into the night, he put a divan bed into his studio and slept there. He even had a new phone line installed, his own phone in his own studio. The calls came to him from Paris; people came to see him from his Dublin gallery; he saw them in his room. He was more like a lodger than a husband.

Once she brought up the subject of her anger in Paris and tried to explain. But he only said that if things had been all that bad, he couldn't understand why she hadn't moved out long ago. 'You could have had this marvellous life you've hungered for! So why didn't you?'

Stung, Joan had retorted, 'With you sick and at death's door? Who was to support you, support this family if I did not?'

She could have killed herself. David had turned and walked out the door saying, 'So it was charity, was it? You were minding the poor decrepit who was about to croak! You were supporting him! Eminently decent, I must say, and something that will earn you the appropriate kudos in that holy never-never land you apply to so regularly. I thought you ran deeper than that, but I won't bother to be disappointed in you. My mistake!'

'No, David . . . It wasn't like that.'

But he was gone, back to his room. When she went up after him the door was closed and she heard the small sounds which told her he was working.

How can he be so black? she asked herself over and over. She tried, as delicately as she could, to heal the breach between them, but he froze her away. When she woke in the night with strange and excruciating abdominal cramps, he was not there to help. She did not tell him about the cramps, but saw the doctor, who told her it was anxiety based. 'It's when you're out of the wood that the reaction sets in,' he said sympathetically. 'You need a rest, a holiday. You have been overstressed for some time.'

Paul noticed the growing impasse between his parents. 'What's going on, Mum, between you and Dad?'

'Nothing . . .'

'Yes, that's exactly what I mean. Nothing is going on between you. You don't seem to talk any more. You don't even sleep together! You're so polite to each other . . .'

Joan looked at her son and, because she had no lies to give him, she did not reply.

Now David was coming back. There had been one phone call from Paris a few days after his arrival there. The exhibition had gone well; there would be a fat cheque at the end. He had met a London gallerist who was interested in his work and an American neuro-surgeon who was a collector and had bought several of his paintings. But there had been no word of love, not one syllable of their old coded intimacies, which they had worked out in their student days and always fell back on, as a private joke, when either of them was away. His voice had been cheerful, but cool. 'So I should be able to repay you some of what you expended on me down the years!'

'Please don't say things like that,' Joan had said in a voice which teetered on the verge of breaking; but he had said a polite goodbye and was gone.

I'm no use to him any more, Joan thought. I'm superfluous. He does not love me any more. Why should he? He is brilliant and original and I'm just a boring lawyer, living between the dusty covers of a thousand files, sheafs of bloody old papers which are archived and forgotten. And she added, finding that the knowledge of it came unbidden, like a black flood: and I'm so weary I could die.

She sat staring at the floor for a while, and then put on her coat and called to Paul that she was going out. His head appeared over the banister.

'Where are you going? Dad will be home fairly soon.'

'Just for a walk.'

'It's raining!'

'I don't care!'

It was a dark, overcast night and raining softly. Joan walked down the suburban road and around the corner and then around the next corner. The rain got heavier, but by this time Joan had left the small housing estate and had directed her steps towards the nearby river.

When David arrived back in Dublin the rain was already torrential. It hissed and frothed down the eaveshoots, ran in mini torrents in the gutters, beat against the windscreen of his taxicab. He was looking forward to his warm house, to his family, to sharing his success. He particularly wanted to talk to Joan; he

247

wanted to apologize; he wanted to explain. Her voice, so small, so uncharacteristically tired, had stayed with him to touch and reproach him. In addition his paintings of her had elicited so much comment, so much admiration – 'your valiant lady' his gallerist called her, while expressing regret that she could not be with them – that his old image of her had returned with new force. He felt that he had behaved badly towards her, that he had taken out on her the fear and rage that had possessed him in the recent terrible crisis in his life. It had, for a while, seemed entirely credible to him that Joan had stayed with him during his years of obscurity and illness only out of duty. Joan was into duty with a capital D. His pride had rebelled at all that this portended; the certainty of her past pity was anathema. And, also, although he had tried to hide it, he had been terribly afraid of death; the thought of oblivion had been, still was, more than he could bear. It was an indignity. But now he felt his recovery in his bones; every day was like a gift, every day he was stronger. He remembered with unease the business of Damion's 'ghost'. Joan had been unable to contain her reaction and he winced as he privately acknowledged that he had provoked it in order to censure it. In the turmoil of his violent emotions it had seemed eminently reasonable that if he could not belong to the living, he would demonstrate arcane knowledge of the dead. He would wield the staff of personal mastery to the end. But Damion's ghost was now laid and he had let him go with love. Call it hallucination, call it auto-suggestion, call it subliminal reality – the fact was that the episode had provided a positive impetus at his life's lowest ebb. He had not, in fact, been as sure of his recovery as he had liked to pretend. He had not, in fact, been sure of it at all.

And when his gallerist had said, as he took his leave of him, to remember him to Joan, 'Who loves you so much', he had been jolted into a fresh perspective. It was easier to believe that she loved him; it made more sense and it answered the certainty at the bottom of his heart. And then he realized, with sudden appalling clarity, that his fury at the indignity of his illness and possible death was something for which he was punishing his wife.

Viewed from this new perspective, he began to see her fortitude down the years as something more than human; to have taken it for granted seemed to him, suddenly, to have been

248

nothing short of criminal. And, as the change in his perspective gained momentum, he tormented himself on the flight home. He had taken and taken and taken, but what had he given? Other than momentary bursts of elation when the nagging pain was in remission, momentary bursts of energy or occasional assurances of love, what had he given her? While she had slaved for years and honed her life around his sustaining, what had he given her? He had been so busy playing the artist, married to his paints, married to the churning shapes and images in his brain, pouring out his vision of the truth on canvas! But art was always inferior to life.

He knew perfectly well that Joan's outburst during that night in Paris, which he had so resented, had been the despairing cry of an exhausted spirit, the demand that life will make of itself. And all he had been able to do was sulk like a child, as though, on top of everything she had given him, she owed him even more. By the time the captain announced the descent into Dublin, he was chafing with frustration at how long it was taking, longing to be with Joan, longing to make it up to her, to kneel and kiss her feet.

Paul opened the front door when the taxi drew up. David paid the fare, hurried to his son, and saw at once that all was not well. He dropped his bag in the hall, embraced his son and looked around.

'Where's your mother?'

'I don't know!'

'What do you mean you don't know? Where has she gone?' David knew the car was in the driveway, Joan's ageing Escort. 'Is she at Lil's?'

'She went out for a walk more than an hour ago,' Paul said in a frightened voice. 'It started to rain after she left!'

'She must have taken shelter somewhere,' David muttered, but Paul saw the sudden haunted look in his face. 'She's not likely to stay out in a downpour like this.'

'I phoned Auntie Lil and also the Kavanaghs. She's not with them,' Paul whispered. 'I don't know where else she could have gone. I went around to Kinsella's shop, but they were just shutting up for the night and no one had seen her. You see, Dad,' Paul added, 'there is nowhere around here for her to shelter, unless she knocked on someone's door.'

David knew this. He turned furiously on his son. 'Why did you let her go out on her own? Couldn't you have gone with her?'

Paul looked at his father in misery and astonishment. 'I thought she was just walking around the block, or down to the shop, or something . . .' He bit his lip. 'She's been so depressed lately.' He dropped his voice to a whisper. 'Do you think something has happened to her?'

'No,' David said. 'But I think we'd better go and look for her.'

The car didn't start immediately and for a moment he thought the battery was flat. But it fired eventually and he and Paul cruised around the estate, Paul keeping a look-out. The roads were empty. The houses were like ships in a typhoon, with hatches all battened down, their warmth and exclusivity something the poor embattled outsider could only envy. The rain continued unabated; parts of the road were beginning to flood, and no matter where he went there was no sign of Joan. He had told himself that he was being foolish; that she was a sensible woman and had taken shelter; maybe she had taken the bus into town and was with some friend or other. But if she had wanted to go into the city she would have brought her car. And then she knew he was coming home. Why would she have absented herself when she knew he was coming home? He tried to evade the answer. And there was something else bothering him too, some kind of subliminal panic which tormented him; it was just out of reach of his reason, prodding him, as though it knew something he did not. And then, for reasons which were part instinct and part fear-engendered by his own history, he turned the car and drove to the river.

They found her almost by chance. It was a narrow road beside the river, a normally narrow waterway, which was now in spate. There was a path and a steep bank and David got out of the car, shone his torch against the slanting curtain of rain, shouted, but, except for the rain, saw and heard nothing. But on repeating the exercise something caught his eye, a form or contour halfway down the bank some distance away from where he was standing with his raincoat over his head. For a moment he thought it was a body and his breath caught in his chest. It was only when he came nearer that he saw it was a sack of old clothes. The relief was so intense that he had to stand still to recover his composure.

And then, further on, hidden by the branches of a tree and the shadows of night, he saw the soaked figure, sitting on a bench and staring into the river.

She started with surprise when he put his hand on her shoulder, put his arms around her, and did not speak as he and Paul wrapped her in their coats and took her home. Then he phoned the doctor.

A hot drink, a warm bath, a heated bed, could they have done anything more for hypothermia in hospital?

The doctor had been quietly scathing. 'Joan has been having problems recently, you know!'

'What problems?'

The doctor sighed. 'You mean to say you don't even know! She's been having classic anxiety problems. People who get life-threatening illnesses seldom know anything about their effects on the people who live with them and love them.'

So David de Barra, tired as was, spent that night awake beside his sleeping wife, holding her in his arms. He held her like that all night. She scarcely moved and he didn't move either, except to hold her a little closer. He did not ponder precisely what had brought her to sit by the river in the pouring rain, like a creature insensible to its own survival. He did not want the answer. Joan had always been strong; it was inconceivable that she could be anything else. But sometimes what was strong was also brittle; sometimes it possessed small, deadly pockets of vulnerability.

He knew how fragile was the narrow band inhabited by humankind, the physical and emotional space within which the vivid miracle of life was possible. How long would Joan have sat there, staring into the curtains of rain, if he had not come; staring at the river as though it possessed some special fascination for her? Something in him shivered when he thought of the sack of old clothes he had seen in the mud of the riverbank.

Towards morning, Joan stirred.

'Silly of me,' she said in a muffled voice, as though she knew he was awake.

'I know, my love,' David, still tremulous with relief, whispered into her hair. 'We're all of us very silly sometimes. I even know a man who went a little mad for a while. He forgot something very important . . .'

Joan did not reply, but neither did she let him go on. She sighed like someone putting down a great weight, reached up and drew his head down to her in the old way.

251

Chapter Twenty

What does a woman's vulnerability inspire in a man? If it's directed at him – probably impatience. If it's directed elsewhere, and if she is also attractive, possibly love. There is nothing surer to kill passion than to be certain of it! Is this true – or a cynical observation?

from *The Horse's Ears*, 1990

October 1990

Pat gazed down at the bright fields of France, saw the French coast come into view, saw the blue of the Channel, and felt the moment when the plane inclined downwards to commence its gradual descent into Dublin. Soon they were into the thick grey cloud mass sitting over the Irish Sea. She looked out and saw only the wispy greyness, the small drops of moisture on the window, and turned back to flipping the pages of *Cara*, the inflight magazine, with its ads for Waterford Crystal and stately Irish hotels. Then they were below the cloud and she saw the Irish coastline – Greystones, the Dun Laoghaire piers, Malahide beach, the airport itself; the landmarks of a lifetime; the familiar faces of homes.

The undercarriage clunked into place, the captain's voice announced their imminent arrival, requesting that seatbelts be kept on, and then they were hurtling down to the runway. Toy buildings became life-sized; reversing engines roared. She was home. The plane taxied slowly to the landing bay. She looked through the small oval window. She knew these mists, these shades of green, these breezes swelling the wind-socks, the accents, soft and rich, which awaited her. She walked through passport control, stood for the conveyor belt in the baggage reclaim, conscious of how quiet this airport was, how small the

253

crowds were, how uniform the racial mix was, how much an island her country was. But it was not her country any more. Paddy was her country and she had lost him. I am bereaved, she thought. This is the same as death.

There was no one to meet her. Gerry was expecting her on the evening flight. She felt the sting of the rain in the wind as she emerged from the airport building, the promise of winter. What did this island know of summer in Paris, the principle of pleasure, the discovery of life for its own sake. She got a taxi, gave the address.

'Have yez been on yer holliers?' the taxi man asked, and she said yes, she had been on her holliers.

When she got home the house was empty. Of course. They were probably at Mass. Gerry occasionally took the children, behaving as though he were a parent with a religious mission, when in reality he was as uninterested in religion as he was uninterested in everything, except success. She was surprised by the sense of disappointment, realized that she had wanted them there, wanted her children, needed them to need her. She brought her case upstairs, began to unpack.

They came back in about half an hour. Simon and Orla came upstairs and she met them in the landing with a curiously nervous pleasure.

'Jesus,' Simon said. 'You gave me a fright, Mum!' But she noticed that he was glad to see her; his eyes, dilating with pleasure, gave him away. She put her arm around him. 'Give your ancient parent a kiss!'

Simon reacted with gauche alarm, but he kissed his mother on the cheek.

She approached Orla, embraced her, saw that she looked pale and tired. 'When did you get home, Mummy?'

'A few minutes ago. I got an earlier flight.'

Patricia expected to be plied with questions about her holiday, about what she had seen in Paris, but her children disappeared into their rooms.

Patricia followed Orla into hers. 'Where's your father?'

Orla looked up at her with hollow eyes. 'He's at the police station. He'll be back soon. I had to make a statement!'

Alarm bells went off in Patricia's head. 'What's happened? Has something happened?'

Orla heaved a sigh. She sat on the edge of the bed with a sob. 'It's all my fault!'

254

'What's all your fault?'

Orla burst into tears, turned her face and buried it in her pillows.

Patricia sat beside her, stroked her hair. 'Darling, tell me . . . Please!'

Orla's sobs got louder. Simon appeared at the door. 'It was that creep, that Mick Clancy . . . He tried to rape her last night.'

Patricia held her daughter in her arms, lay beside her on the bed. Orla kept her back turned. She shook with weeping. Patricia said nothing. She met Simon's eyes. He shook his head. 'Would you like a cup of tea, Mum?' he whispered, and Pat smiled and whispered back, 'In a minute.'

When Gerry came back, Patricia got the whole story.

Orla had been to a disco. Mick had been there and she had accepted a lift home from him on the motorbike. He didn't want her to go in home at once and suggested they go for a short walk. Orla had agreed. They had walked for a few blocks and he had led her into a laneway, a blind alley, and there his true colours had appeared.

'He told her he had a knife!' Gerry said furiously. 'He had her down on the ground. Only for the fact that a dog started barking in a nearby garden and the owner came to investigate, the story would be much worse. He'd have had her! He'd have screwed her. And we might be looking into grandparenthood! Our daughter impregnated by a yobbo like that!'

So like Gerry, Patricia thought, to think only of how it would have affected him.

'Has she seen a doctor?'

'No. She's all right. He was scared off before he could manage to do his stuff. But she'll have to be locked up for a while until she can be trusted to behave herself. We can't have this happening again.' He drew a noisy, angry breath.

Patricia stared at him. 'Hold on a moment, Gerry. This was an attempted rape. Right? There is no blame on Orla. She didn't ask to be raped.'

The light caught the balding dome of Gerry's head, the parallel lines around his mouth, the fury in his eyes. 'She was looking for it, all right! Why did she go for a "walk" with him, I ask you? At two o'clock in the morning!'

255

'She's young and innocent. She probably thought it was romantic!'

Gerry dismissed the argument. 'If you were here, things might have been different. But of course you had to be gallivanting in Paris . . . I should never have allowed it!'

Gerry left the room and Patricia went to the phone to ask the family doctor to call as soon as he could.

'When is the case likely to come to court?' she asked Gerry later.

'Assuming they can catch him – quite soon.'

Pat sat with Orla in her room. The doctor had come and gone, leaving advice and sympathy and a few sleeping tablets. Gerry was downstairs, reading the Sunday papers.

'You stay in bed and get some sleep,' Pat said. 'It's the best thing for shock . . . You heard the doctor. I'll bring you up your supper. Is there anything special you'd like?'

'No, Mummy, thanks. I feel such a fool. You tried to warn me, even the gang tried to . . . but I knew everything!'

'At your age, people always know everything. It's an amazing facility which, thankfully, evaporates . . .' She smiled. 'Never mind. The police will get him and then he'll have to face the music!'

'Will there be a court case?'

'Oh yes. What he did was very serious. He's a criminal! It's a criminal offence!'

'I know, Mummy. I was just wondering. I was wondering if he would get away with it!' Then she added, pushing back her hair and giving her mother a rueful smile, 'We missed you a lot when you were away.'

'Did you?'

'Of course we did. The house felt very empty, very cold. It's nice to have you back.' Then she asked, 'Did Paris live up to expectations? What did you do?'

'This and that. I visited the museums and the art galleries and all that sort of thing,' Pat said evenly.

Orla regarded her from questioning eyes. 'It must have been very queer to be on your own all that time. Did you meet anyone you knew?'

Patricia searched for an answer, aware that her daughter was watching her closely.

256

'You'll never guess whom I saw . . . David de Barra!'

'Who's he?'

'He's Joan de Barra's husband.'

'You mean Daddy's partner, her husband?'

'Yes. He's an artist . . . His work was being exhibited.'

'Oh,' Orla said.

Pat kissed her daughter. 'Get some sleep . . . First day of college tomorrow . . .' She looked down at the soft curve of her daughter's cheek, saw her pallor, how shaken she was, how deprived of certainty. The wilfulness which had been her ruling characteristic was in abeyance; she was more vulnerable now than she had ever been because she no longer had complete confidence in her own perceptions, or in the parameters which she had always taken for granted. She would have to reconnoitre the jungle of adulthood again. But that was for another day.

'It wasn't your fault!' Pat said.

Orla moved convulsively and threw her arms around her mother's neck.

On a Monday morning some weeks later, Patricia lay on her bed, stared up at the witch's face on the ceiling. The house was empty, silent; Gerry was at the office, Simon was at school; Orla was at college. The central heating was on; she heard the occasional click of the thermostat. Outside the year had turned towards winter, 'the Fall', as the Americans so poetically called it. She had written a sheaf of letters to Paddy, torn them up, written more and torn them up. 'The darkness is tearing out my heart,' she said. 'There is a vast silence without you,' and then she destroyed the missives.

This morning she had received a letter from him, written from Richmond, sealed in a typewritten envelope. It was the second letter from him since her return from Paris.

'I was unforgivably insensitive. I love and need you. If we cannot be lovers, let us not lose contact; let us at least be friends.'

She wept. 'Let us at least be friends!' How could he even imagine being just 'friends'? It was an acceptance of the end of their relationship.

She put the letter in with the old ones, glanced at the photograph among the yellowing pages of a young Paddy and a young Patricia, taken after a dinner dance in the Metropole, he in black tie and dinner jacket, she in a black dress with a

257

modest neckline and large 'pearl' earrings, eyeliner on her upper lids. They were smiling at each other, glowing, absurdly young.

She looked out the window at the lawn. The leaves had become gold and russet and yellow and drifted to the ground. The air was full of cold mist and melancholy; beauty and sadness; nostalgia for all the autumns past.

Maybe one day I will wake up and it won't matter any more, she thought. Maybe someday you will cease to possess me.

'Gerry – I want to go back to college!' Gerry was reading the newspaper. He looked up for a moment and then readdressed himself to the article.

'Do you hear me?'

He looked up again. 'Of course I hear you, Pat.' The light from the window caught his glasses, showed the blue sheen in the lens. 'Don't be ridiculous!'

'I need to have my own life, my own job.'

Gerry sighed, folded the paper. 'You live in some sort of pipe-dream! You have made a life of your own – you're a wife and mother! What kind of a job would you get – starting from scratch; a woman of your age!'

'To hell with my age! I don't care about starting from scratch! If I have a job I'll have . . . autonomy!'

'Autonomy! To do what?' He laughed dryly. 'This is a little adolescent of you, Pat! You seem to forget that you already have a job!' His voice became grave. 'That you have responsibilities!'

If the laugh wasn't so dry, Patricia thought, if the voice wasn't so certain and so grave, I could bear it and answer it.

'It isn't a job! And the children are almost grown . . .'

'If you need more money, Pat, all you have to do is say so!'

'I want to study Law,' Patricia said in a dead voice. Gerry raised his eyebrows, glanced at her and laughed out loud.

'My dear girl, there's nothing romantic about Law! Ask Joan . . . Ask anyone.'

'I'm not looking for romance.'

'In fact,' Gerry continued, 'it wouldn't surprise me if she gave it up altogether!'

Patricia sat up. 'Joan? You can't be serious. Why should she do that?'

'She's been hinting about leaving. I think that husband of hers is into a fortune now; he seems to be the new darling of the international art world.'

He leafed back through the newspaper, folded it and handed it to her. 'There's even an article on him in today's paper.'

Pat took the paper, studied David de Barra's intense face looking out from the page and the photo of one of his paintings.

'Mind you,' Gerry went on, 'I don't think much of his stuff. It reminds me of Picasso. When I think how hard some people have to work, while chancers like that get paid vast fortunes for something I could do myself with a few tubes of paint and a bicycle!'

Pat started to laugh. She laughed until the tears ran down her face. She saw Gerry on a bicycle smearing paint on a canvas spread on the floor.

'What's wrong with you? What's so funny?'

Next morning, Patricia opened her letter in the hall, saw that it was from Joan and took it to the kitchen. The letterhead was the firm's: Galligan, Ryder & Co.

'Dear Patricia,' the letter said, 'I would like you to drop in to swear the papers for probate of your mother's estate. I have also found among her personal papers something which I think will surprise you.'

When Patricia went to see Joan three days later, she was presented with some documents for signing. When that had been attended to, Joan put a building-society passbook down on the desk in front of her.

'What's that?'

'It was among your mother's papers!'

'I don't remember seeing it!'

'It was in a sealed envelope.'

Patricia examined the little passbook with its plain brown cover, saw that there was a single sum of money entered: one hundred and twenty thousand pounds.

'My God! The money from the sale of Brierly! So she didn't spend it!'

'No, she didn't. Look at the name on the account.' Patricia looked back at the first page. The account was in the name of Patricia Ellen Galligan.

259

'She put it in my name!'

'She did. It's been there for years, so the interest must be worth a bomb.'

'Maybe she closed the account?'

'It's alive and well. I've checked!'

Patricia leaned back against the tweed chair. 'Do you realize what this means, Joan?' she asked the smiling woman across the desk. 'It means that Patricia Galligan is free!'

Joan toyed with her pen, wrote pound-note signs on the sheet of paper, grinned at Pat.

'Isn't it crazy!' Pat went on. 'For years I have been getting the usual shareholders' bumf from the EBS and never even looked at it. I have a small account with them in Ballsbridge and thought it was apropos of that!'

'You're now a well-heeled woman in your own right, Patricia Galligan.' She glanced at some figures on her file. 'With the interest the account is worth over two hundred thousand! What are you going to do with it?'

Patricia drew a deep breath. 'I don't know! I want to go back to college, finish my degree!'

'And what then?'

Patricia looked at her friend. 'What I would really like to do is study Law!'

'Good,' Joan said briskly, as though this was the most natural thing in the world. 'I'll give you an apprenticeship!'

Patricia harrumphed disbelievingly. 'Gerry would veto it!'

'He can veto it all he likes! I'm setting up on my own . . .!'

Pat sat back, laughed. 'Are you serious? He said you had been dropping hints . . .'

'Certainly! David's raked it in. I can afford to make the break! His Paris exhibition was very successful – my God, the prices were incredible. And you should hear the accolades!'

'I know. I saw the piece about him in the paper the other day and Gerry was telling me . . . that he's made the breakthrough.' She held back the smile, thinking of Gerry and his bicycle. 'I saw David's exhibition while I was in Paris. I thought it might be a bit cheaper to buy direct?'

'It certainly would,' Joan said with a laugh. 'Why don't you call around? He's working on some interesting new pictures. He has another new contract now with a gallery in London and is absolutely immersed. I almost have to make an appointment to see him!' She smiled a private smile, as though these 'appointments' were worth waiting for.

'I'm delighted for him,' Pat said. 'He deserves it. I don't know much about art, but I thought his work had great impact. And I particularly liked the portraits of you!'

Joan flushed. 'Thanks. I don't recognize myself in them.'

'He loves you very much.'

Joan raised smiling eyebrows and fiddled with some papers. 'He's had another scan and everything's fine, you know,' she said, moving the subject away.

Pat sighed inwardly. 'I always envied you, you know, your happy marriage. You gave the impression of never having as much as a disagreement; I know it must have been very hard when he was sick, but you always seemed to be at one with him!'

Joan did not meet her eyes. 'Did I? You might be surprised . . . But I think I can safely say we are now a very cemented pair, very much a couple.'

Before she left, Patricia asked diffidently: 'Were you serious when you offered me an apprenticeship?'

'Of course. I happen to think you would make a very good lawyer. I saw how interested you were in that poor woman, Sarah O'Toole. Why don't you go back to college, get your degree and then apply to the Law Society's law school? You can be articled to me then!'

'Isn't it too late?'

'Rubbish! The years will pass anyway. You may as well be a lawyer in four years' time as festering in domesticity – which isn't doing you one bit of good – if you'll forgive me for saying so.'

'I know. It's like being a trout and expected to live in an ashtray . . .'

Joan laughed. 'A bit of a squeeze . . . Why try to inhabit a space which can't possibly contain you?'

Patricia had a faraway look in her eyes. 'Joan, do you realize that with the money Mummy has left me I can buy that little mews house in Airfield Lane which has just come on the market? I walked past it the other day. It's lovely, with a front patio and a tiny back garden . . .'

'You slut!'

The words came as the light went on. Patricia, jerked from

261

sleep, started up angrily, keeping her eyes closed, squinting to avoid being blinded by the light.

It was Gerry. He was bending over her. His face was cold. She smelt drink on his breath. She pulled herself out of sleep, sat up.

'You slut!' Gerry said again.

'How dare you?' Patricia said when she found her breath.

'Don't you "How dare" me. I heard from John Millar at the club just what you were up to in Paris! It seems I can't let you out of my sight!'

Patricia didn't answer. She was wide awake. In a moment it was clear to her what had happened. John Millar had been at the club. They had all been drinking and Millar couldn't resist asking Gerry about his wife, about how she had enjoyed her trip to Paris. Wink, wink; nudge, nudge. Gerry's wrath was the fury of the cuckold, the outraged rights of ownership.

As she gradually opened her eyes she saw him, saw his twisted, bitter face and, with a peculiar sense of her own absence, saw his anger, as though she were watching from a distance. He lifted his arm and struck her. Then he took her dressing-gown from the back of the door and threw it at her, pulled down a suitcase from the top of the wardrobe.

'Get dressed and get out. Get out of my house.' He stormed out of the room and downstairs.

Patricia gasped with pain. A flash of light danced before her right eye. She put the palm of her hand over it. Her cheekbone was tender and already beginning to swell. After a minute she carefully opened her eyes, realized that she was not blinded, looked at the clock. It was two o'clock in the morning. She heard Orla and Simon whispering together on the landing. She got up silently, went to her wardrobe and began to dress.

There was a knock on the door and Orla's face appeared, looking young and frightened. 'What happened?'

'I'm getting dressed, Orla. Please wait outside.'

Orla withdrew. Patricia packed a case, took her bottles and make-up from the dressing-table and shunted them into a plastic bag, put it in her case, slipped on her watch. Then she picked up the phone extension and phoned for a taxi.

When she left the room she found her children at the return of the stairs. She heard the sounds from below of breaking china and saw in a moment what was going on. Gerry was standing in the dining-room doorway, flinging her collection of porcelain on to the tiled hall. He flung it piece by piece and it shattered with an aristocratic, fine-tuned clink. His face was set and his eyes pink. Only the measured throw of the porcelain pieces evinced his turmoil, but the tight grimace to his mouth and chin and the swelling of his nostrils spoke of emotions in conflict.

Orla looked frightened, Simon subdued.

'You slut!' Gerry said again as Patricia walked down to the hall. 'Get out. Leave my house!'

'I'm not a slut,' Patricia said clearly, picking her way among the shattered porcelain collection of twenty years. 'I am a human being. I will leave "your house" with the greatest pleasure. I have already bought my own.'

There was a thunderstruck silence.

'Rubbish,' Gerry said with a sneer. 'How could you buy a house?'

'With money,' Patricia said.

She turned to her children. Orla looked at the bruise on her mother's face and burst into tears.

'You can come with me, live with me, either or both of you, as you wish. I will always be your mother. I love you both.' She moved towards the door.

'I suppose you think you can take the car I gave you?' Gerry said, holding up the keys, twirling them around on his first finger.

Patricia paused, looked at him, saw the sudden bewilderment in him under the fury, the fear that the situation was heading out of control; that he had precipitated a crisis, when he meant to teach her a lesson, to show who was boss, to hurt and punish her until she was crushed and humiliated. If you have no car you can't leave, his body-language said.

'Mummy, wait! Where will you go; what will you do?' came Orla's anguished voice. 'Will you come back?'

Patricia shook her head.

Simon shouted at his father, his voice trembling. 'Dad! Don't let her go!'

There was the sound of a car pulling up outside. Patricia opened the front door, saw it was the taxi.

'My address is on my dressing-table, Orla, should you or Simon want it. I'm not far,' she added, seeing their stark expressions, 'Within walking distance!'

She looked back at the two miserable young faces, saw the

263

tears on Orla's cheeks, saw that Simon's pupils were dilated with fear.

Gerry turned to the children. 'Don't worry. She'll come crawling back!'

'I don't think so, Gerry,' Patricia said softly. 'My crawling days are over!'

She heard Orla's voice call from the stairs, 'Mummy, will you be in court on Tuesday?'

Pat looked back at her daughter, remembered the imminence of the hearing. 'Of course I will, darling. I'll meet you there.' She closed the front door behind her.

Chapter Twenty-one

The first step in moral courage is simply to open one's eyes.
from *The Horse's Ears*, 1990

On Tuesday Orla got up early. She hadn't been able to sleep. She was dreading the court hearing today, she would be the star witness, would have to go through exactly what happened, tell them what Mick had done. It was humiliating both that such a thing could have happened to her, and that she should have to recount it publicly.

At breakfast Daddy said something had come up and that he wouldn't be able to attend court with her; the best he could do was drop her off. But, later, when she went into the Bridewell she saw her mother already waiting. Hers was the first case called and she went to the witness box and took the oath.

Orla heard the question, heard the drawl of contempt, felt the perspiration breaking out. The courtroom was small and unexpectedly dingy; from where she stood in the witness box she could see its layout in detail: the justice's bench beside her; the table for the court clerk; the place where the accused sat half smirking; the bench where the solicitors sat waiting for their cases to be called, their files open in front of them; the benches for the public, where her mother sat, and her own witness, John Murphy, and several people – mostly men – whom she had never seen before. They watched her expectantly. She gripped the edge of the wooden railing, trying to remain collected. She was being questioned by his solicitor, belligerently, dismissively, in tones of languid disgust; she felt soiled. What gave him the right to talk to her like that?

'Speak up, please,' the justice said. 'If the witness is embarrassed I'll clear the court,' he added irritably.

The justice was wearing a black gown and had white bands at

265

his neck. Orla looked from him to the floor. They should clean the court better, Orla thought, observing the dust between the floorboards.

'Speak up, please,' the justice repeated, raising his voice. 'This gentleman must be able to hear you!'

Gentleman?

The justice had a creased face, strong, middle-aged; he was anxious to get through his list.

Mick, the gentleman, was sitting near his solicitor, who bent over and whispered something to him; they knew she was rattled; they smiled, sharing their command of the situation. She had no one to speak for her. Daddy had told her there was nothing to this: 'Just speak up and tell the truth.'

She wished again that he had been able to come, but he had a meeting with important clients.

Orla's mind feverishly scanned the events of the night. 'I'd better go in . . . thanks for the lift!' She had turned to look at him, but his face was in shadow.

He had lit a cigarette, drawn on it. 'Look, why don't we go for a walk . . .?' He was smiling. In the lamplight his face seemed handsome; the way he held the cigarette was cool. He had been sweet to her tonight, not pushy, not coming on strong. He had changed. Why not go for a walk? It was a nice night.

He took her hand and they walked down the road. They walked around a few blocks, talked about the disco. They came to a laneway.

'This is a short cut,' Mick said, taking her arm and steering her down the dark alley. There were high walls on either side, the back walls of gardens.

'I don't think this is a short cut,' Orla said after a moment.

'Bet you five pounds it is!'

The laneway turned out to be L-shaped, the end being hidden from the street. It was a blind alley.

'You owe me a fiver,' Orla said as lightly as she could, trying to stem the sudden welling of alarm.

Mick pushed her against the wall. His mouth sought hers, not tentatively like the boys she had kissed at parties, not possessively as he had kissed her before, but savagely, so that her lips hurt. She felt him pressing his erection against her and tried to push him away. The wall behind her was hard and pieces of stone were pressing into her shoulder-blades.

266

'Take off your jeans,' Mick ordered.

'Don't be silly.'

She struggled, broke away from him, but he had her again in a moment. His hands moved down the front of her blouse, over her breasts. He pinched her nipples painfully. She heard her blouse rip. He began to grunt.

'Oh please,' Orla whispered; 'let me go.'

'Your jeans . . . take them off, you bitch!'

Orla started to cry. 'Oh, please, Mick . . .'

He laughed, crooked his leg behind her knees and she fell as he pushed her. She screamed. 'Help! Please help me!'

The scream was stifled. His hand was across her mouth. She could hardly breathe. 'I've got a knife,' he hissed in her ear. 'Any more screaming, and I'll use it.' He began to unzip her jeans.

She struggled. He loosened the waistband, tugged.

Suddenly a dog had begun to bark. It was in a neighbouring garden. It barked furiously, self-righteous with territoriality, shattering the quiet. Oh please God let it wake someone. Please, please, please, God.

He was lying on top of her, half tearing, half pulling at her clothes. Her head ached from the way he banged it against the concrete; she saw it all as though it were happening to someone else, like a play on television; it had no reality for her own life. Rape and all its possible ramifications was something that only happened to other people.

Orla studied the solicitor questioning her, saw the curl to his lip. What if she had become pregnant? The embryo conceived at such expense would be treated as paramount. She would have to go to England for an abortion. They wouldn't be able to prevent that, would they?

'. . . wearing suggestive dress.' Mick's solicitor was still talking. 'Be honest now, Miss Galligan, Didn't you deliberately excite my client who is, after all, a young man. You were wearing a see-through blouse . . .'

'No,' Orla said.

'And you weren't wearing a bra?'

Orla flushed. 'I was wearing a bra.'

'And you danced cheek to cheek with my client, pressing yourself against him?'

'I didn't press myself against him,' Orla said in a low voice.

'But you danced cheek to cheek with him?'

'Yes – but only for one dance.'

'And you went for a walk with him of your own free will.'

'Yes, but . . .'

'Thank you, Miss Galligan.' The solicitor glanced at his client in triumphant solidarity and sat down.

She had fought him, hit him as hard as she could with her free hand, tried to bite him. She wished she knew judo or karate, something to give her some leverage against his weight and his strength. He seemed excited by her struggles. He banged her head against the concrete yet again. She was dizzy and in pain. She wept.

'Oh please don't . . . Please. Oh no, no . . . .' The tears trickled into her mouth and she felt their saltiness on her tongue like the taste of blood.

'But what? Miss Galligan,' the justice interposed testily, 'speak up, young lady. Why did you go for a walk with him when he left you back to your door? Wouldn't the obvious thing have been for you to go in to your home?'

Orla was flustered. 'He left me home,' she said, 'and I said thanks and then he asked me would I like to go for a walk and I said OK. It was a nice night,' she added lamely.

'Why didn't you go in home like a good girl?' the justice repeated with exasperation.

Orla stared at him, this middle-aged man with the stern, authoritarian face. Why didn't he understand? Why did he have to put such a dirty complexion on the thing? Why did he have to insinuate it was her fault? She glanced at her mother, saw her tense, angry face.

From her seat in the public benches, Pat watched her daughter. She trusted him, she thought. They are punishing her for that.

There was evidently some onus on Orla, some special responsibility. This responsibility extended beyond her own actions to those of Mick. If she went for a walk with him, if he used this opportunity to sexually assault her, she must be punished for the femininity which was perceived as the cause of the problem. After all, if she had not been female the problem would not have arisen. She wondered why the system, why the men on the bench, seemed to know nothing about women, about how they felt, about how innocent and romantic a walk in the moonlight might be and, if they knew nothing, why were they allowed to sit in judgement? Why should Orla, why should any woman have to live life in a strait-jacket to avoid being culpable for someone else's crimes? Why was only male sexuality used as a yardstick in a court of justice, as though it were the only human sexuality, as though it were the objective truth?

Orla struggled with the feeling that they were closing ranks against her. She glanced again at her mother. Mummy had always been angry and she had always found it irritating. She turned back to the justice, lifted her head and stared at him between the eyes.

'I didn't know the man was a criminal, that's why I went for a walk with him,' she said coldly. 'If he had told me he was a criminal I would have gone in home.'

The justice frowned at her over his glasses and turned to listen to the new witness.

'And what were you doing at three o'clock in the morning, Mr Murphy?' The solicitor was cross-examining the witness, John Murphy, who had come to investigate the barking of his dog.

'Studying.'

'What were you studying?' the justice interposed.

'Chemistry.'

'So you were studying Chemistry at three o'clock in the morning,' the solicitor continued, 'and you suddenly decided to go into your garden.'

'The dog was barking.'

'Ah, so the dog was barking and you decided to stroll in your garden?'

'Get to the point, Mr O'Brien,' the justice said irritably. 'You've just said that.'

The solicitor coughed, checked his notes. 'And when you looked over the garden wall you saw a couple embracing?'

'I heard a girl's voice saying "No, no!" '

'And what did you do?'

'I looked over the wall and shouted "What's going on?" '

'What did you see?'

'I saw a man and a girl lying on the ground.'

'You are mistaken, Mr Murphy. They were merely courting against the wall.' He addressed himself to the justice. 'It slopes, I

269

believe, and in the darkness Mr Murphy must have been mistaken.'

'I've lived in my home all my life,' the witness said, 'and that wall has never sloped before. It was perfectly perpendicular this morning.'

The solicitor consulted his notepad again. 'What position were they in, Mr Murphy?' the justice asked.

'He was lying on top of the girl – head to head. Standard mating position, if you like.'

'Did you hear my client mention a knife, Mr Murphy?' the solicitor said.

'No.'

'What happened when you shouted?'

'The man got up and ran down the laneway.'

'A normal reaction if one is surprised like that,' the solicitor suggested. 'Wouldn't you have done the same thing – run away?'

'Not if I was about my lawful business,' the witness said sternly, directing a look towards the accused.

The dog, a shaggy mongrel, had licked her face while its owner raced indoors. The garden was dark and smelt of safety and damp grass. There were apple trees and overgrown borders and a spill of light from the back door. He came back with his mother in her dressing-gown, who brought her indoors where she gave her brandy and coffee, but it was hours before she could control the shaking. The police came and questioned her.

The accused gave evidence. He spoke nervously in short, jumpy sentences. He didn't look guilty; he didn't even look like the same Mick. He was well groomed, he wore a tweed jacket, his face was expressionless. He said the complainant was his girl-friend. He denied the threat of the knife and admitted to being 'carried away a bit' and to 'feeling her about the breast'. He said they had only leaned against the wall.

'So Mr Murphy's evidence is incorrect?' the justice demanded.

'Yes.'

'Are you saying that Mr Murphy is lying?'

'Yes.'

The accused went on to say that she had led him on and that when he had taken her home she had suggested a walk and going down the laneway was her idea.

Orla stared at him, her face white. She looked around to see if Mr Murphy was still there; he was, glowering. A man in a dirty raincoat leered at her and winked. The justice looked at the young man in front of him and remembered the terrible sexual urgency of twenty. The girl, after all, should have gone in home. However, the evidence was fairly conclusive.

'I find the accused guilty as charged,' he said slowly. 'Any previous convictions?'

'No, Justice.'

'In that case I'll apply the Probation Act. It's not a very serious offence.'

Later, in Bewley's café in Westmoreland Street, Orla leaned across and took her mother's hand.

'Can I come and live with you, Mum?'

Patricia took a spare Yale key off her key-ring and handed it to her. 'You'll find the sheets in the hot press and a spare duvet in the wardrobe.'

Orla took the key, and mother and daughter smiled at each other.

That evening there was a ring on the doorbell and Simon appeared, looking sheepish. He was carrying an old canvas bag which was bursting at the seams and another bag, similarly straining, was beside him on the ground.

'Can I stay with you, Mum?' he asked nervously. Then he grinned like someone who knew the answer.

Patricia embraced him and drew him into the hall. 'I thought you wanted to stay with your father!'

Simon shrugged, smiled ruefully, made a face at Orla who appeared at the kitchen door.

'Well, it's kind of boring. He's at the office all day and when he comes home he's in bad form. I think he would like you to come home, Mum! I think he thought you would. He expected you to look for money or something! If you made any effort, I think he would have you back.'

Pat smiled at her son, saw the hope in his face. 'That's very kind of your father, Simon . . . to have me back if I made any effort . . . Did he send you to to tell me that?'

'Not really, Mum. But I know he would be glad,' Simon said, happily oblivious to irony.

The dirty canvas bag began to wobble, as though it possessed its own life. An interrogative mewling sound could be heard.

'What have you got in that bag?'

'Only the Beast,' Simon said happily. He unzipped the hold-all and a furious Muffy hopped out, glared at them and then stared around at the strange surroundings with dilating eyes, before making a bolt for the corner behind the TV.

'She'll take ages to settle in,' Pat said with a sigh of dismay. 'Cats hate a change of environment.'

'It's a pity about her,' Orla said with heavy sarcasm. Simon ignored her. 'Em . . . any gobblers?' he inquired, looking hopefully towards the kitchen.

When they had finished supper, Patricia said to her children, 'I'll tell you something about life. You cannot go back – any more than a chicken can return to its shell.' She studied the two young faces, read their disappointment. 'But you can, and must, go forward!'

'How is your work going, Mum?' Orla inquired after a moment. She knew her mother had recently used contacts in the profession to get a temporary job as a part-time court-clerk.

'OK. it's only stamping and registering documents and so on – but it gives me a good idea of the system and it makes me feel part of the world. I've also started an evening course in word processing. Joan will be setting up her own practice shortly and then I'll work for her. I'm going back to college next October; too late to apply for this year, but I'll make a start on the books and use the time to advantage!' Simon's face registered astonishment at the calm purposefulness of this new mother. But more pressing matters absorbed him. He reached for second helpings.

'Do you go into court and all that?' he asked with his mouth full.

'Sometimes, just to see what's happening. It's very interesting to actually attend cases you normally only read about in the paper or hear about on TV.'

'Will you go to the trial of the guy who killed his wife?' Orla asked. 'Remember, the poor woman who was pregnant . . . the one you knew.'

'Oh yeah,' Simon said, 'the one who had her brains knocked out . . . what was her name?'

'Sarah,' Pat said. 'her name was Sarah. And yes, I intend to be there. I did little enough for her and feel I owe her that much.' She paused. 'In a way, you see, the trial will be her obsequies.'

The atmosphere in the central Criminal Court was leaden and strangely unreal; so many black robes and wigs and bowing barristers and hectoring cross-examinations. Patricia studied the blocky man in the dock, thought of Sarah with her bruised face and the way she tried to hide it, her fatigue, her humour, her love for her children. She watched the defence counsel address the jury. The trial had been on for a week and was expected to finish today. They had had the forensic evidence, the evidence from the state pathologist as to how the blow from the crook-lock had split her skull, about the blood spattered on the floor and wall, about the other marks on her body, about how long it had taken her to die and how no attempt was made to procure medical help. Mrs Fiona Mc-Dwyer, the accused's neighbour, said she had often heard rows. Mrs McDwyer gave nervous evidence; yes, she had heard him beating her; no, she had never seen it happen but she had seen bruises on the deceased's face; she had been about to get the police more than once. Why hadn't she – because Sarah had always said there was no point and had even told her to mind her own business; yes, Sarah was a spirited woman. 'But she did not deserve the death she got,' she said to the accused's counsel when he inferred that the deceased had been to some extent responsible for her own destruction.

The defence gave evidence that the accused had drink-taken, that there was a history of family violence in his family, that she had provoked him beyond endurance, that she was always finding fault with him, that he had worked very hard to give her and the children everything; he had even recently built her a new kitchen. He had said that he was sorry and had asked his wife and God to forgive him. The accused wept in court. He denied that his son Dara had been present when the incident had taken place. His wife had insulted him, told him he wasn't a man and never would be one. He hadn't meant to do it.

The defence counsel was tall and young. He was quietly spoken; he inferred that the dead woman was always nagging, that she was mentally unstable; he inferred that his client had lived like a saint under constant provocation, inferred that it

273

was a wonder he hadn't killed her years ago. He spoke with conviction, his voice carefully modulated, stressing the words, excusing his client's action, explaining why he had hit her with the crook-lock.

Patricia remembered Sarah smiling ruefully at her across the table in the coffee dock, the livid bruise on her jaw, a woman overburdened and exhausted.

'And she was six months pregnant and not as attractive as she might otherwise have been.'

For a moment Patricia wondered if she had heard correctly. The statement was delivered in a matter-of-fact voice, to convey a matter-of-fact situation, a matter-of-fact problem for the accused. It was conveyed as a man-to-man dilemma, one every man would understand. His wife was less attractive. What was he, the accused, poor man, to do about it? After all, if she was less attractive, what else could she expect?

Patricia watched the accused, remembered the courtroom in the Bridewell where her own daughter had run the gauntlet of the juridical perception of women.

This thickset man who bashed Sarah's brains out with a crook-lock was evidently justified in some way because she was less attractive. Maybe it was all her fault? She should be attractive. She should make his life exciting, fill him with desire. If she did not, the bits of skull on the floor, the concave dent into her brain, the matted, bloody hair, the spattered crimson on the kitchen walls, were the price. Was he saying that it was fair in some way, or, even if it was not, that it mitigated his client's action, exonerated him in part? The barrister was handsome in the black robe and curling wig, like a piece of old underfelt. He had charisma, a certain kind of privilege and grace, and the jury listened to him, were impressed, nodded sympathetically. Poor man, he would never have done it if she had been attractive; he was a good man really; look at the nice kitchen he had given her.

They were shown photographs of the kitchen where Sarah had baked scones, and wiped and scoured and cleaned, and bent over the sink peeling potatoes, and put the baby on the pot, and washed and dried dishes, and washed and ironed clothes, and cooked for five people, while her back ached and her ears rang with the demands of the children, and she wondered what had happened to her life, how had it flipped from rosy expectation to perpetual service. He was young and strong and proud, this barrister, full of the confidence of his black gown and his little wig which marked him out as special, as possessing power. His stomach muscles did not ache with the weight of a gestating child; nothing moved in his belly except his breakfast; he had never writhed in an ecstasy of pain while his body opened in blood and torn flesh to give life; his glands functioned well; he had pleasure without cost; his brain was trained for the main chance.

Not for him the endless drudgery of motherhood. Not for him the eternal giving without return, the void of a life plundered and unfulfilled. He stood there in his pride and strutted a little in his black robe under the ridiculous wig which gave him power, and let his voice ring out these certitudes. She had been given a nice kitchen; he was a good man really; she was six months pregnant and not as attractive as formerly. He said these things as apologia for her death. He did not check the words lest they disgrace him; whether he meant them or not, the contempt and privilege that made them possible imbued the exchange, man-to-man to the jury, man-to-man to the judge. Never mind the exhausted, overtaxed life; the scream, the thud, the crack of her skull; the spurting blood, the bits of brain and matted, bloody hair; the silence. He had no brief to give her justice; he was counsel for the accused. He was the accused's man. He had taken the accused's gold.

Pat studied the wig, the gown, the crisp white bands, the badges of what was just and reasonable, and wondered could any mercenary, for sale to the highest bidder, have put it better?

The jury came back after an hour's absence and found the accused guilty only of manslaughter. The judge impressed on him that the jury had been merciful. He sentenced him to ten years penal servitude.

The judge stood up. 'All rise,' the tipstaff said. Patricia did not rise. She sat there, staring at the varnished benches while the courtroom emptied.

Later, having left the court, Patricia walked in a half daze along the quays, checking the tears. What kind of a country is this? she wondered. Are we mad or blind? Is the evil bred in the bone or do we learn it?

275

She passed a Muslim couple. They stood out in the Irish street as a little exotic. He was in suit and shirt. His wife was in grey coveralls, walking the regulation number of paces behind her master.

Epilogue

Patricia went back to her house and her children and her books.

Some weeks later she went to work for Joan in her new office, looking forward to the day when she would be apprenticed. Joan had a small practice, beginning to burgeon now as her old clients followed her. Patricia thought of Gerry's face – his wife apprenticed to his former employee – and laughed. It wouldn't hurt Gerry, except in his pride, and he would go on from strength to strength until the day he woke up and found that his life was nearly over and he wondered what it had been about.

As for herself, she was careful. She accepted the occasional invitation. But she kept the prospect of any new relationship at arm's length. She wanted no more mistakes. Better to be cold and safe. Better anything than the emotional roller-coaster to which she had subjected herself.

She had not answered Paddy's letters, not even the last one when he wrote to tell her he and Susan were separating. Susan, it seemed, had succumbed to the charm of one Patrick Rouvier and wanted a divorce.

On Patricia's forty-second birthday – a Saturday – Orla answered the doorbell at lunchtime and returned looking embarrassed.

'It's a man; he has a bouquet of flowers for you!'

'What kind of a man?'

'An . . . oldish man!'

'She means he's a crumbly,' Simon offered. 'A member of the disintegrating generation! She means that he's at least thirty!'

Patricia went to the door, knew, before she saw him, who it was. He was wearing the same suit and trench coat he had worn for their lunch in the Shelbourne.

'I won't come in,' he said, presenting her with the flowers. His grey eyes dwelt on her hungrily. 'But I'll be back . . .'

277

He turned and walked away, his steps leaving a crisp pattern of sound and echo in the laneway.

Patricia shut the door. She felt the sudden void in her stomach, the old sinking sensation. She handed the flowers to Orla, who went to the kitchen to put them in water.

Pat sat down.

How useful and cool it would be to say that I have exorcized it all, she thought. That I could claim total disinterest, the absence of any vestige either of delight or desire. That all that passion and fury of communication was merely a bubble that burst. That I am free.

She smiled to herself at the ritornello of living, at the tension between mind and spirit and body, the three remorseless creditors.

'Are you going to see him again?' Orla asked in a low voice when she came back to the kitchen.

Patricia thought of Glendalough and Paris, two ends of the same spectrum. But the space in between had hardly been explored. She turned to her daughter, reached out and gently touched her face.

'We'll see,' she said. 'We'll see.'

Author's Note

The court sequences in this book are based on real cases where I was either present myself or was furnished with details by a reliable eye-witness.

The rape cases and cases involving domestic homicides referred to in newspapers are based on real Irish cases within the past ten years, though not in the time frame in which they actually occurred.

Sarah's story is ficitious. However, the comments of the defence counsel at the trial of her killer contained in the last chapter were actual words spoken by defence counsel at a similar trial.

I wrote this novel in 1991/92. Various important events of a constitutional and legislative nature have since taken place relating to some of the issues touched on which are outside the scope of this book. However, only time will tell whether any real change will occur in what seems to be the prevailing juridical attitude to women in cases where their interests, as women, confront those of men.

Mary Ryan
Dublin, April 1994